The Contraband Shore

The Contraband Shore

DAVID DONACHIE

Allison & Busby Limited
12 Fitzroy Mews
London W1T 6DW
allisonandbusby.com

First published in Great Britain by Allison & Busby in 2017.

A CIP catalogue record for this book is available from
the British Library.

First Edition

ISBN 978-0-7490-2165-8

Typeset in 12.25/16.25 pt Adobe Garamond Pro by
Allison & Busby Ltd.

The paper used for this Allison & Busby publication
has been produced from trees that have been legally sourced
from well-managed and credibly certified forests.

Printed and bound by
CPI Group (UK) Ltd, Croydon, CR0 4YY

To the memory of Bryan Cooper
author, scriptwriter, journalist and a true bon viveur,
whose company I was often invited to share

PROLOGUE

With Elisabeth Langridge returned from the West Indies, Cottington Court had come back to life. A mansion and extensive estate which, in her absence, had rarely held a sizeable dinner was this day hosting a fete in the grounds; the guests, people who made up a goodly selection of the quality families of East Kent: parents as well as sons and daughters of an eligible age, but no small children, given their propensity to run riot.

As far as those attending were concerned, this early springtime gathering was being hosted by Elisabeth's brother, Henry Tulkington, but he failed to be present to greet them. When he was finally dragged outdoors and away from his paperwork, he did his best to appear as though he was appreciating the activity. In truth, to a person who held himself to be a serious man of business, it was all so much frippery.

No one remarked on his coat and hat on a day reasonably mild; those who had known Henry for years were well aware he was inclined to be very careful of his constitution. Others, less conscious of his concerns, were either too polite to mention it or so busy enjoying themselves they barely noticed.

All were invited to play bowls on the lawn or skittles on a wooden track fetched in from a local tavern, to throw horseshoes at a stake or try their hand at archery on targets set up against the backdrop of a tall and tight hayrick. When not engaged in such activities, they could repair to a marquee and partake of the rum punch and cordials provided, this a concoction of some strength.

Elisabeth, known as Betsey to her friends was, in contrast to many of her female guests, soberly dressed, as befitted her situation. Being a widow imposed upon her certain social and sartorial restraints; there could be no colourful and extravagant silks or gaudy turbans. It was a sadness to her that the mother of her late husband had declined an invitation – indeed she had been made to feel uncomfortable visiting her at nearby Sholden. She was, no doubt, still grieving the loss even after a period of over two years, as was, if not to the same crippling extent, her daughter-in-law.

Elisabeth suspected the Widow Langridge had always found her a tad frivolous. It was certainly the case she had never seen her as a fitting bride for her son; what mother ever does? She would have had no cause for concern on this occasion. To ensure the bounds of proper and acceptable behaviour were never crossed, Betsey's Aunt Sarah was always close by, especially when any male showed an intention of acting in too familiar a fashion. This was a distinct likelihood, her niece being both a beauty, as well as a young woman of substantial independent means.

It was impossible, however, for the aunt to carry out her watchful duty in the archery butts as men, both married and single, took the rare opportunity, by tutoring their aim, of physical contact with women to whom they were neither married, engaged nor related. Sarah Lovell was not alone in her gimlet eye when it came to ensuring no liberties were allowed to go unremarked. Several wives could be seen storing up a later reprimand for an errant spouse, who, having imbibed more punch than was wise, took to exhibiting an excess of familiarity.

One who was certainly in for a later roasting, and this had nothing to do with manhandling women, was the Reverend Doctor Joshua

Moyle, who had probably been at the bottle before he arrived. The Vicar of Cottington, a man hard to find sober, sought to hide his broken-veined cheeks with thick whiskers, which left his cratered nose and rheumy eyes ever watering as the most prominent features.

His wife took less pleasure in his antics than the rest of the guests, as he sought to line up and plant an arrow on the bull, his aim obviously unsteady merely from the fact he struggled to avoid a slight stagger as he released his projectile. As a result, it thudded into a neighbouring target, not his own. The gales of laughter this produced was not taken as an affront; indeed, Moyle turned to those watching and bowed.

'Does not the sound of laughter cheer you, Henry?' Betsey asked, as she dipped a cup into the huge silver bowl before handing it to her brother.

'Of course, Elisabeth, most certainly.'

The reply, given after a mere sip of the brew, failed to satisfy. Betsey felt slightly frustrated for, despite her best efforts to place her brother within the orbit of the unwed females present, he had yet to fully engage any of them in a meaningful conversation. Her quip when pushing him into this event, which had not been easy in itself – that a chateau required a chatelaine – had engendered a response, which, while politely delivered, told her to mind her own business.

'We can always rely on our good vicar for amusement, if not example.'

Betsey questioned the word 'good', and as for example, Moyle to her was a bad one, the only saving grace she could recall his ability to deliver ferocious sermons promising hell and damnation for sins numerous, in many of which he was himself a transgressor. The living he occupied was in the gift of the Tulkington family, in reality her elder brother, and she could never fathom why such an endemic soak was tolerated. Comment on that was also not taken well.

Henry had always been hard for her to connect with; a twelve-year difference in age, added to a birth that had taken from them their mother, was only one factor to affect their relationship. He had been sent away to a school noted for its hard discipline; she had been tutored at home by a benign governess, as well as fussed over by servants.

In attitudes they were chalk and cheese, Betsey with her optimistic nature and love of the outdoors, contrasted with her brother's addiction to business, aversion to fresh air or outdoor pursuits and what she called his hypochondria. If he was genuinely ill, she could and would show sincere sympathy, but most of his supposed ailments were the product of his imagination. Often these were prompted by things he had read of in avidly consumed medical tomes.

If they had quarrelled in the years gone by, it had arisen from his controlling nature, as well as an absence of anything approaching gaiety. With their father also gone by the time she grew to maturity, he had been the head of the household and so sought to act *in loco parentis* to a sister intending marriage – one who was having none of it. That, however, was all in the past. She was determined, home again and older, that things between them would be different.

'Will you aid me in the butts?'

'I reckon your aim would be best without it, Elisabeth. It is not a sport at which I have any skill, if indeed a thing of that nature exists. I would make Moyle look like Robin of the Hood.'

'While I have none at all with the bow,' Betsey insisted. 'You know you are the only person I can ask.'

That remark seemed to please her brother, though the twitch of his lips quickly disappeared. She thought to mention it, only to conclude a misreading of the expression. Her situation did not permit for even the most restrained of the male guests to hold her elbow, place a second hand around her waist and whisper closely in her ear to tell her when to release the bowstring. Skittles she could play, as long as no excessive exuberance was demonstrated if all the pins tumbled, likewise success in the other entertainments.

'Perhaps,' she added, 'if you are seen assisting me, it might encourage some of the other ladies present to ask for a touch of tutoring.'

'Which would surely dampen their enthusiasm. That is, if they demonstrate any in the first place.'

She tried and failed to avoid a cross look, but Betsey Langridge possessed a brow that did not furrow unobtrusively. Back in England due to unforeseen as well as unfortunate circumstances and with half a mind to remain, she longed for her childhood home to be like her house in Jamaica: a place of social repute, an estate of which people talked, if not in wonder, then at least in appreciation of the amusements, table and sparkling conversation it provided.

This would surely never happen with Henry unwed and, she had to admit, it would take a singular creature of a wife to change him: he was too solemn of disposition and worked too hard for his own good. If anything of that nature were to transpire, it must be down to her to bring it about, which led her to ignore his obvious reluctance and adopt a chastising tone.

'They will not if you fail to engage with them.'

'I agreed to your request to hold this and have met the expense. Settle for that, dear sister, and accept that whatever kind of life you enjoyed in the Caribbean is unlikely to be replicated here.'

'So you will not even take my arm and a tour to be introduced?'

'That would be too churlish, but please, Elisabeth, no romantic effusions.'

It was obvious, as they circulated, she was the object of more interest than her brother. Or was it that Henry produced in the younger women present a degree of reserve, brought on by a rather uncompromising countenance? This was not helped by his constant recourse to his handkerchief, while Betsey's radiant smile encouraged the eligible males to hope their attentions were more than merely politely received.

The time came to consume the roasted pig, which had been cooking over a charcoal pit since early morning and was now being carved, to be eaten sitting at tables freshly set up by the estate servants in the marquee. There was a certain amount of jockeying amongst the young men to secure a place beside her, all seen off by the basilisk stare of her aunt, who ensured that, at each elbow, Elisabeth was obliged to converse with an elderly couple, long wedded to each other and thus no threat to propriety.

By now a number of the more mature male guests were drunk; Roger Colpoys, married to her good friend Annabel, was loud as the inebriated tend to be, one of telling prominence but not alone amongst many who'd overindulged at the punch bowl. Dr Moyle exceeded others even in this; the vicar was face down in his plate and snuffling through apple sauce, luckily at a place far enough away from Betsey for her to be able to ignore it.

Her brother was clearly taken by it – enough, anyway, to produce a rare bout of laughing. He called for a couple of servants to lift the divine from the danger of suffocation and carry him back to the vicarage. As they lifted his head, it came away with a long piece of crackling entangled in his white whiskers, already stained by gravy. Once more this occasioned laughter; Henry rocked in his chair, as did a majority of the men. The women, especially those married, showed overt sympathy for Moyle's long-suffering wife.

The meal, consumed, including a syllabub and a choice of cheeses and with port doing the rounds, allowed several of the bachelors, at least those who were sober, to circulate. One by one they manoeuvred to come within Betsey's orbit. Sat opposite, Aunt Sarah's expression was enough to make any approach stiffly formal and definitely non-tactile.

Only in the departure could those who wished to pay court to her be allowed any physical contact, no more than a touch of her fingers and a brush of a kiss on the back of her hand. If that proved to be more than perfunctory, a cough from the same relative would bring on a swift termination.

Guests gone and alone in her bedroom, Betsey, in reprising the day, was not sure to what extent she had truly enjoyed herself, given the constraints on her behaviour. In summation, she saw it as only a beginning, a first dip of the social toe. Cottington Court, in time, would be as she wished it, never mind Henry and his misanthropy. When the period of mourning for her late husband was over, perhaps she could put her mind to her own future and cease to concern herself with that of her brother.

Inevitably that took her thoughts back to Jamaica, to its warm climate and life of ease. If there was sad recollection of a spouse lost to the endemic fevers of the region, there were more recent memories of a warmer nature to help her over into sleep.

CHAPTER ONE

Edward Brazier was puzzled. The stable yard was crammed with open carts, coaches and covered vans; also busy were the lanes surrounding the inn – inexplicably so. Being situated in a country location on the edge of a far-from-substantial village, well off the main routes to the east coast of Kent, it scarcely warranted such traffic. The obligation to call upon an old superior had brought him here in a hired hack, when the simplest, most comfortable and quickest route to his destination would have been the regular stagecoach through either Dover or Sandwich.

Rear Admiral Sir Eustace Pollock, who had been his captain aboard HMS *Magnanime*, had taken up a country residence, having bought a vacant parsonage in the village of Adisham. Having never married, the admiral was being cared for by a housekeeper and various other servants and he had, in his letters, alluded to a degree of loneliness. It would thus have been remiss for one of his former midshipmen, as well as the man who had helped him rise to officer rank, not to call and pay his respects when he was in the locality.

The recollection of the conversation the pair had engaged in was enough to bring a smile to Brazier's lips; Pollock, a grizzled old salt long past his prime, who struggled to recall where he had put his pipe or his eyeglasses, seemed able to remember and relate with startling clarity every misdemeanour of his one-time subordinate.

'You were a damned nuisance, Brazier,' he had growled, gathering a shawl around his shoulders while poking his fire, on a day in which the necessity for either was questionable. 'You cannot know on how many occasions I regretted giving in to your father's pleading that I take you on board.'

'I seem to recall, sir, that you had me mustered as a servant for two years before I set foot on your deck.'

There was no resentment in the statement, nor for the fact that Pollock had been pocketing the small sums provided by the navy, this to both clothe and feed him when he was still onshore and at school. Such a practice was common, one of the ways for a naval captain to enhance his income, and was not to be remarked upon.

'I sense it left you with an obligation.'

'An obligation to have you kiss the gunner's daughter more than a dozen times in your first twelvemonth. Damn me, my arm ached from chastising you. Still, you turned, by some miracle, into a competent officer.' Poker still in hand and staring at the fire, Pollock added, 'And now you're a post captain, though only the Good Lord knows how since, as a shaver, obeying an order seemed alien to your nature.'

These memories had been delivered with gruff good humour, manufactured anger and very loose recollection of the truth; the conversation turned less pleasant when it moved on from amusing recollection to Pollock's present status. Like every flag officer in the King's Navy, he owed his admiral's rank to time served. He had reached the top of the captain's list during the American imbroglio, to then become the victim of a far-from-uncommon consequence: no employment.

Fortune and decades of service had failed to favour him with the kind of reputation that rendered notable a fighting sailor's name, added to which, any connections he could call upon were not of the social or political standing to make a pressing case on his behalf at the

Admiralty. So he drew his pay and lived comfortably enough, while the next round of promotions, depending on the number of admirals above him who had expired, could well see him promoted.

Even then his hope of ever again holding a sea command were slim to non-existent, while even a shore appointment seemed a distant prospect. He was that pitiful article, a 'yellow admiral', a flag officer without benefit of service. While Edward Brazier commiserated with Pollock as he listened to his litany of complaints, he kept hidden the fear that he too might be in much the same boat.

'You're welcome to stay, Brazier, of course.'

'Thank you, sir, but I'm pressed for time.'

Not wishing to tell the truth, he produced a previously arrived at excuse. Pollock had always been dead set against naval officers marrying, seeing them as 'lost to the service' when they tied the knot, worrying on home and family instead of the complex needs of their command. Brazier was on his way to pay court to a beautiful widow he had met and become very attracted to in the West Indies, a quest he hoped would lead to nuptials. It would scarce go down well to say so.

'I have bespoken accommodation in Deal, for which I am already overdue. Also I have a hired hack waiting in your drive, as well as the coachman. He will be anxious to get back to Canterbury, from where I engaged him, and I must allow him time to do so.'

'A pretty penny that must be costing you.'

'I am lucky enough, sir, to be able to meet the expense.'

Pollock had nodded but did not press, though his expression failed to hide his disappointment. What was left for an old sailor but to reminisce and relate well-worn stories, best done with a fellow officer, someone who both understood the nature of the tales and could counter with their own?

'I was looking forward to hearing of your adventures in the Caribbean,' had been the actual response. 'And of course that lucky stroke that came your way.'

17

The temptation had been to say it had not just been luck, though that certainly played a part. HMS *Diomede* had taken a valuable prize through inspired guesswork, good seamanship, as well as a crew at the peak of their abilities. Such a response had to be suppressed, not least in that it would sound like boasting. In truth, he was somewhat weary of recounting a tale he had been obliged to repeat several dozen times already.

'I will certainly come by Adisham on another occasion, sir, and ensure I allow myself more time.'

'That would be most welcome.'

'Best step down, your honour. With this commotion, it looks to be a time afore we get a suitable swap.'

These words from the coachman brought his passenger back to the present and the reason for their stop. The horse pulling the hack was spent and, since his man could come back by this route, it made sense to seek a temporary replacement. Removing the overall he was wearing to keep his uniform clean, Brazier complied, alighting to stretch his limbs.

'I will have something sent out to you if that serves.'

'Kind of you, sir.'

The tavern, when he entered, was so crowded he was in want of a place to sit, which made him wonder what could possibly be going on in this rural backwater to justify so many conveyances and seemingly prosperous customers? Every table near to the entrance was full, so Brazier headed deeper into the warren-like hostelry. Finally, in an alcove, he espied a booth for four with only two occupants, fellows with heads close together and in deep conversation.

'Gentlemen, would it trouble you if I were to occupy one of these vacant places?'

The act of lifting his hat should have been courtesy enough for a pair of strangers. Expecting a smile and a nod of acceptance, he received the very opposite. Both heads were raised to glare at him, which gave him a chance to inspect features he had not previously bothered to examine, characteristics not aided by less-than-friendly expressions. Obviously these two did not wish to be disturbed and anticipated the stricture would be complied with. Irritated by the incivility of not even a spoken reply, Brazier sat down anyway, put his hat on the table and looked out into the well of the tavern for a serving girl to see to his needs.

'We are engaged in a private conversation.'

Rough voice and tone, with a grating quality, and decidedly hostile.

'One in which I have no interest, sir.'

'While we would be more content if you was to park your arse elsewhere.'

The second voice was different; wheezy, as though the fellow had an affliction of the chest. Yet for all that there was nothing weak about the delivery or, when Brazier turned to respond, the look that went with it. Had there been another seat he would have, in the face of such malice, moved. He had come in for a pot of ale and a bite to eat for himself and his coachman, not a dispute.

'If you can identify anywhere else to sit, I will most happily oblige, but as you can see there's no room in this place to swing a cat.'

That naval expression got both men eyeing him up and down, taking in the blue broadcloth coat with white facings and gleaming brass buttons, as well as the twin epaulettes on his shoulders, there to tell anyone who cared to look he was a post captain in His Majesty's Navy of over three years' seniority. With a deliberate desire to send his own message, Brazier put a hand on his sword hilt to ease the scabbard away from his leg, while also allowing himself, with a direct look, a deeper appreciation of the features of these fellows.

Gravel voice had a large head and a heavily pockmarked face, with eyes rendered small by the setting, though it had to be admitted the whole was supported by a broad and substantial frame, so did not seem excessive. Weedy was cursed with a protruding lower lip under a too-large nose, which had a drip of fluid forming at the tip, while his weak-looking eyes were rimmed red as if he had been weeping. Both were still utterly ill-disposed. With a couple of smiles and a kindly plea, Brazier would have obliged; he prided himself on his manners after all, but this rankled.

There is a moment, many a time previously experienced, when what could be called an impasse might just become violent – and that applies to fighting dogs as well as humans. The tension becomes palpable, and right now it was on the cusp of spilling over, with Brazier deciding gravel voice, with his bulk and muscle, should be in receipt of the primary blow. Weedy would get a hard elbow in that fulsome, dripping nose as an immediate follow-up.

'Gentlemen, you will have observed I am a naval officer and, as such, I have shared a midshipman's berth over many years and a wardroom even longer with many like souls. I am thus perfectly capable of shutting my ears to the private conversations of others, as one is obliged to do in the service. So I pray you carry on your exchange, to which I do assure you, I will pay no heed.'

The mood lasted several seconds before gravel voice put his hands flat on the table to push himself upright.

'T'is as well we are done. Come, Jaleel, let us leave this high-and-mighty merman to his ale, on which, if there is a God, he might choke.' The wheezing laugh from his companion was overdone for such a feeble sally, while the words that followed lacked any humour at all. 'I have marked you, matey, you may count on it. It would serve you well not to cross my path again.'

Edward Brazier had stood at the same time as gravel voice, to face a man of a height equal to his own of six foot plus: if there was to be a bout it would never do to be caught sitting down. By habit he created a gap between them that would allow him his sword if it was required, replying in a very controlled tone of voice.

'That, sir, is a stricture that applies in more than one direction. It is my fond hope, for the sake of my soul, that I never clap eyes on you again.'

There followed a second moment when violence was on the cusp, the two men standing with eyes locked. Gravel voice flicked a glance to Brazier's sword, while the man under scrutiny was equally aware of bunched fists with their distended well-used knuckles. What broke it apart was the need to move, this to allow the fellow called Jaleel to squeeze past; he was much smaller and stringy in his build.

Outside the alcove the rest of the tavern had gone quiet, the babble of indecipherable conversation dying away; all eyes were now on the two men facing each other. It became a crowd who, in anticipation, seemed taken by the fact that there might be a contest, while those closest were wondering if it was safe to stay within the orbit of its coming violence. What they got was a snort from gravel voice as he spun on his heels and marched out, his companion at his heels.

'Sir?' asked the serving wench, to the customer still on his feet.

The stern expression evaporated at once as Brazier responded, asking for a tankard of ale and some bread and cheese, the same to be sent out to his coachman, before sitting down again. The spare seats were soon filled; clearly another conveyance had come into the yard. As he munched and sipped, Brazier listened with no more than half an ear to the inconsequential talk of his seemingly well-contented fellow travellers, marking only that they, by what he could not help but overhear, saw this place as their destination.

'Captain Brazier, sir, ready to go at your convenience,' came the loud call from the out-of-vision doorway.

Sat in the hack again, once more clad in his duster coat, Edward Brazier put out of his mind the pair of bad-tempered locals. Also relegated were any concerns about his own professional future. Given he was heading to Deal for a purpose closer to his heart than his head, it was that to which he sought to turn his mind, conjuring up images of a decent-sized house, outside which, on a well-tended lawn, he would play with his future wife and children.

The onward journey was without anything to be remarked upon other than discomfort. A seat in a hack designed for short town journeys was far from comfortable, rendered less so by being buffeted about while traversing rutted tracks full of deep potholes. He did reflect on the alternative, only to conclude his backside would have been even more afflicted had he chosen to travel on horseback, a mode of conveyance that did not favour the thighs or buttocks over distance, especially for a fellow who had not mounted such a creature in several years.

With darkness creeping over the landscape, all he could observe, even with a full moon and strong starlight, outside the minimal pool cast by the tiny carriage lanterns, were the lamps and candles of the dwellings they passed – he assumed a stream of isolated farmhouses or tiny hamlets – until finally he reached his destination: the Three Kings Inn on the foreshore of Lower Deal.

His sea chest having been taken inside by the porter, he settled his bill with the coachman, with an extra coin for his attention, then saw him off on his way back to his home city. Brazier stood for a moment sniffing the familiar scent of the sea on a blustery, easterly wind, one that served to blow away from him the odour of rotting fish as well as a dozen other noxious smells. He stood for a while, eyeing the mass of lantern-illuminated ships in the roadstead: ghostly shapes in the overhead light, numerous merchant vessels of all shapes and sizes, filling the waters between the shoreline and the great protective bar of the Goodwin Sands.

Amongst them would be the vessels of the Royal Navy's Downs Squadron, which led him to wonder if that would include people he knew, or a ship within which he had served. Given the reason he had come to this place, was that something to be welcomed or avoided?

Common courtesy demanded he make his presence known to the man who commanded in the Downs, and, from that, contact would flow and spread, whether he liked it or not, as well as an interest in the previous activities of this new arrival. That being a problem for another day he went indoors.

'I bid you a hearty welcome to our establishment, Captain Brazier. I'm happy to say that the rooms you sought, the best we have, with a view of the sea and a private place of easement, are free for your use and ready, with a goodly fire a'burnin' in the grate.'

The owner of the Three Kings, who introduced himself as Garlick, was a fellow with a visage that went with his vinous occupation. He had the purple nose and blotched skin of the serious imbiber, these under a shiny bald pate, to which was allied the necessary obsequious nature of the trade. His smile exposed stained wooden teeth as well as a lack of sincerity so, on the whole, it was unpleasant.

'I must apologise for being a full day late. I was held up on the way.'

'What does that matter, sir?' Not at all, was the Brazier thought, given it will appear on my bill anyway. 'Your sea chest is already in your rooms and, if you desire it, I will send up a wench to stow away your possessions.'

The gleam in the puffy eyes told Brazier he was required to respond; what type of wench was now his to indicate. One that would see to his clothing as stated, or a person of another profession altogether, who would meet requirements of a more personal nature?

'Some indication of your wines will serve, Mr Garlick, plus an idea of what I can partake of in the article of food.'

'To be taken in the parlour, sir?'

'No, tonight I will eat in my rooms. And I am accustomed to laying out the contents of my sea chest without assistance.'

The flicker of those same eyes, the way they turned away from this new guest, spoke of a disappointment to match that of Admiral Pollock, albeit for a very different reason. Garlick and his ilk made extra money from folks with certain needs other than a place to eat and lay their head.

'And am I allowed to enquire how long you will be staying, sir?'

'There you have me, fellow, for I have no idea. And could you ensure I have the means sent up to write? I have some messages to pen, one of which I would like delivered as soon as it's composed.'

The rooms, in contrast to the man who ran the place, were charming and comfortable, while the food – a pair of mutton chops and a pigeon, accompanied by a heap of spring vegetables – amply met the Brazier cravings. The wine he chose, a pitcher of Burgundy was, by its name, of such a quality as to make him suspicious. Produced from a cask to be sniffed at, his nose hinted at true quality, so much so that he took care in the pouring, though not in the consumption. By the time he sought his bed, the pitcher was empty.

CHAPTER TWO

He was, by naval habit, up before first light, the half-glass panelled doors, when the heavy drapes were pulled open, soon filling the room with the glow of a rising eastern sun, which in time turned the sea from grey to blue. Silhouetted against it lay a large vessel under bare poles anchored not far off the Naval Yard, one he had not noted in the dark. It being a brand new third-rate ship of the line he examined it with a degree of yearning.

The seventy-four-gunner was surrounded by boats, this to service much deck activity, and looked to be in the process of its final fitting-out. Finished and ready for sea, she would be handed over to some officer favoured by the Admiralty. In his heart, even if he reckoned his next command should be of such a size and rating, he doubted it would be him. He also espied a 28-gun frigate and a pair of sloops, they too being worthy of close and professional examination.

A tug on a bell alerted the establishment, which brought first a young skivvy to clean the grate then lay and light a new fire, along with a lad to remove the chamber pot from the side closet. Next a bowl of hot water arrived in the hands of the fellow who would shave and towel him. That done, food in ample quantity, as well as a pot of coffee, was laid out on the table.

Brazier was able to take his breakfast with the double doors open and, provided with a telescope, to look out in strong sunlight at an anchorage filled with a couple of hundred cargo vessels, boats by the several dozen moving to and fro carrying people and stores. He paid special attention to a couple of merchantmen under reefed topsails, slowly and with great care making their way through the throng of their fellows to get out to sea on a southerly course, he naturally wondering at their destination.

The glass was switched backwards and forwards as he sought the purpose of each craft, including those hovelling the seabed for lost anchors, chains and cables. In the larger supply boats there would be canvas and cordage, pork and beef in the barrel, fresh bread in both loaves and ship's biscuit, nails, timber, turpentine and vinegar – indeed a thousand articles without which a vessel could not sail. Then there were the water hoys, pumping their precious commodity into barrels knocked up by the ship's cooper, these then lowered into the hold by lines that led, through blocks on the yards, to the capstan below.

Lacking a harbour, everything required to supply the ships laying off Deal had to be taken off the open beach; this was trade on which the prosperity of the town must rest, so he had to wonder how it had been affected by the nation now being at peace? In the American War, after France and Spain had joined the fray in support of the colonists, a system of convoys had been forcibly imposed by the government, in order to satisfy the London insurers of ship risk, this to contain soaring losses.

Thus ships in the hundreds, once gathered here, were escorted to their journey's end by the Royal Navy. Heading down the Channel, they came under the protection of the patrolling frigates of the Channel Fleet as they weathered the headland of Ushant. This being close to the French naval base of Brest was thus an area of great danger, ameliorated by the line-of-battle ships in the offing, ready to intercede should the enemy emerge in strength.

Once clear of the Bay of Biscay, those engaged in the port wine trade would hive off for Lisbon, the next area of risk off Cádiz, though the Spaniards had been less active than their French allies. At Gibraltar those in the Italian trade, plus the Levanters, would head into the Mediterranean, the remainder carrying on south to the Cape Verde Islands. Finally the East Indiamen would part company with those on course for the Caribbean.

Such convoying had been unpopular with those it was aimed to protect, just as much by the naval commanders tied to the coat tails of merchant captains. Not only was it frustrating for a serving officer to be denied the freedom to act as they saw fit, they were dealing with ship's masters accustomed to command their own vessels, men not prepared to bow the knee to any Tom, Dick or Harry just because they carried a King's commission.

By repute they were a damned nuisance and utterly lacking in discipline when it came to sailing at either the right speed or in the correct order. Brazier was glad it was a duty he had been spared, not least because of it being related to him by his fellow officers their desire to string up the master of a merchant ship from a yardarm as an example.

Deal, with its huge anchorage protected by the Goodwins, had become the primary location for convoy assembly and would have prospered by it, so the end of hostilities would have affected more than the navy. The Three Kings was, in itself, an indication of absence; in wartime it would surely have been full to bursting, unlike now, when he could bespeak a room by letter and be cosseted like a royal on arrival.

A knock brought a reply to his letter from the commanding officer at the Downs, Rear Admiral Sir Clifton Braddock, with a wish for him to call and pay his respects at a time convenient to the recipient. An hour later Brazier was walking along the road fronting the shore, hemmed in by fine-looking houses of all shapes and sizes to one side, with more dilapidated dwellings on the edge of the shingle beach –

buildings at the full mercy of the elements and showing it – these interspersed with gaps full of fishing nets strung on poles to dry.

If he did not know Deal, there was nothing unusual to remark upon: the sound and, least of all, the smell of a seaport was familiar. Likewise common was the fellow tasked with supervising entry to the Naval Yard, one-pegged and ex-service, who being out of his tiny guardhouse, eyed the approaching officer with an eagle and far from friendly eye, a look that disappeared as the rank became obvious.

He said something unheard to the armed marine sentry at the actual gate then, forelock touched, he enquired as to Brazier's business, apologising that he was required to do so. A whistle brought a youngster out of the guardhouse: a clean lad in naval garb of white ducks and a kerseymere striped top, tasked to escort him to his destination. He went ahead through the mass anchors and piles of chains, plus a series of outhouses, passing horses pulling carts, skipping over their yet-to-be-swept-up dung, until the solid and handsome brick edifice, which housed the headquarters of the station, came into sight.

Outside the double doors, fronted by a pair of brass cannon on either side of a flagstaff on which fluttered a Union Flag, stood another two marine sentries who presented arms at his passing, while inside a second ex-tar manned access to the inner sanctum. Brazier was directed to a side room to wait while his name was sent up to Braddock. He was not left for long.

'Damn me, I'm surprised to see you, Brazier. How many years has it been?'

'Must be near seven, sir.' Brazier responded with faux enthusiasm, suspecting it being a question to which the admiral well knew the answer, despite an enquiring expression on the bluff, ruddy face.

'Premier on *Hero*, if I have the right of it.'

'Indeed, sir.'

'Dined aboard often. Commodore kept a good table, I must say.'

'He was fond of entertaining, sir.'

Knowing what was coming after this opening exchange, Brazier sought to delay the shared memory, one larded with mixed feelings, by turning to look out of the large windows. He and the then-Captain Braddock had first met just before an expedition to the Cape of Good Hope and subsequently on the voyage, many times in Commodore Johnstone's dining cabin.

The squadron had been tasked to take the Cape colony from the Dutch, a notion scotched by the French under the formidable Bailli de Suffren, first off the Cape Verde Islands. It was a fight that might be claimed as a draw, but one which favoured the enemy more than Britannia. Admiral Suffren then got to his Dutch allies at the Cape first, to deny Johnstone the harbour, leaving him no choice but to sail on to the Indian subcontinent.

Braddock was no different to Pollock; he would want to reprise the whole expedition. Total deflection would be impossible, but it could be put off. 'That's a fine third rate you are overseeing, sir.'

'*Bellerophon,* they've named her. You should go aboard, Brazier, and look her over.' Braddock produced a rather forced laugh. 'How long is it since you sniffed a ship's timbers and smelt anything other than rot?'

'I don't recall ever doing so. She's fitting out, of course?'

'Aye, safer to do so in this neck of the woods than at the Medway dockyards. I will not say nothing goes missing in this yard, that's never to be stopped, but it's a fraction of what the Chatham dockies would pilfer. Come, man, take a seat, have a glass of wine and tell me what brings you into my bailiwick.'

The question brought disquiet; as with his old commanding officer, if not for the same reason, he had no desire to discuss personal business. He could hardly say he had come to take the sea air when he had just been paid off in Portsmouth from long service in Jamaica. After several thousand miles sailing the Atlantic that was a commodity of which he'd had an abundance.

'I came on from visiting Admiral Pollock at Adisham, sir. Having never anchored here and close by, I was curious to cast an eye over the place.'

It did the trick as Braddock, with Pollock mentioned, was required to manufacture interest, as well as regard, for a long-known fellow officer. 'And how is the old rogue?'

'Longing to be active, sir.'

'Don't we all, Brazier, don't we all? I have always meant to call upon him myself, but the time . . .'

The consequence of the lack of that commodity was left hanging, for it was unlikely to be factual. If he and Pollock had been cordially friendly once, it was doubtful such an attitude would be maintained now, it being a truism that the higher you rose in the service the less amiable became your relations with your peers, due to endemic competition for increasingly limited opportunities.

'Still you came on?'

'Curiosity, sir, as I say.'

That got a raised eyebrow as Braddock clearly tried to imagine what was worth exploring in such a backwater. 'Not much to see, less you're an aficionado of Tudor castles, gun bastions and the shoals of fish.'

'I'm at present without encumbrances, sir, and have the time to act with a freedom I have not enjoyed for many a year.'

'Ah, blessed freedom,' Braddock responded, which was as good a way as any of covering the fact that he was at a loss as to what to say next.

'Since you are based here, sir, you must know Deal well.'

'Too damn well, Brazier, and it does not render me fond.' A raised eyebrow obliged the admiral to continue, though he acted to gather his thoughts by indicating the decanter, issuing a silent invitation to partake. 'It's a confounded place and full of the worst kind of villainy.'

'Worse than Portsmouth or the Nore towns?' was the disbelieving response: both the main fleet bases of the Royal Navy were hardly virtuous, quite the reverse.

'Most certainly. What do you know of smuggling?'

'I am hardly unaware of what it entails.'

He was tempted to add he had spent the last three years acting against it in the Caribbean; he sensed that would not be welcome, given it was an extremely lucrative station on which to serve and therefore a source of envy.

'Well this place is wedded to it. There's barely a soul in the town who's not either a perpetrator or a beneficiary and it's a damned nuisance. I rate it as no business of the navy to be seeking to stop the perpetrators, which is a task for the Revenue Service. Should we catch anyone, we are obliged to hand them over, with no certainty we will be rewarded for the value of what they carry.'

Braddock would be thinking of his own purse, not anyone else's; that was the way of flag officers.

'I'm nudged by the Admiralty for the sake of appearances,' he continued, with a sly look, 'but I happen to know they share my view. Trouble is, I'm plagued by demands from Billy Pitt to act forcibly.'

'I would think the King's First Minister would have more on his plate than people running contraband.'

'He has and he should stick to it. I make a show of some effort, but I'm damned if I'm going to wear out the ships I command by having them beat up and down the Channel, to then have the Admiralty clerks demanding an explanation for the wear and tear on wood and canvas, with a demand that I and my captains make good any losses.'

The admiral slapped the top of his desk. 'Let Pitt propose, but in this area of the briny, as far as the navy is concerned, I dispose. I'd be chasing shadows anyway, for the sods are damn clever, which I must admit even Pitt acknowledges. It would be better for his well-being if he didn't spend so much time here—'

An expression of obvious ignorance changed the admiral's line. 'You do know he desires to be Lord Warden of the Cinque Ports?'

'I did not,' Brazier replied, seeking and failing to recall what such an office entailed.

'Pure flummery, of course, and not worth much more than a brass farthing. Lord North has the title now, but he resides in Oxfordshire when not on Parliamentary business. So Pitt uses Walmer Castle as a retreat when the House is not in session. Likes the sea air, he says, and is ambitious to have full possession when North goes to meet his maker, it being a lifetime appointment.' The decanter was visited again. 'Trouble is, what goes on is right under his nose, which is no doubt why he's become obsessed.'

Braddock shook his head at such perceived idiocy. 'Inclined to go off the deep end too. He called in the army to burn every seagoing boat on the whole strand a couple of years back, trying to put a cap on it, which my predecessor wisely declined to be part of. We have to live here and I don't want my tars being at risk of a beating by the locals on a run ashore, and for something we should not be part of.'

That brought another artful look to the older man's face. 'You ain't come to the Kent coast with that in mind, have you?' The look of mystification had Braddock add, 'To have a word in his ear?

'Sir,' Brazier replied truthfully, 'I didn't even know he used Walmer Castle, so why would I?'

Braddock made an attempt to look as if he believed his visitor and failed, given what he had proposed made sense to a competitive and devious mind. William Pitt's elder brother had recently been offered the post of First Lord of the Admiralty, and might in future be able to dole out employment to the likes of Brazier and Braddock. What better way to apply pressure on Lord Chatham than through his younger sibling, who just happened to also be, as the King's First Minister, his political superior?

'Wasting your time, mind you. More wine?'

Brazier nodded and held out his glass, deciding it was time to get to the nub of his reasons for calling. 'I was wondering how you were fixed in the article of spare mounts, sir. I will require a horse while I'm here.'

'Dire, Brazier, dire. Half our nags are near to spavined and asking the Navy Board for the funds to retire and replace the creatures falls on deaf ears, which means of course the fit horses are asked to do too much. That said, you tickle my curiosity. What good would one of our shire horses be to you?'

'You have no others?'

The response was sharp. 'Only coach horses, and they are for my personal use.'

'Then I wonder perhaps about stabling a hired animal?'

'Town's not short on places and we are surrounded by farms who would oblige you.'

'If I could stable here, it would be convenient for the Three Kings and I can be sure your men would look after any hire properly. I will of course pay for feed.'

Braddock waited for some indication of what length of time that would be; he waited in vain, not responding till after a deep gulp of wine.

'I daresay we can find you a stall. As for feed, a few oats and some hay, it will not rate the time it takes to calculate a bill. Now, let's put our minds back to the Cape Verdes, for I don't recollect talking it over with you after Suffren humbugged us, French swine that he is. I do recall your name being praised by the Commodore for your taking back of the *Infernal*.'

'That was a hot affair.'

Braddock's shoulders shook with mirth. 'Very good, Brazier, a telling pun.'

'Unintended, sir,' was the honest reply, *Infernal* having been a fireship. 'But I will add there were many others who should have had their names recalled in that and subsequent encounters. The men I had the honour to lead deserved recognition for it.'

'Luck, Brazier, it all comes down to luck: whose name is put forward for praise and who's left out. Only the Good Lord knows how I have suffered from that.'

* * *

33

By the time he exited the Naval Yard, Edward Brazier and Braddock had refought three engagements: the one against Admiral Suffren off Porto Praya in the Cape Verdes, another at the Cape of Good Hope and a third battle to take the port of Trincomalee in Ceylon. The last was where Brazier got his step to post rank, leading the successful assault to take the fort, which dominated the harbour.

He had partaken of too much of Braddock's wine and, his host not being choosy in the article of quality, it sat ill on Brazier's stomach and even worse on his tongue. The remedy was sea air and legs fully employed, so he set off along the busy street fronting the beach at a pace – an object of some curiosity to the locals, who must know every officer who oversaw the yard and wondered at a newcomer.

The strand itself, shiny pebbles glimpsed through the numerous alleys which allowed access to the shoreline, was busy as goods were loaded to be carried out to the waiting ships. That acknowledged, there were just as many craft idle as employed; those who crewed them, bearded, weather-beaten fellows clad in dirty and well-worn oilskins, sat on the gunwales smoking their pipes.

Brazier knew ships sailing down from London took on much of what they required here, not least hands for blue-water sailing, in numbers not necessary for the trip down the River Thames. These were men who had been discharged from other merchant vessels on arrival in the roadstead, and for the same reason.

Many of the buildings on both sides of the street advertised themselves as ship chandlers, while one was very obviously a place to recruit hands, given the clutch of tars milling around outside. There would be competition for the more experienced: those who could hand, reef and steer. Also numerous tables were laden with several varieties of fish, dead on the slab but with the seawater smell of freshness. Others held piles of live crabs and lobsters, these manned by females of such brutish appearance and formidable build that they looked sure to get the best of any bargaining.

He passed a pair of armed bastions placed to back up, with cannon, those of the old twin castles. These occupied the only spaces not given over to dwellings, going on till he came to the most northerly of the local Tudor-built fortresses: a very run-down affair, with its moat gone and its walls at the mercy of the sea.

What lay beyond looked to be flat scrub and marshland dotted with sandhills all the way to a distant set of chalk cliffs, so he decided to make his way back by a different route, taking a gentle slope through a jumble of gimcrack dwellings, hovels really, until he came to what seemed to be some kind of main thoroughfare: a long and straight, lower-level road.

At this north end of the town there were buildings only on the seaward side, opposite a series of market and vegetable-growing gardens. The road itself was not short on ruts, through which various conveyances, hand- and horse-drawn, sought to manoeuvre by each other with no set order. Thus the air was replete with shouting and endless disagreement on the right of way, with no shortage of blaspheming. There was also no scarcity of equine filth, both fresh and driven into the mud, which gave employment to a series of crossing sweepers at each junction.

The east-side houses turned to an untidy set of more trading emporiums, each with its beam and double block to raise and lower goods from the upper floors. Just like the front, all the trades that serviced seagoing ships were here; sailmakers and purveyors of canvas by the bolt, emporiums selling rope from whip lines to multi-stranded anchor cables, businesses suppling vinegar and turpentine spirits. There would be a woodyard and bakeries for ship's biscuit somewhere, as well as a slaughterhouse for meat.

Interspersed with these emporiums was a ready supply of places in which you could buy drink, some no more than a sign and a single open window, behind which probably sat a naval widow, granted the right to earn the means to eat by vending spirituous liquor, mostly gin, in lieu of a pension.

The dominant building was the church, solidly constructed in brick on the landward side and with no pretentions to the excessive elaboration of the Papist tradition. It was of a design popular in the reign of William and Mary – a style Brazier, as a midshipman, had seen replicated in what had been the American colonies. His ever-curious nose took him down the side street to reveal a large graveyard to the rear and, knowing it must contain the remains of sailors like himself, he was drawn to examine the headstones.

The sight of the parasol and two bonneted females exiting a narrow gate made him stop and, if he was surprised, that was as nothing to the look of sheer shock they displayed. The older of the two, as he lifted his hat, bent to whisper in the ear of the younger woman and, by her expression, the urgent words she was saying were not praiseworthy, though any strictures she issued were not obeyed.

'Captain Brazier. I cannot adequately express the depth of my astonishment at seeing you here.'

'Mrs Langridge, my amazement is equal to your own. Yet I welcome it, in that I should meet you so fortuitously. Knowing you resided hard by the town, it had been my intention to drop you a note asking if it would be fitting to call.'

As a touch of colour came to the cheeks of Betsey Langridge, Brazier turned a fraction to look at the older woman, her Aunt Sarah. If her niece showed no malevolence, it was not replicated in a woman saddled with a most inappropriate name.

'Mrs Lovell.'

'Why do I sense your presence is no coincidence, sir?'

'I do assure you, this meeting is just that, madam.'

'You will forgive me if I take leave to doubt it.'

It was Betsey who spoke next, her pleasant tone annoying her aunt, who sucked in irritated cheeks. 'It does seem strange, Captain Brazier, given the last time we met was some three thousand miles distant.'

'A meeting that I fondly recall.'

Another hint of a blush was followed by a twirl of Betsey's parasol, as a clearly exasperated Aunt Sarah spoke once more. 'We came to lay flowers at the memorial to Mr Langridge.'

This was forcibly delivered to remind him of the situation of her niece.

'I was given to understand Mr Langridge was buried in the Caribbean?'

'That does not preclude recollection of his fine nature, as well as a plaque to his memory, in the graveyard of a parish church in which he worshipped many times and to the building of which his family generously subscribed.'

'Please feel free to call, Captain Brazier, though I would take it as a kindness to be allowed some prior warning.'

'Perhaps in a few weeks' time?' posited Aunt Sarah, with an attempt at, and an utter failure to produce, a sweet smile.

Brazier was looking very directly at her niece. 'I doubt I could delay that long.'

'And neither should you, sir.'

'Elisabeth! We must be getting home.'

'Of course, Aunt Sarah,' was the reply, but her eyes were still on Edward Brazier, who had just told both women where he was residing.

CHAPTER THREE

It was a much-cheered fellow who returned to the Three Kings, the immediate task to write to Betsey Langridge. The doubts he had harboured as to his reception, which had plagued him for some time, could be put to rest. From where he sat now, they looked to have been absurd, yet that had to be acknowledged as hindsight. The last time he had seen her had been thousands of miles away, which took no account of a twelve-month gap.

Added to that, their last parting had held no firm indication that any future suit would prosper. Folk in the old country might suspect the moral standards of the colonies to be lax, when the truth was the very opposite: in such small communities reputations could be shredded on the merest whiff of damning gossip, so care to avoid scandal was rigid.

On first meeting her, Betsey had been too recent a widow to show open interest in anyone. Aware of these restrictions and the number of prying eyes had tempered Brazier's attentions; he had to keep the fact of his immediate attraction to her in check. Early conversations had naturally been hedged by a high degree of formality, so it had been impossible to be sure anything more pointed would be entirely welcome.

Time and repeated contact, in a constrained social milieu where the same people met all the time, had thawed that somewhat, but not enough for him to be sure if he could progress to a more familiar exchange. He had tested the limitations as far as was possible, finding a conversational companion who appeared to see humour in his sallies as well as one who had reacted cordially to his attentions.

These certainly, even in their early, guarded manifestation, had been much frowned upon by Aunt Sarah, sent to fetch Betsey home and to act as her chaperone in the process – and for sound reasons, Elisabeth Langridge having inherited her late husband's lucrative sugar plantations. So Sarah Lovell had her work cut out, for not everyone of the resident colonial bachelors had been quite as guarded when it came to her niece's reputation.

A few shameless opportunists made plain their intention to pursue her, only to be effectively rebuffed. The worst of the lot had been the hardest to deal with: none other than King George's third son, Prince William. Not that it was her property that drew him to her, or the prospect of an advantageous marriage; he was attracted by her manifest beauty and, in terms of attention, she was not alone.

William, touring the Caribbean in command of the frigate HMS *Pegasus*, had gained a reputation as something of a satyr and Jamaica was not the only place where his gross attempts at seduction had caused a stir. He had outraged folk in Antigua and Bermuda and, from what had been gossiped about since, he had continued his habit of excessive drinking, coupled with overfamiliarity, in the Leeward Islands.

If the amount he drank was not unusual, the effect upon his behaviour was, pointing to an exceedingly light head. In his orbit, when so affected, no woman, married, single, young or mature, was safe from his risqué sallies and outrageous suggestions, not least that irregular intimacy with a royal prince was a gift to be prized.

Brazier had been forced to intervene to stop one of the local port officials from calling the prince out. A duel would have caused a scandal in any event; if he had been wounded or expired – not impossible since his challenger was a crack shot – the result did not bear thinking about. Then there was the dispute Prince William had with his premier, to which Brazier had become an unwilling party.

As captain of HMS *Pegasus*, William was a martinet and by no stretch could he be described as a fully competent seaman; he owed his rank and command to his bloodline. His first lieutenant and a highly competent officer, Mr Schomberg, who had been placed aboard to counter the prince's inexperience, had occasion to intervene in the case of an approaching hurricane, questioning his superior's orders in terms of precautions to both secure the ship and seek a safe harbour.

This had led to a public dressing-down from a choleric royal on the quarterdeck, witnessed by the whole crew, followed by an official complaint from the prince to the senior officer on the station. This meant it had landed on Edward Brazier's desk, given the Jamaica Station was between commanding admirals, one having died suddenly and the man already designated as his replacement not yet arrived.

A dogged Isaac Schomberg demanded a court martial to clear his name. In examining the case and prior to the event, Brazier could plainly see from the logs of HMS *Pegasus* that Prince William was in the wrong and he gave an opinion under oath that said so. This did not go down well either with the miscreant or, he was subsequently to discover, at Windsor Castle; officers of his rank did not take the side of a mere lieutenant against a Prince of the Blood.

Brazier put aside these thoughts to concentrate on composing his note. He must eschew any hint of overfamiliarity, for her aunt would surely insist on seeing whatever he wrote. Her hackles were ever on show, as they had been earlier, and, given he was acting with a haste she would deplore, nothing must be provided as an excuse to fob him off. Finally satisfied, several scrunched-up attempts at his feet, he gave a final critical perusal, sanded the letter, folded and sealed it, then went downstairs to arrange delivery. Garlick was stationed at the hatch just inside the entrance, obsequious as ever.

'I require this to be delivered as soon as feasible. Charge any cost to my account and I must know it has arrived and has been accepted.'

'Never fear, your honour, I'll see to it.'

Garlick took the small square of folded paper to examine the destination. That he looked at it for some time and was still while doing so caused Brazier to wonder. 'Is there something amiss, Mr Garlick?'

The reply was slow in coming and unconvincing when spoken; indeed, the man seemed to have acquired a frog in his throat, so hoarse was the word when he said there was nothing wrong. With no time to wonder, Brazier moved on to his next concern. He needed to hire a horse – it was too early to buy one – and it had to be an animal that reflected his standing.

'I cannot turn up anywhere on any old cob, I need a pure-bred.'

He was about to add that it would need to be a passive beast as well, but that was something for a stable yard owner, not an innkeeper. He had not ridden a horse these six years past and knew from experience anything in the least bit sprightly would tax his rusty abilities to control it. It would not look good turning up at Cottington Court on a feisty mount he was struggling to keep in check.

'If I can make so bold as to suggest the yard of Mr Flaherty for your needs.'

'Irish, I would guess.'

'He is that, sir, with the gift of his race when he speaks.'

'Honest in his dealings?'

'I would have a care to purchase from him, sir, yet that would be true of anyone dealing in horseflesh, for it is the occupation of scoundrels. But for a hire, he will see you have what you need and, if it is not in his own paddocks, he will know where to find it.'

'Then all I require is directions.'

'Best I send a lad to show you the way, your honour. Beyond habitation, one road and field round these parts looks much like another.'

'Make it so, I will wait for him outside.'

'There are seats in the parlour and you can partake of refreshment there.'

'No, plain sea air for me.'

Having seen the parlour and the near-impenetrable fug of pipe smoke which emanated from the occupants, he had no desire to inhale it. If the Three Kings lacked folk to fill the rooms, it was obviously a venue for the more prosperous citizens of the town, to gossip, take a turn on the most recently delivered journals from London and perhaps to transact business.

That very thing was in the air at another location. The arrangements for the meeting between two very suspicious parties had taken near a month of talking to finalise and, even now, the lack of mutual trust was evident. Both the principals had arrived with armed escorts, while the agreed location had been set at the top of a hill dominated by a windmill.

This overlooked the fields that dropped away to the strand of buildings forming the southern end of Lower Deal, and height allowed for a complete view of the approaches; no one was taking a chance on being surprised, but it did fully expose the hilltop to any breeze going and there was a brisk easterly on this day.

A hired coach stood empty at the crown, with each party taking one side of the slope, in their centre the conveyances of the men who had come to talk, neither trusting the other to use their own. By the middle coach two men stood talking, though their conversation was not of long duration, merely a check that all the conditions had been met. That established, a waved arm was a signal to proceed.

The principals alighted and headed uphill, throwing wary glances all around to ensure their security, before entering the meeting coach through opposite doors. Very different in appearance, they eyed each other as two cats would do when defending a territory, to then rest on opposite padded seats without a word exchanged. Henry Tulkington, as ever with a handkerchief in his hand, held it to his mouth and coughed before speaking.

'I do think, Spafford, since you pressed that we meet, it is up to you to commence proceedings.'

'Proceedings you call it. Fancy term.'

The voice, unlike that of Tulkington, was heavily local and, if that contrasted, so did their appearance. The man speaking showed the rough skin and red face of a one-time sailor, as well as the physique of a bruiser: stocky with wide shoulders, rough hands added to the lumps and scars of a hard life and physical contests. The fellow he was addressing wore with ease the air of a gentleman; tall, slim of frame even in a thick coat and muffler, with an ascetic, pale face, hair hidden under his tricorne hat and a powdered wig.

'To a purpose, I hope. It would not please me to be dragged out to face the elements for no reason.' Tulkington coughed again, as if to underline the effect of the cool breeze on his chest. 'I doubt you appreciate I am a far from well man, and having you in close proximity does nothing to aid my maladies.'

'And what if it's not just you that can lay claim to a malady?'

That took a moment to absorb. 'You render me curious.'

'The Grim Reaper might be standing by my shoulder, so close I can near feel him.' Tulkington recoiled so his back was pressed hard against the body of the coach, while his face registered alarm. 'You reckon yourself to be suffering from a whole raft of disorders, which many put down to imaginings. I know I am for certain, just as I know it could be a telling one that might see me gone within a twelvemonth.'

'Is it an affliction to carry by proximity?'

'Never worry, it will not afflict another. It's well hidden too and able to be kept undisclosed as yet.'

'So much so that I remark this. You look in rude health.'

'Which will not last long, and that's the cause that made me press for this.'

'I hope you didn't come expecting sympathy.'

'Do you rate me a boob?'

'I reckon you a vexation and one who has deprived me of a deal of money by your locally undercutting my prices.'

'There you go bein' high and mighty. You don't own this coast, an' your line never has.' That brought forth a bout of coughing and employment of the handkerchief from the man so accused. 'I want an assurance, Tulkington, that what I tell you in this here coach stays a'tween us. Not even your right hand is to know.'

'A lot to ask, Spafford. What if it's not to my advantage?'

'It will be in time to come.'

'Something you've failed to get around to mentioning. If what you say is true, I will not rejoice to see you go from this world – that would be un-Christian – but I would not have you hope me mourn.' A fearful face followed and a hand covered and rubbed at his heart. 'Besides, who knows, I may precede you.'

'Not claiming to be a God-lover I could then celebrate, but you'se been dying since the day you was born and there was a time I fell for it. Now I don't; I reckon you to see old bones, where I will not.'

The reply was delivered with rare passion: Henry Tulkington hated his lack of good health to be questioned. 'Have you turned physician, man?'

'Don't need to, when I has eyes and hopes so many times dashed. But this ain't gettin' us to where we need to be.'

'*You* need to be.'

'Fair enough. If I peg it, it will be my lad Harry who will be in line to take my place.' Tulkington tried not to smirk, but it was impossible; he knew Harry Spafford too well and so did his pa. 'I don't reckon him to last long afore one of my own topples him, which won't be done gentle – can't be.'

'How charming,' Tulkington opined, before chuckling, and then added, 'You can share a plot, perhaps with his mother too, if he was ever to find out to where she fled to get away from you.'

'It's not a matter for jests.'

'Get to what you want, Spafford.'

'To die in peace, knowing my lad will not follow me to the grave.'

'I can hardly prevent that.'

'You can if I give all I have to you a'forehand.' For the second time Tulkington was forced back against the body of the coach, though less violently on this occasion, it being brought on by astonishment, not fear of contagion. 'If I know I'm goin', I'll cede my business to you and lead my lads into an alliance. Once I've perished, you'll have this stretch of the coast to yourself.'

'And Harry?' A nod. 'You reckon me to be gentle with him and fund his drinking?'

'My offer is only good if I can get him out of harm's way – an' can I say now, as matters stand, I would reckon you to drop him overboard with roundshot in his breeches.'

'So what you offer comes with a tariff.'

'It does. What I will gift you is my share of the trade and with it the freedom to price goods as you choose. In return I need to see a way to fashion Harry's future, out of your way and no trouble to anyone.'

'I'm intrigued.'

'What does that mean?'

Tulkington felt a surge of superiority then and could not hide a smirk. He was educated, Spafford was not and it was always a cause for pleasure to have such a fact confirmed. 'You have pricked my interest.'

'I need to be able to leave my Harry enough to get by on, and away from East Kent as well.'

'Is there such a sum to be had? His consumption of drink is legendary, as are the debts he obliges you to pay.'

'We both know business has been harder since the peace.'

'For you, maybe.'

'You might not be suffering as much, but suffer you do.'

'I will allow you your assumptions, Spafford, and long may you hold to your delusions.'

'Let me in on a part of yours, a few good cargoes, so I can make

Harry a legacy which, over time, will return to you tenfold when I am set to expire.'

'A notion that renders the word "delusion" insufficient. You should be grateful I don't bury you early, which is well within my power to effect.'

'Not without bloodshed and that would serve us both ill, as you know from past encounters in your father's day.' Tulkington fought to keep on his face a look of indifference, but Spafford was not fooled. 'Folk who will turn a blind eye to cheating the Revenue will not do so if there are bodies to explain, will they? Your pa understood that and so do you.'

'Get to the point.'

'I need to ensure my lad is out of reach of those who would do for him and, try as I have, there's no getting away from the fact that someone will. He's not strong and is too tempted by the bottle.'

'You forgot the trollops,' Tulkington sneered. 'I doubt there's enough in coin to secure for Harry both his drinking as well as his whoring.'

'Crow away, Tulkington, but think on it an' you'll come to see the sense, for whoever tops my Harry will not hesitate to seek to do like to you. They'll have to, for that will be the promise they must make for support. You'll have that war I spoke of on your hands, even if you don't want it, and we both know what it will mean.'

'One in which I'd expect to easily triumph.'

'But at what price? Money well get even tighter and the Preventatives will be forced to pick up on it. They'll see a purpose in getting off their bone-idle arses an' happen, if it gets bloody enough, the army will be called in, as it was on the instructions of Billy Pitt. And where's he half the time? Not in London, but sitting in Walmer Castle just waiting for an excuse to crack down hard and for good.'

'I rate him of little account in my affairs.'

'Now, maybe, but fighting don't allow for that. Not even you can hide when you're in a bloody struggle. Folk who are close-mouthed now will talk to save their own skin if they are at any risk of being seen as being accomplices to murder. Names will be given out, so I wouldn't be surprised to see a whole host at Tyburn, queuing for their turn to dangle, with the only way out to put others up for the drop. What if you're exposed for what you control, an' happen be one of the party?'

'I sense it would be a sight to cheer you.'

'That I give you, the only pity is I will not be there to witness it.'

That occasioned a long pause; Tulkington knew what Spafford was thinking, for his aim was obvious. Did the sod know what he was reflecting on, that was more important? What he was being told required to be thought about, for the outcomes outlined were not utterly fanciful but, right now, it was necessary to be blunt and dismissive.

'What a picture you paint, Spafford – and that's what it is, nothing more than imaginings. The fate of Harry Spafford is no concern of mine and let the devil have him when his time comes. It will do hereabouts a favour, for he carries your blood and that is foul enough, without adding the afflictions he has picked up in his debaucheries.'

'You don't see what I propose as advantage to you in the long run?'

'No.'

'I ask you to put your mind to the matter, for I might not have long.'

That was received with a vehement shake of the head, which elicited from Spafford a bitter response.

'I didn't have you for a fool, Tulkington, but happen I was the one all along, seeing I pressed for this meet. If you won't do what is goin' to be to your gain, I ask only this. That what we have talked about you keep to yourself. I reckon to read your mind, but know this, I'll start a war afore I go if you seek benefit from my ailment, an' I'll make sure it keeps goin' when I'm in my six feet of earth, to be carried through till you're taken down. So give me your word.'

It was a long time in coming, but come it did.

'Then our business is done,' Spafford said in a flat tone, head bowed and eyes down, which hinted at his disappointment. 'Happen we will never clap eyes on each other again and it will end up in regret for my boy and you too. The last will be some recompense to me when I meet my maker, if I am so blessed.'

Tulkington opened the coach door, shivering at the blast of wind that swept in, stepping out to deliver his parting words. 'Given you're a product of pure devilment, I am sure you will meet your maker the second you expire. Satan will welcome you to the fires of hell with open arms.'

He turned away, pulling his coat and comforter tight around him as he strode back to his own coach and the safety of his men. John Hawker, the man who led them, looked at him quizzically only to get a shake of the head. It was not that Tulkington intended to keep his promise to Spafford, but it was not yet time to break it for a man who always kept his cards close to his chest.

'Let us get out of here.'

His long-time adversary sat still in contemplation until the fellow he had set to arrange matters could hold his curiosity no longer. The Tulkington coach was heading away by that time, with the men he had brought as escorts following on foot.

'Well,' Daisy Trotter asked softly, a sleeve crossing his nose to remove a drop. 'Did he fall for it?'

'He says not, but from what I know of Tulkington, fast thinking is not his way. Happen, when he reasons on the matter it will be seen a notion to act on. Let it stew for a few days.'

'It's either that or we have to do for him, at whatever cost.'

Spafford looked at Jaleel Trotter, called Daisy, with his stringy build, wheezy breath, watery eyes and the near-permanent clear drip on the end of his nose. He appeared to be weak and, in truth, he was not sturdy. But he had a reputation as the master of the sly knife in the ribs, backbones for choice.

'If it comes to that it has to be.'

CHAPTER FOUR

Not expecting an immediate reply from Cottington Court, Brazier had time to reacquaint himself with riding a horse, not that the basics were a mystery. You do not forget how to hold the reins, or the need to use thighs and heels, backed up by the voice, to get the mount to obey a command. But he was conscious that after such a long absence, the muscles employed would ache after too long in the saddle, that part of his anatomy in contact with leather the same.

The Irishman, Flaherty, had put forward to him a near-perfect mount called Bonnie, a bay mare of some eighteen hands and one that showed no inclination to tug at the bridle, so the trot around the paddock promised to be pleasant. This proved to be the case, the owner – an inquisitive soul who had already asked several questions – standing in the middle with a keen eye and the odd suggestion.

'So what would be bringing a Jack tar to this neck of the woods, with him not having a ship in the Downs?'

'You discount mere curiosity, sir,' Brazier replied, as he nudged the animal into a trot. 'A desire just to see the sights.'

That got a smile. 'How could I, when it's me posing the enquiry?'

Flaherty had a hair colour to match the mount, though unlike the smooth coat, his wild ginger mop looked to be untameable. With that went pale, freckled skin and bright-green eyes, alongside an easy manner. Brazier had to remind himself it was one which could be used to deceive as well as charm. Garlick was right: horse dealers were a highly suspect lot.

'You sit reasonably well, I will say that, but I would suggest a straighter back.'

Brazier pulled himself upright and was pleased to notice the effect as it increased pressure on the stirrups; he seemed more connected to the horse as he urged it into a canter, taking her over some poles lying on the sand, something he did a dozen times, while declining the Irishman's suggestion that they be raised a few feet. When he finally dismounted, the session – conversation included – had lasted, to his surprise and by his watch, for near a full hour.

As he held the timepiece in his hand he saw Flaherty looking at it keenly, which made him realise he had been unwise, it being a new and expensive gold-plated Hunter bought on the way through London. A man who traded in horseflesh was well versed in picking up the signs of a customer's means by his possessions. Quickly he snapped it shut and put it back in his waistcoat.

Bonnie was put to a hay net, Flaherty leading him into the empty stall he used as an office. 'How long will you be wanting the beast?'

The possibility of being rebuffed existed, as did the reverse. It would be unwise to show confidence on a mere smile. 'That is uncertain; I could not even say it would go to a week. I would therefore posit that a daily rate would serve.'

'Fair enough.' The green eyes narrowed then and the lips thinned. 'With, of course, a sum in indemnity, for the tack and lest the horse suffer in any way. Strong they might appear, but they are frail creatures and much given to ailments. This here Bonnie is of value to me – a favourite, you might say.'

Brazier wanted to say pigs might fly as the two men locked eyes, not in any rancorous way, but in that fashion folk do when they are seeking to discern the limits of what one can charge and the other can contest. If the Irishman was good at it, so was Brazier; a man could not rise to be a captain of a fighting ship, dealing with admirals, a crew of three-hundred-plus men added to a dozen officers, every one ambitious, and not be well versed in the rules of the mute encounter.

Edward Brazier had learnt long ago that his best weapon was silence; the first to speak was usually the first to give ground. It was plain that Flaherty had studied at the same academy, for he said nothing, the only indication of his knowledge of the game a slow spreading smile until finally he realised he could not win.

'I sense I am dealing with a fellow who is not of the swaying kind.'

Brazier grinned. 'While I sense a worthy adversary, Mr Flaherty.'

A hand came out. 'Vincent in the name.'

'And a commendable one for your race,' was the reply as it was grasped. 'A fair price I will pay, but—'

'Such a price will be provided. I suggest three shillings a day for both mount and tack, with an indemnity for me to hold of five guineas, plus the cost of stabling.'

'Done. But I will be stabling at the Naval Yard, where your favourite will be well cared for in the article of feed and grooming and at a cost not inflated by avarice.'

Flaherty threw back his head and laughed as Brazier reached into his coat for his purse, an act which caused the Irishman to cap his humour. Looking stern, he raised ginger eyebrows.

'You carry such sums on your person, sir?' The look Flaherty got implied the obvious, given his customer was quickly counting out the guineas. 'If I could be so bold to advise you, I would not maintain it as a habit in a place like Deal. They teach filching in the cradle hereabouts.'

'As they do in every port I've ever set foot in, Mr Flaherty.' Brazier nodded to his weapon, lying on the man's trestle desk. 'But as you see, I rarely go abroad without my sword and we sailors are not known to be gentle with our knuckles, regardless of rank.'

'I would still advise double purses, one for small coin and another for gold.' Flaherty began to smile again as he looked at Brazier's breeches. 'The one you'll have to resort to in order to get yourself some boots.'

Brazier had not thought on it beforehand, and so had arrived at the paddock in his uniform breeches and white stockings – adequate for the roads hereabouts, dry paths and the deck of a ship, but no good for a horse. The inner part of both calves, which had not been protected by the saddlecloth, were now streaked with dirt, he having ridden Bonnie when she had been fetched in from grazing, without her being groomed first.

'There's a cobbler opposite St George's Church who has pairs for loan. It's quite common for men of the sea not to have any with them, often their bein' stuck here for a month or more.'

The still-saddled mount was led to the gate where sat the lad who had guided him to Flaherty's paddock, now waiting to show him the way back. Brazier saw the light of wonder in the youngster's eyes, for the animal was handsome, which caused him to pose the question.

'Your name, boy?'

'Ben to all.'

'Well, Ben, would you care to sit atop her?'

'Why that would be sure fine, your honour. Ain't never got up on anything but a donkey.'

'Then let me hoist you aboard.'

Which he duly did, settling him on the saddle and taking the reins to lead Bonnie down the lane. If the boy was delighted and excited, Brazier forbore to tell him that it was he who was doing the favour, this for a man whose lower limbs were aching.

The note he had written was being waved with some irritation. 'I feel I must forbid you to respond, Elisabeth.'

Betsey Langridge put much effort into keeping calm, which was far from easy. 'I think, Aunt Sarah, you exceed your responsibilities.'

'I do not. It is my task, given to me by my dear nephew, to see your reputation is not sullied.' A loud sniff saw her fingers entwined at her waist. 'I daresay it is easier here at home than it was in that heat-blasted island on which you lived, but the limits of proper behaviour do not alter.'

'A gentleman of some standing, a highly respected naval officer, asks merely to call and renew an acquaintance. What harm can there be in that?'

Her much older relative did not have to work hard to display displeasure; the cast of her features – pinched pale lips with the creases of her years, hollow cheeks and catlike eyes – naturally leant towards it. The assemblage was fully deployed now for she could see harm as plain as day.

'If Henry were here he would back me up.'

The tone hardened; Betsey was heartily sick of not being able to go anywhere without her aunt in tow. Likewise she hovered on the perimeter of any conversation, even with a woman, never mind a man. Betsey reckoned she had no role in life other than satisfying her brother, so was taking comfort from the one with which she had been tasked.

'He has no more right to rule my behaviour than do you. Is it necessary to remind you that I am no longer some inexperienced maiden, but a woman who has been wedded and also mistress of her own household?'

'You are a widow.'

'Something of which I hardly require to be reminded.'

Sarah Lovell changed tack, her tone less entreating. 'What do you think this Captain Brazier thought of your behaviour outside the graveyard?'

That touch of rouge on the cheeks appeared again, which had Betsey turn to face the mullioned window to hide it. 'I cannot fathom what you mean.'

53

'Fiddlesticks. You know precisely what I mean. I would not say you actually simpered on seeing him, but it was not far from that. And what is the fellow doing here, anyway? I do not recall him saying he was in a ship.'

'I have no idea and neither do you.'

'You do not see yourself as the reason?'

Betsey spun round again, making no effort to hide her resentment. 'Now it is my turn to say fiddlesticks to you. I recall, as I am sure do you, that Captain Brazier was punctilious in his manner from the very first time we met in Jamaica.'

'On that occasion he was in the Governor's House and on his best behaviour, as he needed to be. I would not say that he held to that standard every time you met subsequently. In fact, he became increasingly forward.'

Seeking distraction, Betsey mentioned another pursuer. 'You mean like Prince William!'

Aunt Sarah fell for it, saying with some vehemence, and throwing her eyes to the ceiling, 'May the Good Lord forgive me for lese-majesty, for that's a fellow who needs to meet the birch rod he was spared as a child.'

Betsey could not say, dare not admit, she had taken a liking to Edward Brazier on that first occasion and it was one that had grown with further acquaintance. On the island it was impossible not to meet at every event when his ship was in harbour; horse races and regattas, the balls that followed, and celebrations such as the Governor's or the King's birthday.

Within the bounds of good manners, he had shown himself to have a telling wit, which never strayed into the vulgar. There was, too, an attraction to him beyond that, a certain presence that went with his rank and responsibilities, fortified by a modest self-confidence. Betsey had observed he was respected by both his inferior officers and fellow captains, an attitude that extended to the Governor of Jamaica himself.

What she hid, even from herself, was the fact of a physical attraction, for he had a figure good to look upon. When she had searched for a word to describe him to herself, it settled on saturnine. He had regular features on a dark skin made more so by the Caribbean sun, under straight black hair tied at the rear by a silk ribbon, for he eschewed a wig. Even his height, a bit over six feet compared to her own five foot and a half, seemed to feel right. He also had a penetrating and steady way of looking at her and spoke with a deep and attractive voice; it was that which she recalled above all.

'I will reply, inviting him to call; to do otherwise would be a want of the good manners you so prize. Added to which, you will be present, so nothing that might offend the sensibilities can occur.'

As Betsey swept out to go to the library and pen her note, she was thinking not only would Sarah Lovell never leave them alone, but her mere presence would drain out of the meeting any possible pleasure.

Sitting at the desk, quill in hand, it was some time before it was dipped in the inkwell. Betsey looked around the book-lined walls and reflected how much she had loved being in here as a growing girl. It was in this very room that her governess had taught her embroidery. The Reverend Moyle was held to be incapable of much in the education line – indeed he often demonstrated staggering ignorance.

So the nearby Vicar of St Leonard's in Upper Deal had been engaged to impart Latin, Greek and mathematics. It was rudiments, naturally, and not to a standard of a fully educated cleric, but good enough to allow her to engage in conversation with people of some erudition without sounding foolish.

It was impossible, too, not to recall her life with Stephen Langridge, a much-loved only child whom she had known from infancy, his family being nearly as prominent locally as her own. Deal and its surroundings were not overgifted with folk of quality, so they formed a somewhat incestuous circle that had met often, in the same manner as people in Jamaica. The two had grown up together and had meandered, on reaching maturity, into a mutual attraction without really noticing.

This had not met with brotherly approval, he acting as though the man asking to marry her could be some kind of threat, which was absurd. Henry did like to command those around him, but how could he see gentle Stephen in that light? He was handsome and graceful of manner, qualities that her brother had always lacked, so she rated him jealous.

Betsey could see and hear Stephen too, in her mind's eye, right now: a flop of fair hair dropping over his brow, a hand uselessly and continuously employed to sweep it back into place, his voice light and kindly. There were the soft eyes and the lazy smile, at its best when she caught him gazing at her unawares and, if the place had been discreet, with no servants to observe, they would fall into each other's arms to allow spontaneous mutual pleasure to follow.

That aspect of their life together, of which she had been warned in the most alarming terms by Aunt Sarah, amongst others, had turned out to be the very opposite of the tales of painful and unpleasant duty. Stephen had been a gentle but eager lover and had found in his wife someone who returned his desire in full and enthusiastic measure. How she missed that.

He had been mounted the last time she saw him in full health: astride his stallion, wearing his broad-brimmed straw hat and blowing her a kiss as he set off to tour the plantations, a journey that would take a week. It was impossible to not contrast that with the speed of his decline, for within the month he was a near skeleton, whose hair had gone, the lazy smile more of a rictus.

She felt tears pricking her eyes and a thought came to her that she could never quite suppress. When Stephen passed away, the same when he was committed to the ground, Betsey could not be sure for whom she felt more remorseful: him, or herself for being left in limbo. It was hard to push the shame of that out of her mind, but with effort she did so, beginning to write.

My dear Captain Brazier

* * *

He having returned, Sarah Lovell went straight to see her nephew to appraise him of what had happened outside the graveyard and, what's more, his sister's response in writing to invite this fellow to visit at his own convenience, which to her was on the very edge of respectable acceptability. She found him occupied with a visitor: a local mill owner, she was informed, who had already been kept waiting to see him, obliging her to go away and return, so she heard very little of what was a heated exchange.

Sarah Lovell was absolutely certain Henry would share her view once the fellow had departed and she was admitted to tell her tale. Yet the attitude he adopted, as he went to stand before the fire to couch his first question, did not much indicate any firm opinion.

'A navy man, you say?'

He listened without much reaction until he posed the next question, which was an obvious one. What did his aunt know of the man? Sarah Lovell was obliged to say that when she arrived in Jamaica Brazier had been the naval officer in command at Kingston, his admiral having died in horrible circumstances. If he was popular with the governor and his inferior officers, he was not much loved by the colonials, plantation owners and traders.

'And why would that be?'

'Due to his diligence in enforcing the Navigation Acts, Henry, which had those same islanders paying higher prices for that which they wished and, very often, needed to purchase. The talk was of combining to sue him for their losses'

Further than that she could not go, but his interest in Elisabeth, if not singular in a society she saw as lax, had been manifest.

'How my sister reacted has more bearing,' was the considered response; that not leading to a rebuttal told him all he needed to know. 'I sent you to Jamaica to protect her from this, did I not?'

'You did, nephew, and I did what was necessary to discourage not only Captain Brazier, but all those who sought to show untoward attention to Elisabeth – a task not easy, but one in which I was sure I had succeeded.'

'Evidently not.'

Sarah Lovell was stung and desired to tell Henry that with a headstrong sister he would have done no better. Yet she was in no position to challenge him, even if she thought him mistaken. It would do no good, and she was given no chance, to tell him of her successes: of the others she had seen off, the ones with the gleam of golden guineas in their eyes. She was required to further dwell on this proposed visitor in regard to that very subject.

'I doubt he has need of Elisabeth's plantations. It was the talk of the island when I arrived. Brazier had taken a Spanish ship from some French pirates, one they had previously captured. In its holds was a cargo of silver and, given the gap between its capture and rescue, this was accounted as prize goods. Brazier got his eighth share of the value as per custom, which was, as you can guess, substantial.'

'And now he has turned up in Deal?'

'Had there been correspondence, I would have seen this coming, Henry. But those who wrote to Elisabeth from the West Indies were very obvious in their intentions and aspirations, so as to be a subject of much amusement between us. They were clearly just in pursuit of her money.'

'Where is Elisabeth now?'

'Perhaps in the library. She went there to pen the invitation to Brazier.'

'Ask her to come and see me. It would be best that it is not sent.'

Sarah Lovell found Elisabeth was not where she thought and was not even within the house. On enquiries being made, it was established she had gone for a walk in the woods, the dogs being missing too, a common enough occurrence and one quite regular. Sarah also found out the lad who helped in the stables had been sent off on a pony, his instructions being to carry a letter to the Three Kings.

* * *

Walking did little to ease the ache in his thighs, which led Brazier to wonder if his hostelry had a bathing machine, for he had often found a dip in the sea to be efficacious in the article of tired hams. Not that it would be as pleasant or as warm as the waters of the Caribbean, into which he had often plunged, with a lookout aloft and a pair of men with muskets to guard against sharks.

Idly he wondered if Betsey was of the type to swim, for if it was uncommon in men, anathema to most sailors, it had become a popular pastime with the fairer sex, who saw benefits to their health. He imagined she would, and that they might take to it together. Being unable to control the thought, he soon had them both naked and delighting in the experience, these becoming imaginings it was hard to control.

He sought to turn his mind to other, less lubricious thoughts. Was it worth composing another round of letters to those who might exert interest on his behalf? The question would be the same: could they see their way to writing to the Admiralty and recommending him for a ship, the fact that such pleas were necessary being deeply annoying.

He had a good record of both service and action under a number of still-living commanding officers, be they captains, commodores or the admirals. They would never have sent in a report containing anything other than praise for his application to his duties. Old Pollock he naturally included, for the misdemeanours of a midshipman were long in the past.

In action under Commodore Johnstone he had distinguished himself on more than one occasion, the first time at Porto Praya in taking back the ship Admiral Braddock had referred to, which had been captured by the French. At the Cape of Good Hope he had led one of the parties that boarded and destroyed a group of eight valuable Dutch merchantmen, there being no way to take them as prizes. Added to that he had been the subject of a Gazette for Trincomalee.

'Best jump down, Ben,' he said, putting aside these recollections as they came in sight of the Three Kings, 'I doubt Mr Garlick will take to me walking and you riding.' Raising his hands he lifted the boy off. 'Nip in and tell him you're back, while I lead her to the Yard stables.'

'Happy to oblige you in that, sir,' the youngster squeaked.

'What, enter a naval yard?' Brazier jested. 'Might be a press gang in there, evil coves just waiting for the likes of you with a cudgel or a shilling, a prime hand in the making.'

'Won't need no press for me, your honour. Come a war, an' I'll put myself forward right off.'

'You'd like to go to sea?'

'Not half.'

It was hard not to say, 'So would I.'

'Perhaps another time. I need to speak with those that will care for her.'

Bonnie was soon stabled and in the hands of those men who would brush her coat, pick her hooves and carry out the dozens of procedures needed to keep a horse healthy. Brazier made his way back to the Three Kings and, on entering, got a look from Garlick that implied he had something of interest to impart, which brought him close.

'We has Mr Pitt with us, your honour.'

'*The* William Pitt?'

'None other. He often comes here for his midday victuals if he's down from London and has no one of family to care for his needs. Happen it would serve to acquaint yourself.'

'Which would require an introduction, Mr Garlick, given I am not one to press myself on anyone, high or low, without one.'

'I did tell him you was recently arrived and I reckon he knew your name.'

'I cannot fathom why he would.'

'With a bit of promptin', I will admit. If I was to say you had returned, happen he'd want to exchange a word.'

Edward Brazier felt a deep reluctance to oblige Garlick, who was, no doubt, seeking to engineer a meeting for his own purposes, not that he could be blamed. It was in the nature of the inn-keeping beast to take advantage wherever it could be sniffed. Introducing men of standing to each other could result in them dining in company and spending money.

Brazier's mind then went back to the suspicions of Admiral Braddock and his reasons for being in Deal. Much as he disliked the prospect of that which Garlick was proposing, smacking as it did of opportunist grovelling, William Pitt was a powerful man, second only to the sovereign in his authority. None but a fool would pass up such a chance.

'Lead the way.'

CHAPTER FIVE

Garlick led him through the parlour, past several tables at which people were eating – less smoky now because of that – then on to a separate dining room. After a discreet knock, he opened the door to reveal William Pit. He was sitting facing the entrance and lifted his head, made curious at the sight of a tall, uniformed officer at the owner's back.

'Saving your presence, sir, there is, as I told you, a senior naval captain a'staying here and he is anxious to make your acquaintance.'

Brazier wanted to curse the man; he had been well and truly humbugged, led to believe it was Pitt's desire to meet with him when it was clearly not the case. This was made doubly embarrassing when a furrowed brow showed his surprise at this intrusion. Sat with his back to a window, overlooking the seashore, beside his plate lay a pile of papers, which he had probably been studying while he ate.

'Sir, this interruption is not of my doing.' If the King's First Minister had looked confused before, he was doubly so now, especially since Garlick quickly and expertly slipped away, leaving him the sole occupant of the doorway. 'I will, of course, leave you to your labours and food in peace.'

The lips, which tended to the downturn, lifted a fraction. 'Am I to judge you are a victim of our overeager host?'

'Perspicacious, sir. He assured me you wished to make *my* acquaintance.'

'He is wedded to his incorrigible trade, but he has put you in a position of some mortification, so I feel it would be churlish merely to send you away. If you wish you may come and join me.' Brazier's eyes flicked to the pile of papers, a look perceived by Pitt. 'You will rescue me from these confounded reports, sir, which are inclined, if I study them while eating, to badly affect my digestion.'

The desire to decline was strong, but the original reason for complying with Garlick was solid too.

'Pray take a seat and I will send for a second goblet. That said, it might serve if we formally introduced ourselves.'

'I well know who you are, sir.'

'Aye, Garlick would have boasted of it.'

'I would have without his swaggering. I saw you once at St James's Palace, during a royal levee.'

The memory was of a salon full of men in uniform, either red or blue, so military, or functionaries in coats of many colours, with just as many ladies of rank and varying levels of age and beauty, from the seriously beautiful to the downright frightful, and all in awe of bustling King George. The monarch had looked to Brazier, even with all his stars and decorations, like quite an ordinary person, albeit one easily driven to barking at people.

'I think you were being much put upon by a very agitated sovereign on the subject of the Prince of Wales, and he was far from discreet in his condemnations.'

'A normal estate, sir, when it comes to his male children, none of whom meet his standards. Please, come in and take a chair . . . ?'

'Brazier, sir, Captain Edward Brazier.'

The look went quizzical only to turn to a non-committal smile, which led his visitor to conclude it had not registered. Why would it? There were too many officers of the Captain's List for them to be at all familiar. Acceding to a hand gesture Brazier took a chair, this as Pitt rang a bell, with silence maintained for the few seconds it took for a servant to appear. He lifted the glass flagon by his side and peered to see what was within.

'Another of the same and a goblet for my guest. Have you eaten, sir?'

The positive response was a lie. In truth it was a mite early for a man accustomed to having his dinner at the naval time: four bells in the afternoon watch and not, as civilians did, around noon. He could dine early, but to eat now would fix him to the table for perhaps too long. Brazier wanted to depart when it suited him, although a couple of glasses of wine from Garlick's surprisingly good cellar would be happily consumed.

'Are you here on duty, Captain?'

'No, sir. I merely came to Deal on a visit.'

Another quizzical look led to a sketched explanation of his recent service, added to the fact that his frigate had just been paid off at Portsmouth. If it left hanging in the air the fact that he was now free of employment, no new ship being mentioned, it was not taken up.

'Three years you say?' Pitt enquired, as a second flagon and a goblet appeared, he then pouring for both of them from the old one, Brazier able to register it was then empty. 'You must have been in Jamaica when Admiral Hassall died?'

'I was, sir; a most unfortunate event.'

'Sudden.'

'Very. His valet saw him to bed a healthy man, but found him dead in the morning.'

'I was informed of his demise by Admiral Lord Howe, in Cabinet. The despatch told us he expired from the bite of a venomous snake?'

Brazier had to hope that Pitt did not notice his very slight hesitation; he had to compose his reply as carefully considered, on a subject he would really like to have avoided.

'That was the conclusion of the physicians. The bite marks on

64

his jugular were obvious, while they insisted the contortions and discolouration of his countenance indicated, when they reported to me, they were correct in their conclusion.'

There seemed to be an element of morbid fascination in the next question. 'You did not observe these effects on the cadaver yourself, then?'

'I trusted the doctors to tell me the facts of the matter. I did, however, see him as he was being sewn in canvas, before he was placed on a board for burial at sea. That did not disguise his face, which proved he died a horrid and painful death. My task was to take over his duties, pending the arrival of his replacement. It was I who wrote home the despatch, regarding his passing, from which Lord Howe read.'

'Onerous, Jamaica, in terms of the responsibility of command, I daresay.'

Brazier replied when he had supped some wine; Pitt had gulped and then refilled his empty glass to near the brim, his guest declining.

'It's a busy station, sir, as much in peace as in war, especially now the Americans are barred from trade with our colonies, not that they don't try. Added to which the traffic from the Spanish Main brings the wolves in abundance and they are singularly far from particular in whom they attack. Our own merchant fleet is as much at their mercy as a Don, for any cargo will serve, given it is easy to sell on. We did our best to curtail that, sir, for the Spanish possessions can be lawless too. Or, shall I say, those who govern them are not given to interference as long as their own vessels are not involved.'

'Nothing short of piracy, in other words, which the King's Navy is surely tasked to prevent.'

'We did have our successes, one or two of them striking.'

Pitt's expression changed to one of sudden enlightenment, the gaze lifting a fraction, as if the answer to what had occurred to him lay above his head. 'Brazier you say? You know I think I've smoked you out now, sir. Were you not the lucky fellow who took a Spanish ship carrying bullion, not long after poor Hassel expired?'

'HMS *Diomede* was fortunate in that regard, sir, but entirely due to an excellent crew and a fine set of officers.'

'While I was not, Captain. Your modesty does you credit, but we had strong representations that the vessel should be restored to Spain and not treated as a prize. The demand was declined, of course, but it did nothing to improve our relations with Madrid, not that they are ever happy as long as we hold Gibraltar.'

Fully expecting to be asked for details of the chase, battle and recapture of the *Santa Clara*, in which he would show as much humility as he had demonstrated a moment past, Brazier was surprised when Pitt changed the subject. It was one that threw his guest.

'How does the navy take to the office of First Lord being filled by a soldier?'

'We are here to serve, sir.'

That was an ingenuous reply: the navy was furious at the appointment of the Earl of Chatham to such a post, a fellow who had purchased a mere captaincy in the Foot Guards, which was stretching the term 'soldier' to the limit. It meant he had nothing apart from his title and his parentage to distinguish him. Pitt did not come across as much of a laughing man, but he did so now, his shoulders gently shaking in mirth.

'I cannot believe you are in ignorance of the furore, sir, for I, the man who appointed him, am not.'

'While I cannot believe we are bereft of an admiral with which to replace Lord Howe.'

Brazier was thinking that the Admiralty was run by a board made up mostly of sea officers; Chatham might chair it, but he would likely find his ability to get his way severely constrained. Pitt was thinking on another matter entirely, obvious by his following heated exclamation, one which missed by a sea mile Brazier's point.

'Damn me, you're right about the numbers of flag officers. That is a pack that could do with a cull.'

The man opposite could not help but frown at both the tone and the sentiment; he would one day, if he lived long enough, hold flag rank and the reaction was noted.

'If I offend a sensibility, Captain Brazier, I will forbear to apologise. The number of elderly admirals unemployed and drawing pay are a drain on the public purse, which is much strained already. You will have seen the 74' fitting out here, I daresay?'

'Impossible to miss a ship-of-the line laying just offshore.'

The tone of the response became too overly empathic, which led Brazier to wonder if Pitt was affected by his consumption of wine. He was well into his second flagon of a very good claret and his glass was never left empty.

'Over thirty-six thousand pounds of the navy's budget to pay for it, sir. And what will happen when she's complete, now we are at peace? It will likely be laid up in ordinary, to sit in the Thames Estuary and give the rot a good chance to take hold.'

'I suspect the keel was laid when we were at war, sir.'

'Before I took office and under Lord North, it is true. Not that I could have stayed it, for the navy is a law unto itself, as my predecessor found. They will spend every penny granted them in their budgets, the estimates of which grow every year and are never constrained by any thoughts to the other requirements of the nation.'

'Without our ships to protect us, Mr Pitt, we'd be at the mercy of our enemies and perhaps no nation at all. France is still a powerful enemy and so, as you have already mentioned, with Gibraltar in our possession, is Spain.'

He recognised Brazier's touchiness and he held up a hand to acknowledge he had been somewhat rude. 'You make a good point, but I sense waste and it irks me.'

Pitt sat back and dropped his chin in contemplation, which

allowed Brazier to examine him more closely than hitherto – here, or previously at St James's Palace. If his eyes spoke of high intelligence, the cast of the lower half of his face showed it as not designed by nature for mirth. He also had the pallid skin of an indoor man, the whole topped with swept-back hair and a rather indolent manner. It gave him the look of a person of no great account, a man about the town and, given his dress was of excellent quality, one of some means.

Nothing could be less apposite. Pitt was exceedingly young for his office, a mere twenty-four years of age when he became First Lord of the Treasury. By repute he was damned clever and very active, quite happy with his reputation as a miserly guardian of the Exchequer. He had inherited a startling national debt of near two hundred and thirty million in pounds sterling, this from the American War, and he was busy, with some success, seeking to pay it down.

It was imputed by his political enemies that, to the detriment of the nation and having raised taxes on imported goods, he hated to spend so much as a penny when a farthing might serve. His response, as reported – for he was a lively debater both inside and outside parliament – was to term them corrupt spendthrifts, many of whom had lined their own pockets from wartime contracts, while others had been openly sympathetic to the American rebels.

'I hope that my elder brother, being a civilian, can constrain the excess, for he will not be swayed by sentiment or the pleading of admirals. I know it will be seen as nepotism and that does concern me, but King George is with me on this. There are many things we must get a grip on and the Navy Board, along with the Admiralty, are but two.'

The voice altered slightly to become less friendly, more pointed, while his look at Brazier was fixed. 'He will, of course, not act in a high-handed fashion. My brother knows he will be required to take advice from his naval colleagues when it comes to appointments.'

'Very wise, sir,' Brazier replied, draining his goblet, to hide the fact he was somewhat put out by the tone; it implied he declined to intervene in such matters and this for a fellow not asking for any favour. He shifted in his seat preparatory to moving on. 'Now, if you will forgive me, I have matters to attend to.'

'You may know, Captain, I come to Walmer Castle for the sea air. Feel free to call while I'm in residence. My younger sister, Lady Eliot, is soon to arrive to take the air for her condition of pregnancy. She will do the honours at my table and is an avid seeker of new sources of conversation, of which the Kent coast has something of a dearth for me.'

'That is kind of you, sir, though I fear I might bore her.'

'Nonsense; having smoked your name, I can now recall it was worthy of a Gazette for Trincomalee, and in recounting that alone you will entertain her.'

'I have no idea how long I will be in Deal, but if it is of length and time permits, I will certainly request permission to call.'

Once outside the private room, Brazier felt he had just played a bad hand, indeed he had been foolish: he should have jumped at the chance to visit Walmer Castle, for who could say where it could lead? When Pitt alluded to his elder brother Chatham seeking naval advice, he had reacted in the wrong way. He should have had a refill and talked of something else to kill the impression he was seeking an intercession on his behalf. That accepted, the offer to visit had seemed genuine.

Garlick, once more at his place, got a black look and a sharp instruction to deliver dinner to Brazier's rooms at three of the clock.

Daniel Spafford was eating in his isolated farmhouse outside Worth, with him the man he held as his right hand. He and Daisy were again discussing the events of the morning, which had been a disappointment. The idea, a false one, that Spafford was ill enough to be at risk of dying, had been thought up by Trotter as a notion to appeal to their rival.

69

Being obsessed with his own health, forever intoning the doom-laden words that he reckoned to be not long for this world, Tulkington might fall for the notion that Spafford was in worse straits, as well as be attracted to the idea of seeing off competition in the long run. On reflection it could be seen as desperate from the start, a case of hope and need overcoming common sense.

'I hope you has some other thought in that head of yours, Daisy,' Spafford growled. Being in rude good health, he cut into his beefsteak with gusto, meat to be washed down with a tankard of porter, part of a jug brought to him from the local tavern. Speaking through a mouthful of both rendered his words indistinct. 'I cannot abide that matters should rest as they are.'

'I could just seek to knife him, Dan – be a pleasure to.'

'What makes you reckon you'd get close? I wouldn't let you within ten feet if I thought you might blade me, which is why it took you near a month to even get to talk to Hawker.'

Trotter's thin frame swelled at those words for he was proud of his reputation, one that made most men cautious when he was close by. How often had he been asked the number of souls he had seen to perdition? The questioner would get nothing but a wolfish grin, along with an invitation to make up their own number, he saying he could not rightly recall. That was more of a scare than any figure.

Trotter and Spafford had known each other for over a quarter of a century, meeting as ship's boys, sailing mates on the Baltic run where they had bonded to be something akin to brothers. The seal of friendship came when Daisy had, one dark night, knifed a huge brute of a bastard who was seeking to prey on Spafford, then a young and comely lad.

The two had just managed to toss his weighty bulk over the side into the German Sea and, being a bully to all aboard, few asked where he had gone, even with his blood staining the deck. Never mentioned was why Trotter had acted as he had, when he himself was suffering no oppression. But from then on he was never far from Dan Spafford's side.

The move into smuggling had come naturally to a pair grown to be prime seamen and coming into their late twenties. This was at a time when, with a war on, sailing to the Baltic risked being taken by French or Dutch privateers, villains as like to slit your throat as take you for a prisoner. Spafford had been in receipt of a small windfall, enough money to put down for the hire of a lugger, the precursor to the two he now owned.

When England was at war normal trade was impossible, so the profits were high and the number of buyers abundant enough to allow for competition with Tulkington. Not any more; the coming of peace and the difficulty of contending with his rival's smooth operation had, over three years, dented what had become a far-from-deep Spafford purse, this to the point where it was becoming bare.

To trade at all he now had to sell much lower to undercut the competition, and while the gang of a dozen souls he led were loyal, it was only because he had kept them sweet. Without support he could not operate at all, which meant, as of now, too much of what profit he made was going to them. In the presence of the only person with whom he could share his concerns, he was obliged to mull over what to do next.

Every leader needs an ear to which he can open up without concern, as well as a voice to warn him, one not afraid to speak openly, when he might be approaching shoal water. Daisy loved him and that had, from their early years, been his shield, not broken in any way by the disinclination of Spafford to oblige his cravings. The other protection was simple: Jaleel Trotter was not called Daisy for nothing. He was no leader of men, as well as no Hector with his fists or a sword, while being more dangerous to himself than others with a pistol. Dan Spafford had grown from that slight and put-upon lad, to become a rough-and-tumble bruiser no one would dare seek to bully.

'You would have knifed him if you'd been in that carriage, Daisy, had you been there to hear him. Can't think of a time when not havin' a weapon hurt so much. He talked to me like I was shit on his shoe.'

'He sees a gent when he passes a mirror glass.'

'An' I see a turd in fine cloth,' Spafford spat, simultaneously stabbing at his meat as if it was his rival.

'Yet one who can bear his costs and easy.'

The nod was a weary one, Tulkington being able to maintain his enterprise in a way Spafford could not. The sod had been at the game all his adult life, as had his father before him. Years of cross-Channel dealing meant he had contacts a bit of a johnny-come-lately could not match, as well as the use of larger vessels he seemed to have no need to own.

He also had something of a lock on the town of Deal as well as the charitable ear of those who held official office, many fellow Freemasons, men who had benefited over years from the Tulkington family's largesse. If many of his contributions were to municipal causes and above board, there existed the gifts he and his father before him had made to men supposed to uphold the law, from loans at questionable rates or in some case outright bribes, which put them under his power.

Not that any real pressure was required when it came to trafficking contraband. Above anything else the Mayor and Jurats of Deal abhorred disturbance and, living cheek by jowl with easily aggrieved boatmen, violent demonstration and disturbance – which included house burning – was always on the horizon. The making of anything even close to a living was fraught with difficulty and nothing led to unrest quicker than scarcity of income, so smuggling and the monies generated and spread was reckoned a keeper of the peace.

A blind eye to the smuggling trade, from which, in some way, all drew benefit, was seen as good for the prosperity of the town, certainly for the tavern and alehouse owners, as well as the various trades that dealt in common commodities. It was all very well for the likes of

William Pitt and a few moneyed souls in London to rail against it, but they would not suffer the consequences of interdiction. Unless they were prepared to provide an alternative way of fashioning a living, it was something, to the more prosperous folk of Deal, best left alone.

Tulkington himself also benefited from the clandestine income smuggling brought to the town. He owned several enterprises, which supplied both the anchorage and the inhabitants with necessary produce. Less open was the way he drew monies from other sources so he did not just depend on contraband to pay his more numerous hirelings, which he had and could maintain in numbers. Spafford was acutely aware that something had to be done to alter the present situation. It was the means that was lacking, given today's attempt to delude him had failed.

'We could link up with Romney Marsh,' Daisy suggested, 'they've no love for Tulkington and would aid us in seeing him off.'

'How long would that last afore they were at our throats too?' A bit of a sigh and a long chew on his beef. 'But we can't just go on as we are, Daisy. If we have to get hostile, let it be so, but it would aid us to be making some money when it happens and there's only one place that can be got.'

'Am I smoking this right, Dan?'

'You are, Daisy. We're going to have to lift and sell some of Tulkington's own goods.'

'How's it to be done?'

'By bein' bold, brother; there's no other way.'

'You has to know he has a cargo due.'

'Easy to sniff that, Daisy, and are we not at a good time of year for calm waters and long nights?'

It would not have pleased Dan Spafford to have any inkling of the thoughts of Henry Tulkington on the same matter. When he described the man he had met as a pest, it had been in the nature of a

73

householder referring to a mouse, something easily solved by a terrier and, given he was in possession of such an article in John Hawker and the gang he led, not one of great concern.

Tulkington had always possessed the means to squash Spafford at any time of his choosing. Yet he had good grounds to allow him to trade, though not with complete freedom to challenge his supremacy. It was the same with the opportunist smuggling carried out by the boatmen on Deal beach; they too might sometimes think they were cocking a snook at a superior operation, when in reality they served, for his enterprises, a definite purpose.

Though by no means able to completely control the Revenue Service, Henry Tulkington had the resources to in some ways bend their activities. It was essential for his prosperity they had more than one target for their efforts. Without multiple potential culprits to chase, they would be obliged to concentrate on his activities, which operated on a much higher plane in both quantity and value.

It was necessary to ruminate on what Spafford had told him, to first ask himself if the supposed approach of his passing was true: a lie, it could be ignored. Yet if the man was truly on the point of expiry, what he had said about subsequent trouble had the merit of presaging trouble. Son Harry could not exercise control over his own bad habits, let alone the kind of ruffians his father led. It then followed that Spafford's conclusion also had weight.

Nothing stimulated Preventative activity like bloodshed and at worst that would extend to the army being called in, as it had in the past, in cases like that of the Hawkhurst gang. Active thirty years past, his father had taken and passed on the lesson of their demise as a telling example. Too successful for their own good, they had not only allowed their smuggling operation to become obvious, their leaders had acted with no sense at all, resorting to bloodshed when the Revenue sought to curtail their activities. It had ended with many of the gang dead, either from a weapon or a rope, and their operations smashed.

The sprite of violence, once out of the bottle, was impossible to control, especially when folk were disturbed or harmed who should be left in peace. Never a man to act in haste, Henry Tulkington knew he might have to craft a solution. As yet, as a problem, it was not pressing; he had other concerns much closer to home to worry about.

While Edward Brazier was at his victuals, William Pitt was making his way from the Three Kings back to Walmer Castle, behind him a pair of musket-bearing soldiers, as well as a clerk carrying his papers. There were endless folk prepared to tell him this kind of perambulation was unwise, that he should travel by coach, even more prepared to spit at his passing, for he was singularly unpopular in these parts.

It upped the abuse, which tended to become highly vocal, when he forced himself to smile at the irate boatmen he passed, some of whom were owners of craft they had been obliged to build as a result of his actions. Pitt cared little for the fact that he was detested, even when informed he had been burnt in effigy in retaliation. He was unwavering in his wish to put a complete stopper, by hook or by crook, to their villainous trade, forever cogitating on ideas or actions that might bring that about.

Many would have wondered at his dilemma. He might be the King's First Minister, but he did not enjoy untrammelled power, his actions dependent on supportive Houses of Parliament and the fragile coalition that made up the Cabinet. He could not call out the army without risking the kind of censure that might bring down his administration, and the navy were able to politely ignore his requests to intervene. The trail of influence and interest worked against an easy solution and many a Member of Parliament shared the common view that taxes were vile and smuggling contraband could never be stopped, so what was the point of trying?

There was another thought to occupy him, which was the name of the naval captain he had just met. It took him back to the Cabinet at Downing Street in which Admiral Lord Howe had informed those present of the death of Sir Lowell Hassel, the commanding admiral at Jamaica.

In itself, such a passing was not uncommon; the West Indies were a graveyard for Europeans, and sailors, – if they suffered less than soldiers – were not immune. Yet the manner of the expiry was odd. Even more troubling was the unsigned letter addressed to Howe which had come in the same packet as the Brazier despatch. It made the whole affair much more perplexing.

'Oh yes, Edward Brazier,' Pitt said to himself, in a non-carrying whisper, 'I knew your name alright, as well as the responsibilities you took on after Hassel died. The question to which I do not have an answer is the reason the death occurred.

'Was it as your despatch said or was it, as the anonymous letter implied, foul play?

CHAPTER SIX

The fellow in question was left to enjoy a solitary meal, which was far from unusual given his rank. Aboard ship he would regularly have his officers to dinner, as well as the ship's sailing master, and if the vessel warranted one, the surgeon. It was generally a pleasure to do so, yet it was not something to be undertaken every day, so eating alone was part of the loneliness that went with command.

Such solitude always left him with his own thoughts, and it did so now, on his prospects both romantic and professional, which bounced, as they always did, from the positive to the negative. He was in the latter state when there came a rap on the door and there was Garlick, utterly unabashed, holding a small square of paper in his mitt, showing a bright-red seal.

'Not long come, your honour, from Cottington Court, the lad said.'

Again there was an air of enquiry, an indication the innkeeper was deeply curious about the contents. Brazier took it then gave him a look that brooked nothing other than dismissal. He broke the seal as soon as the door closed, rising to stand by the glass-panelled doors to read Betsey Langridge's note three times, seeking some warmth in the tone, only to conclude it was utterly formal.

When to call? It was late in the day but not impossible, for he had been told Cottington was not far off: no more than an hourglass of sand at most when walking, less mounted. But would that show too great a degree of eagerness? If he was keen to meet with her again, he knew that an excess of haste might be unwise. The encouragement he had sensed from the meeting outside the graveyard could be put down to wishful thinking.

He sat to write and to say that if it was convenient he would call on the morrow mid-morning. Then, too restless to stay indoors and feeling the need for some air, he dressed in civilian clothes, this in order to attract less attention, leaving behind his distinctive naval hat for the same reason, looked at then discarded the notion of wearing his sword, locked the bulk of his coin in his sea chest and essayed out, ignoring his host's ever-present inquisitiveness.

With the tide out he chose the foreshore and, it being twilight now, boats that had spent the day plying stores out of the ships were full of human cargo coming ashore, most bearing catcalling sailors prettified up for a night of revelry – nimble fellows who leapt from prow to shingle so as to keep their shore-going shoes and stockings dry. Those of greater standing, ship's masters and their passengers, conscious of their superior status, were dragged in, their craft hauled up onto the beach and dry pebbles by willing hands, eager for a copper reward.

The tars quickly disappeared down the numerous narrow alleys. Their talk would be full of excited anticipation, which Brazier knew from his own experiences as a young man were rarely fulfilled. There was no well-found beauty with a heart of gold just waiting for a handsome sailor to carry her off for freely given favours, no tavern owner willing to feed them ale at no cost in exchange for tales of far-off and exotic parts. Likewise the lottery ticket they might buy would not have the numbers to make them rich, indeed it was just as likely to be forged as genuine.

He followed them up to the road that formed the highpoint of the town which he now knew to be called Beach Street, then down yet another narrow alley to exit into a narrow street, well illuminated by lanterns or tallow wads in every window from ground to upper storeys, with inns so packed that the custom, gathered under lamps, spread out onto the street.

Being so crowded it was far from easy to make his way and, given the jostling as well as the number of urchins charging around in what appeared an aimless fashion, a firm hand was kept on his purse: he knew the realm of the pickpocket when he saw one. Progress had him pass hucksters selling gimcrack trinkets, Romany women seeking a coin for a tiny bunch of good luck heather, windows from which food and drink, mainly roasted chestnuts and gin, were being dispensed, while noisy, banter-filled bargains were being struck with the indoor prostitutes of the pricier kinds.

There were ten times more on the street itself, backs to a wall or stood in a proprietary way on an alleyway corner, all calling for trade: varying types, from the mature and large-bosomed to waiflike creatures, some who looked to be mere children, so every desire was there to be catered for. Their numbers increased in density as he came to and looked down a constricted, short sloping street of small cottages, cut off by a wall at the far end, which was full of sailors striking carnal bargains.

Another alleyway he passed probably led to a Molly-house, judging by the knot of fellows round the entrance. It was hard to appear overfussy regarding dress in a town full of titivated sailors, but they managed it by being outrageously outré in their ribbons and multi-feathered hats. One or two were bold enough to eye him as a potential partner, looks that he ignored.

A side street took him once more onto the main thoroughfare housing of what he now knew to be St George's Church. This was no place for common trades now, but dedicated to entertainment or at least the promise of such, with invitations being called to passers-by that their night would not be complete without witnessing bear-baiting, dog and cock fighting or a bare-knuckle bout between two 'famed boxers', bruisers of whose names this naval officer had never before heard.

He passed the Baptist Chapel set back from the road, an odd-looking building with something Moorish about its design, fronted by folk who adhered to its tenets, who, Bibles in hand, were beseeching those passing to enter the chapel and save their souls. Some obliged, very likely men who had just come from the company of a whore, who thought it a place to assuage their guilt.

There was no beseeching or saving of souls outside St George's. The Anglican faith was too secure in its establishment to feel the need for harvesting. It did have the requirement to protect its walls from human fouling, however, so there were burly souls there to guard the brickwork as well as the closed doorway.

'Captain, I scarce spotted you in this crowd without your blue coat and naval topper.'

The voice had him turn round and look down at the Irishman. 'Mr Flaherty?'

'Do I perceive you're taking in the sights?'

'Who would not?' was the only possible reply to such an irony-filled enquiry, delivered with a wry expression.

'And does Deal impress you?

Brazier laughed. 'I would suggest that hectic as it is, its offerings would pale beside an Indian bazaar or even a Moorish souk.'

'This I cannot contest, never having been near either.' Flaherty took his arm, but with no pressure. 'I am about to enter the Playhouse and partake of some wine. It would please me that you should join me. It has entertainments and a card room, but it is also a fine class of beverage.'

'Even to match the Three Kings? I cannot fault his burgundies.'

'Claret man, myself. Garlick has a good supplier, and so does the Playhouse; indeed, they're one and the same, I suspect.'

Flaherty led him a several dozen yards to where a pair of pitch torches, flaring in high sconces, lit up a knot of potential customers outside a set of double doors, then into the foyer of the building, crowded, with loud and raucous singing filling the main hall, finally entering a side room to seek a spare table at which they could sit.

The room was occupied by quiet card players as well as those ship's masters Brazier had witnessed coming ashore: men of the dress, manner and attitude of those who issue orders and expect them to be obeyed. All were in deep conversation with fellows of a like standing, no doubt talking of freight rates and insurance costs, or the difficulties attendant with finding a trustworthy and experienced crew.

'Or where to find a superior lady of the town,' Flaherty insisted, when Brazier alluded to the matter. 'One who will not lay out her wares for less than a guinea. Will you join me in what I choose?'

'Happily.'

A gesture brought an apron-wearing fellow to the table and Flaherty engaged him in a discussion regarding what was available in the claret line, one to which Brazier barely paid attention, that being taken by the fellow who had just come through the door carrying a leather-bound folder, to stand and look around the room in a manner that seemed to challenge everyone present. Having placed his order, Flaherty turned to observe the direction and intensity of the gaze and thus the object. He provided a name, just as Brazier was about to enquire.

'John Hawker, a man by repute it is best to avoid.'

'I failed in that but yesterday, Mr Flaherty. I came across the sod on my way to Deal and found him singularly unpleasant.'

'It would be uncharacteristic that he should be seen as otherwise.' The voice lifted from a gloomy tone to a hearty one. 'And here comes the lovely Saoirse.'

The woman who entered the room took more than just the Brazier eye, for she was striking in a green dress of rich velvet. A full head of auburn hair was worn loose, framing a pale but comely face and she bore herself with such a degree of confidence it was to be remarked upon. Nodding to the man named Hawker, he, carrying the leather-bound ledger, followed her through a side door, one quickly shut behind them.

'The owner of the establishment,' Flaherty said. 'The sole owner.'

Brazier looked around and evinced some surprise. 'A woman on her own?'

'A very remarkable one, Captain.'

'She would have to be, Mr Flaherty. If I do not know Deal I know seaports. They are rarely places where one of her sex can hold her own without the support of a spouse or powerful protector.'

'Believe me, Saoirse Riorden requires neither, and as for protection, if you had paid attention on the way in you would have observed the pair of brutes who had station under those torches, men bound to her service and ever willing to act on her behalf.'

'And she's Irish, like you.'

Flaherty responded with a wan smile, this as a decanter of wine and two goblets, all crystal, were placed between them. 'Aye, she's from the old country.'

'Do I sense a more intimate connection?'

'My, you're sharp, sir,' Flaherty replied, adopting a slightly thrown look as he poured out a drop of wine, to then raise and sniff at it. The sip he took was rolled around his tongue before it got a nod and the two goblets were filled. 'A fine brew, a little sister to Lafite and Latour and not shamed by comparison.'

'You know your clarets, sir.'

'A lifetime's occupation, Captain, and one that has seriously inhibited prosperity.'

As they drank, and Brazier showed his appreciation, their conversation shifted to the general and again, the mildly inquisitive. What was a captain doing here with no ship and no position at the Naval Yard? How had Flaherty got into the business of dealing in horses? Brazier was guarded in his response, the Irishman less so, he having been a paid jockey who had ridden for the aristocratic and wealthy owners who frequented Newmarket and Epsom Downs, folk either too fat or too frightened to contest on their own mounts.

'For a percentage of the purse, of course, and an introduction to the kind of brew our betters enjoy, though too many sink it without appreciation. They are as careless about the women in their company, while I admit I was not.'

'I would take issue with the expression "betters", Mr Flaherty. From my experience, a claim to superior blood does not necessarily elevate a man. I can think of one case in particular and his is reckoned blue.'

'You have the right of it, but you will not be surprised I find in that statement a lever to curiosity. In one particular case, you say?'

The opening of the side door and the appearance of Saoirse Riorden and Hawker dented the need to reply and name the royal prince. Brazier, a naturally acute observer, was taken by two things; a sort of hunger in Flaherty's expression, but more so by the stiff manner of the pair being examined, which hinted that whatever had happened behind that door had not been pleasurable.

This made him realise that which he had not considered, probably because it did not fit in with his perception of the fellow Hawker; that there might be an attachment between them, one which was under some strain, a point he made quietly to Flaherty.

'Never in life,' was the empathic response. 'They are not even friendly.'

So you are carrying a torch for her, Brazier reflected, knowing it would be something that would not be welcomed if mentioned. Added to that was the secondary realisation they were both in the same position. The pair under their gaze were exchanging quiet words but no smiles before Hawker turned to look once more around the room, demonstrating a flicker of something short of recognition as it rested for a second on Brazier.

Then he was gone, with the owner of the Old Playhouse staring at his back with no hint of regard, more a stiff posture. Then the face cleared and she smiled, a more professional expression than joyous, and began to work the room, pausing at tables to ask if all was well with the service being provided. Naturally, in time, it brought her to theirs and an immediate glance at the crystal decanter. It meant an expensive brew, which justified its use; most of the other tables ran to glass flagons.

'There you are, Vincent, beggaring yourself once more.' The green eyes flicked to Brazier, which elicited the required introduction. 'Then I bid you welcome, sir, both to the town and my establishment.'

'The captain here has rented Bonnie from me.'

'Indeed. You will enjoy her, sir, for she's a fine and steady mare.'

'You clearly know the beast.'

She laughed and it was a head-thrown-back peal. 'Holy Mary, how else would I recover the bills my friend here runs up and cannot pay?'

The response was spontaneous. 'Then he will not be troubling you tonight, madam; that decanter falls to my tally.'

'Captain—'

Brazier cut off the protest with a quickly raised hand and a determined look.

'Sir, you have been kind enough to take me in hand when I am alone in the town and know no one. In gratitude, I could do no less than treat you to something in which you take such pleasure. Might I add that I too am enamoured of your choice?'

Another laugh from the hostess, though this time a chuckle. 'Sure, it would be odd for a man of your trade, Vincent, to go lookin' a gift horse in the mouth.'

'I feel I should protest.'

'While I am of the opinion, Mr Flaherty, it is time you refilled our goblets.'

'Would you join us, Saoirse?' he asked as he went to comply.

'Kind, Vincent, but no. The place will not run itself.'

'Will I see you in the morning?' Flaherty asked.

'Why would I, when you have gone and given this fine gentleman my favourite horse?'

'I have others.'

'Which never ceases to amaze me. When I come to your yard, I half-expect to find the bailiffs have cleared it out.'

The response, for the first time in a while, was made with the kind of flippant tone that was Flaherty's normal manner. 'While I know that something always turns up.' The eyes went to the ceiling. 'Does not Jesus love me?'

'They say he loves a sinner,' was the sardonic answer, 'so sure, you should be close to his heart. Captain, it was a pleasure to make your acquaintance and I hope, while you are in Deal, to see you once more at my tables.'

'I think it would be safe to assume so, madam.' She departed to talk to another group of customers with Flaherty's eyes on her back. 'A striking woman, Mr Flaherty.'

'And a kind one, Captain.'

'I did not sense any kindness in the exchange she had with the fellow you called Hawker?'

'No.'

Brazier waited for more; he waited in vain, which left him foundering for a moment, the cover for that an invitation and a hand on the neck of the decanter. 'I'm sure the Playhouse would run to another?'

'I would be disinclined to impose, sir.'

'Come, Mr Flaherty, so formal. I will call you Vincent and you shall know me as Edward. We will sit here and exchange pleasant conversation in which you can impart to me why this man Hawker is so to be avoided.'

'Captain, you say a refill. Knowledge of the tariff might give you pause.'

About to reply that it would not even begin to dent his means, Brazier stopped himself. He was a man to make friends quickly, most sailors being inclined that way through the transience of the profession. He liked Flaherty, but it resurfaced that the man was a horse dealer and he could not put out of his mind entirely the reputation of that trade.

'I too am a slave to quality in the article of wine, so let us think not of consequence but of pleasure to be taken.' An arm was raised to summon the servitor. 'Calon Ségur, I recall you named it.'

It was a jolly pair who downed the second decanter, with Brazier being informed that Hawker acted as a government tax-gatherer, so was unpopular merely for that. Then there were the rumours, though it had to be admitted they were nothing more, of some of his more devilish activities. He was a noted bully, bad enough in his own incarnation but ten times more so, for he could call upon others of a near-to-equal stamp to back him up. If it could not be proved, it was common gossip that to cross him was to risk a one-way journey in a wherry with a length of heavy chain round your feet.

'He is suspected of murder?' was Brazier's startled comment. Flaherty nodded. 'Is there no law to haul him up?'

'None, it seems, that would dare. He walks proud and evinces no fear.'

'Surely the magistrates would not allow him such freedom?'

'I would not go putting any faith in that quarter,' Flaherty replied with some vehemence. 'You don't get to sit on the bench in this neck of the woods if you're not connected to the right people, and that tells you certain folk are looked after, Hawker being one.'

'I cannot be sure he did not recognise me a while back. His gaze rested upon me for a short time. Perhaps not wearing my uniform would throw him, of course.'

'It should perhaps concern you that he might.'

'Vincent, understand this. I have faced people seeking to harm me with cannons firing grape and round shot. I have swung a cutlass and fended off knives on an enemy deck and come away with little more than a few scratches. The fist of a bully does not alarm me unduly.'

'I'd avoid him, as do most if they can.'

'Your Saoirse does not seem to fear him.'

That at least brought back some good humour. 'Sadly, she's not my Saoirse and second, I don't know that she fears anyone.'

'I suspected you were attracted to her.'

'Given you're not blind, I would be surprised if you did not.'

'Without reciprocation, I sense?'

The voice changed to one of suppressed anger. 'I think you wander to areas that the purchase of wine does not entitle you.'

'Yet it would do no harm for you to know that I may be in similar straits, and being so, I comprehend the state in which you find yourself better than most.'

'I think that requires you explain.'

'I hope you will forgive me if I do not.'

'Having denied you the right to pry into the aim of my affections, I would scarce be fair if I did so in yours.'

'Could I say, Vincent,' Brazier posited, smiling and picking up the decanter, 'that sounded utterly and completely unconvincing.'

Flaherty threw back his head and laughed loud enough to turn nearby heads. 'You have the right of it, for sure.'

Henry Tulkington had decided not to make a point of asking Elisabeth to talk with him; he reasoned with the note gone and it being too late to stop it, the idea of this Brazier visiting Cottington was now inevitable, so haste would disclose his disquiet. He waited until dinner to raise the subject and did so in a normal conversational manner, to have the supposition confirmed.

'He has asked to call in the morning and stated it was only necessary to respond if it was inconvenient.'

'And is it?'

'Henry, we are not overburdened with either callers or duties, are we?'

'You're not, Elisabeth; I on the other hand—'

Sarah Lovell nodded as if to confirm the unfinished point, both having it dismissed by Elisabeth with brio. 'If you would attend less to business and more to pleasure, not least in the article of female company, I'm sure you would be a happier soul.'

Henry was not to be drawn on that subject and he looked crabbed it had been raised, his expression quickly corrected to one of enquiry. 'Do you have a notion of why Captain Brazier is so keen to call?'

'Keen?'

'I sense a degree of haste and so does our dear aunt.'

'He is close by, we met by accident, he wishes to renew the acquaintance, to which I have no objection. This is a house that could benefit from a few more visitors – social ones, that is.'

'I merely wonder at his intentions, Elisabeth.'

Betsey responded to both that and the crabbed look on her aunt's face with total dismissal. 'Intentions? I think you're running ahead of the hounds there, Henry.'

'But you would not object to my finding out?' Betsey shrugged. 'Perhaps if you were to introduce me when he arrives.'

'You won't be too busy?' was the sarcastic response.

'For matters concerning the family, no.'

CHAPTER SEVEN

A third pint of claret had been consumed, so fuzzy-morning head was treated by a substantial amount of coffee to accompany his breakfast. Shaved and in uniform, a hotel groom having been sent to fetch Bonnie, she was saddled and waiting when he returned from acquiring a pair of boots. He had clear and straightforward directions as to where to go: a ride away from the crowded town, through orchards in the main, the trees showing abundant apple and cherry blossom. There was also some pasture: cattle, sheep and goats, in small fields dotted with a few people tending to animals and the trees.

Paths of bare earth or gravel led to isolated houses of, he assumed, the tenants or landowners of the local farms; either low old dwellings, with thatched roofs or, for the more prosperous, four-square red-brick, pointed with white lime. They sat under red roof tiles, with smoking chimneys, small canopied porticoes and low sash windows, some bricked up to avoid the window tax.

Not far from such houses sat large barns, also constructed of brick, and by them the meaner dwellings of the farm workers, surrounded by chickens, dogs and in some cases grubby children. The carts carrying produce to market were, at this time of day, mostly going in the opposite direction and, seeing a King's officer, he was given way to and treated to indications of respect.

A gentle rise took him up to the upper part of Deal – the original settlement he had been told – which boasted its own imposing red-brick church with a white belfry, next to a substantial rectory. It was just one of a number of substantial houses, many looking recently built and boasting a variation of the design of those already passed, occupied no doubt by folk who found the bustle and commotion of the lower town distasteful. There was, however, an old thatched alehouse opposite the church, virtue and wickedness, as ever, living cheek by jowl.

Beyond that lay a stretch of rising road hemmed in by open fields, grassed at the edges, over which he could put Bonnie to first a canter then to a short gallop. This she took to with relish and speed, moving fast enough to near remove his hat. Even if he was less than sure of his seat, he enjoyed the sensation, one he had not experienced in years – a motion which, if it was not as exhilarating as a fast-sailing frigate on a stiff breeze, was yet stimulating.

Cottington Court, he had been told, lay in forested ground, with only its roof visible from the road. Gaps in the trees provided an occasional glimpse of wave-filled anchorage and, with the tide very low, the extensive sandbars of the Goodwins showed as a light-brown shade in the water – a potential burial ground for those who, even with charts, did not know the safe passages through to deep water. From the shore he had already seen the masts and part-hulls of ships wrecked over many years; slowly sinking into the soft and shifting sand they were a constant reminder of the risks.

Advised to look out for a pair of stone greyhound figurines, there they sat, on either side of spiked metal gates set back from the road, the neatly curved wall encasing it in a deep arc. A pulled bell brought from the gatehouse a living, snarling dog on a thick rope, held by a fellow carrying a heavy cudgel, who enquired in a hissing way on his business, in a manner far from either servile or friendly. Brazier thought about producing the note of invitation, only to reason this toothless cove would be unlikely to be able to read.

'Captain Edward Brazier to see Mrs Langridge. I have good reason to believe I am expected.'

That brought forth a grudging nod, then a large key with which the gate was unlocked, to be swung open and allow his entry. With Bonnie's hooves scrunching on the neat gravel, he caught sight of the house at the end of a long drive. In fact it was more a mansion, set back past a second set of more ornamental gates, framed by sturdy brick pillars topped with recumbent eagles. Closer to, he had sight of the formal gardens on either side of the central pathways, the beds being tended to by a couple of elderly men, bent double.

Clearly the abode of a wealthy man, it was built in the style redolent of the reign of the second Charles, slightly more elaborate than the modern fashion for squared-off regularity, but still of the kind of red brick that favoured sunshine. It boasted three-storey twin bays projecting from the main body on either side of the double doorway, their tops decorated with stone fretwork. The windows were well proportioned in the whole, mullioned and small-paned. More telling was their sheer number; there was no worry about window taxes here.

The gate being opened, he trotted through to be faced with a pair of spaniels running at him eagerly, lolling tongues evidence of the benign nature of family pets. A lad in a leather apron ran forward to take his reins, allowing him to dismount, which permitted the dogs to sniff at his boots. Bonnie was led away without a word being said and he knew, in this kind of establishment, she would be watered and put to a bag of hay without the need he request it.

Betsey came out of the house, to stand at the top of a set of round stone steps. She was clad in a plain grey dress, which was a nod to her widowed state, but not one to contain either her beauty or his admiration. If the sourpuss Aunt Sarah was just visible to her rear, it did nothing to dent his pleasure. His hat came off and he executed a slight bow, aware his heart was beating a little faster.

She had come to greet him personally and not left it to a servant to announce the arrival, a more common way for anyone to be received, certainly for the first time of calling. The fellow who would have normally undertaken the chore was to one side, in decent domestic livery of a frogged coat and black breeches, tasked now to merely hold open the door.

'Mrs Langridge, it is kind of you to allow me to call.'

'Captain Brazier, how could I refuse such a request and from someone I consider a friend?' The face of Sarah Lovell registered her deep disapproval of those words and, in truth, it was a bold greeting, one to be taken as encouragement he was sure, dented when Betsey then pursed her lips to add, 'I informed my brother of your intention to call and he is impatient to meet with you.'

Those words repressed a desire to skip up the steps, Brazier taking them at a deliberate pace, to hold and kiss the back of her proffered hand, feeling an odd sensation run up his arm as his lips brushed the skin. Betsey then turned to lead the way indoors, her voice carrying a hint of mischief as she added, 'My Aunt Sarah welcomes you also and is eager to renew the acquaintance.'

If it was the case then it was not evident in her retreating back, which was singular in being so rigid as to make clear her feelings, while her actual words were replete with distaste, as was her desire to get away, she making no attempt to disguise what was an excuse.

'Forgive me if I decline to join you, Elisabeth. I have pressing household matters to attend to that cannot wait.'

Neither Brazier nor Aunt Sarah saw the stuck out tongue; he was being relieved of his hat and examining his surroundings, the object of the slight swiftly disappearing. The inside of the house was as impressive as the exterior, the hallway wide, its walls and a wide staircase lined with portraits and landscape paintings. Floored with polished, wide and gleaming boards, these carried the deep patina of their age, the space set off by a couple of modern settles of carved mahogany, upholstered in lively blue velvet. On a central round table of the same wood sat a huge punchbowl with elaborate handles, made of what he took to be solid silver.

Betsey led him on and into a room that suggested a very masculine air: heavily curtained, ceiling to floor windows, deep leather chairs, a card table as well as a large desk; a fire in an inglenook grate, the basket full of glowing red logs. The high trees outside rendered the interior somewhat dingy after the sunny ambiance of the hall.

'Captain Brazier,' Betsey said, 'my elder brother, Henry Tulkington.'

The man standing before the fire responded with a keen look and one hard to read for disposition. Tall, slightly built with a hollow chest and a sallow countenance, he was wearing a freshly powdered wig, which stood out stark in the gloom. Brazier examined what he could see of the face, seeking a likeness and failing to observe one. Where Betsey radiated happy vivacity, her brother seemed to be cut from a more melancholy cloth. His shoulders were slightly stooped and, still under examination from his visitor, he put a hand to his chest to rub it, a look of slight concern crossing his face.

'Close the door on the way out, please, Elisabeth. I think I need to speak with our visitor alone.'

'Henry, it is stifling in here. I reckon it cooler in Jamaica.'

'Would you have me catch a chill?' The sigh of frustration from his sister could not be disguised, this while her brother looked at Brazier as if he would approve. 'I suffer from a delicate constitution, Captain, which I fear my own sister does not fully appreciate.'

In no position to take issue, Brazier merely acknowledged the statement, feeling the need to smile, though he had to agree with Betsey; the room was too warm for comfort. Her brother having asked her to depart, they were to be left to talk, which had apparently been a prior condition: that the head of the house should cast an eye over him. She smiled at him reassuringly and exited, closing the door behind her. There was no invitation to sit.

'You met Elisabeth in the West Indies, I gather?'

'I did.'

Tulkington adopted an air of abstract curiosity and produced a large handkerchief into which he coughed, that followed by a vigorous blowing of the nose. 'And you have chosen to call upon her, I am led to believe, almost immediately upon your return to England?'

Not liking the tone of the question, Brazier answered with a curt statement. 'I have been home for several weeks, sir.'

The handkerchief being closely examined, eye contact was broken. 'Come from?'

'Deal, where I have lodged at the Three Kings.' Brazier could see, by the slightly cast-up eyes, the answer was insufficient. 'I travelled to there from Portsmouth.'

'Where I presume you are domiciled?'

'Naval officers are rarely domiciled, Mr Tulkington. We are, by the very nature of our service, nomadic creatures. I have rarely been in England over the last twenty years and, when I have, my family home in Hampshire has been where I have resided. Sadly my parents are no more, so that has new tenants. Naturally, if I was to anticipate a lengthy sojourn onshore, I would need to find my own house. As of yet that does not merit a decision.'

'Quite a way off, Portsmouth. I am minded to enquire if your coming here is merely to renew an acquaintance?'

'There is that, of course.'

'But it is not all?'

Was the tone of that enquiry inauspicious? It was hard to tell, but this brother had not engaged in any of the normal niceties – in fact there had been no polite preamble at all. He was asking, and within a minute of meeting, what were his intentions. Would it be wise to state them openly or to equivocate? That depended on factors of which he had no knowledge, like how much power did this brother hold over his sister. Best to go slowly.

'I found your sister's company congenial on those occasions on which we met. I have good grounds to believe she felt the same way.'

'She was certainly all aflutter at the notion of your calling, sir.'

'I sense by the way you relate the fact, such an attitude does not entirely meet with your approval.'

'It may, it may not.'

Betsey's Aunt Sarah would be behind this. He could not believe it was a personal animosity towards him on first acquaintance. She had made plain her low opinion of anyone who showed the slightest interest in her niece, to leave them in no doubt their attentions were unwelcome. In every conversation he and Betsey had engaged in, the older woman had sought in various ways to break it up. It was almost as if Tulkington guessed the line of his thinking, while his visitor had no way of knowing he was engaged in a complete falsehood.

'I knew of you before Elisabeth told me you were intending to call, indeed your name was mentioned as soon as they returned home. Our aunt was most concerned that of all the fellows who paid court to my sister, you were the most assiduous.'

'Which would surely have been rebuffed, if it had been unwelcome.'

'My sister is given to enthusiasms and, quite often, they are far from wise.'

'Odd, I found her to be eminently sensible.'

Delivered in an even way, flat almost, it produced the first troubled expression on a face that had remained studiously bland. 'I do not take kindly to be told by a stranger to us both that my impressions, indeed my deep knowledge based on years of experience, are erroneous.'

'I cannot question your familiarity with your sister, sir, though I would perhaps posit that her having been married and older than you may recall, as well as her having spent some time away from your gaze, she may now be very different.'

'Her widowhood has left her a wealthy woman. Such an estate

95

will attract those whose intentions are more to do with her money than her being.'

'Despite her very marked beauty?' That was waved away as if it was of no account. 'I take it you suspect me of being cut from such cloth?'

'I do not mean to impute your motives, sir—'

Brazier cut right across him, sick of the game being played. 'Really. I find that hard to countenance, given you have just as good as done so. Your aunt has no doubt told you of the number of fellows in Jamaica who sought to pay court to your sister and she would be right to term many of them fortune-hunters. If the source of your concern comes from there, sir, your aunt has no right to include me.'

'You seem very sure, Captain.'

'Mr Tulkington, I will no longer beat around this particular bush. I have come here to not only renew your sister's acquaintance, but to find out if a suit put forward by myself would be welcome to her. Indications so far lead me to a conclusion they might well be, not least the alacrity with which she accepted my intention to call.'

The handkerchief was produced once more, to again be coughed into, hiding what his visitor took to be a flash of anger. The material muffled his response. 'I suspected as much.'

'I would also point out something your aunt should have told you, for she could not have failed to be informed by those she met while acting as chaperone of my situation. I am a wealthy man in my own right, sir, and I have no need of your sister's plantations.'

'You think it is merely that, sir? Quite apart from her wish to possibly dispose of them.'

'What else could it be?'

'My health, sir, which, unless you are only partially sighted, you will observe is delicate. I am not a well man and may not be long for this earth. I am also unmarried as yet and without issue. Should I pass away, all my substantial holdings will be inherited by Elisabeth. Should she decide to wed for a second time, not only will her new husband have possession of what she already owns, but he can anticipate control of my fortune as well. It is therefore, to me, a legitimate concern that I would not wish that to pass to a frivolous fellow who might gamble it away.'

'Then, sir,' Brazier replied, seeking to sound emollient, 'I see it as necessary to act to put your concerns at rest. First I must seek from your sister a firm indication of how she feels regarding my attentions. If her response is encouraging, I would indeed propose marriage, formally asking for your approval, even though I cannot see you have the right to object.'

'I assume that right as her elder brother and protector.'

'Betsey—'

'Elisabeth,' Tulkington barked, showing real passion for the first time. 'I hate that childish tag, given to her, I might add, by Langridge when they were naught but children, something to my mind they never ceased to be.'

'I do not seek to dispute your feelings, sir, but your sister is past the age of majority and, as you have pointed out, a woman of substantial property. I know I would be happier to have your blessing should she give me her hand. The mere fact that I am here talking to you indicates to me that Elisabeth would like it too.'

'And if a blessing is not forthcoming?'

'Then we would be required to do without. As to your concerns regarding my being a fortune-hunter, I am perfectly willing to acquire from my prize agent an up-to-date account of my own substantial holdings in three per cent government consols, so as to put your mind at rest.'

'I have to tell you, Captain Brazier, I am minded to do everything in my power to dissuade my sister to reject any offer of marriage made by you.'

'On what grounds?'

'Your profession, sir, if being a sailor can be so termed?' Brazier was confused and it must have shown, as Tulkington continued with a more-in-sorrow-than-anger tone. 'I have known quite a few of your nautical breed in my time and, to a man, they have been whoremongers and, I would not be surprised to find, diseased by the pox because of it. Would a man of integrity hand his sweet sibling over to such a person?'

The response was icy and the heat of the room, which was making Brazier prickly without the need to dispute, did nothing to mitigate it. 'I think I am forced to tell you to have a care, sir, for if you continue in that vein, your sister will inherit all you possess in very short order.'

'You threaten me?'

Tulkington should not have allowed himself a twitch of the lips – not a smile, but one suppressed – for it was foolish: it told Brazier he was deliberately trying to provoke him. How could Betsey ever agree to wed a man who had called her brother out with the intention of killing him? He could easily envisage the rest of the scenario, which would end with a hasty apology on some dawn field. This man, with his weaknesses and slender frame, unless he was a superb shot or a devil with a sword, was not stupid enough to let a challenge go ahead against a fellow who made his way in the world by fighting his nation's enemies. Yet perhaps whatever damage he sought would have been done.

'I think I will go and find your sister, sir, for she, not you, is the reason I came to your house today. Nor, might I add, will I let you indulge in provocation, which leads me to suspect you see me as a simpleton.'

'I do not think you will marry my sister, sir, for she will listen to me.'

'Let us put it to the test.'

Brazier spun round and left without another word, though he did take the liberty – after all, it was not his house – of slamming the door. He left behind him a deeply troubled man for, if any suitor seeking the hand of Elisabeth was unlikely to be welcomed, a serving naval officer was anathema and one who could live off his own means doubly so.

He had left no doubt of his intentions and even less about how he expected they would be received, with which Henry Tulkington could only concur. His sister had been like a skittish colt at the prospect of this visit. Tulkington's aunt had made plain that he had a sound reputation – indeed his character, according to those who served with and under him and had spoken of him, was unimpeachable.

Added to which he had been assiduous in pursuit of those seeking to break the Navigation Acts, the statutes that forbade anyone from trading into the British colonies with a cargo or vessel that did not originate from a home port. At the conclusion of the war in America that extended to the nascent United States, who, as colonies, had depended for their prosperity on the trade with the sugar islands. This left them no recourse but to seek to break the embargo, and the fact that he had seriously interdicted what was by any other word smuggling might have been a recommendation to others, but not to Henry Tulkington.

This would have been no concern with them out of the way, but Elisabeth had hinted at selling her plantations and remaining at Cottington, uncomfortable with the use of slave labour to make them profitable. She had even expressed strong views on emancipation, which to her brother was evidence that she was beyond frivolous: she was irresponsible.

If she did sell – he had no means of stopping her outside persuasion – and then did marry Brazier, where would they reside? This naval sod had said quite plainly he had no home of his own, while Elisabeth had admitted to being homesick when in Jamaica, missing the friends with whom she had grown up, the very same people she had invited to that stupid fete.

What if they desired to live here in this house? If he refused, what would be his grounds? Even if they resided close by it was too dangerous, so it had to be stopped. There was another emotion coursing through his mind: he had been threatened, and that never stood well with Henry Tulkington. He was a man of parts and very prominent locally, not someone to trifle with, a fact he had made plain to others. He found it no trouble to imagine himself bloodily chastising Brazier for his effrontery, until the sod begged for mercy.

If anyone had told him it was the reaction of a weak fellow when faced with a strong one, and common to humanity, he would have laughed out loud. The more time he spent in the reverie of retribution, the greater became his need for vengeance until he felt consumed by it.

'Damn you, sir, no one in this part of the world speaks to me in such a tone and neither will you.'

CHAPTER EIGHT

The liveried servant in his short, powdered wig, the fellow who had been by the front entrance to take his hat, was now waiting outside the room, not close enough to listen at the door but, despite a demeanour no doubt honed over years, unable to avoid a wince as he reacted to the reverberating sound of it closing. The fellow was swift to readopt the required servile air, which meant he should always have his eyes cast upwards and never make contact with those of his betters he was addressing.

'Mrs Langridge is waiting for you, sir, in the drawing room.'

He moved to lead the way and Brazier, still seething, followed him, seeking to calm his mood, for it would not do to carry it to Betsey. The servant knocked, opened the door and sonorously announced him, which given he must be the only person visiting seemed excessive. Brazier's heart was racing again, but asked, he could not have said what caused it – anger or anticipation. She was standing by another fireplace, this unlit, and looking at him with an air both amused and quizzical. More importantly, being in her own home allowed her to receive him alone, as long as the door remained open.

'Am I to judge, by the way the whole house shook, the meeting with my brother did not go well?'

He could not but respond in a like manner. 'I allowed my temper too much rein.'

'It is something Henry is inclined to provoke in people.'

'Yet you agreed to my being interrogated.'

The brow furrowed and any good humour evaporated. 'That's a very forceful word.'

'I fear your brother used words that make it pale by comparison.' There was temptation to add what had been imputed regarding his character, but he suppressed it, for it would serve no purpose. 'But let us put that aside. I came, as I have just informed him, to call upon you.'

'And have I not already said how welcome that is to me, Captain Brazier?'

'I'm curious as to how you would react if I asked you to call me Edward?'

The lack of an immediate reply, added to a bonny hint of a blush, told him she got the drift, which served to mightily encourage him. Yet, for any woman of intelligence he had posited a hurdle to be crossed with care. It also had to be admitted, by the man proposing the idea, that it smacked of excessive impatience for, in the game of courting, incremental steps were the norm, so it was necessary to soften the effect.

'Let me say, a life spent at sea does not prepare a man for lethargy. I am aware my request borders on the breaching of accepted norms. But that is, to those who reside on land, another quality sailors often lack.'

Her body movements and facial expression, somewhat confused, told Brazier he had made her acutely uncomfortable. Before he could continue she spoke, and it carried a whiff of her being nervous.

'You have not seen the grounds, Captain Brazier, and you must, for they are my arbour: the place, particularly the woodland and lake, where I played as a child and I recall with fondness. I try to go for a walk through the woods every day and it would be pleasing if you would accompany me.'

He should have just agreed, but his nature forbade it. 'Just you and I?'

The roughish smile accompanying the sally rouged her cheeks once more, which, as always, he found enchanting. Betsey did not.

'I am bound to say I admire a certain degree of boldness—'

'And I have gone too far.'

'I must ask my Aunt Sarah to accompany us,' allowed her to avoid an answer. His expression must have been telling in the disappointment line, for she was quick to qualify her point in the face of his obvious displeasure. 'I will also request that she does so at a discreet distance, which will allow us to converse without being overheard.'

'Then I am yours to command.'

That lightened her mood and produced a nautical quip. 'So I have the quarterdeck, Captain?'

It was too good an opportunity to miss. 'Madam, you have the entire vessel from keel to mainmast cap.'

This being outrageous, it was enough to once more fluster her. Betsey moved to pass him, saying, on her way to and out of the door, 'I must change into more suitable clothing. A servant will fetch you some refreshments.'

Left alone and in contemplation, Edward Brazier was obliged to examine recent events and, as ever, he was aware of a certain amount of speculation. One clear fact could not be disputed: Henry Tulkington was dead set against his sister remarrying, so it might not be personal to him and, very likely, Aunt Sarah took her cue from the dominant character at Cottington Court.

A wandering mind, served with a pot of coffee, could conjure up any number of possibilities for his attitude, even some quite salacious conclusions, though he was swift to suppress such thoughts. What had Tulkington been like when Betsey married Stephen Langridge?

That sharp remark regarding her and the childhood friend who had become her husband was revealing. Or was it?

A knock, then the sepulchral face of the servant. 'Mrs Langridge and Mrs Lovell are waiting in the garden, sir. I took the liberty of fetching your hat.'

There was a sore temptation to ask this stick of misery for the truth of what he had been wondering upon; servants knew everything about their betters: their moods, accidents, disputes and secrets. They shared that with common seamen, who seemed to know what went on in the great cabin, as well as what was afoot in the destination line, long before their captain deigned to inform them.

Sadly, it could not be, so, taking his scraper, he went to join them, going through the ritual of polite greetings before they set off, accompanied by the spaniels, exiting the formal garden by a side gate, which would take them towards the wooded part of what Betsey assured him was a walled estate. He did not speak until they were out through the gate, and there was no physical contact; he and she remained a minimum of a foot apart, which frustrated Brazier, who harboured a strong desire to take her arm.

'I am tempted to look round and check on your aunt's mood,' he said with a touch of mockery, as they moved into a tree-lined path, the foliage taking away much of the light, the dogs racing playfully to and fro up ahead.

'Would that be necessary?'

'You do know why I have come here? It wasn't just your brother making guesses, I hope?'

'No.'

'I am now left to wonder at which question you're answering.' When she glanced at him, it was to see a diverting smile, not the complaint she had suspected. 'That said, they will both suffice when it comes to a response.'

She emitted a small laugh. 'You're little changed from Jamaica.'

'Why would I be? I'm the same fellow. Did you wish to find me altered?'

'You must know I saw you as very different to most of those . . .'

It was not an interruption; she had hesitated and failed to finish the sentence.

'Who sought to engage your attention. How so?'

'Very much more subtle, especially in that look you ever had in your eye.'

'I was the soul of discretion,' he protested. 'Both verbally and otherwise.'

'You may have thought yourself that, sir, but I can say it was not so, for I was on the receiving end of what I can only term your refined audacity.'

'Your aunt would never have allowed such a thing to occur. Any discomfort and she would have intervened.'

'I did not say I found it unsettling, did I?'

'But you are saying my own impression of my behaviour towards you was at complete odds as to how it was perceived?'

'I suppose I am.'

'Then I am bound to wonder which one of us carries responsibility. I might assume that you read the things I imparted in a light never intended.' Brazier was quick to correct himself; telling her she was being foolish would not serve. 'No, strike that. Let us just accept that my view of my discretion is not as I thought.'

'I felt it refreshing to find someone who was neither a stranger to rigid formality, a manner evident even in your fellow sailors, or so bold as to cross several lines at once, like the late Admiral Hassel.'

'I did note he was a touch free.'

'He was ever eager to play to old roué, which was nothing more than a disguise for taking unwarranted liberties and that was the case when my poor, dear husband was still alive.'

'You never spoke of your husband when we met and that's the first time he has been mentioned now.'

'To do so in the Caribbean was only to reprise grief. I cannot begin to count the number of times we came this way, on this very path, as children, and that brings forth memories too.'

'I would like to know of him.'

'What's to say? He was sweet to me as a child, like a brother, and we grew to love each other as man and wife. But Stephen was never robust and you know, as well as I, the air of the Caribbean can be mortal to Europeans.'

'Do you miss Jamaica?'

'Only the good times, and there were many.'

'Your brother intimated you're considering selling the plantations.'

'Did he say why?'

'No, but I assumed a dislike of slavery.'

'How astute you are. I was never at peace with the means by which they were managed. Stephen was a gentle soul, who treated people well, but the overseers he inherited along with the cane fields were a brutal lot. A stronger man might have curbed their excesses, but . . .'

The pause was telling, for she had bordered on criticism of him. 'In my capacity as owner, I managed to dismiss the two worst offenders, which was a matter my husband had discussed as being desirable. I felt it necessary to do so as a legacy.'

Brazier's mind was not on cruel overseers. He had been taken back to the time his ship had encountered a Dutch slaver in the mid Atlantic, a vessel so malodorous the smell could be picked up for miles if you were downwind. The trade was legal, but he was obliged to send someone aboard to inspect any vessel heading towards the Caribbean islands, slaves being a commodity as likely to be smuggled as any other. Such a vessel, heading on a course that could take it to a colonial possession of King George, was required to have a home port in Britain.

It was not a duty he wished to inflict upon his inferior officers;

in any case their reluctance was palpable. All the crew had heard of conditions on such craft and were in no great rush to witness them. So, he had chosen to go himself, taking his barge crew, they being amongst the toughest and least sentimental crew members, which left him with a vision that, recurring now, and in this company, was unwelcome.

Men and women chained on racks, so tightly packed as to make breathing difficult while the decks ran with piss and watery shit. They were fed, but there was no charity or quality in it, for they were required to be a saleable commodity once they reached their destination. It was well known that in extreme bad weather, the slavers would dump them all overboard to save themselves.

His abhorrence of the trade, as well as the exploitation of innocents, which he had never taken to in any case, stemmed from that day, so he was tempted to laud Betsey's possible course of action, yet he stopped himself. Having already overstepped the mark more than once this day, by too-flagrant hints regarding the future, any opinion advanced in that area would sound as though he reckoned her consent to his approaches to be a foregone conclusion. It was as well she changed the subject.

'Henry was not happy about Stephen and I marrying either, which I could never comprehend.'

Brazier nearly blurted out: 'So I should not feel singular.' He bit back those words too.

'He is overly possessive.' A pause. 'Can I ask why you never wrote?'

'I feared to put too much of my sentiments on paper, which might have driven you away, given I find them hard to convey with a quill. One untoward sentence can do untold harm, so I reckoned talking would serve better and, as of now, I have little idea if that notion holds water.'

'Would it help if I was to say nothing that was said by my brother today renders me disenchanted?'

A harrumph from their rear indicated that Aunt Sarah had surreptitiously closed the gap. It was Betsey who increased her pace suddenly to reinstate it, just as they came onto more open ground by a small tree-lined lake. Still, being cautious, she spoke softly.

'My Aunt Sarah only follows his instructions and you must not blame her, for she is dependent on him for everything – a roof over her head and even the food she eats. I doubt she would have come out to the Caribbean if he had not demanded it, for she is a particularly bad sailor. I saw her misery on the way back to England and it must have been the same on the outward passage. Added to that she has been very kind to me in the past.'

'If there's an aunt, there must have been an uncle.'

'Gone. Disappeared. Went out one day and never returned, with no word since. Aunt Sarah has no idea if she's a widow or still a wife.'

'Then I feel I must promise to be nice to her.'

That got a full laugh. 'Lord, she will test you on that.'

'Elisabeth! Decorum,' came from the very source, as if to underline Betsey's assertion.

The subject closest to Brazier's heart had to be put to one side, for he was shown the church, which lay in the estate grounds: a small rectangular chapel with a square steeple and patch of ground filled with gravestones of various age. The living was in the gift of the estate and Betsey also described the incumbent, a Reverend Moyle. Though she tried to make her impression of the divine and his addiction to the bottle sound humorous, Brazier sensed an underlying dislike of his inability to behave in a manner befitting his office.

'Your brother could dismiss him, surely?'

'He could but declines to do so, which is, to me, a mystery. And here we have the lake.'

He was taken round to be shown where she and her childhood friends had fished and swum as children. *Did she still do so now* was

108

one of those questions that could wait, though again it rendered him uncomfortable to contemplate they might do so together.

Besides, he felt the need to listen acutely to what was being imparted, for she was back on the subject of her late husband, he gaining the impression that she and Stephen Langridge had grown into marriage. If there were constant references to his kind nature and quiet good humour, as she pointed out where they had climbed trees and plaited flowers, or set terriers to dig out rabbits, ferrets and stoats, there was no hint of any deep passion.

Other childhood friends were referred to, names that meant nothing to him, girls and boys now married and one or two with children of their own, which brought a wistful tone to her voice, for her union had clearly been childless. Again he had to bite back the question and for the same reason. To ask her if she wished for children was impossible.

'Your father?'

'If I was to say Henry is his true heir, would that suffice? Though he had none of my brother's obsessions with his health and was a more stalwart creature altogether. My papa was kind in his way, but so taken up with his affairs and projections that he barely ever spent time with us. He was extremely hard on my brother, which perhaps explains his present behaviour. Henry was sent away to school, which I suspect he hated.'

She fell silent in contemplation. Betsey should have gone on to describe her mother, but that did not happen, which he found strange. Was it because he might ask that she changed the subject abruptly?

'You must stop me blathering.'

'Why would I, when I enjoy it?'

'You have listened to me talk for an age, yet have not once referred to your own family or upbringing, and I am curious.'

A positive sign, to which he responded in the only way he could. An only child, son of a naval surgeon, often away at sea though, he had since been informed, much respected professionally. This was why he had been taken onto the books of the ship of the line commanded by the then Captain Pollock. Prior to that he had been raised by his mother, whose memory he revered, with both parents now deceased.

'There was schooling prior to going aboard, of course, so I can stab at Latin and Greek, but it was mathematics that counted, for that subject is the very bedrock of naval service. If you struggle as an officer with numbers, you will struggle to properly navigate and keep your logs. It never does to be fully at the mercy of the ship's master, so you must be able to check his calculations. Likewise a clerk handling your logs.'

As it had been with slavery, his mind was partly elsewhere in reaction to his own recollections, in his cabin as Lieutenant Schomberg demanded he convene a court martial to clear his name of unwarranted accusations made against him by Prince William. He was quick to put that out of his thoughts. Best to talk of the joys and miseries of being a midshipman, which he went on to do.

'I have already alluded to my lack of – what shall I call it? – discretion, in the manner of my calling here.'

'I reckoned it bold in alacrity, sir,' she replied, with a wry twist of the lips. 'Nothing has occurred to change that opinion.'

'Then I must tell you where I learnt it. You cannot imagine life in a mids' berth on a man-o'-war, and I would hesitate to seek to fully enlighten you.'

'Surely it is no worse than conditions on any ship, for instance the vessels on which I sailed on the triangular passage?'

No was his immediate, unspoken thought; the navy was very different. How do you describe an existence surrounded by endemic bullying; unwarranted and unwanted sexual advances; finding your possessions, so lovingly packed in your brand-new sea chest by your mother, stolen and with no redress possible? There were many who succumbed to such and left the service.

Edward Brazier had been a fighter at school and he held to that one from the first day aboard, earning, with his dark looks, black hair and ferocious temper the soubriquet of 'The Turk'. Most of those canings Admiral Pollock had referred to came from him fighting those who sought to oppress him. What he gave her by way of explanation was much filleted and full of happier memories.

'And now you are a full post captain.'

'Suffice to say, I have been favoured by a degree of luck.'

'Your luck was the talk of the island.'

'I meant prior to that, though I do not deny the good fortune of the *Santa Clara*. I have been blessed enough to have been in action many times and, given they were generally successful, I have risen in the service at a rate much faster than many who, like me, lack influence where it counts.'

'Captain Edward Brazier,' she said. 'I like the sound.'

'Ah, I do have a Christian name.'

Her voice dropped to a low timbre. 'You enquired earlier if I would call you by that name?'

'And?'

'You must know what such familiarity implies?' There was no need to reply to the question with anything other than a penetrating look. 'It speaks of some kind of understanding, which is a step full of meaning and could leave me a hostage to fortune.'

'I feel inclined to quote the Bard and refer to that commodity being taken at the flood.'

The pealing laugh was delightful; it was bound to upset Aunt Sarah, which made it doubly a thing to enjoy. 'Quoting Shakespeare. Are you erudite as well as lucky and brave?'

It was his turn to laugh. 'I am certainly not a person inclined to bat away flattery.'

The voice was even quieter as she spoke again. 'If I do agree to call you Edward, it can for the present only be in private and when it cannot be overheard by anyone. You must recall my present estate and the need to give no room to malicious tongues.'

'Then it is probably best if I say to you that I am bent on seeking your hand in marriage. I know there are better and more proper forms of uttering such a proposal, but I need to know for my own sake if my intentions are not going to be rebuffed. I add that I am aware of the constraints on your ability to respond, but I have calculated the time it has been since the unfortunate demise of your husband.'

'You would not expect me to accept here and now?'

'I can think of no reason not to.'

'Allow me a little time, Edward.'

'If I must, of course.'

CHAPTER NINE

He rode out of Cottington Court in fine fettle, near certain his proposal, even if it had not been openly acknowledged, was going to be accepted. There were particulars to be observed and they would take a while, but as of this moment time was a commodity he had in abundance. Of course, he could be called back to service at any moment and he had to hope in that event Betsey would understand. But the chances of a ship were slim: the nation was at peace and the Royal Navy had been run down accordingly.

What he left behind was not so blissful; Henry Tulkington, who had avoided Brazier on his return from the walk, was still furious at the way he had been spoken to. No one else in the locality would have dared, yet here was this stranger treating him as if he was of no account. He was also determined to challenge his sister as soon as he was gone and it was not a tranquil exchange, made worse by the way Aunt Sarah backed up the brother so forcibly.

'You hardly know the fellow, Elisabeth.'

That she had to admit was true; she had met him on a dozen or so occasions, yes, but today was the only time in which their talk had been in any way private and not carried out under the public gaze. Given that, her reply was slightly defensive.

'I intend that I should get to know him better – and you too, Aunt.'

Betsey deliberately looked at Henry as she uttered those words, the implication plain: he was included. He was stood with a shawl around his shoulders which, given his piqued expression, made him appear like some old crone. The look he gave her said in no uncertain terms he was not in any way interested in getting to know Brazier better, quite the reverse.

'I would like to know how far your folly has taken you.'

'Folly!'

'It is nothing less. A near stranger to you, as Aunt Sarah says, whom you met on a few occasions in Jamaica, and one who has the audacity to turn up at our house—'

'He was invited Henry. I invited him.'

'I refer not to his presence, but his effrontery. I found his manner insufferable.'

'I daresay he felt the same about yours, and I would remind you that you have no say in the matter of whom I meet and converse with, or for that matter whom I like or dislike.'

'As your elder brother I have responsibility to see you do not do anything you might later regret.' Henry looked away, breaking eye contact, his voice wheedling and his manner that of a person deeply hurt. 'Not that your Brazier fellow even came close to acknowledging that my opinion counted for anything. I daresay he is accustomed to berating the common seaman and lacks the discernment required for polite society. Even now, as I think of the words he used, I shudder at the thought of his clear intentions.'

'Is it not that you're feeling chilled?'

'Elisabeth,' Aunt Sarah interjected, 'attempts at levity will not aid matters.'

'Nor will it help to impugn Captain Brazier's intentions.'

'At least,' Henry said, with a direct stare and growl meant to appear fierce, 'tempted as I was, I didn't stoop to threatening him.'

'What are you talking about?'

Eye contact was lost again. 'I made reference to his being a serving officer, who could be off to sea at the drop of a hat and for months if not years, which would leave you all alone, not that he would care. I made it plain that you are not some trophy to be taken up as an ornament. His response was a clear warning that speaking in such a way, which I took to be my right, I risked being called out to provide satisfaction.'

Betsey was genuinely shocked. 'You surely don't mean he challenged you to a duel?'

'Not in his exact words. He is easily insulted, I suspect; touchy in his character.' Henry looked her in the eye again, to drive home his point. 'Pistols or swords at dawn was implied and we both know what the result would be, from one who seemingly would stoop to kill a member of your own family to achieve his ends. Is that the sort of ruffian with whom you are happy to consort?'

'Consort? So far I have not done anything but share a pleasant interlude and a walk with a man whose company I enjoy.'

Aunt Sarah cut in again, her tone more pleading than hectoring. 'It is a short step from that to a greater degree of familiarity, which, even though I could not hear the words you exchanged, led me to believe was taking place.'

'I am minded to forbid this, Elisabeth.'

'While I will remind you I no longer require your permission to do anything, and nor do I need to come to you for money, Henry. I have my own.'

'But I do reserve the right to say who can and who cannot enter my house. I am quite prepared to issue an instruction that Captain Brazier is not to be admitted onto my property.'

'And when did you arrive at that notion?'

'At this very moment.'

Betsey wanted to shout liar but held her anger in check, to answer calmly, although it sounded forced even in her own ears. 'Then I shall arrange to meet him elsewhere.'

The air of self-satisfaction in the response was infuriating, underlying his threat was no spontaneous notion. 'Then it best be close by. I own every horse in the stables, likewise the carriages. They are for your use only if I can be sure it is not to meet that man.'

'You would confine me to Cottington Court?'

'It would be for your own sake, Elisabeth,' Aunt Sarah pleaded. 'Henry means well.'

Betsey pushed past her brother, emitting a reply, made more in sorrow than anger. 'How can you say that when you know it is the very opposite of the truth?'

Stood in the doorway she spun to address Henry again. 'I wonder what people will say, brother, when they see me walking to Deal like some common churl. They're bound to ask what is amiss and I will be happy to tell them that I am going to visit, against your express wishes, a certain Captain Brazier in Lower Deal. No great wit will be required to deduce from that why I would be so determined.'

For the second time that day the house reverberated to the sound of a slammed door.

The journey back to the Three Kings was tediously slow. Brazier found himself behind a herd of cattle being driven, he was told by the herder, towards the Deal slaughterhouse. There they would be slain, butchered, the majority salted and packed in barrels, doubtless for sale to the ships taking on stores. He was obliged to hang back to avoid being totally enveloped in the cloud of dust created, but at least the time could be employed in the making of some decisions.

To stay where he was made no sense, when he would be in Deal for some time. Whatever bill Garlick presented to him he could afford but it was a poor use of funds. Matters with Betsey could not be rushed: the rituals of proper courtship must be outwardly observed and he was determined to give no one an excuse to question his behaviour, which applied most to her brother.

It would be better to rent a house and to do that he required his needs to be met by at least one servant. Anyone local he would not know, while he envisaged two very good reasons not to employ such people. First they might gossip, and the notion of his comings and goings, as well as those whom he entertained, being talked about in the gin shops and taverns of the town was not to be contemplated.

Added to that, complete trust was necessary – a hard thing to judge in any person you did not know intimately. All he interviewed would claim saintliness in that area, but experience told him the people who protested their honesty with the greatest vehemence were often the most light-fingered; besides, the alternative was much more attractive.

The men who had served him aboard HMS *Diomede* had also been discharged and might be still unemployed. He had the means to contact those who would be keen to serve with him again, not that in such an event it was necessary. At the first hint of a new conflict, with ships of war being commissioned, he would surely be in line for a command. Then the nautical grapevine would be activated.

At once, country roads would then be full of volunteers making their way to whatever port the captain they favoured had berthed his ship, with no fear of press gangs so early in an outbreak, the more likely threat coming from recruiting parties seeking to get them drunk and aboard other vessels.

Any house would have to be of a size in which he could entertain, and not just Betsey Langridge and her ever-present chaperone. There was Admiral Braddock, who had already intimated he would have Brazier to dinner and that must be reciprocated. Other naval officers of equal or lesser rank resided in Deal and good manners and tradition obliged him to invite them to dine as well. It would be possible to get Admiral Pollock over from Adisham for any gathering of blue coats, which would ease his isolation.

It was a stiff naval officer who dismounted at the Three Kings, for he had been too long in the saddle this day. Ben was out front and he requested the lad take Bonnie back to the Naval Yard, with Brazier hoisting him astride the beast, ignoring the lad's protests.

'Never mind Mr Garlick, young 'un. I will tell him I insisted you must ride her and he will not argue with me.'

'Hope my mates see me, your honour,' he called gaily as he trotted away. 'It'll make them right green.'

Garlick was in his usual spot and once more the owner showed what Brazier thought to be excessive inquisitiveness. He had sought directions, so his destination could be no mystery. As before it was ignored in favour of instructions that a bath should be provided and his dust-covered uniform required to be sponged and pressed.

'And dinner, Captain?'

'After the bath.' The lack of a bathing machine belonging to the hotel already established, Brazier added, 'While that is being prepared, I require a number of towels and a gown to wear down to the seashore.'

Garlick visibly shuddered, a reaction to which Brazier was well accustomed. All of his crews had reckoned him deranged to go swimming in the sea and risk not just drowning, but seizure by some many-tentacled or sabre-toothed creature of the deep. Sailors might bathe in a sail slung over the side, but they remained sure that just below the surface of the water lay any number of threats to their lives – and what they could not witness, they were prone to imagine.

In his room, divested of his clothes, he donned a pair of cotton ducks. At sea, he plunged naked, but that would not serve on an open beach in sight of humanity of both sexes.

'At least,' he said to himself, 'I have no need to fear a shark.'

In which he was utterly correct. Such a creature would never have borne the temperature of the water, indeed Brazier was unsure if he could himself, for it was still winter cold, icy enough on entry to make him gasp. Once he was fully immersed and moving, that eased, as did those aches he had garnered in the saddle. To then,

118

still chilled, lower himself into a bathtub full of hot water was bliss indeed and a very strong aid to contemplation of a happy future.

Betsey Langridge, from her bedroom window, saw her brother depart in the company of his coachman and postilion, her lips pursed at the thought of what he had said about confining her, which would not occur. It was an empty threat; Henry had never been physical in that way. Indeed, with that twelve-year gap between them he had always been something of a distant and indifferent presence in her life, until it had become plain she intended to wed Stephen Langridge.

He had objected quite strongly and he had proved obdurate for many a month. Yet he had come round eventually, to provide her a fitting ceremony in St Saviour's, the quality folk of Kent, from the Lord Lieutenant down, invited to Cottington Court to toast the couple and wish them God's Speed to their new life in the West Indies.

Joshua Moyle had even been sober throughout the ceremony, which Betsey put down to the restrictions placed on him by his wife. He had, of course and as usual, reverted to type at the subsequent feast and got thoroughly drunk.

Her mind inevitably turned to Edward Brazier. Would Henry come round in the same manner once he saw how determined she was? Unavoidably this led to her examining her own feelings, naturally wondering if it had been wise to be so openly encouraging. She did, in reality, hardly know him, so perhaps it would have been better to hold back on his desire that she use his Christian name. But then, it had felt right at the moment of saying it.

She could not avoid conjuring up an image of him as a darkly handsome suitor. That acknowledged, Betsey reminded herself it was not only his appearance she admired: it was his whole presence, especially his voice, so deep and warm. It would be less so on a quarterdeck, no doubt brisk and commanding; that too stood in the credit column.

It was impossible to think in those terms without wondering again what her late husband would think of such fancies. Would Stephen approve? Surely he would not have wanted her to remain a widow after he was gone? Betsey was utterly certain that was not her wish, for she missed not just Stephen but the whole gamut of the married estate: the companionship, the need to run her own house, even the shared silliness and, if it made her blush to think on it, the intimacy of the bedchamber.

Henry was right about her being a desirable catch, but wrong about Edward, as she now allowed herself to think of him. It had been very evident in the Caribbean how different he was and how she had reacted to his presence. Of any number of suitors who had made plain their feelings, some surely genuine, many obviously not, the only one to induce any kind of emotion in her breast had not long left her side.

Was the feeling real, was it the first stirrings of true affection? Honesty forced her to admit she was unsure.

Henry Tulkington was a man of business and not singular in his interests. He had any number of matters that took up his time and attention, determined, as he was, to present to the world, like his father before him, a facade of wealth, success and respectability. Many of his activities could be carried out openly, either at Cottington Court or in various places in the surrounding towns, but the enterprise that made him the most in terms of money had to be clandestine.

The slaughterhouse-cum-tannery, which he owned, just outside the north-west end of Deal, was not a place to excite visitors or invite folk of quality to reside nearby, so it was surrounded by mean dwellings and even they gave it as wide a berth as they could. Still, being poor, they could not avoid the stench of either rotting offal, a river of congealing blood, or the drying hides of leather. It provided a location for Henry Tulkington to do business without it being observed or overheard.

As ever, it was noisy with the sound of cattle and pigs, never more so than when the latter were having their throats cut, which had to be done not long after arrival, given the creatures were barred from the town unless they came for immediate butchering. Tulkington hated it too, abhorring the sight of so much blood and, as ever, he hurried to John Hawker's second-storey workplace, where on any day, hot or cold, there was a tray of herbs above the stove, the scent of which fought the noxious odours from below.

'You're content with the arrangements?'

Hawker, being a man of few words, merely nodded at what was an oft-asked question, habitual rather than essential, regarding a coming shipment. This attitude was repeated when Tulkington queried the transport that would later take the contraband to where it could either be sold or collected by customers regularly supplied. Hawker apart, those seeing to the landing would not know those locations; goods, once brought ashore and stored, were distributed by men who never saw the carrying vessel.

'And the master's payment?'

Hawker held up an oilskin pouch heavy with coin, this as Tulkington eased closer to the stove, backing to it in order to enjoy the heat on his thighs, confirming he had done what he could to prevent problems. Tulkington dealt with those, locally, who were tasked to enforce the law, people who never saw any reason to expend effort to interdict smuggling: the magistrates, Justices of the Peace, members of the town council and even some of the local clergy, which included Moyle, who enjoyed fulminating against wrongdoing from the pulpit to the same level he enjoyed drinking untaxed brandy.

Outsiders reckoned places such as Deal were so steeped in crime that every hand, from the lowest to the highest, was stained: the truth was less stark, but no less damning. Every soul in the town knew what went on and would, in conversation and with outright hypocrisy, condemn it heartily. This they did before either spending their illegitimate proceeds or, in the higher reaches on the social scale,

121

contracting for delivery of their own illicit and revenue-free supplies.

An occasional head might be raised, Temperance Societies or Baptists seeking to curtail smuggling as well as drinking by prayer and the threat of providing information. This was a good way to have your meeting house torched by an angry mob of the local boat fraternity, who would claim, with an apparently clear conscience, to depend on the trade to provide for everyday food and shelter.

Corcoran, the fellow employed to superintend the activities of the Kent Preventatives, had a near-Herculean task and was poorly rewarded for his efforts by the sinecure holder who, in theory, was supposed to carry out the work. Corcoran did not operate on the coast, but had his station inland, from where he could oversee the work of those patrolling the Thames Estuary, the east coast centred on Dover, added to the southern area of his responsibilities, which ran through Folkestone all the way to the Romney Marshes, with active smuggling taking place along the whole coast, not that he ever had the bodies required to be truly effective.

There was always a shortage in the number of men covering Deal, but another method existed to ensure the activities at a certain location stood at a very low risk of interruption. That task fell to Hawker and he now outlined how the local Revenue would be diverted on this occasion. The method was simple, for they were not overeager, hardly surprising given their miserable stipend, but obliged to stir occasionally in order to justify it.

The strategy was to grant to them an occasional morsel of success. Deal Beach was a community and one in which everyone sought to know the business of everyone else. Thus gossip was rife, albeit never allowed to take place in the presence of anyone not recognised: a strange face stuck out and brought about immediate suspicion, given the Revenue had over the years tried to slip in spies.

Competition for employment was rampant, given there were too many boats and too little trade in porterage, while jealousies, as well as long-standing family feuds, abounded. This led to loose tongues, if the ears listening were held to be safe, and Hawker was seen as very sound indeed, as well as a fellow it could be profitable to be in with, so he picked up hints of what was being planned.

Thus he could alert the Revenue and give them the occasional smuggling sprat, which would both ensure they were busy and, if Tulkington's men were in a period of being active, divert them away from the landing of any cargo Hawker was charged to oversee. Not that they were always presented with an easy success; that was too risky. He often chose to tell the owner of any lugger set for a Channel dash they were on to him. This left them either in the wrong place or on the wrong night to intercept, while mightily enhancing the standing of Hawker.

'They should be chasing their arses when we're busy. I've told them a tale 'bout three hundred pounds of tea coming in by the Albion, but it will really land above Sandown Castle. They might see a rate of moving lanterns, but will be too late to put a stopper on it.'

Tulkington stated himself to be fully satisfied regarding weather and the arrangements, only to then change the subject, to get lifted eyebrows from a fellow not much given to showing his thinking.

'I have to own to a problem, John. My foolish sister has become enamoured of an adventurer fellow, a naval officer, and I reckon his pursuit of her should be discouraged.'

'An' how far does this being discouraged go?'

There was meaning in that, which had to be cogitated upon. Hawker's reputation served both him and Tulkington well and it was not just for taking anyone needing to be seen to out in a boat. He was the man who ran the slaughterhouse and tannery, very happy with what the more lurid minds gossiped about. Rumour had it there were bodies who had gone through the slaughterhouse doors whole, to either emerge in pieces or not at all. Even more terrifying was the thought of human parts being salted and mixed in with barrels full of pork.

'A warning only, perhaps,' Tulkington said finally. 'That failing, who knows.'

'Best tell me, Mr Tulkington.' Which he did, to get a doubtful response. 'Navy is tricky, bound to stand out.'

'He's not attached to the Downs Squadron, but a visitor newly arrived, a rogue of a captain come with the express desire of seducing Elisabeth and getting his hands on her possessions.'

'What's he look like?'

'Your height, black hair and I'd say a swarthy complexion, a haughty manner too. He was at my house today and, I have to admit to you, the fellow is lucky to have got away unscathed. The way he addressed me was enough to have him depart bleeding and bruised but I could not act as I would have wished in the article of chastisement, with my sister and aunt in the house.'

Tulkington was now looking at the stove and warming his hands, back turned, which allowed John Hawker to smile without being observed, for if the sister was the excuse, it would be her brother who felt insulted. That would warrant a beating and it was not the first time; it did not do to show disrespect to Henry Tulkington, for he took it ill.

Traders in the town knew to their cost what happened if they tried to dun the owner of Cottington Court; even a lawyer who sought to bring a suit against him was physically so discouraged as to drop it. Then there was his near neighbour, a farmer called Colpoys, who had got into a trifling boundary dispute, only to wake one morning in a ditch, bloody and battered.

Even if he insisted upon discretion, Henry Tulkington liked it that folk were cautious of him and his name, as well as a reputation inherited from his sire. Both, as it was with contraband, were whispered about rather than openly stated. He was ever talking bold when, in truth, in the physical line, he was a true fraidy-cat. Anything of that nature thus fell to his factotum Hawker, who was happy to oblige, taking pleasure, as he did, in chastisement – and even more, if that was required.

Lack any aggressive ability he might, but Tulkington was still the man in charge, the brains who arranged everything Hawker was tasked to carry out, never ever to get his own hands dirty while the fellow he trusted to execute those responsibilities was more than content with the arrangement.

'I have a notion I might have already seen this cove. If it's the same bugger, he was at the Griffin's Head two days' past and he deserves a cudgel.'

'Why would he be there?' was the apprehensive enquiry.

'Passing through, I reckon, not prying – and besides, if he were, it would not be in uniform.'

'He is residing at the Three Kings, for it was to there my sister sent him a note.'

'Sweet on him, is she?' That got Hawker a look that told him that was none of his concern; his enquiry was unwelcome. 'So a sound beating, happen.'

'That will satisfy me.'

'In your name?'

'I don't want my sister to know anything about it.'

'You're sure you don't want him seen to proper?'

'The Good Lord knows I'm tempted.'

Hawker could smile fully and openly then at that piece of hypocrisy; if Tulkington was a regular at St Saviour's and St George's, as well as generous when the plate came round, he was not one to obey any commandments.

'I hope that a beating will send the message he is not welcome hereabouts – that and maybe the loss of his purse. If he does not desist . . . well.'

'He's bound to connect with you, Mr Tulkington. Just arrived he is, you say, and that means there likely ain't nobody else he's crossed.'

The Tulkington brow furrowed. 'You said he deserved a cudgel. Why?'

'Not one to take a hint, politely given. I was talking close and quiet with Trotter, regarding your meeting with Spafford, an' he comes barging along to take a seat, without so much as a by your leave. I would have laid into him then, sword or no, if we had not been making the arrangements.'

'So you have an antipathy of your own?'

'While he has a face I know, as does Daisy Trotter.'

'Then it would be a good idea to leave him with Trotter's name as the one handing out the beating, not yours or mine.'

'Clever that,' Hawker replied with real feeling; the notion was typically cunning of Tulkington. 'How soon?'

'The weather is good and the sea reasonably calm, so we can expect the promised landing to come in on time. If it can be done before you go to meet the ship that would serve.'

'Can't say fer certain, Mr Tulkington. Sod has to be where we can get at him and it'll not be much good, given your notion on Daisy, if I is spotted.'

There was truth in that. John Hawker was a too-well-known face in the town, being the man charged to collect taxes on behalf of the King's Treasury, a well-rewarded government sinecure actually held and delegated by Henry Tulkington. As a cover for shifting contraband – the folk being taxed for legal vending were often the same people selling the superior products Hawker had to offer – it could not be bettered.

'Then don't get involved.'

Hawker nodded slowly. 'Makes sense, even if it be a pity.'

CHAPTER TEN

Brazier came back to an invitation from Admiral Braddock asking him to dine the next day, and quickly accepted. With the aim of renting a house now decided upon, he turned his mind to the need for a servant. Of the several men who had acted in that capacity aboard HMS *Diomede*, Joe Lascelles stood highest in his estimation. The son of a slave he was rated free, this after the judgement of Lord Mansfield that no man in England could own the body of another. His father had been brought to England, with John in tow, by a West Indian customs official and slave trader, from whom he took his surname.

He had joined the navy as a volunteer to get away from, as he had it, a life like that of his sire, as a household servant albeit free, only to end up fulfilling that role in the great cabin of Brazier's frigate. His one problem being in the West Indies was his inability to go ashore; it was too risky despite him carrying written proof of his free status. If he had ended up on a plantation, there would be scant chance of getting him back.

What marked him in Brazier's mind was his unfailing good humour and saint-like patience, an attitude severely dented on the day they came across that Dutch slaver. It was the only time his captain, who described to him the things witnessed, had seen him shed a tear. Had the Lord Chancellor's judgement not become law, John could have shared the fate of those being transported.

The slaver, it had transpired, was on course for the Dutch colony of St Maarten, but the conditions for Joe would have been the same, only he would have been forced to work in the fields of a British colonial possession, at the mercy of an overseer whose income was decided on a good crop yield. Brazier asked him once why he never complained. The response was simple: fate had been too kind.

His normal demeanour was a wide, white-teeth smile or a deep-throated laugh, easily invoked, which made him of inestimable value to a commander who, generally good-humoured himself, disliked having misery in his orbit. There were a couple of others to whom he sent letters, men who had acted as servants and whom he trusted, all with a promise to bear the cost of a reply, but he had high hopes that John would respond positively.

The temptation to ask Garlick for advice on the renting of a suitable house did not last; the man would look to personal advantage in the matter, either by seeking to profit from any transaction or finding him an abode designed to drive him back to the Three Kings.

It duly struck him the only person he could seek aid from was Vincent Flaherty, simply because he might know whom to ask, so, having had his dinner early, Bonnie was taken out again for a ride to the Irishman's paddock.

'That would be best asked of Saoirse, for sure, Edward. Not much going on in the town she don't know about.'

Brazier, having sent Ben and his mount back to the stables once more, decided to call upon the lady prior to the start of the evening trade; it would be too busy later. So he made for the Old Playhouse determined to arrive before any torches were required to be lit, completely unaware that he was being followed. John Hawker had been well placed to see who entered and left the Three Kings and he had with him a couple of true hard bargains, men who would be guaranteed to avoid gentility in the task set for them.

'Listen for the St George's bells,' was the instruction, as Brazier entered the doorway, for Hawker and these two were needed elsewhere in the hours of darkness. 'If it counts past seven of the clock, we'll have to let it slumber for tonight. An' keep them cudgels out of sight.'

John Hawker had allowed cudgels only in case matters went awry and they were required to both defend themselves and get clear; this was to be a beating with fists, not one to maim or kill.

'Wait till he's down an' out afore you go for his purse too.'

Brazier was welcomed by Saoirse Riorden, who remarked on his being in uniform and, with the tilt of her head and a droll look, how it was suited to him. This was taken to be the normal manner in which a tavern-cum-playhouse owner talked to a potential customer, especially one who appeared to have deep pockets. For the coming evening she was dressed in red velvet, which set off her hair and skin, making of the whole a warmer hue than the green in which he had seen her previously.

He followed her to a place in which they could converse, which turned out to be the very room she had entered with the fellow called Hawker. It was a small space lined with shelves groaning with bound ledgers, and a tiny desk with ink and quills. Following behind her, he could not but eye the grace with which she moved, as well as the gentle sway of her hips. Her air of confidence was attractive too, a trait very necessary given her occupation.

'You'll be looking for something grand, I suppose, to fit your wondrous prosperity?'

That got a questioning look, quickly responded to, only to be told his good fortune in the Caribbean was no secret.

'Sure, it does not take much to find out about a new arrival in this place, especially one well found and with the rank you enjoy. If we are overrun with sailors, few are captains in the King's Navy.'

Edward Brazier, a bit piqued, wondered where such knowledge came from; he also knew he would whistle for an answer if he enquired. A post captain would have been remarked upon at the Naval Yard as soon as he visited Braddock, while Garlick looked to be a stranger to discretion. Then there was his open generosity to Flaherty in the article of his wine bill. Whatever, it was out and there was nothing to be done about it.

'I need to accommodate myself, an occasional guest in comfort, and at least one servant, while it has to have the means to lay and maintain a good table.'

'Would close to the Naval Yard serve?'

'It would indeed, given I must entertain Admiral Braddock and what officers he has on station.'

'Not many these days, as I remarked. There's a property, Quebec House, near the gentile southern part of Middle Street, not free from all noise, but quieter than the North End. It was home to a marine officer until recently, is spacious and comfortable and, as of this moment, not occupied.'

'Quebec House sounds very grand.'

'It is, enough to impress.'

'Do I want to impress?'

The smile was enchanting as well as impish. 'That would depend on what you seek at Cottington Court.'

'I sense someone has been talking too much.'

'Captain Brazier, everyone in this town talks too much.'

'Everyone? How well do you know Garlick of the Three Kings?'

Her expression was made mischievous by her look of false innocence. 'A fellow purveyor of hospitality is someone I meet from time to time and one it pays to be friendly with, as it is with all the tavern keepers.'

The air of confidence now rankled: he knew he was being teased and also suspected it was a habit she had with the men she met. With her being comely and unwed, they would tolerate it. The thought of him being sharp in his response was held in check for it would not serve his needs.

'I would need to add,' she continued, 'that we do not live in a place where a great amount of interest occurs, which means that every event assumes proportions it far from warrants.'

'Does it extend to common knowledge?' She shook her head slowly. 'And would it be possible to maintain that?'

'I will not gossip, if it brings concern.'

Brazier was silent for a moment, contemplating the notion of a grand dwelling instead of one more in the utility line. He did not require such a house for himself, but one thought did surface: it might impress and temper the animosity of Henry Tulkington, while the effect on Betsey – a house which, if she chose could become her own – could not be other than positive.

'I need to look it over and talk with the owner.'

That caused her to emit a chuckle. 'Captain, you are talking to the very person.'

'Why do I feel I have been made to look a dupe?'

'Have you?'

'I would reckon so.'

'Men react like that when they are bested by one of my sex.' Seeing him frown, she added, 'Allow me my games, in which I mean to do no harm, other than redress the balance between men and women.'

'By playing on the former.'

'Who prey on the latter by habit and expect praise for it.'

'Not a tag I am willing to wear.' The expression he adopted was one he hoped hinted at humour, but the words were unforgiving – they had to be if he was going to pay her back in kind for her disdain. 'I admit I found myself surprised when Flaherty told me you ran this place without a man to aid you, a husband perhaps. Now I am less so. It takes more than physical charms to snare one.'

131

'The first thing it requires is the desire to do so.'

Her look had switched from amused playfulness to outright resentment and it was a telling change; the skin was now tight on her cheeks, while the narrowed eyes held something akin to scorn. Brazier was being told that Saoirse Riorden was not a plaything of any man.

'I think we have perhaps got off on the wrong foot, which I have already had experience of this very day.'

'Vincent will tell you I'm not one to be trifled with.'

'I doubt I need his validation.' A hand was held up palm forward. 'Pax?'

'Pax, indeed. If you want to look at Quebec House, I will take you there now, or on the morrow.'

'Soonest done.'

'I will fetch my cloak but it will be of short duration, for I am not gifted with much time till I must open my doors to custom.'

'I would not wish to inconvenience you.'

'Do I not owe you some consideration, Captain, for the way I have teased you?' She held up a hand to kill off his reply, which in politeness would have been negative. 'It is a habit of mine, and I admit a far from attractive one, as Flaherty is ever reminding me.'

'Manifested for protection, perhaps?'

'A sharp observation, though not from him, for he is a sweet man in a world not over-gifted with such. If you wait at the door, I will join you once I'm sure all is prepared.'

It was beginning to get dark outside now and as he stood under freshly lit torches, he found himself being examined by the pair of squat, wide-shouldered toughs who minded the Playhouse doorway. Their long clubs, attached to their wrists by leather straps, swung menacingly from their hands. Typical of their breed, they eyed him as they did everyone, those passing by included, as persons on the very edge of committing unwarranted violence; in their occupation, the notion of peaceful contemplation was alien.

With deliberate irony, rating them miserable sods, he raised his hat and moved away; he would be able to spot Saoirse as soon as she exited the building. So ferocious was the way he was grabbed, his hat flew off and he was dragged backwards into some kind of dark recess devoid of overhead light, the first blow of a fist taking him on the side of the head, immediately followed by one to wind him and bend him double. Having been in many fights in his career, he knew he had to retaliate and he also had to keep his feet, which could only be achieved by the wild flailing of his own fists in order to seek to gain some room, his fear that if he went down he would never get up again.

His knuckles connected with bone, which hurt his hand as much as it did whoever the punch landed on, that followed by more blows traded, this while he was trying to make sense of the spittle-flecked words he was hearing. The foul cursing he could comprehend, but what in the name of creation was the meaning of 'Daisy sends you love', or 'Learn where to park your arse, polite, mate'? And finally, 'Best you leave Deal behind, or Daisy reckons this will rate mild'?

In a fight the brain becomes remarkably clear, while what was being inflicted upon him hurt less than it would subsequently. Edward Brazier had noted such facts from his early years in the navy and it mattered little if the contest was with or without weapons. As blows rained down on his head and body, he managed to fend away enough to raise his eyeline and see his assailants silhouetted against the buildings opposite, those already lit by lanterns in the first-storey windows to provide light to the street.

Staying upright he decided would not serve after all, for he had to get out into the twilight. It took all his strength to push one man back enough to create the space to dive under him and, once on the ground, to roll away, though he was taken by a telling boot in the process, which thudded into his back. He kept rolling until he felt the earth of the road under his hand, then yelled for help.

Saoirse Riorden had come out, cloak round her shoulders, to

wonder where her prospective tenant had got to, the look she got from her doorman a smile rather than a glare. Her question as to the whereabouts of a naval officer was answered by a finger pointing up the road and she moved in that direction, just in time to see a figure tumble out onto the street.

She knew it was him by the white facing on his waistcoat, though it took a second to realise he was *in extremis*, as two black-clad fellows came out behind him and started to wildly kick at his body. Brazier was on his back now, using his feet as he had previously used his hands, to deflect as many of those boots as he could, shouting loudly for assistance, which was not forthcoming from those passing locals who moved away from danger, not towards it.

He was aware of a female scream, then the sound of those boots, which had been seeking to do him serious damage, pounding off on the hard ground and diminishing. It was not just those he heard, for if he could not identify them, the two Playhouse doormen were rushing past his inert body, while the woman who employed them knelt beside him, asking what he reckoned was a senseless question.

'Jesus, Mary and Joseph are you hurt?' Her next words were aimed at others, her returning retainers. 'Help him up and take him indoors, where we can see what harm has been done.'

The stab of real pain across his back, as he was lifted, came out as a moan. He could taste blood in his mouth and, when a run of the tongue followed, it told of a split lip. Brazier tried to say he could walk, and to brush off support, only to begin to fall as soon as he was obeyed.

'Will you for the love of God be quiet now,' Saoirse insisted.

Her face became visible as, despite the pain in his back, he lifted his head, the whole quartet now illuminated by the flaring overhead torches. So was her horrified expression, quickly modified, one which told him he had a badly battered face.

'Upstairs with him, Tally. Proctor, find someone to go and get the doctor, then fetch hot water and cloths. If he's sober they're to get him here, in fact drunk as well, and with no excuses.'

The stairs were a trial, too narrow for him to be supported, so a hand on the wall and a lengthy pause was required more than once to steady himself. At the top he was eased into a room, before being helped to lay back on a long settle and that was when the pain really began to kick in, all over his upper body, this while his head began to throb.

His eyes were closed when the damp cloth was applied to one of his injuries, which brought forth a curse as the pain of contact stabbed into him. Then came the really hard part, as she and the fellow who had fetched the hot water tried to get his coat off, even more painful when it came to his long white waistcoat.

The slow thud of feet on the stairs brought the doctor, this heard by Brazier rather than seen, for he had his eyes closed, one through his own volition, the other because it was so swollen he could not see out of it. The smell of drink, on the breath of the man who bent over him, was strong and it was upsetting to hear him ask for that very commodity; was he planning to drink even more!

The assumption was not entirely correct; there was another purpose and one that brought torment as his various afflictions were dabbed with the spirit, to then be washed with water, he assumed to clear away blood or the grime he had gathered in his attempt to roll to safety. The worst point of pain was when he was raised so his back could be examined and, once inspected, it was announced he might have a cracked rib.

'We'll need the shirt off as well. Saoirse. Send someone to the apothecary for bandages, enough to encase his torso. And happen we should allow your fellow here some of this brandy to ease his distress.'

The bottle was put to his lips, to sting the split lip before any of the liquid made it on to his tongue, still less his throat. When it got there it made him gasp, even as he realised it was far from being a rough spirit.

'Would I be permitted, Saoirse?'

'Jesus, how could I stop you, without I drag the bottle out of your hand?'

'Not often I get to drink such quality.' That he had done so was established by a satisfied gasp, followed by, ''Tis a pity to waste it on a wound, is it not?'

Brazier opened his one good eye to find the face of Saoirse Riorden looking into his with a concerned expression.

'We will have to lift you when the bandages come, will that be withstood?' The nod was slow. 'You rest here tonight. There's no way to get you back to the Three Kings without you passing out.'

'Which,' he hissed, trying to make a joke, and regretting it for the pain, 'will give your gossips something real to talk about.'

CHAPTER ELEVEN

Danial Spafford had sent his lugger crews out in pairs throughout the day, some to scour the alehouses of Deal, others to various dwellings, each with instructions to look out for the whereabouts of certain people. The way Tulkington landed and moved his goods, and who oversaw the unloading, was no mystery to men who had been in the same trade for years. His rival had been picking up information all that time, which eventually amounted to a picture. The where and how he had, but not the when.

It was a matter of deep envy that Tulkington's operations were so well organised. The ships he used were larger and his cargoes more varied: not just tea and brandy, but fine wines in the cask. He brought in quantities of tobacco, ladies' leather gloves, bolts of silk and lace, added to which he had a secure place to land his cargo outside the midsummer months. It was also one Hawker's men could defend as well as get clear from if they were required to escape.

Most smugglers landed their contraband and carried it to where it could be quickly stored. For the owner of an individual lugger and small quantities, that had to be Deal Beach itself, or very close by. There, with speed and in darkness, a number of brandy barrels or tea-laden waistcoats could be quickly hidden in the cellars and attics of the houses, before any lawful agency could intervene unless pre-warned.

For Spafford, with a couple of luggers' cargo, it was the Sandwich Flats a mite more than a mile north of Sandown Castle, his stuff borne by hand over the scrub and sandhills by willing locals for a copper reward, to be hidden behind false walls in various barns or, at the right time of year, under hayricks, with the men he led around to guard them until it could be sold.

Tulkington had the use of St Margaret's Bay, a place hard to approach unseen by land and near impossible in numbers along the shoreline. The base of the high chalk cliffs at either extremity were boulder-strewn at low tide, under at least a half a fathom of water when high and often more. With a strand in the centre free from obstructions, the bay had only one steep path as landward approach, while the area was riddled with long-employed tunnels, which, being in chalk, required no supports.

Tulkington's father had hewn out a series of chambers, with wooden beams to keep in place the roof and, into these, the products disappeared to be stored for later distribution. This meant he had no need for constant cross-Channel journeys at inclement times of the year – indeed if the spring and autumn importations went well, he could often avoid the middle months.

The window for the landing of large-scale contraband was constrained by both weather and the hours of daylight. Midwinter provided few opportunities, while in midsummer the few hours of darkness favoured a swift approach by smaller boats and an even faster unloading, this being achieved by a line of as many as one hundred souls in a passing chain. Thus it became an activity from which much of the town took benefit, which in turn guaranteed silence.

The same applied to Spafford and the folk who lived around Worth and Ham, but Hawker oversaw those who carried out the unloading at St Margaret's, each pair of hands known to and depending on him for the means to eat and drink, better than that allowed by the meagre pay they drew as farm labourers or apprentices.

What required no explanation were the possible conditions prevailing under which such activities could be carried out. The state of the moon was important: full or near full meant the need for heavy cloud cover; nothing but a sliver was best. Then there was the sea state, which mattered just as much for a Deal chancer as it did for Tulkington or Spafford.

A really heavy swell had to be avoided. Not only was unloading dangerous and, from a full-sized cargo vessel, time-consuming: it was too easy for a vessel to be driven so far onshore it would struggle to quickly refloat, quite apart from the damage inflicted upon the hull. It also needed to be reasonably calm, though not utterly so, and the tides had to be favourable.

For all these caveats, there was no guarantee, even if conditions were fair, when Tulkington's cargoes would be expected and that was what his smaller rival was seeking to discover. It was cheering to find certain parties – Hawker's close gang members – were missing from their usual haunts, which had Spafford ask, once everyone was back from their tasks, where his son was.

'Last time I saw him he was outside the Albion,' was one reply.

'Not for long,' was a sniggered response from 'Dolphin' Morgan.

This was a soubriquet given to him because he was held to be as thick as the wooden posts that sat in a line along the high point of the beach: bollards, to which boats could be secured. It was as well he took it in good humour, for he was massive of shoulder and fist, while being short of temper.

'Any hope of getting him back an' sober?'

The look that got was that pigs might fly, while if he wanted to chastise Dolphin there was no point. If Harry was not present there was no time to fetch him, and besides, if he had gone into the Albion it could only be for one purpose, one which would render him a liability. Not even Daisy could tell Dan Spafford his son was that.

Suppressing his irritation, Spafford told his men of the intention to rob Tulkington.

'An' tonight looks to be a good 'un for the deed.'

This was followed by a slow look around the dozen men whom he held to be loyal, for not one of them could but wonder where this would lead; a fellow like Hawker was not one to take matters lying down and behind him stood Tulkington, who was way more powerful in terms of resources. Candlelight made grimmer what were serious faces and Spafford knew they would need bucking up.

'Time I let you in on the truth, lads. The cupboard's near bare. It's this we do, or it'll be goin' back to portage, hovelling or you all grubbing for enough sea coal to fill a sack you can sell.'

Not normally a man of many words, Daniel Spafford observed the shock the truth caused, taking some comfort from the fact he had kept his situation so well hidden. Now he laid it out plain and he was not shy on the alternatives. These men had come to him to get away from the lives they had led before, which was relentless toil on the beach or in the water and never knowing for sure where the next bit of coin was coming from.

Smuggling with Spafford had allowed them a life of some ease for the occasional risk of being had up by the Revenue and even, given they were sometimes armed, being maimed or killed. If they had been well rewarded, it would have been spent as soon as it was paid; that was the nature of the beast and Spafford knew it. There would likely be not a saved guinea between them.

'So where's the money to buy a boat, an' you need that to eat? Where's the coin to pay the Clerk of the Council for a spot on the beach? And even if you could run to it, what kind of living could you make with everyone out to cut each other's throat for portage or a passenger? I daresay there are ways to eke a crust, as a crossing sweeper or a night soil man, happen.'

A pause heavy with meaning was followed by, 'You're with me, Daisy?'

'As ever Dan.'

That got the assembly a gimlet-eyed examination of those same faces, which left in more than one mind the thought that disloyalty could make it unsafe to show Daisy your back.

'Right, let's get dressed as we need to be.'

The men who made their way to the shore, carrying the oars that would propel their boats, were uniformly attired in long dark coats and tricorn hats, while half of them were armed.

John Hawker, having set his toughs on Brazier, had picked up his horse and a pair of pistols at the slaughterhouse, to then make his way to St Margaret's Bay, riding along a path running along the high point of the chalk down, a task that became increasingly difficult as twilight turned slowly to night. So it was by lantern light he made his destination: a dilapidated cottage halfway down a cliff-side track, already occupied by one of his gang members.

His primary job had been to assess the sea state in daylight and, if it looked suitable, to hoist an ensign on a flagstaff only visible out at sea, which would tell the vessel cruising out in the Channel it was, weather-wise, safe to come in. Tulkington was adamant no chances be taken, so only if the flag remained flying would the operation proceed, which meant it was necessary to ascertain that was still true and that there were no sightings of Preventatives trying to assemble in the village half a mile inland.

They should have been strung out halfway between Deal and Walmer Castle, waiting for a cargo that was never going to arrive, but it was best to be sure. Nothing had been reported so, certain it was safe and that the men he needed were in position, he lit and handed over one lantern, then took another himself.

A lifted trapdoor exposed a set of steps, which took him and his companion down to a narrow tunnel, in which the light he carried bounced off the smooth white of the chalk, this providing good illumination. As the crouched pair made their way, other lanterns were lit at intervals until the point came where they must split.

'Remember, wait till you see the light flash out to sea.'

The instruction got a look, which said the listener was no fool and knew what he was about. In the face of a glare from Hawker, who was no more a man to leave matters to chance than his employer, it quickly disappeared and so did he. Going on alone Hawker eventually felt a breeze on his face as well as the smell of the sea in his nostrils, which told him he was close to the high opening, one covered by a gorse bush growing out of the chalk cliff.

He shaded his lantern prior to moving the edge of the bush to one side, just enough to let him see out, using a tie left on a ringbolt to keep it from swinging back. It was near to blackness now, broken clouds in the sky hiding the stars and too little moon to silver the edges. Held up, his lantern was unshaded three times, with no response, which did not cause worry.

The time a ship could make its landfall could never be fixed, regardless of tides – indeed it was not unknown for there to be no arrival at all and with no way of telling why. All he could do was wait.

Spafford was in no rush to execute a plan he had worked out a long time past, as well as one he had dreamt many times of carrying through. It was a long slow row, in a pair of oared cutters, from the boathouse at Sandwich Flats to where he needed first to be. He had no intention of having his men bend their backs to throw up spray, which might pick up what little light existed and be visible to watchers on the Kingsdown cliffs.

Being in the smuggling game required that he know every bit of the coast and Spafford hove to a cable's length short of the headland called Leathercote Point, the south side of which formed the northern extremity of the destination bay. He needed to wait out of sight to even the keenest eye, rocking on the swell, the oars only used to steady the boats, keeping them from drifting, while he sang softly to himself, which he hoped would reassure his bound-to-be-nervous companions.

The winking light out at sea came after a long wait. Spafford knew that would be responded to, even if he could not see the pair of lanterns spaced wide apart on either arc of the bay, of which he had been told. This gave the ship's master a way to make his landfall close to, if not exactly in, the middle of the bay, thus avoiding the huge rocks at the edges. Even with an onshore breeze there would be no sail; the ship would be edged in on its sweeps, dropping an anchor in deep water and paid out on the capstan until she grounded. Once unloaded and lightened, the same cable and capstan would be employed to silently haul the vessel out to deep water again.

'We're on, Dan,' Daisy whispered. 'You was right. Hear that lads, he were right.'

'We'll stay awhile, yet.'

If the approaching vessel was hard to see, it was not, in increasingly close proximity, impossible to hear; creaking cordage and straining timbers, plus the odd command, floated across the water, until eventually an outline of triced-up canvas on the yards could be faintly detected. Then came the splashing sound of the long sweeps dipping into the water to provide steerage way. The noises grew, grunts and possibly curses, with bodies moving about to tell Spafford the holds were being opened and emptied, the cargo being brought on deck so that transferring it would be as swift as possible.

There would be men on the strand now and they would cast a line to draw ashore a thicker cable, this so the ship could be hauled in and held fast to a dolphin. That would be followed by the dropping of a long gangplank, down which the contraband could be speedily taken to a pair of long ladders. These led up to the entrances, twin tunnels through which it would be carried at the run. Speed was essential; the ship needed to be a goodly distance offshore by dawn, an innocent-looking trading vessel on a course for a French home port.

Hawker was well aware this was the time of maximum danger, so his nerves were taut. You could take all the precautions you like, but you could never be sure it would not all go ahoo. If the Revenue were waiting where they should be, in anticipation of what he had told them was coming ashore, all would be mustered in the wrong place. Thus there would be none to man the other possible concern: the Revenue's armed cutter, berthed in Dover Harbour.

A vessel that carried four small cannon, it was to be feared. Out at sea it was invisible and, being a swift sailer if well handled, it could quickly spring a trap, at which point the ship and what it carried would be abandoned. The tunnels, quickly sealed to keep their entrances hidden, would be full, not of cargo, but men seeking to escape capture.

The silence, which had mostly held, was broken by the rasp of the keel on the pebbles. Then came gasps and the occasional cry, added to the scrunch of a multitude of feet, both the ship's crew and Hawker's locals, slithering as they tried to run on a rising bank of shingle bearing a load, with Dan Spafford listening hard and seeking to time what would come next.

The chambers in which the cargo was stored were nowhere near sea level; they were halfway up the cliff side and access to them was wide enough for only one man at a time, so once the first loads were on their way, the numbers on the beach would be few and that was when he could strike.

'Haul away,' was a quiet instruction.

The oars were dipped to take the Spafford boats in to the shore. Once they heard the hiss of water on the shingle it was pull hard, with his men being led out before the lead cutter even beached, to splash along the shoreline yelling 'Surrender in the name of the King', with their leader firing off one of his pistols, the crack of which echoed around the bay, this while the second cutter was heading for the side of the cargo ship to board.

That pistol shot had John Hawker, who was on his way to pay the vessel's master his fee, returning to his opening to peer out into the gloom. He was now trying to grasp what was happening, as well as seeking to make sense of it. He had got to his present position of trust for several reasons, not least his willingness to do whatever was necessary in the chastisement line. But he also possessed a good brain as well as reliable judgement and his instincts, as well as the lack of loud, shouted and repeated orders to yield, indicated to him this was no Revenue raid.

The lantern was abandoned as he hurried back down his tunnel and, knowing the various routes well, he was soon scurrying through the one that led to the main storage chambers, for it was off these that all the others ran. Inside the feeder routes there were men by the several dozen carrying the cargo uphill in a long line and, given the varied objects some were having to manoeuvre, seeking to avoid getting stuck.

Most were so far inside the dense chalk that the sound of Dan Spafford's pistol going off was muted; only those at the very rear heard it and that did not produce any willingness to turn and find the source, quite the reverse. All knew what to do if they were threatened, which was to haul in the ladders and close off the entrances.

There would be no rushing out into darkness and possible arrest. Above their heads were locals set to keep watch and they would know how lay the land. Having been told what they might face, they would then get to the surface and disperse over time, using a multitude of concealed exits, some of which ran to the next headland.

Part of Spafford's plan was to have the pair who once worked for Tulkington get to those entrances quickly – they knew well where they lay – and discharge a fowling piece full of buckshot towards each. Aim was not important: it was designed to induce fear, and if some of the shot struck home so much the better. The real object was to ensure those entrances were quickly sealed, this while the main body ran to intimidate those still on the ship.

They could then get their cutters alongside and unload as much cargo as they could carry, a task made easier given that the few sailors remaining, being unarmed and taken utterly by surprise, had rushed below at the sound of the first shot to man the capstan and seek to get the ship off the shingle. Only the master stood his ground, slashing at the holding cable with an axe until he was felled by Dan Spafford's pistol butt.

For all his screaming imprecations, John Hawker, having made one of the main chambers and seeking to get down to ensure all was secure, could not get past the lumbering and ignorant men portaging the cargo, even when the news of what was happening to the rear rippled forwards. The narrow tunnels had been hewn out of the self-stabilising chalk for one-way traffic, with only the occasional cut-out niche where a man could sit and rest, a seat provided. If Hawker managed to turn the man before him, it did little to persuade those following, which ended with everything coming to a complete halt.

The Spafford thieving was not leisurely: it was ferocious and far from organised. What could be grabbed was flung and only occasionally lowered to the cutters, until there was barely enough room for those who were required to row. Eventually a halt was called and a retreat ordered. The escape was messy and quite a few were served a ducking as they tried to get aboard with too much haste.

That accepted, they were not disheartened as they rowed out the now low-in-the-water boats – quite the reverse. For blood-up and coursing ruffians, who hated common toil and sought profit in adventure, elation came from having just tweaked a very powerful nose.

Hawker got to the strand level eventually by allowing all the cargo in the tunnels up into the main chambers. He had his twin pistols out, ready and cocked as he made the sealed-off exit, to listen hard for evidence of activity. None being apparent he had it opened and

146

the ladder lowered to come gingerly out, lantern held aloft, into the blackness of the night, several of his men following.

There was an eerie silence at first, yet on the soft breeze there carried the faint sound of cheerful singing and, had he been able to see in the dark, Hawker would have been given sight of two cutters full of merry men and purloined contraband. Up the gangplank he came across the laid-out captain being tended to by a couple of his sailors, one of his gang opining, as he saw the mess of cargo that had been abandoned, bolts of silk and a keg of brandy rolling back and forth on the slight canting of the deck.

'That weren't no Preventatives, John,' said the man with him. 'This was thievery.'

'Throats will be slit for this,' was his spoken response, as a couple more of his men joined him.

'Who was it?' That got a slow shake of the head but the verbal response was vehement. 'But I will find who it is and butcher them.'

CHAPTER TWELVE

The night was uncomfortable once the draught of laudanum by which Brazier had been sent to sleep wore off. Every time he moved, the pain caused him to wake. In a room with heavy drapes, which cut out any daylight, he more than once wondered where he was. The apothecary had been asked to supply more than bandages; various ointments and pain-dulling preparations had been ordered and applied to his afflictions and if they had eased matters when first used, it did not last all the hours he was comatose.

Fully awake he had to reprise what had occurred, not least the supposition his twin assailants might have been intent on robbery, yet that was dismissed not only because of the words they had uttered but the fact that he still had his purse and his watch. Those words played out in his mind, so often they became blurred by repetition, but the one on which he never lost focus was the repeated name of Daisy.

Who was she and why had he so offended her? Could it be a case of mistaken identity, for he knew no one of that name and certainly not in Deal, or anywhere else for that matter? It took some time before the other words he recalled moved to a point of any clarity, which finally put him back in the tavern at which he had stopped on the way. Park your arse? Leave Deal? Nothing made sense.

He dropped off again, tired of reflection, this till the drapes were dragged open, the rasping on the pole enough to have him open his one good eye. Saoirse was by the window, to then turn and gesture over him. He spun his head to see a female servant she had brought with her, in her hands a steaming bowl.

'Beef soup, Captain, to restore you. It would be best you down that before I treat your wounds again with the apothecary's creations. If you can sit up, you may spoon yourself; if not, Harriet here will feed you.'

'Try me,' Brazier replied, his voice both rasping and made thick by his swollen lip.

Saoirse came round to take his outstretched hands and pull, her face showing concern at the obvious discomfort caused. But Brazier was firm in his resolve and was soon sitting with his back to the upright part of the settle, looking at his hands and his bruised knuckles. A small table was set down next to him on which the bowl could be placed, followed by a spoon, before Harriet disappeared. As soon as he leant forward cushions were slipped behind his back.

'Do we have a mirror glass?'

'I'm not sure you'd be wanting to see yourself. Anyway, take the soup first.'

'I have other needs to attend to beforehand,' he croaked, with a meaningful look.

And he did, these being the call of nature, which obliged his hostess to fetch for him the chamber pot. Vacating the room, she was not there to observe the difficulties incumbent of him relieving himself but must have guessed, and so he was given time. She was also careful enough to knock and ensure he had completed his toilet before entering once more, happy to see the soup bowl empty and the chamber pot full. Harriet was with her to take the latter to be emptied. Saoirse had fetched with her a small mirror, which he took and lifted gingerly to look.

'Not a pretty sight.'

'Was it ever that?'

'Sure, there's a time when a body can be too modest.'

Brazier examined the swollen eye, now surrounded by a black bruise, the lump on his forehead and the upper lip already beginning to form a scar. His nose too seemed a mite wider than normal.

'This would not be one of them and that applies as much to my body, I suspect.' His tongue employed in inspection, he added, 'at least I still have my teeth.'

'There's more than soup if you wish to employ them.'

He shook his head slowly, then looked down at his bloodstained shirt. 'My uniform?'

'Taken down the street to be attended to by a washerwoman. The breeches we declined to remove and they are, as you can see, filthy and, like your stockings, torn, so I have sent to the Three Kings to fetch replacements.'

'How very discreet,' was his mordant response; he could easily imagine Garlick arriving at certain conclusions when hearing the request and where it was from – this as, with some difficulty, he got to his feet, swaying slightly. 'I can assume that will be all over the town too?'

She laughed out loud as an amusing thought struck her. 'Happen when you're seen, they'll think it was I who did this to you. But seriously, sit down once more and I'll ointment your bruises. There is no rush for you to leave.'

'I seem to recall mentioning discretion.'

'The point of that is long past. Your uniform will be a while, so settle yourself down, let me do as I said, then I'll have you sent up a proper breakfast, as well as someone to shave you.'

He lifted the mirror again to look. 'Which will not be easy.'

'God knows you look rough enough without you have a day's growth as well. Since you're bent on seeking discretion, it might be an idea to take you to look over Quebec Court. The Three

Kings is no place to be staying with a black eye and a split lip.'

'Given the garrulous nature of Garlick, it's no place to be staying at all.'

Still holding the mirror, Brazier wondered at the effect it would have on everyone, not least Betsey. But there were others too, and no man likes to admit to being given a sound beating, regardless of who was dishing it out.

'Saoirse, I have mind to put this down to a fall from my horse.'

'And you ended up here how?'

'As luck would have it, a Good Samaritan came across me by a high hedge, on my back and in distress and took me in.'

'It makes a good tale, though I'm far from sure I'd be one to believe it.'

'You don't have to believe it, only to relate it, if asked.'

'Male pride?'

'Call it what you will.'

'Not much to ask.'

Betsey Langridge was not one to be easily dissuaded, neither would she give her brother the satisfaction of refusing her a conveyance to take her into town. Sure he was occupied with a visitor, and her Aunt Sarah busy overseeing her domestic duties, she made ready to go out in a dress-cum-riding habit. The first act was to raid her cash box, then, clad in stout shoes, under a wide bonnet and a medium cloak, she left to make her way down to the gate, a couple of pence in her hand for the keeper, he being her only concern. Had Henry forbade him to let her pass?

The dog, as he came out at her approach, snarled and strained to get at her, to which she paid no attention, given it was seeking to impress Tanner, the gateman. Its main function was to deter callers, especially the indigent in pursuit of charity, and anyway, it was on a thick rope lead. Of more concern was the look the gatekeeper gave her, for it carried a clear thought: to him quality, outside their own property, unless they were children, never walked anywhere.

'Please open the gate, Tanner.'

She said this, hoping the tremor she felt in her voice did not carry. His hesitation was obvious, the reason less so and since he gave no immediate verbal response, Betsey felt it safe to assume he had no instructions. The coins were proffered and accepted, albeit with a tinge of doubt, the great key produced and the well-oiled lock released.

Betsey Langridge found herself out on a road she had not walked along since the time she had ceased to be a child and started to become a woman, which was seen as unbecoming. The mere act brought back the same kind of recollections she'd had when walking round the lake with Edward Brazier and, with it, a sense of freedom.

Her destination was Long Farm House, which had been the home of her childhood girlfriend, one of that group of which she and Stephen had formed a playful portion and had been part of the guest list at Cottington on the day of the fete. She was let through the gate to be welcomed at the door by Annabel Colpoys.

'You came on foot?' Annabel asked, after a hug of greeting, shocked, as if to do so was to court the risk of being murdered.

'I have fallen out with Henry, Annabel, and I refuse to beg from him a carriage to take me into Lower Deal.'

'Your brother,' Annabel sighed, for she had known him nearly as long as her friend and could well recall being troubled, on the rare occasion he joined them, by his presence, which was death to gaiety.

'I will walk if I must, but I was hoping you and Roger might be able to aid me.'

'He is out in the carriage, but I can give you the dog cart or a donkey,' Annabel laughed. 'Neither of which will enhance you in the public eye.'

'A donkey was good enough for Jesus, I recall being taught, so will serve. I only need it to get to the yard of the horse dealer I have heard about, a Mr Flaherty, where I am hoping he will rent me a pony.' A bit lip followed; what she was about to ask for was bound to be revealing. 'If he does, I wonder if I could stable it with you?'

Annabel frowned. 'That speaks of more than a tiff, Betsey.'

'He wishes me to be beholden to him, as he has always, and I am determined not to. I have been, like you are now, mistress of my own house and married.'

'Poor Stephen,' was inevitable, so hands were held, eyes were dropped, for a ritual moment of silence. 'You must miss him so.'

Her silent nod was a formality, for Betsey Langridge had conjured up an image, not of her late husband, but of Edward Brazier. Could that be because of time passed? She told herself that in order to assuage her feeling of guilt, but it failed to convince.

'If you will permit me, I will take the donkey and leave it with Mr Flaherty for later collection.'

If Betsey was curious as to why Annabel hesitated, she was not about to be enlightened – not to be told that Annabel's husband Roger had said many times that Henry Tulkington was a man to be very cautious of. Indeed, if he had been present, he might have declined to assist.

'Of course you can,' was finally said with determined force. 'And I will lend you my saddle.'

Given what had occurred, John Hawker had been tempted to break a prohibition, which forbade him from visiting Cottington Court. Henry Tulkington kept his connection always at one remove, so that at no time could he personally be linked to illegality, so Hawker had to wait out the rest of the night and most of the morning. His employer would call at the slaughterhouse in any case, to find out if the previous night's tasks had been successfully completed, which was something of a routine and had been for a very long time.

On being given the news that it was not so, he reacted with an unsettling degree of composure before turning to the stove to once more warm his hands, a position he held for some time as he cogitated on what he had just been told. After the farrago in the coach, it pointed to Spafford.

He had deliberately kept Hawker in ignorance of the exchange, which had nothing to do with promises – it was habit. Should he tell him now? He decided not to, slowly spinning to face him, and talking in a voice not much above a whisper he finally asked the question for which Hawker had understandably been waiting.

'How much did they get away with?'

His man was looking at him keenly, obviously seeking to find in his expression, added to the tone of his voice, anything of the nature of blame. He had been thrown by the calm way his employer had reacted, expecting instead a blast of fury directed at him for allowing such a theft to occur. All he could do was hand over a slip of paper.

'Not close to a mite of the whole, by my reckoning, as you'll see, but it weren't the quantity, it were the boldness of it.'

Tulkington moved away again to study the list, mentally calculating the value, only to conclude it was not enough to fund Harry Spafford for a couple of months, let alone the kind of legacy sum at which his father had hinted. It did not preclude them from being responsible, quite the reverse: it did raise a troubling question. Was it merely a provocation, an attempt to draw him into a reaction? Or could it be just a ploy to get that for which Spafford had asked?

Once more he wondered about sharing these thoughts with Hawker, to tell him not only what was discussed, but that Spafford might be dying? His man, fully appraised, would be bound to draw the same conclusion as he, as well as give the expected response: nothing less than an immediate punitive raid on the farmhouse at Worth. Was that what Spafford wanted, the opening bout in a war? Expecting trouble, he would be ready and waiting to drive them off, which would certainly provoke unwelcome consequences.

A confrontation was bound to spill blood and that drew attention, which could only be unwelcome, given Spafford was correct: those who commonly turned a blind eye to the trade, and even profited from it in some cases, could not ignore the lawlessness this would produce. Both would suffer, yet Spafford might feel he had little to lose: if it brought him down, it could do the same to Tulkington. For what had been stolen, it was not worth the risk. He turned to look back at Hawker, his expression giving nothing of these thoughts away.

'It could not have been done without they knew there was a cargo landing last night.'

It took no great wit to realise that moving contraband the way they did was bound to be whispered about; Tulkington knew that as well as John Hawker. The Kent coast might be a secretive community, but that was not a seal on talk – how could it be otherwise? Too many folk drew payment for concealment or being part of an unloading chain, helping to move on hidden goods, as well as those who kept watch on the paths leading to the bay.

'I take it not one of our people saw a familiar face, or heard a voice they knew?'

'They were stuck in the tunnels,' Hawker responded, with a shake of his head. 'An' the ship's crew wouldn't know the thieving bastards from Adam, even if they was from round these parts. I suppose it could be some fool from Deal chancing his arm, but how do we find out?'

'Stealing is one thing, John, but to be profitable it will have to be sold. Surely we will smoke who's suddenly got brandy and tobacco to trade.'

'Good thinkin', Mr Tulkington. We'll soon smoke them out if they're from these parts.'

The subject was changed abruptly once all that needed to be said about the previous night had been aired. 'There was the other matter I asked you to attend to?'

'And it was.'

Tulkington was pleased to hear Brazier had been given his due, less enamoured when he found out it had taken place in the Lower Valley Road close to the Old Playhouse, it being a spot reckoned too public, though the man who had arranged the affair was in no way abashed. His employer had wanted Brazier seen to quick and it had been done. That being so, it left no time to act choosy as to where.

'As I said, it had to be as and when. He didn't get the full ticket, I admit, he kept his purse, our lads being disturbed, but enough was handed out to make him hurt.'

'It is to be hoped he gets the message.'

'As it is to be hoped he don't connect it to you and his dealings with your sister. Might be he causes trouble, in which case . . .'

Hawker did not have to finish, for it was the same fate as he expected would befall those who had carried out the previous night's thieving.

'My sister will likely tell me of it, so I'll write to him and commiserate on his misfortune to allay suspicion.'

'And the thieving?'

'Ear to the ground, John, as ever. But I need to think on how to play it, if you find the rogues.'

'Only one way as I can see.'

'Perhaps,' was the enigmatic response.

A hand was held out to take from Hawker the key that would give Tulkington access to the tunnels. His next destination would be the chambers where his contraband was stored, every item checked against a manifest to ensure no further pilfering had been added to theft, that providing a perfect opportunity for light fingers.

As was his habit on these occasions there was no coach, just him on a less-favoured mode of transport, for he was no lover of the discomfort of riding a horse. There was no choice if he wanted to keep certain things secret and it was not just stored contraband. That checked, he could then go on to a place and a person it was necessary

156

to visit when success raised his needs. This would be followed by a second destination: the house he had acquired for meetings of the Downs Lodge.

Not that tonight would be a formal occasion, more one in which he could meet and converse with those of like standing, drinking abstemiously while others did so copiously, which allowed him to listen carefully to what was said. It was from such gatherings he sometimes gleaned information that could later be put to use, and also the place where he stayed in touch with those required to be kept sweet.

At home, his Aunt Sarah was wondering what to do. Elisabeth was nowhere to be found and it took no great leap of the imagination to guess where she might have gone. Henry needed to be told, the trouble with that idea being she had no idea where her nephew was either.

Vincent Flaherty was no stranger to odd apparitions and they were not always brought on through overimbibing. But the sight of a well-dressed lady, sat side-saddle on a donkey, caused him to blink, for the quality of the riding garments, bonnet and cloak did not match the means of transportation. Added to that was the way she waited for him to help her down, the act of someone accustomed to respect and attention. That done, he found himself looking into a pair of corn blue eyes and a very comely face, which piqued a more-than-normal degree of interest.

'Ma'am.'

'You are Mr Flaherty?' If he nodded he was unsure it was necessary, for it did not sound like a question; she seemed to have no doubt about his name. 'I have come here in the hope of hiring a mount, a decent-sized pony perhaps – nothing above fifteen hands, which is a height to which I'm accustomed. The saddle on the donkey will fit such an animal, I think.'

'Then I may have just what you need.'

157

The trading was brisk for, if his pretty visitor looked to be gentle and pliable, she was anything but. The name she gave him, Mrs Langridge, did not register, while her address at Long Farm House was close by, but never by him visited; Vincent Flaherty was not of the standing to be invited to such dwellings. Luckily he had a pony, said to be from Ireland originally, black in colour and just below fifteen hands, a gelding that went by the name of Canasta. So a bargain was struck for a week, with rent added to a deposit to ensure the animal was returned whole.

'Canasta?'

'Spanish for basket, I'm told, Mrs Langridge. This I will say to you, for I have ridden him. He is a good mount, friendly, but he is strong. If you do not have a firm hand, he will run with you.'

'I am sure I will manage, Mr Flaherty; I have been riding ponies and horses since I was a child.'

As she left Flaherty jingled her coins in his hand, thinking they would serve to pay back Edward Brazier if he returned Bonnie. The captain's deposit had gone on his debt to the feed merchant.

If his coat and waistcoat hid his body bruises, Brazier's hat, which had been recovered the night before, even pulled low, did not do much to hide his face, so he was subjected to a raft of stares. This meant he was constantly raising a hand to hide it as he and Saoirse made their way from the Playhouse to the southern end of Middle Street, which ran to the wall of the Naval Yard.

Quebec House was of three storeys, solid in construction in the middle of other dwellings, with dormers jutting from the roof tiles, and entered by a low doorway. It sat on the down slope, which led from the beach to the shallow valley behind. Brazier already knew of its age; besides, the name would have given it away. It was being built when the news came of the capture of Quebec in the year '59 by General James Wolfe, which gave it a tinge of sadness; Britain's best general had been killed taking the capital city of French Canada, to be much mourned.

Inside, the furniture was covered in sheets, quickly removed, without filling the air with dust, which signified the house was regularly cleaned. Once revealed, what was there spoke of comfort and quality while the whole had charm. The brick-lined inglenook fireplaces were high and wide, stacked with logs, but not for cooking. There was a proper and separate wood-fired range in a small rear chamber, and a second large-windowed parlour facing south from which to catch the sun in the evenings.

The dining room and drawing room were panelled in high-quality waxed pine and Saoirse had even purchased some portraits and a couple of landscapes, to make it look like an old family residence. Two small cupboards lay either side of the fireplace, one for powdering wigs, the other a storeroom for crockery and cutlery, while the walls boasted several sconces for candles.

A mahogany dining table could sit four, six or ten with the leaves extended and there were the chairs needed to accommodate that number of guests as well as a sideboard for everything required to entertain, including a small metal-lined cupboard for the necessary pot.

'It must have been a well-heeled marine to have afforded this.'

'He was, and an amorous soul to boot. I think he thought I came with the house.'

It was hard to appear inquisitive with his altered face, so the look he gave her was one to which she did not respond. If she perceived his curiosity as to how the marine officer had fared, Saoirse was not about to satisfy him.

'Linen and bedding I will provide, there's plates and cutlery in yon cupboard and, if you wish, I will send the required traders to call upon you, the people I myself use.'

'Do I sense I am not allowed to haver?'

159

'You'd be a fool to, Captain, in my opinion. This is the best you will find in the town and I am not one to seek to sting those who occupy it, even hot-blooded marines.'

'Speaking of which?'

'Ten guineas down afore, to be held, and four shillings per week, with a guarantee of three months' tenancy.'

'On a handshake?'

'Never in life. I have been dunned before and obliged to chase flitters gone to sea and with poor results. So it will be from here we go to my lawyer in the Western Way and a written agreement drawn up, signed and witnessed.'

Edward Brazier was thinking about the three months. Had he been asked this two days ago he would have said no, but having seen and talked with Betsey, he was more confident and he had already acknowledged matters could not be rushed.

'Very well.'

Flaherty had not been wrong about Canasta; he was a pony requiring a firm grip on the reins and no soft voice of command. That accepted, and she knew her horseflesh, there was a charm about him, most evident when she dismounted and found herself nuzzled affectionately, which led to a degree of slapping and rubbing, taken well. Looking into his huge brown eyes, she was sure she saw intelligence.

Entering the Three Kings, Betsey found a singular-looking fellow behind the hatch opening; bald head, purple cratered nose and heavy whiskers, who was most obliging and positively fawning when she asked for Captain Brazier; he too could spot by her garments she was quality.

'Not here, ma'am, but if you wish I can direct you to where he is now.'

'That would be most kind Mr . . .'

'Garlick, ma'am, with a k to end it.'

'Singular, sir.'

'Never let the stuff pass my lips. French and Papist muck to me, though the Romany folk say it's handy for warding off evil.'

'Captain Brazier?' was the repeat question, the tone a mite terse.

'Old Playhouse, ma'am, in the High Street.'

'You're sure he is there?' Conscious of the effect of the question as well as the nature of the establishment, she added, 'At this time of day?'

'Certain, ma'am. That's where a messenger came to request his spare breeches be sent this very morning.'

CHAPTER THIRTEEN

Returning to the Three Kings, Edward Brazier was keen to get to his room without either being spotted or having to engage in conversation with the owner. He nearly managed it by moving swiftly, while ignoring the back pain this caused, his hat held to the side of his head to hide his bruises. The voice of Garlick calling his name stopped him.

'There was a lady calling for you, Captain Brazier, not much more than an hour past and eager to see you. She should have found you, seeing I sent her on to the Playhouse.'

There could only be one lady calling on him and he half-turned, hat still disguising his wounds. 'You did what?'

'Sent her to where you was, as I was bound to.' Garlick looked to Brazier's lower body. 'I knew you was there, for I sent your clean breeches, did I not?'

'Which I hope was not mentioned.'

'Well . . .' Garlick responded with hesitation and a look of slight remorse, which was as good as saying he had.

He turned to face Garlick full on, hat dropping. 'Describe her.'

'My lord, your honour, what has happened to your face?'

'Never mind my face, tell me of hers.'

The sinking feeling he experienced as Garlick spoke was as emotionally troubling as his physical afflictions, while it took no great leap of the imagination to work out what such a combination of information would lead Betsey to deduce. He was prepared to wager at any odds wanted that the Playhouse was a place she had never set foot in, but being brought up locally she would know of it and its function.

Not that it was a bawdy house – he had discerned no evidence of such activities – but it did exist as a place of drinking, gambling and, in the main room, raucous entertainment, not exclusively male, but certainly a venue no respectable female would visit. Those who did would be ladies looking for a night of free provision from the better class of sailor. Jack tar, having disbursed his coin, would expect his reward.

'Did she go to there?'

'Can't say, sir. When I mentioned it, she gave me a very crabbed look and left sharp.'

'By coach?'

The owner paused, his head sinking to his chest. 'No, I seem to recall she might've come on a horse; must have been for she was carrying a crop. I can find out from the yardman.'

Brazier waved that offer away then strode out and collared the fellow who saw to the carrying of guests' luggage as well as a dozen other tasks, one being to mind any mounts tethered in the yard. Given there had only been one lady calling, he was quick to confirm she had arrived and departed on a lively pony.

'Gave the little bugger his head too, which got a few curses aimed at her back from those she obliged to scatter. Reckon she was in a right strop.'

'Find young Ben for me. Tell him to get to the Naval Yard and fetch my horse.'

Back inside he barked at Garlick to send up a bottle of brandy before taking, with some caution, the stairs to his room. There he eased himself into a chair, this when pacing to and fro would have been more satisfying, the trouble being that walking pained his rib, to which was added the dull ache of his other body bruises whether in motion or still.

Yet nothing compared to the agony brought on by his imaginings and, if the delivered brandy eased his aches, it did nothing for the scenes playing out in his mind. There was only one place Betsey would go – home to Cottington Court – while he was unsure if he was being wise in his intention to pursue her and explain. Would he be required to – would not his damaged face do that for him?

Realising that was his best card, he changed his coat, with some effort, from military to civilian, at the same time as mentally rehearsing what he would say, relieved when the knock at his door told him Bonnie was outside and saddled up. He tried to get onto her unaided, but that brought on agony, so he was obliged to lead her over to the mounting block and get astride her gently. Not that he was free from torment; the mere motion, as Bonnie went from a walk to a trot, made him gasp and haul her back. Thus it was at a slow pace he took to the road out of Deal.

The blow with the birch cane was calculated to cause hurt, but not to break the skin and, had the female administering it been able to see her customer's face, and the grimace which appeared at each strike, she would have been sure she was doing that for which she was being paid, this whipping the preliminary for what would follow.

Henry Tulkington could not be said to be taking pleasure in this, but it was, to him, necessary, and carefully examined it might have been seen as a counter to the rigid control he held over the life he led, a place and situation where he was able to freely surrender to the whims of another. The buxom lady he visited regularly had a fecund imagination for the infliction of pain and instruments that could be applied to various parts of a body to induce delightful anguish.

Even the conclusion of a session, which lasted two hours, was a combination of ecstasy and agony, as she extracted a price for the pleasure of culmination, her final act to stand him in a bathtub and wash her client's pale frame with a stiff brush and lye, which, if she had properly carried out her commission, would seriously sting.

Little in the way of talk had taken place in those two hours, if you excluded the foul and diminishing insults spat at her client, as well as commands to obey her instructions, these accompanied by a sharp blow from a riding crop. None at all were exchanged on conclusion; the session was known to be at an end and she departed the chamber in silence.

Tulkington then dressed himself with stiff care, his thinking returning from submission to its more normal state of superiority. A guinea was left on a rough bench to which he had so recently been strapped and pounded. With his appearance checked in a mirror glass and found to be as it had on arrival, he went out to his waiting horse.

Given the exceptional circumstances of this day, prior to meeting with men he saw as associates and fellow masons, he had to go by the slaughterhouse to see whether Hawker had discovered anything about his missing property. Even with that in his mind he was, for a short while, content.

'I's been asking around as you required and there's no sign of any bugger selling owt we ain't supplied. I even hinted that I had bought some spare brandy off the beach, which needed to be got rid of quick, an' was taken up on it sharp. If there were excess around, it would have been refused.'

'So no one is talking about what occurred?'

'Not a one and they would if they knew when it's me askin'. I gave the hard eye to a couple of Spafford's boys and they just stared back, innocent-like, and I'd reckon them to avoid my eye if there was guilt. The sods ain't working out of our patch is my guess.'

They speculated on Ramsgate and Margate, both with harbours. Dover was not included, given the Revenue worked out of there, only to come to no conclusion. Other possibilities, like the Romney Marsh crew, were unlikely to be the culprits, due to the distance for boats, it reckoned to be too far to row. The conclusion arrived at, and aired by Tulkington, was it should be seen as a one-time affair and a loss they must stand.

'It hurts to have you say so, when I take it personal.'

'You carry no blame, John.'

Full eye contact was necessary in the delivery of such reassurance. The business could not be carried out without the likes of this fellow, unless Tulkington chose to take charge personally. Hawker he had inherited from his father, who had taken him as a young tough, from a lowly gang member to his present rank, having him taught to read and write as well as paying for tutoring in numbers, something for which he had shown a decided aptitude.

Tulkington was suddenly made uncomfortable by the realisation of dependence, which sparked another thought. At some time Hawker might require to be replaced. Did he need to get to know the men Hawker led better, for if a substitute was required, it would have to come from amongst them?

Did any of them possess the necessary qualities of blind obedience and easy brutality allied to an ability to absorb education?

Betsey Langridge had taken the route before Edward Brazier and, if his mind was in turmoil, hers was no better, while giving Canasta his head did little to assuage that. The only thing that distracted her was the distress visited on those obliged, quicker than would be normal, to get out of her way.

Brazier's supposition regarding the Playhouse was accurate; she had most certainly never crossed the threshold and would have been shamed to be seen doing so. If she thought about the place at all it was in lurid hues: the kind of images that in themselves were shaming, wounding enough to cause a tear when she conjured up a vision of him indulging in such merriments and more beside.

'Clean breeches, indeed,' she cried, as her progress scattered a flock of sheep, the curses of the lad shepherding them ignored.

Never mind the Playhouse; Lower Deal was not a location to

which anyone of quality went in the hours of darkness, if you left out St George's for an occasional evening service in winter. In daylight the Lower Valley Road was a place to confer with certain tradesmen for the artefacts required to maintain a decent establishment, emporiums that were shuttered at night to avoid having their doors and windows broken by revellers.

Even then Betsey could count on one hand the number of times she had bought there, it being confined to hats, cloths with which to make dresses, as well as shoes, purchased or taken for repair. Anything else was a male reserve, and for food, what could not be produced at home was brought to the house by a vendor obliged to respond to a written order.

Past St Leonard's Church she hauled on the reins to slow Canasta, realising that to take him to Cottington was a silly thing to do. Not that she could see any further use for the fellow, given his purpose now seemed redundant. There was a temptation to turn round, ride back to Flaherty's and hand him in. Yet to do that was bound to engender questions, nosy enquiries she most certainly would not answer. They would be unwelcome nonetheless.

Annabel had offered stabling; Canasta could be left there until the terms of her rental were complete and when returning the pony would arouse no comment. The fellow who saw to the gate at Long Farm House did give her an odd look when she called to be admitted; she realised why when Annabel came out to greet her.

'I see you have put that equine through his paces, Betsey.'

The evidence was not only around Canasta's mouth; some of his foaming saliva had streaked his flanks. Even having been walked for a bit, his chest still heaved too much for it to be seen as calm. As Betsey slipped out of her saddle, Annabel called to her gateman to take the beast and first lead it to the trough, before stabling him and washing him down.

'Come, Betsey, let us unlock the caddy and have some tea.'

To refuse was impossible: to say she would rather go home would be rude in the face of the offer of what, to a house like this, was such a valuable commodity. Worse was the need to engage in polite talk about old and shared experiences, when her mind was still in tumult, a discomfort deepened when they heard the carriage in the driveway, which told her Roger Colpoys had returned.

Being burly, with a rubicund farmer's countenance under bright-red hair, Roger was incapable of entering a room with anything approaching refinement. He added to that a step of such force it was inclined to make the older parts of the manor house shake. With that went a voice to match and language bordering on the vulgar.

'By damn, Elisabeth, how nice to see you present.'

The 'damn' got closed eyes and pursed lips from his wife, who suffered every time he blasphemed, and they were frequent. Roger eyed the china cups and the pot, which brought on a scoff.

'Wasting money again on that muck, I see. Can't stand the brew me'self.'

'Which shows on your face, husband. I do not expect you to take tea instead of claret, but it would serve if you sat down.'

The door to the drawing room was only partly open; the first child through sent it crashing back to hit the wall, he followed by two siblings, another boy and a girl. Every time Betsey saw the Colpoys' brood, she was never sure whether to be jealous of her friend's fecundity, or happy that her own lack of it had spared her the sort of behaviour this trio displayed; they were as unruly as their father and carried his colouring.

Then there was the effect on Annabel, who had never been a beauty, but had been a valued friend two years her senior and one who made up from the lack of looks with a wonderful manner and a sharp wit. Motherhood seemed to have quashed that, for she was of a more serious mien now. Or was it the years of living with her coarse spouse?

'Behave, you lot,' reverberated around the house and brought the children up short, more for the way Roger's crop slapped his boots than the voice, given he was prone to employ it. 'Say hello to your Aunt Elisabeth, by damn.'

The responses came out as meek and mumbled whispers before they were, as Roger called it, sent packing.

'Surprised to see you, Betsey, with no carriage in the drive.'

'She walked down from Cottington,' Annabel said, handily forgetting to mention the time at which this had occurred.

'What! Walk! Why in God's name—'

'She fell out with Henry.'

'Not hard, by damn,' was the response, before Roger sought to correct himself, his face slightly contorted. 'He's a good fellow, mind you. Honoured to know him, what.'

'I lent Betsey the donkey to ride.' A pause, 'It was not to take the whole way into Deal.'

Ginger eyebrows went up at the thought of Elisabeth Langridge on such a beast. If Roger Colpoys was known for his coarseness, she was seen as the soul of refinement, not in the least affected by time abroad. They had barely settled back in place when he demanded Betsey recount what had happened, which she was obliged to do, including her renting of Canasta, added to the fact that the pony was now in his stables.

'I had intended to pick the donkey up on the way back, but I forgot.'

'Fallen out with Henry, eh? Rum business.'

Roger enunciated that before throwing himself into a chair and fixing his wife with a stare, soon turned on Betsey, it being one which invited further explanation. Since none was forthcoming, an awkward silence followed, with Annabel looking at the floor and her husband eventually lifting his eyes to the ceiling, as if in contemplation.

'I should be getting back to Cottington.'

'Damn it, had I known, I would have left the carriage harnessed.'

'I walked here, Roger, I can walk back.'

He hauled himself upright and barked unconvincingly, 'Won't hear of it.'

'Please, Roger, it is not far and I would appreciate the air.' The tone of that being firm enough to brook no argument had Roger's mouth working without anything emerging. 'Henry will be wondering where I've got to.'

'Yes,' Roger said with a frown, which Betsey sensed was brought on by worry, one to which she felt it inappropriate to respond.

'Annabel. Thank you for the tea and your aid with the animals. I will call soon and take the pony back to Mr Flaherty, fetching your donkey back.'

A servant was called to bring her cloak, kisses were exchanged, and Betsey departed with the feeling she had left behind her an atmosphere. It was evident in the stiff way Roger was now behaving, added to the air of apprehension exhibited by a wife who had picked up the mood as well, much as she tried to disguise it. Unknown to their recent visitor, Roger Colpoys was berating his wife for getting involved before she even got out of the gate.

Walking head down, she did not see the bay mare until she was close and when she did, it occurred to her the man astride it seemed to be asleep, head lowered and rocking gently with the motion. Then she realised the hat he was wearing was jutted front and back, it being a scraper, a singular design worn only by naval officers.

The combination of the human shape and the familiarity of the horse, seen only the day before, registered and she let out an involuntary gasp, loud enough to be heard, also strong enough to lift and turn that head, which brought from Betsey Langridge a scream.

'Edward, what has happened to you?'

With his lip in the condition it was, the smile he produced did not still any anxieties. 'I fear I have been the victim of a fall. I set Bonnie at a hedge and while she pulled up, I did not.'

'Poor you,' was the response as she looked up at him, mixed with deep shame at her previous condemnations, which made her next words seem very feeble. 'I called at the Three Kings.'

'I am well aware of it, just as I know that what was imparted to you was not well received.'

'The Playhouse?'

'Is where I was taken, having been rescued from the field where I lay by the owner, who was passing and was good enough to take me in, see to my immediate needs then to call a doctor. Unable to move with ease, I rested there overnight.' Her hand was to her mouth. 'I can guess what you thought.'

'If I could tell you how sorry I am for such imaginings.'

'I would dismount to hear them, but without a block I'm not sure I could get back on the horse again. Please forgive me if it looks like bad manners, or even resentment.'

'Stay mounted, Edward. It would please me to be escorted to my gate in that manner.'

Betsey came close, to take a firm grip on a stirrup leather as Brazier put Bonnie to walking once more, then asked in a soft voice that he recount everything that had happened, which he did with as little invention as possible. This had her conclude that, when he talked of the owner of the Playhouse, he was most certainly a saint. It did not seem politic to Brazier to disabuse her as to his saviour's sex.

'I sense you are in pain, Edward.'

'The physical manifestations of which will pass.'

She got his meaning. 'I feel I have behaved very badly. Perhaps if I explained—'

'There's no need. I am aware that we sailors carry the burden of poor perception and I would own in many cases it is well deserved.'

'My brother tarred you with it after you left.'

'Then I hope he was more careful in his language than he was when speaking with me.'

'He said you threatened to call him out.'

'I warned him to be careful of his tongue, which I have to tell you was loose enough to warrant such a reaction. But I realised fairly

171

quickly it was no more than an attempt to provoke me, so that you would see me in a bad light.'

'To which I have just found myself prone.'

Brazier did not want to go there, did not want to admit to his disappointment she had jumped too quickly to a condemnatory conclusion. He surely had the right to hope she would trust him, for if that was so lacking, was there a future? Best to put the thought to one side and return to Henry.

'Did he specifically say I challenged him?' She nodded, looking up at him with sad eyes. 'Well, I can say to you it was not that overt.'

How could she say now that the words of her brother regarding sailors had coloured her thinking as soon as she was told his whereabouts?

'I came to put your mind at rest and also to tell you I have rented a house in Deal: Quebec House in Middle Street, hard by the Naval Yard.' The direct look accompanying those words required no explanation, but she got it anyway. 'What your brother thinks, I care not, but you? I am serious in my intentions towards you; I hope you know that and, if it takes time for matters to be resolved, so be it. I will be here.'

'Edward,' was all she could say and it was close to a whisper, before looking meaningfully at the gate to Cottington Court, no more now than a few yards away.

'You have no idea, Betsey, how much I would like to bend down and kiss you, but I fear if I did, I would fall off.'

'Then this will have to suffice.'

She put her fingertips to her lips, kissed them, and then stood on tiptoe to bestow them on his. He had to bend to make contact and to do so was agony, but that he masked, for what she was imparting indicated to him that all doubts were laid to rest.

'I look forward to visiting you at Quebec House, Edward.'

'While I look forward to the day I carry you across the threshold, which I have to say, will not be soon. More likely, as of this moment it would be you lifting me.' Brazier laughed as she smiled; it hurt like hell to do so but it was of no account. 'I intend to move in tomorrow and I hope you will call.'

'I will, Edward, but I fear I must ask my Aunt Sarah to accompany me. It would not serve either of us to risk scandal.'

'For your company, the price is worth paying.'

She produced that blush of which he was so enamoured. 'Goodbye, Edward.'

The walk to the gate was slow and she turned once she had pulled the bell to smile at him, which stood in stark contrast to the glare he got from the keeper, severe enough to make that of the ever-snarling dog look welcoming.

'Mr Henry was in a rare passion to find I let you out this morning. Threatened me with a whipping.'

'Then he will just have to get used to my coming and going as I please and so, I fear, will you.'

Brazier got a final wave as she went through the gate, aware he was being examined by the gateman, pulling on the reins as Betsey disappeared, to turn Bonnie round for the slow ride back to Deal. As she walked down the gravel drive, Betsey was thinking that two people could rent houses, though she would not consider Lower Deal as suitable for her. Wherever it was, it would be more convenient than residing at Cottington Court and certainly more comfortable, being without the constraints of her brother, which she knew on entry she was going to be exposed to.

It was thus a pleasant surprise to find him out of the house and, according to Aunt Sarah, who delivered the message with barely disguised annoyance, not expected back until late.

CHAPTER FOURTEEN

The rider who returned to the Three Kings was exhausted and in physical pain, for which his emotional well-being hardly compensated. Even the ever-eager Ben, who quickly appeared to take Bonnie to the stables, did not get the accustomed smile of greeting. Indeed, one look at the swollen face had the lad declining to meet his eye and bustling away. Thankfully Brazier was spared the nosiness of Garlick not, as normal, at his hatch.

Food he ordered by bell, only half of it consumed and washed down with brandy to dull his aches, which was followed by a restless night with little sleep, taken only partially undressed. The dawn had him writing a note to Admiral Braddock as he ate a slow breakfast, asking to be excused dining that day due to an unfortunate riding accident. He also enquired if the surgeon on station – there was bound to be one – could attend upon him, a request to which Braddock responded to with alacrity; the fellow in question called within the hour, introducing himself as Thomsett. A second note had, in the meantime, got off to Vincent Flaherty requesting him to visit, if possible before midday.

Thomsett was a small fellow with a pair of spectacles perched on a snub nose who came over as excessively fussy and apologetic, with any number of unnecessary expressions of regret. It was sorry this and sorry that. His wig was a far from perfect fit, while his coat showed that when he ate or took snuff there was little care in ensuring it all went to mouth or nose.

He was, however, brisk when it came to his trade: a complete change of demeanour, quick to get off the garments in which his patient had slept and unwind his bandages. This exposed the heavy bruising at the point where he had taken that swinging boot. Gentle probing was accompanied by stifled gasps as Thomsett sought and found the seat of the crack in the rib. The face had already been examined with the pronouncement that only time would heal his lumps and contusions.

'You were attended to by a local doctor, Captain, and not long after the time of your fall?'

'I was and, while I will not say he did me harm, his interest in the brandy bottle was an equal part of his ministrations.'

'He wrapped you well, more like a mummified body than a patient. Was the man being paid by the bandage yard?' The surgeon sniggered at his little joke, then went to his bag to dig out a couple of small bottles, holding one forward. 'I would recommend a tincture of laudanum to relax the muscles, which I will also rub with this herbal preparation, known to ease pain.'

'A concoction distilled from Melissa leaves, herbs and brandy, by any chance?'

Thompsett was surprised. 'You know of it?'

'My father was a naval surgeon, sir, and swore by it. He was less enamoured of laudanum, saying it could become an addiction and I did have some last night.'

The surgeon pulled a spoon from his waistcoat pocket and tipped a small amount of the opiate out, holding it forward for Brazier to consume. 'Then you will be pleased to know I use it sparingly.'

Next he dripped liquid from the second bottle onto a hand and gently began to massage it into the area around a large bruise shown to his patient with a mirror, the effect first cooling, to soon become numb around the pained area.

'A riding accident, I was told, Captain.'

'I was a fool to try the hedge.'

Out of Brazier's eyeline, the fact that Thomsett did not respond was taken as concentration on his task; he did not see the look of scepticism. He did, however, hear the low, serious voice. 'Given your parentage, you will know the ailments with which we naval surgeons normally deal, and I do not refer to the pox.'

Getting no response the surgeon carried on. 'Most of our work is on wounds caused by falls and accidents, both aloft and in the holds, bones breaking, skulls cracked or fingers and limbs lopped off. But, given the nature of those who man the ships of the navy, endemically prone to dispute with each other, I am no stranger to what happens when the infirmities are brought on by a bruising physical contest.'

'Is it so obvious?' Brazier said after a gap of several seconds; there seemed little point in denial.

'To an eye accustomed to the results, yes.'

'I would ask you to oblige me in holding to the notion of a riding accident.'

'Even when Admiral Braddock asks me how you fare?'

'Especially then.'

'Very well. Time to bind you up again, though I will use only half of what I removed.' Another snigger. 'The rest, when washed, the navy will take as a gift.'

Was that agreement regarding Braddock or not? It seemed that to ask would underline a thing Brazier wanted kept quiet – and tasked to explain why, he would struggle, apart from the fact he especially did not want Betsey to know.

Having finished, the tight bandage being pinned on his chest, he was looking at the top of Thomsett's scrub wig when the surgeon spoke again. 'I wouldn't recommend riding for two weeks, Captain Brazier; we would not want you taking a tumble again, now would we? I will call on you again at your convenience.'

'Will that not interfere with your duties, sir?'

'Captain, we are at peace and the level of the establishment is low, so my responsibilities are slight. Send for me when you feel you might require another examination, which will save me from boredom.'

'It will not be here, Mr Thomsett: I have rented Quebec House. Do you know it?'

'I do, sir, having had the good fortune to dine there once or twice.'

'Then I hope to be able to offer you the chance to do so again.'

'Should I leave the laudanum?'

Brazier shook his head. 'The Melissa water yes. I can ask one of Mr Garlick's servants to apply it.'

Flaherty, when shown up, found him sitting dressed in clean linen, writing, with half a dozen notes sealed, addressed and ready to be sent, Brazier asking to be excused so he could finish the last. That sanded and sealed he turned in a rather stiff manner to face his visitor full on.

'You don't seem eager to ask about my condition.'

'Saoirse went out riding this morning. Naturally we talked on her return and your name was mentioned.'

Brazier made a poor fist of hiding his irritation. 'She told you the truth?'

'She told me you'd fallen off Bonnie when attempting a too-high hedge, which I must own to, made me laugh.' The look of curiosity from his host obliged Flaherty to explain. 'Two things did not make sense. The first was a man trying a hedge who, only two days past, was careful just trotting over a grounded pole.'

'Two reasons?'

'I have hunted on Bonnie and she has only two modes of behaviour. She will either take a hedge with brio, and one you would doubt she could clear, or pull up well short thinking the person on her back a fool. These points I made to Saoirse, who knows the beast as well as I.'

'And then she told you what happened?'

'I reckon only part of it and with reluctance.'

'Then I will tell you the rest. Knowing you as I do, I best order up some wine from Mr Garlick's cellar.'

'A long tale, then?'

'Not long: painful to both body and soul.'

It was not the telling that took time, but the speculation that followed. Flaherty was sure no one would ever refer to Hawker as Daisy if they wished to stay whole, while the only people of that name would surely be female. He would struggle to recall any he might have met, what they looked like, and would have no idea where they lived even if he could.

'You could ask around, Edward,' Flaherty said. 'To find out.'

'I could, but not without bringing attention to myself. I would stick out like my black eye, which could well earn me another or worse.'

'Whereas I?' Brazier nodded, adding a quizzical look. 'It may be a risk to do so. If someone arranged to have you duffed, they will not take kindly to enquiries of the person making them. I have made a few friends here in Deal in the two years I have been here and, as far as I am aware, no enemies. This seems like a good method to uncover and create some. And what if I do find this mysterious Daisy?'

Brazier lifted the sealed pile. 'These are letters to some of my old barge crew, including my coxswain.'

'These men read?'

'No, but the letters are addressed to a local scribe or a person who reads for them and pens their replies. I have already sent asking my servant to come to Deal, but these fellows are scrappers, men who have stood alongside me more than once and probably are, at present, without a ship. I am asking they stand by me once more.'

'Are you looking to start a war?'

'I'm looking for the person who inflicted a beating on me for no reason I can fathom. I would like him to know that to do such a thing does not come without retribution.'

'That sounds very like war to me.'

'Will you do as I ask?'

'Up to a point, Edward. But I will heed any warnings which come *my* way.'

It was a stiff Edward Brazier who made for his bed when Flaherty departed, to seek to sleep, which did not come easily. It might have been an idea to hang on to the laudanum Thomsett had offered.

Betsey faced the morning and the dining room with a firm jaw – at least it had looked so in the hallway mirror – as well as deep resolve to change matters to her advantage. She came across Henry and her aunt already at table, going to the sideboard to take a plate and helping herself from the silver serving dishes: kedgeree, kidneys and smoked ham. Sitting down to silence, and receiving no return to her looks of enquiry, she employed the staple opening gambit, given it was raining outside.

'Not such a nice day, I observe.'

Henry did not look up from his plate. 'Not, then, a day for walking? But yesterday was hardly that either, which did nothing to deter you.'

A glance at Aunt Sarah showed her eyes glued to her food, but there was no movement of cutlery.

'I found it quite pleasant, Henry. A rare chance to experience a habit of my younger self, to see the world in a happily remembered light. I really would recommend it, for I came home far from weary, but refreshed.'

'And not alone? I am told that your Captain Brazier accompanied you. He also looked to have been brawling, hardly a surprise given his profession.'

That information could only have come from Tanner, who would have been still on duty when Henry returned home, asleep probably, but obliged to rise and unlock. Betsey had lain awake listening and according to the clock chimes; when the horse's shod hooves rasped on the courtyard gravel, it had been past midnight.

'I was fortunate enough to have an escort, yes, and one who was willing to be that even after a heavy fall from his horse.'

Tulkington was genuinely shocked, so it was not a faked response. 'He fell off his horse?'

'A brave man is inclined to try high hedges, Henry.' There was a dig implicit in that; Henry was no hunter. Being delivered with a mischievous smile, it was wasted; he wasn't looking, so Betsey added, 'For all his travails he is yet gallant and chivalrous, for which you should be extremely grateful, as I suspect you were concerned for my welfare.'

His cutlery was thrown noisily down, to have him finally look up to glare at her. 'There seems little point in my having any concerns at all, since you choose to flout any notion of my legitimate reservations.'

'Legitimate, brother? Can I tell you what they are to me? A complete mystery.'

'They would be.'

'This is all most distressing,' pined her aunt, her voice weak and hinting at the approach of tears. Betsey thought it might well be an act, then castigated herself for her unkindness. Sarah Lovell liked harmony at Cottington Court, which meant, for her, security.

'I agree, Aunt Sarah, but I might suggest it is more distressing for me to be treated like a child than that you should be obliged to hear me remind my brother I am not.'

'You have no care for whom you hurt, do you?' Henry demanded.

'Given I am not the cause of the pain, why would I?'

'You consort in a public place with that scoundrel Brazier, with no thought to the reputation of this house or the feelings of your relations.'

Now it was Betsey's turn to chuck the cutlery. 'You will oblige me by never referring to him in that manner again, Henry. Perhaps it is you that is so warped that you cannot see virtue when it stares you in the face.'

Her brother threw his head back, to emit a very forced and insincere cackle.

'Virtue forsooth. I would be willing to hear how such an appellation can be applied to a man who could well be a grubby fortune-hunter. He says he has no need of your fortune, but I take that as smoke and mirrors. He insisted his prize agent would provide figures on his holdings. Such things can be drawn up in a moment but need not necessarily be true.'

'If you do not know that to be a falsehood, let me set your mind at rest. Edward Brazier—'

'Edward now, is it?' he barked.

'Most certainly so and the familiarity is of my choice. I have no idea how much to the pound or penny Edward gained from his capture of a Spanish plate ship, which, our aunt will tell you, was the talk of Jamaica, but I suspect it is enough to match what you can muster. I would also remind you that he is a post captain in the King's Navy. If anything, it is I who would gain from our union, not him.'

'Elisabeth,' Sarah whined. 'You surely have not gone so far as to—'

Sarah Lovell could not complete the sentence; it was, to her, too terrible to contemplate. Henry was visibly shocked, rendering ashen a face already pale.

'Captain Brazier has made his intentions towards me clear. I have made no formal acceptance, but I am comfortable in the knowledge that his desires are reciprocated and you should be too. If not, it is my decision and I cannot help your feelings.'

'Just two years a widow and you can contemplate a step such as this?'

'Yes, Henry, and welcome the prospect of no longer suffering loneliness and grief. It is two and a half years since Stephen passed away, so I am closer to the time when I can respectably contemplate a second marriage, and that to a man who is well aware of what society will accept. He is also happy to wait for the required period of mourning to pass.'

'And what if he gets bored?' Henry sneered. 'Will we find him trawling Portobello Court like every other sailor who comes ashore in Deal?'

'Henry!' was the shocked response from his aunt; such places as Portobello Court were not mentioned in polite society. Betsey was thinking of the Playhouse, and her unwarranted suspicions, of which she was now reassured. Edward would never voluntarily visit an establishment like that. Even less would he be seen near Portobello Court, a den of true iniquity.

'How dare you!' Betsey spat, with no decorum at all.

Aunt Sarah's sensibilities were utterly ignored; indeed, they were further degraded by her nephew. 'Tars are not of the kind to keep their breeches buttoned for long, regardless of what they protest, which is followed, as sure as night follows day, by the surgeon's probe.'

Sarah Lovell's napkin was now at her lips, and her face was drained of blood.

'Forgive his gutter mind, Aunt Sarah, as I do, for I know of whom he speaks and he does not.'

'What I do know is this,' came the reply, delivered just after a strong blow of the nose into the ever-present handkerchief. 'He will never pass through the gate to my house again.'

Betsey chose to sneer, the tone of her voice full of mirth, in an attempt to control her anger. 'And I would refrain from asking him to, brother, for fear he might put a ball or a sabre in your chest for your effrontery. A man who knows how to behave as a gentleman will not stand your insults and it is as well he is not here to witness them.'

Henry stood up, rubbing hard at his stomach. 'I cannot bear more of this. My digestion is in turmoil.'

'I might add, Henry, that Captain Brazier has taken a house, in which he is looking forward to receiving me as his guest.' In an aside to Aunt Sarah, she added, 'Properly chaperoned, of course.'

Henry, still rubbing at his gut, saw his chance to sneer. 'What a pity you will be unable to return the compliment.'

Betsey rose, threw down her napkin and stormed out. On the way to her room, she wondered if Henry had issued instructions to the gatekeeper to keep her from leaving; he was perfectly capable of it, Tanner having made it plain he had been angry the previous night. Also in her mind were the kinds of tales she had heard of sisters and widows who had fallen out with their family, usually over an inheritance, to be branded insane and confined in isolation, with no idea whether such tales were lurid inventions or the truth.

With such considerations it seemed politic to take precautions and a plan came to mind, which she knew she must act upon immediately or at least when the house moved into its mid-morning somnolence. The rain had stopped and the sky had begun to clear, so she resolved to depart when the servants were at those duties – things like polishing the silverware, preparing food and laying out crockery – which kept them away from the major rooms and common areas unless summoned.

Dressed once more in a cloak and bonnet, a heavy fur muff to keep her hands warm and what she carried hidden, she quietly left the house and, having made sure the ever-eager dogs stayed by the stables, exited through the kitchen garden and set off down the long path to the exterior gate, her heart beating increasingly faster at the approach. Tanner emerged with his ill-tempered mutt and a look on his face that boded ill.

'I has instructions, Mrs Langridge, from the master, to not let you leave Cottington without his say-so.'

Fury would not answer and there was no point in returning to the house to challenge Henry, so she tried a calmly delivered threat.

'I wonder, Tanner, if you know the penalty for holding a person in confinement against their express wishes?' The toothless face, creased already, took on the appearance of an aged and desiccated prune. 'At the extreme, it can lead to the gallows, at the very least to a prison hulk, now that we lack transportation to the Americas as an option.'

'Mrs Langridge I—'

'Of course, if my brother has given you written instructions, he will bear the opprobrium.'

'I don't have letters, ma'am, never have had.'

'So nothing in writing?' A shake of the head. 'Never mind, I'm sure he will support you when you're had up. Open the gate?'

'Can't ma'am.'

'Very well,' Betsey replied, 'I have made you aware of the consequences.'

That imparted she turned and made her way back towards the house. Halfway up the drive she looked over her shoulder to check Tanner had gone back into the gatehouse. With no sign of him, she skipped off the path and into the woods, thinking her brother was not just a misanthrope, he was a fool.

Henry had never been one to play outside – she was told it was the case even before she was born – so he did not know his own estate as a place of adventure; she had and did, so knew of the old postern gate hidden behind overgrown hedges and ivy on the southern wall. At this time of year the hedge was far from fully grown so it only took the bending of a couple of branches to give her access to a door, one that had been in poor repair years past.

Now it was so rotten it nearly fell apart as she pulled at the rusty ring handle, the outer frame getting stuck on the roots of a nearby tree, though not enough to prevent her creating a gap through which she could squeeze. The next-door field was ploughed, which meant muddy ankle boots and that had to be borne.

CHAPTER FIFTEEN

It was a contemplative Henry Tulkington who sat by the fire in his study, staring at the flickering flames and seeking an answer to a set of worrying conundrums, one of which was how to deal with his being robbed, while still lacking any solid information. If it was Spafford, that had to be put to one side, for the most pressing problem centred on Elisabeth and her infatuation with Brazier. It was obvious he would struggle to control her, but could he contemplate within the family a serving naval officer, especially one who was known to be upright in pursuit of his duties? If he had interdicted smuggling from the newly formed United States, he would scarce accept it here in England.

Had he been an impecunious naval officer, it might have been less of a worry; his putative brother-in-law had the means to ease his purse, while any man who took such gifts and became accustomed to them would scarce wish to see them curtailed. Yet not only was Brazier well heeled it seemed, but in marriage he would gain control of Elisabeth's property. Thus the means to suborn any principles he might possess was severely restricted.

It was too risky to just let matters take their own course, but barring Elisabeth from leaving Cottington could only be a temporary measure; if they were not an overly social family, him especially, there were still attendances that could not be avoided, Sunday worship being just one at which the whole family was expected to show – and if the Reverend Moyle had no control of his consumption of alcohol, he could hardly fail to remark on the lack of a showing by his sister.

His mind turned, as hers had done, towards the prospect of declaring her mentally unfit enough to justify confinement, given he was sure he could find a medical man amongst his Freemason fraternity who would do his bidding. But such a declaration would be too easy to challenge and the same fellow who presented the problem would be sure to do so, no doubt, in a very public and noisy manner.

Henry Tulkington had business interests outside the running of contraband and he was determined that they should not be exposed to public gaze, especially the activities of John Hawker. When his factotum collected monies due to the government on taxable goods, every legitimate penny raised was paid over to the Exchequer by Tulkington, though he took a percentage as profit. But a proportion of what was sold in the various outlets was smuggled goods, so the man collecting their taxes was the same fellow who said what was available in revenue-free contraband.

Those who declined what Hawker could provide were well aware he could call on a strong band of hard bargains to do his bidding – it was no secret in the Lower Town. His pitch was simple. If you decline to sell run goods, pay a regular fee to ensure your business prospers and no harm can be done to you, for I will ensure that is so. Refuse, and you are at the mercy of every villain in town.

Few had the ability to stand up to him and it was not just the implied threat of property or trade ruined. There were the rumours of other things Hawker had done to those who crossed him, which were enough to include terror in some and compliance in many. By such means Henry Tulkington kept a grip on the trade of Lower Town, his name never openly mentioned, but his influence acknowledged, even if only in whispers.

Hawker and the others who worked for him were rewarded from the extracted income, without the need to touch other sources. Much

186

of these, because of their illegal provenance, needed to be discreetly hidden away and quietly invested, bar a certain amount disbursed to buy the goods he required from his suppliers in France.

That exchange was not done in carried guineas, as Spafford in his luggers was obliged to carry, with all the attendant risks of being apprehended in possession of money that could only be for one purpose. It was and had been, since Tulkington Senior's time, facilitated by seemingly normal transfers through Jewish banking intermediaries, via a reputable enterprise based in the City of London run by his father's illegitimate half-brother.

Frustration at the lack of a firm conclusion to the problem of Elisabeth took him from a seat by the fire to his desk, so he could distract himself by turning to other opportunities. He was in the process of seeking to buy the last mill he did not already own in the area, sat on a hill near the hamlet of Northbourne, driven by both the stream of that name, as well as the wind. Achieved, he would have a monopoly on locally milled flour, and so be able to supply the bakery he already owned.

With the supply of meat also under his control, he could then sell his products at any price he chose, the main customers to be fleeced not the locals but the merchant vessels using the Downs. No ship could sail for foreign parts without it had the requisite supplies of salted meat in the barrel as well as ship's biscuit, and they would be obliged to pay what was asked.

If a national war and the convoys came again, the income from that would be huge. The fellow who owned the Northbourne mill, who had been in this very room two days previously, was disinclined to sell, even when Tulkington had considerably upped his offer, to still be rebuffed. Was it time that the man got a visit from Hawker – and would that work, for he was a stupidly stubborn cove? There was another solution, of course: the employment of torches to burn him out.

'Henry,' his aunt said from a flung-open door, to take his mind off such ruminations. 'I have been looking all over for Elisabeth.'

There was no need to add more, given the look on her face, while it was clear she expected her nephew to be alarmed. It threw her when he smiled; rare enough in itself, doubly so now.

'Fear not, Aunt Sarah, I have given orders she is not to be allowed to leave.'

'Then I am tempted to ask you where she is. There is no sign of her in the drive.'

'She likes to walk the grounds of a morning, does she not?'

'With the dogs, yes, yet they are within the house gates and whining to be let out.'

'Send a servant down to Tanner to remind him of my instructions.' There was no smile now. 'If he has failed in his duty, the only person going out of the gate will be him, at the end of my boot.'

To arrive on foot at the Colpoys house a second time occasioned less surprise than the first. The gate was opened and the servant's forelock touched in respect, though he could not avoid a glance down at Betsey's mud-caked footwear, half-covered with good dark-brown loam. She used the boot scraper to get the worst off before ascending the steps to use the polished knocker.

A glance upwards immediately showed three eager faces as the Colpoys' brats looked to see who had come, but not for long, no doubt called to order by their governess who, apparently, was a demon with the birch and needed to be. A liveried servant opened the door and, knowing well the caller, stepped aside to let Betsey in while announcing his intention to fetch madam from her boudoir and her embroidery.

Betsey was left for much longer than she would have expected, which at least allowed her to remove her still-mud-caked boots, which revealed the bottom of her dress had not escaped the same degree of impairment. When Annabel did finally appear, the servant at her back, there was something discomfiting about the cast of her features. There was certainly no effusive welcome, quite the reverse.

'Have you come to take away your pony?'

'Partly that, but I have an even greater boon to ask of you.'

The response should have been as it was the day before, immediately concerned, but it was not.

'Henry has sought to confine me. The gateman had instructions not to let me leave so I had no choice but to sneak out. It may be that I will have to abandon living at Cottington, which means I must find a place to lay my head, should it come to be necessary.'

'Abandon?'

'If I cannot remain there, Annabel.'

Her voice rose to a higher pitch in reply. 'Such an extreme reaction, merely because of a quarrel with Henry?'

'I have not yet told you of the seat of our difference.'

Annabel looked down at Betsey's now stockinged feet, as well as the filthy hem and said in a distant way, 'No, you have not and I am at a loss to know, as is my husband, who was surprised I did not enquire.'

It was in a slightly terse voice with which Betsey responded. 'Am I to be invited in, or will I be obliged to explain my reasons in the hallway?'

She meant in front of a servant, who had already heard too much, all of which would soon be gossip below stairs in any number of houses.

'Take Mrs Langridge's cloak.'

This being said over her shoulder, Annabel headed for the drawing room and a disrobed Betsey followed, to find her friend stood by the fireplace looking rigid in her posture. There was only one way to shake that, which was by employing a jolt, but first it was essential to close the door so as not to be overheard.

'Henry objects to the notion I might marry again.' There was no response and, more tellingly, no invitation to sit, so it was with some trepidation that Betsey continued. 'I met someone in the Caribbean whom I found to be congenial company and he has followed me to Deal.'

'Someone?'

'A naval captain.'

'And he wishes to marry you?'

'Henry doesn't only object to the notion of my marrying, he has taken violently against Captain Brazier, to the point of threatening to bar him from entry to Cottington Court. Also, prior to his latest strictures, he declined to allow me a coach or a horse, which is why I arrived on foot yesterday.'

'So you wished to borrow a horse to go and see this fellow?'

'Do I detect a note of disapproval?'

'I would be bound to say, Elisabeth, that such an action as you undertook borders not only on the rash, but is enough to ruin you if it became public knowledge. A widow running after a prospective lover, forsooth, and with scant discretion.'

'I think I implied a prospective husband,' Betsey said, her heart stung by the use of her proper name by such a close friend.

'I fail to see the difference. If you are prepared to throw yourself at this man's feet, who's to know what silly acts will follow? Or the ramifications that will flow from them and who they will affect.'

'What has changed, Annabel? Why are you so very different today, when yesterday you were glad to see me and, as one of my oldest companions, eager to help?'

'Perhaps, with what you have just told me, I can see that your brother has just cause to seek to restrain you from your own folly.'

'I came hoping, indeed believing, you would give me temporary shelter if I required it.'

Annabel turned her back and laid a hand on the mantelpiece. 'Which would make me and this house party to your behaviour.'

'Is not that what friends are for?'

'Real friends do not risk the reputation of those they say they hold dear.'

'I sense my request for shelter is not welcome.'

Back still turned, Annabel replied in a strained voice. 'I'm sorry, Elisabeth, I cannot in all consciousness oblige you with such a promise.'

Stung, Betsey responded. 'I trust at least I may retrieve my pony?'

'Ask the stable lad to get him out for you.'

There was no goodbye from either. Betsey went out into the hallway, shutting the door behind her, and sat on a chair to replace her ankle boots, cursing under her breath as she buttoned them up, while being equally dismayed at the exchange in which she had just engaged. Inside the room Annabel was leaning on the mantelpiece, her head against the hand that rested still on the carved wood; she was weeping. Never a woman to tolerate blaspheming, she was doing so in a vehement whisper now.

'Damn you, Roger Colpoys, damn you.'

Even if she hated having to do so, Annabel Colpoys was obliged to obey her husband, who had been furious when Betsey left the day before. Any suggestion that an act of his house should cause grief to Henry Tulkington was not to be allowed to occur. Her pleas to be told why not were ignored and, when she pressed, found her threatened with the riding crop.

Canasta was led out on a simple rope halter, the bridle of the same material. Given there was no saddle, it was an abashed stable lad who had to respond to the questioning look.

'Mr Colpoys' orders, Ma'am.'

Betsey took the rope and turned towards the gate. 'Do remember to thank him for me.'

She held her tears till she was far enough away not to be observed. Only then did she lay her head against that of Canasta and cry, feeling an acute sense of isolation. There were other friends from her past, but none that lived so close as to be of any help. And they too might react like Annabel. The thought of Stephen's mother rose up to be dismissed; how could she consider asking to stay with her when she was contemplating a union with another man?

It would have possibly cheered her to know that, back at Cottington Court, her continued non-appearance had become the subject of consternation, with Henry Tulkington quite changed from the sanguine mood of earlier. His aunt, having made sure Elisabeth had not left by the main gate, had sent the servants out to search the grounds and check if anyone had seen her at the various gates – kitchen garden and access to the farms or in the church – all to no avail. A long-walled estate had other exits, doors that had been checked and were barred from the inside.

Henry's first response was to harass those same servants into getting his coach horses into their harness but, that done, it stood waiting for a master who did not appear. He was back in his study, hands on the mantle, staring once more at the fire, having suppressed his immediate desire to go in pursuit of Elisabeth and, if need be, drag her back by the hair. It simply would not serve. Experience, both above and below the legal line, had convinced him that, just like dealing with Daniel Spafford, time was an ally.

According to his aunt, the association between Elisabeth and this Brazier was of short duration. She was besotted by a fellow she did not really know and one, moreover, who had shown no compunction in lying to her about how he had come about his cuts and bruises. These had been described to him in detail by Tanner, which moderated his anger towards the gateman on the previous night.

A complete reversal of his position would not be wise; Elisabeth would smoke that as an invention. But he could soften in the face of such determination, as he had appeared to do with Langridge, then set enquiries afoot as to the nature and reputation of Brazier. It was typical of an enamoured woman to describe the man they admired as being a paragon, while he had never in his life met anyone who could truthfully claim the tag. All had flaws; the trick was to find them.

Added to which, and the thought produced a rare smile, he could always set Hawker on Brazier again; let the scoundrel explain that away as falling off his horse! First he would write to his uncle in London, requesting that he gather information which, in his capacity as a King's

Counsel, and one who moved in the highest social and governmental circles, might produce something of use in the denigration line.

That arrived at, he still had to go after Elisabeth and try to persuade her to return with him so, rising from his chair, he went out to his waiting coach only to see her, in the distance, coming up the driveway, leading a pony. He waited by the traces, his Aunt Sarah, having been alerted to this apparition, taking up station in the front doorway.

Both observed, as she came closer, the shoulders were far from square; there was a physical attitude to go with the tear-stained face and partly unpinned hair. Two servants opened the gate to let her through, one taking the rope and leading Canasta away. She looked at her brother with nothing even hinting at regard, only to hear him say very softly,

'I was going out to find you, Elisabeth. You may not take it as true, but I was worried and, seeing you now in a somewhat dishevelled state, it seems my concerns were justified.'

'I must go and change, Henry.'

'Of course. But that done, please come to me so we can talk.'

'What point is there in that?' she asked, with eyes on the ground.

'If we exchange views, it may be there is one. Within the hour, shall we say?'

'Very well,' she replied, passing by him, only to stop and turn, straighten her shoulders and meet his gaze directly. 'Tanner, at the gate. Do not overly chastise him. I threatened the poor fellow with a prison hulk and worse if he did not let me pass.'

Henry was able to manufacture a kindly look, while recording the fact of her blatant lie. Tanner reported he had seen Elisabeth approach the gate, but he had refused her permission to leave as instructed, his last sight of her heading back up the drive. This meant Elisabeth had taken another route out and, given the various gates were barred from the inside and had been seen to be so in the last hour, it implied she had assistance from one of the estate servants.

That was a problem to be dealt with, but not right now. For the moment a touch of blandishment was more appropriate. 'Few would be formidable enough to gainsay you, sister, if you were determined, would they?'

As ever the study was too hot and Betsey, in an initial act of defiance, left open the door and waited for the reaction; there was none, or at least not what was expected. Having been sat, Henry stood to greet her.

'Now you look much more yourself. I shall order tea.' He waited, obviously for a response, but none came, though it was clear by her posture the spirit that animated her was back in full force. 'It would be best to sit.'

Betsey made for the card table, this set at a decent distance from the burning logs, while Henry occupied a chair close by but facing her. 'Would it be possible to say we have both been foolish, Elisabeth?'

'It is not a word I would want to apply to myself.'

'Headstrong, then?' Seeing her face close up he was quick to add, 'It matters not, really. We are where we are, and I for one have come to the conclusion matters cannot stay the way they are.'

'If you seek to confine me to the house, they most certainly will.'

'I do not expect you to accept that I was only concerned to protect you.'

'From?'

'Yourself?' Again she frowned. 'And I admit to perhaps overreacting to what I perceived.'

'Which is?'

'Let us not reprise what we already know. Suffice to say I knew before he walked through the door to this room why Brazier had come to Cottington and so, I suspect, did you. I count you as headstrong, and I use that word in memory of how you were in the matter of Langridge.'

'Surely you mean Stephen.'

'Forgive me – a habit and a bad one, to refer to someone become a relative by their surname. When he asked for your hand you were in your minority, so I had the right to ask if such a union was both wise and proper.'

'One I can recall only too well: a right that you exercised to the full.'

194

'But I did come round in the end, which at least you must acknowledge.'

If the face was set and she was silent, her response so obviously had to be yes Henry did not wait for it to be confirmed.

'I am at an earlier stage with these proposed nuptials, but experience tells me I will not quickly change my view, even if I am prepared to admit to the possibility. All I ask is that you show discretion. Allow time for your real feelings to be established beyond peradventure. It would be tragic if you were mistaken.'

Betsey had to hold steady in the face of that advice; she had harboured similar thoughts regarding too much haste. Henry seemed not to notice and continued in his placatory tone.

'You are free to come and go as you wish, and to use whatever mode of transport you desire. I have been too harsh in my restrictions.'

'And Captain Brazier?'

He had to admire her refusal just to accept his mellowing, but noted her caution in the naming of the swine pursuing her. There was no Edward!

'You may receive him as you wish, properly chaperoned, of course.'

'And you?'

'Not yet, in time perhaps. For now it would be best to invite him on those occasions when I am absent. Meanwhile, you may wish to see to the sending of this.'

Henry rose and came close to hand over a letter, which caused raised eyebrows when Betsey read the superscription.

'It is, in part, an apology to Captain Brazier for my previous manner of addressing him, though I would admit it is far from effusive. Oh, and I commiserated with him, of course, for the injuries he suffered falling off his horse.'

195

CHAPTER SIXTEEN

It was commonplace for a naval captain to keep a list of men he could call followers – prime hands and petty officers who, in the event of his getting a ship, especially should there be the threat of war, he could call on to join him – and Brazier was no exception. Among them were the contact addresses of the men who had formed his barge crew aboard HMS *Diomede*, provided so that their dependants could draw upon their pay warrants and to which would be sent any notification of death or injury.

These men went everywhere with their captain; in ship visits to colleagues or admirals or to take him ashore and off again. More vitally, if he took part in an opposed landing, or boarded an enemy vessel, they were the people at his side. Those who volunteered to man His Majesty's ships hailed from seaports in the main and, when discharged, it was to those they returned, Chatham and Portsmouth being the most common, though there were numerous others: Plymouth, Falmouth, Harwich as well as a dozen more of the size of Deal. It was to such places the letters were sent, some never to be read, given the intended recipient was absent, possibly having taken service on a merchant vessel, but others found their mark.

The coxswain of HMS *Diomede*, Tom 'Dutchy' Holland, who had commanded his barge crew, had been at Brazier's side in some hot actions and he was a doughty fighter, which was required now. Post for him went to the Old Quay Inn, which lay at the head of Restronguet Creek off the Carrick Roads above Falmouth Harbour, a place where there was work and pay from private boat owners for a man with Dutchy's skills.

He was working on the rigging of a private yacht belonging to a Mr Dobson when alerted, which took him to the Old Quay Inn to find out what was afoot, the notion of his receiving a written communication enough reason for gossip well before the contents were known. Once read to him he requested a reply be sent at once, pledged his credit to the innkeeper for some silver coin, before going to his lodgings to pack a ditty bag and tell his woman he was off to serve his captain. Given he had spent much of their time as a couple at sea there was no protest, as long as she could be sure of a supply of money to feed her and their three children.

'Take my regrets to Mr and Mrs Dobson, for he is a good man and she a kindly soul, but when such as Captain Brazier calls, it cannot be ignored. The Turk has said he will make arrangements as soon as I get to his side, so you drop by the Old Quay regular until how it's to be done is told you.'

Of the dozen letters Brazier had despatched, four had engendered replies. This put the recipients, from various places around the country, on the road to Deal, walking where they must, hitching rides on carts if they were available. Within a short time of taking occupation of Quebec House, Brazier could reckon on having not only his favourite servant to see to his needs, but also a trio of hard-fisted scrappers to watch his back.

Having Betsey visit his new abode after a week of occupation was welcome, if stifling; her aunt was in the far-from-spacious drawing room the whole time, which made any kind of conversation stilted and replete with banalities, this as tea was offered, infused and poured.

Brazier had visited Cottington once, at a time when the brother was away on his affairs and they, with the obligatory and very welcome walk in the grounds, had been freer in terms of exchange.

Betsey had made use of the church in order to distract her aunt and so he had met the old soak of a priest, the Reverend Doctor who had the living. The navy had its serious drunks and Brazier had been exposed to a number of them, but he wondered if any could hold a candle to Moyle. It was mid-morning and, if he was not actually so drunk he could not function, he was very obviously far from completely sober.

This kind of visiting demanded he pay his respects to the man's wife and, in Mrs Moyle, he found a cause for true sympathy. The length of her suffering was in her face and body, she being a woman who looked as if she scarcely ate, while her manner was fussily remorseful. Tea was offered but declined and off they went to continue what conversation could be managed.

Yet there could be no physical contact apart from a bestowed kiss on the hand when departing, a restriction that he knew was troubling Betsey as much as he in an increasingly obvious way. Did she perceive the level of frustration in his eyes as much as he discerned in hers? The only person he could even talk to about this was Flaherty, a man equally smitten and even more frustrated by it.

'It would be easier if she had never been married, Vincent. But she has and is therefore accustomed to a relationship that is physically unhindered.'

'Sure I am that, having met the lady, my patience too would be sorely tested.'

'Enough of my moans. Have you found anything out?'

'For a place where rumour is rife and gossip a way of life, the folk round here can be mighty tight-lipped, even after my having lived here come two years. I mentioned care to you before, Edward, and I worry that I don't know the whys and wherefores of to whom I am talking. It is a place where it is wise to know the cousinage, who's related to who, when you query to a body.'

'You said to me that Saoirse knew everything that went on in Deal.'

'Well, if she has knowledge of this, she is not saying. When I asked her I got a look that said to mind my own business.'

'Does that not imply she does have information?'

'None she's willing to give out. Happen if you asked on your own account, she might be more forthcoming. I have to beat around the bush, whereas you can enquire direct.'

Brazier might acknowledge the truth of such an assertion, but he also had to admit the notion of him visiting the Playhouse and asking was impossible. On receiving the note of commiseration from Tulkington, he had deduced he would be a fool to accept the sentiments expressed. Could it be such a man had performed even the half volte-face to which he alluded? This implied he still disapproved, but would not stand in his sister's way.

Was he being cunning, which led to an examination of what he might be up to? If the folk of Deal were not being open about the fabled Daisy, they were very much willing to claim to know Henry Tulkington and in a way that indicated familiarity with his prominence.

The lawyer to whom he would pay his rent had initially shown surprise bordering on alarm at the mention of the name, only to then praise to the rafters a local worthy so very successful in his enterprises. He was also not shy, it appeared, when called upon to gift funds to local projects, the most pressing presently being the aim to lay the three main, prone-to-mud thoroughfares with cobblestones.

The tradesmen who called at Quebec House to supply food and drink also responded with respect when the name was mentioned. So he now knew the family had been prominent in Deal for several generations, the father having enhanced an already high standing in the community. The commendations he heard were hard to square

199

with the misery guts he had encountered, a point forcibly made to Flaherty who sought to advise his friend.

'Even I know you won't hear much said against the Tulkington name, Edward, but does it occur that that might be because he's rich and thus not a man to cross? Money makes cowards of us who must sell our services, be it horseflesh or tea.'

'Speaking of which, I have become a dab hand at the making of the brew, which would astound some who know me.'

Brazier alluded to the brewing of the leaves in a deliberate change of subject, He had no desire to include Flaherty in the train of his thoughts: recurring ones in which he speculated that folk who talked freely to him of the Tulkington family virtues would be just as willing to talk to Henry about him and, in a small town like this, there were people present to observe his every move.

'And what about the fellow who taxes it so to render it a luxury?'

'I'm off to see the Pitt tomorrow – to entertain his sister, I suspect, more than any desire on his part.'

'It's as well your black eye is fading.'

Brazier automatically moved his back, as if checking it had ceased to cause discomfort, noting the hesitation before Flaherty spoke again: not just the gap in his conversation but the look on his face, which appeared embarrassed.

'I hate to bring this to your attention, but in pursuit of what you seek, I have taken my eye off my business these last ten days.'

'I also suspect it has occasioned some expense?'

'That grin you're wearing looks mighty self-satisfied, Edward.'

'It is not intended to be, I assure you. I didn't raise it for fear of causing offence. You recall when we first met with Saoirse, she referred to the – what shall I call it? – the impecunious nature of your affairs. I trust you not to have been indulging in high-value clarets, but I'm aware, even on such a short acquaintance, almost all of what takes place in Deal, both socially and in business, does so in proximity to drink.'

'Very true.'

'Some of which you are obliged to purchase in the hope of loosening tongues?'

Flaherty grinned. 'I will own to it not always being a duty.'

'It is nevertheless on my behalf, so must fall to my account.'

'It is a sum I cannot demonstrate.'

'You don't have to, Vincent. I will take it on trust.'

That took away the grin, to be replaced with contrived wonder. 'From a dealer in horseflesh?'

'Even in such a benighted occupation, there must be one honest fellow.'

'Not a wager I would take.'

Flaherty produced a list of his outgoings, passed over for Brazier to examine, which was brief and non-committal. He left the room for a short period to return with a written note.

'Take this to Mr Davies, the advocate in King Street. He is treasurer of the council and has a stout safe for municipal funds. He is acting as my banker on remittances sent to him from London.'

'So you've taken my advice?'

'About not carrying around a purse full of guineas? Yes I have. I cannot be sure that for all that was said about Daisy, the pair who came at me were not just set on robbery. They were, after all, disturbed.'

The frustrations of Edward Brazier could not compare with those of the woman he was intent on marrying. While hating to admit her brother had been right, Betsey occupied a great deal of her time thinking of the man in pursuit of her and what might transpire, with all the caveats she could conjure up surfacing regularly, not least that she might be deluding herself to thinking of marrying a man she really hardly knew.

Their meetings in Jamaica were constantly reprised as she sought clues for the point at which pleasure in his company had morphed into something more profound. Likewise here at home, though exchanges, which might be overheard by her aunt, did nothing to establish enlightenment. Yet on the chaperoned walks she could feel that strange sensation brought on by his proximity and his voice.

Activity would have helped to fill a portion of her day but, being a lady of leisure, she was not required to do much, even in the domestic line. At Cottington Court, that was overseen – and the role tenaciously hung on to – by her Aunt Sarah. In the West Indies, Betsey had run her own household, which included overseeing the recruitment or, in very occasional cases, the dismissal of house servants. The latter a matter for very careful consideration, given it would send a household slave to back-breaking field work on one of the plantations.

Betsey had to have her tolerance tested to the limit to even think of imposing such a fate on someone who had ceased to be just a face. If she felt uneasiness now, it had not surfaced as readily back then. How easy it had been to forget, mostly down to their obliging manner, that the servants who worked in the Langridge house were not present by choice.

Here the household servants occupied the attics or, in the case of the gardeners and stable lads, a cottage for the first and a loft for the latter. In Jamaica they had occupied a thatched sort of barracks, well away from the house – further even than the stables – a long hut split in the middle to keep apart the sexes, with one of the estate guards on duty overnight, tasked to ensure they stayed that way.

Part of her responsibilities, early in the morning, had been to meet with the head retainer to arrange the running of the day. Were she and Stephen in or out for dinner? If not, were they expecting guests? If going out, at what time would the carriage and the master's horse have to be ready, her maid already alerted to the required clothing for the occasion?

Entertaining would involve a discussion around place settings, chairs etc., and then a session with cook to plan the meal, with messages being sent to the various providers to supply what could not be accessed within the bounds of the home farm and vegetable beds, which she took to and enjoyed inspecting regularly; to do that here at Cottington was seen as prying.

There was, of course, endless visiting, which Betsey now undertook diligently, calling on the very same people who had attended her spring fete, all except Annabel Colpoys, who had shown her a cold shoulder at St Saviour's these last two Sunday services. Her husband, Roger, had made a point of ignoring Betsey too, and kept his children from engaging with her, which was wounding. Odd that Moyle's sermon had been gentle for once, his subject the benign nature of the Holy Spirit.

The fear they had gossiped and mentioned her intentions was ever present. Thus every visit to an old friend of herself or the family was an occasion of acute observation, seeking for the slightest hint that her reputation had been compromised. Duty demanded she visit Stephen's mother and there her antennae were acute for any hint of scandal. If she thought it irrational, and Edward had quietly on their walk dismissed it as nonsense, it was nevertheless one of the norms of the society in which she lived.

A widow must show respect to her dear departed and not go husband hunting, or even be seen to enjoy the company of an unmarried man, until a decent interval had passed. If she showed the slightest inclination to stray from those constraints, her Aunt Sarah was there to remind her. Henry, on the other hand, had taken to never directly referring to the subject.

'I shall be going away the day after tomorrow, Elisabeth, to London,' he murmured, fork poised halfway to his mouth. 'For several days and possibly a week.'

She had to suppress a feeling of excitement, which was not easy; luckily Henry went back to concentrating on his dinner by the time she replied. 'To visit our Uncle Dirley, no doubt?'

'Partly that, but there are other matters to address.'

'Am I allowed to enquire as to what they would be?'

The superior smirk was infuriating. 'Nothing to worry your pretty little head about.'

It was not vanity that made her accept the 'pretty'. She never considered herself in that way: Betsey knew she had been favoured in the article of looks allied to health but, to her, gloating on it or seeking advantage was reckoned improper. But fury at the 'little' had her grip her cutlery very hard and nearly brought on an outburst. She had to tell herself to change the subject; condescension almost counted as natural behaviour for her brother, something she would bear in silence for the sake of her greater goal.

'Why is it Dirley never visits us here?'

He seemed to require time to answer that question, which was odd. It should have come readily, since he knew his half-uncle very well and had been doing regular business with him ever since their father passed away. To Betsey he was close to being a stranger, even although he had handled the Langridge will, seeing to the transfer and continued smooth running of the plantations, all of which had been carried out through written correspondence.

'He dislikes the country and prefers the town, but then there is the question of his . . .' There was a pause and a feebly waved hand, as his aunt breathed heavily enough to ensure no untoward expressions were uttered, which led to an evasive conclusion: 'You know.'

'Do I? He seems like a mystery to me. I've not seen him since I was a child and can scarcely conjure up an image. To call him a distant relative is an understatement. He did not even attend my wedding.'

'It might be a misnomer to name him as a true relative at all, Elisabeth,' was the quiet opinion of Sarah Lovell. 'The family repute might be tainted by his too-obvious presence.'

'Surely the time for the shame of his birth is long past?'

The response was more forceful. 'Is there ever such a period, dear girl, when shame is diminished?'

The hint was obvious: never mind your illegitimate Uncle Dirley, think of your own situation and guard it. Her brother started talking about the possible price of wheat, given there was the prospect of a good harvest at home and a poor one in France, at which point Betsey went back to her own private ruminations; the subject was of no interest to her whatsoever.

Joe Lascelles was the first of Brazier's old crew to arrive, just as his one-time captain was in the act of departing for Walmer Castle. Indeed the door was open, Bonnie was outside, saddled and being held by a moonlighting Ben, who eyed Joe suspiciously as, ditty bag slung over his shoulder, he enquired for Quebec House. Africans were not unknown in Deal and neither, with the East Indian trade, were Lascars, but they were far from common.

'Who be askin'?'

'It is in the nature, young fellow, of my being polite, for I can now see very well that the name is writ over the door.'

The one-time son of a slave had not only the ability to read but, for his social position, a refined manner of speech, picked up in the houses of his father's master and, given one of those residences was in Yorkshire, there was a tinge of the accent in his voice.

'Is that you, Joe?'

Brazier voiced this enquiry as he approached the door from within and heard the exchange. He was greeted on exiting with that smile he remembered so well, which was one to light up a dark room.

'None other, and about to clip this brat round the ear.' There was little actual threat in that, not with a deep laugh to accompany it. 'Do I detect I am come at an awkward time?'

'I am bent upon an engagement for which I cannot delay.' Brazier took the reins from Ben and introduced him to his new servant. 'He's a good lad and willing if you need anything.'

'Food and a place to lay my head for an hour will suffice. I have been on the road for over two weeks and, being told I was close, I was up with the birds this day.'

'There's a spare latchkey hanging in the rear passage and food in the larder.'

'And duties?'

'You will see to them without aid from me and we can talk upon my return. Make yourself comfortable in one of the upper rooms. If you require water, use my name to draw it from the Navy Yard well. Also, keep an ear out for a trio of old shipmates coming to the house.' That got a look and the names: 'Dutchy Holland, Peddler Palmer and Cocky Logan.'

'Which will have me head scratching worse than Peddler as to why.'

'Later, Joe,' Brazier said, hauling himself into the saddle. 'I must be off, given a late arrival is to be avoided.'

CHAPTER SEVENTEEN

Prior to travelling to London, Tulkington called upon John Hawker. Another shipment was due and his man required a list of the expected contraband which, on this occasion, would stand as a test. The next task was to work out the possible dates on which it could be landed, this dependent again on the state of the moon and the height of the tides, albeit with the constant risk of bad weather, for traversing the English Channel was rarely straightforward even in high summer.

It was not unknown for a crossing, if the prevailing westerlies blew strong and continuous, to take a week, which normally would be spent waiting in harbour for the winds to moderate or shift. The very devil was to be caught out at sea in storm conditions so severe that they barred a run for a port too dangerous to enter. This could be harmful even if the vessel did not founder. Tossed about for days on end, passengers had been known to expire from sheer exhaustion.

The boat people of East Kent knew their waters and rarely put to sea if instinct, based on years of accumulated and handed-down knowledge, indicated gales in the offing. What would be a mystery to a landsman – the run and colour of the sea, the sniff and direction of the breeze, added to the shape of the clouds – was an open book to the best coastal seafarers and none more so than smugglers.

Unloading had always been less of a problem; with an eight-mile stretch of shingle coast from the fishing hamlet of Kingsdown to the Stour estuary, there was no shortage of places to land illicit cargo and many an enterprising individual had done so over decades when circumstances permitted, goods to be eagerly snapped up locally. It had been Tulkington senior's genius to make regular in supply what had been haphazard, so now traders came from far and wide to collect their purchases.

Hawker also reported what he knew of the man he was tasked to keep an eye on, something he was too wise to undertake personally, especially when he had no need. Brazier would eye with suspicion any adult showing interest in him, but the town was full of parentless urchins who would do his bidding for a small reward in copper, or even better, a flask of gin. So every move had been marked, the information passed back to Tulkington, who found it deeply disappointing.

'Are you sure this man is a Jack tar? No drunkenness, no women?'

'Not much like those I've encountered, right enough,' Hawker replied. 'Had your sister to visit, but not another female and has not gone near a whorehouse or even the Playhouse or the Paragon. Flaherty the horse dealer seems to have become a companion of sorts, though I reckon it will be because Brazier bought a good cellar from Parkin.'

'I wonder what he would say if he knew Parkin's wine casks were supplied by us.'

'Should I keep watchin' him?'

It was impossible to miss the hint in the way that was asked; Hawker reckoned it a waste of time.

'Until I return from London. He will discover from my sister where I am. Perhaps my absence for near a week will flush him out.'

He did not feel it necessary to say he had taken other precautions. That was no one else's business but his own.

The notion of flushing Brazier out was not without foundation, though mistaken in its conclusion; Betsey had penned a letter to

Brazier as soon as Henry's carriage departed the driveway en route to Dover and the mail coach, again using one of the younger stable boys as a messenger, waiting till her aunt was occupied to despatch the lad on a cob, her message being that with her brother absent, the time must be used to become better acquainted. This was hard to achieve at Cottington but his parlour would never serve; their walks were accompanied, while a public place, even if she could shake off her aunt, was barred by convention.

So, enclosed in her note was a small sketch showing the location of the old broken gate, previously used by her to escape. Edward could gain access to the grounds, while her walks would be timed to take her within sight of the location at an agreed morning hour. Alone they could converse freely and find time to become better acquainted.

Not mentioned, or even alluded to, was the need she felt to reassure herself that the course on which she was set was a wise one. It was obvious that proximity to Edward Brazier caused her to experience a feeling of anticipation in her lower stomach, even a current of some kind running through her arm as he kissed the back of her hand on departure.

She thought him of fine character, as well as kind and considerate, but her own limited experience still allowed caution to intrude; she had really only known and been close to one man in her life. Common tales spoke of prospective husbands who had appeared perfect gentlemen prior to the nuptials, only to become drunken ogres and gamblers once the knot was tied.

There was no indication Edward Brazier was anything other than he appeared, but surely no amount of contact could be too much to lay even a slight worry to rest. Betsey was also aware of his profession, with a sure feeling it was something to which he was attached. Called to serve, it would surely be accepted with alacrity, which would take him away from her side.

If elements of that troubled her, it also induced a feeling of pride;

no man of parts should shirk serving his country. Was that to be a portion of her life – wedded, comfortable, but alone for a period of unknown duration while he was at sea? Were the feelings they might share enough to stand up to what could well be a strain on any union?

The lad who watched Brazier as he took the Lower Valley Road out of Deal was not happy to venture into the open country. Scrubland was no place for the kind of waifs who gathered to drink their gin and sleep in the alleyways of the town, the rough spirit, together with huddled humanity, warding off the cold. But there was a craving for his reward, so he stayed with him till he saw the horse turning into the drive which led to Walmer Castle. Destination marked, Hawker's ragamuffin decided that was enough, so set off for the slaughterhouse.

Walmer Castle had a captain who held the command; not that the Marquis of Waldron, who held the post, bothered to execute the duties of his office. He took the pay and delegated the work to another, a fellow who had scraped the money together to purchase a lieutenancy. That officer oversaw the small detachment of soldiers, two of whom were on sentry duty on the bridge spanning the moat, smart enough drilled to present arms to a naval officer whose equivalent army rank was that of colonel.

There was a man to take Brazier's hat and sword and another, superior fellow in black coat and breeches who led him through the stone corridors to the main chamber, in which there was a pair of flaring and very necessary fires; solid-stone walls did not do much to admit warmth from outside. It was a room in which to both relax and entertain, furnished with comfortable seating near, but not too near, one of the fires. A long, heavy oak dining table with high-backed chairs sat halfway between the two massive grates. Brazier noticed the table was laid for three at one end, so deduced he was to be a solitary guest.

'Captain Edward Brazier, sir.'

Pitt rose from one of the fireside chairs to come forward and greet him, the woman who came out of another he guessed to be Lady Harriot before she was introduced. On first impression she was, as had been indicated by her brother, so heavily pregnant as to be close to term. But there was a secondary examination of a woman who was neither a beauty nor the converse.

The eyes were lively enough, but her nose was too prominent and she had her brother's lips, which tended to that downward humourless tilt. The voice was strong and there was something about her carriage and demeanour, even with her prominent belly, which indicated such was replicated in her character.

Brazier was not entirely in ignorance of the lady: she was after all prominent socially and thus spoken of in the journals. Her husband, Sir James Eliot, was very conspicuous in the anti-slavery movement, a close associate to William Wilberforce, as was Pitt himself. Even if he knew it to be a subject fraught with pitfalls – it aroused strong passions – and given it was a fair bet the wife and sister shared their views, he knew it was bound to surface.

'My brother was very eager to have you as a guest, Captain Brazier, which leads me to suspect you must be entertaining company indeed. He is choosy as to whom he has at table and is, in the main, obliged to feed politicos, dreary as they are in their speculations on the state of the nation.'

'I fear he is mistaken, madam,' Brazier replied, taking a glass of wine off a tray presented to him. 'I'm a sad case when it comes to being amusing.'

Pitt had drained his glass and taken a second from the same tray.

'Amusement is rarely what my sister seeks, Brazier. Those who have acted with bravery or witnessed strange phenomena are more to her liking. She is an avid student of the world and corresponds regularly with Sir Joseph Banks, who, you will recall, sailed with Captain Cook.'

'How I wish I had done so too,' Lady Harriot said. 'There is a great deal outside these walls, and what have I seen?'

'East Kent,' was posited as a wry and amusing response by her brother. 'The centre of the universe, so how can you complain?'

'Pay him no heed for his poor wit, sir. Come and sit with us a while, for dinner will be some time. You have, I believe, seen service in both the East and West Indies?'

'I have been fortunate in that regard, yes.'

'I find the notion of India and the Spice Islands fascinating. Then there are the places visited by Cook, not least Australasia.'

Pitt interjected. 'Perhaps I should send you and James there as envoys.' A nod to Brazier. 'But, of course, the objects first have to be gained by our soldiers and sailors.'

'A task of oversight I would carry forward with greater brio than most of the men you might favour, my husband James notwithstanding.' She turned to Brazier. 'As you can see, Captain, he tends to patronise me. It is no secret I find the confining nature of my sex a burden.'

'Then hope for a son, sister, to live through.'

The response was a manufactured expression of exasperation which did not convince, given it was not intended to. Brazier felt he was witness to a dispute that had been long in the making and probably went back to childhood. Their father had been the Great Commoner, William Pitt, the architect of victory, who had led the country to triumph in the Seven Years War to be then ennobled as the First Earl of Chatham.

His second son could be eager to emulate Pitt senior, although the nation's finances must be able to sustain the burden. But what of Lady Harriot? She would have been raised in a household at the centre of national affairs, at a time when great events overseen by their father were taking place and, being very likely as bright and engaged as her brothers, mightily narked at having a lesser role in the world being created.

Prior to moving to the table, the conversation was as Brazier expected. He was gently questioned on his service, the enquiries posed in the main by the sister. With mention of the West Indies came the inevitable interrogation on slavery.

'It is the most pressing cause of the age, Captain, do you not agree?'

'Important yes, Lady Harriot, but I think your brother would be the best person to address with the term "pressing", for I have only opinion while he has the ability to effect change.'

'It certainly merits attention, that is true,' Pitt responded. 'Had I the power to force it through the House it would be law in a trice, but the sugar lobby is exceedingly powerful, which curtails whatever ability you ascribe to me.'

'They are even more powerful in the Caribbean islands than at home,' Brazier insisted.

The fellow who had shown him in arrived to say dinner was about to be served, so the trio moved to the table, Lady Harriot easing herself in with care and Pitt, once the first glass of wine had been served and a tureen of soup disbursed, immediately taking up the conversation where it had left off.

'I seem to recall you had several run-ins with the plantation owners.'

Brazier smiled, though he did wonder at such facts landing on such an elevated desk.

'They want the law enforced to keep their slaves under control, but not to stop them buying cheap goods, smuggled in from the United States or the Spanish colonies. It was my job, and that of my fellow captains, to stop it.'

'And how successful were you?' Lady Harriot enquired over a soup spoon.

The temptation to snap 'Not as successful as we should have been', was not expressed; instead it was replaced by a softer answer. 'We enjoyed moderate success, more towards the end of my commission than at the outset.'

'And to what would you attribute that?'

Pitt was looking into his bowl and there was no eye contact, while the tone of voice carried no emphasis, yet his guest still felt the need to be guarded in his response. Things had happened in the West Indies upon which he had no wish to dwell, matters he certainly had no desire to openly discuss.

'I would posit good intelligence as the cause.'

'That and no more? It would not, then, be a question of leadership? It seems to me that matters improved markedly following on from your taking over the command.'

'It surprises me you are so well informed.'

'I read a precis prepared for me of what despatches come in from all our overseas possessions, and with the Caribbean I would say the conclusion of better intelligence was there for all to see. Your captures went up markedly in number and Lord Howe was mightily impressed. I'm sure you, and those you took command of, made a pretty penny in prize money, even excluding the recapture of the *Santa Clara*.'

'For which the locals threatened repeatedly to sue me.'

That was a deliberately evasive reply; he had no notion to be questioned on prize monies or to defend a practice that often saw naval officers accused of greed, in effect putting their purse before their duty, given it was not what had motivated him to be so active.

'They have leverage on the colonial courts, and the judges own plantations as well. I'm far from certain they would not have succeeded in having me locked up.'

'A case that would have ended up being appealed in London, where it would have no merit. The Lord Chancellor would have thrown it out.'

'Good Lord Mansfield – a saint in my eyes.'

Pitt's face was a picture as he reacted. If his sister esteemed the man for his judgement on slavery in Britain, it seemed obvious that her brother held him in somewhat less regard. Pitt led a fragile coalition of competing interests, the holding together of which would likely be taxing. Mansfield was, by repute, something of a weathervane.

Conversation was put in abeyance by the removal of dishes and the arrival of several more, as well as a different wine. Pitt had behaved in a more abstemious fashion than at his Three Kings meal, but his glass was never empty and neither was Edward Brazier's, while Lady Harriot was still sipping her first pouring. The conversation became more general and wide ranging than hitherto, this over several courses, more a reflection of society at present until, food consumed, Lady Harriot announced her intention to walk the battlements and take in the air, prior to laying down to rest.

'If you will excuse me, Captain Brazier. My condition demands it.'

He raised himself from his chair, a mark of respect not replicated by her brother.

'I seem to recall your service was not without complications,' Pitt advanced, as soon as she was gone. Given a querying look by his guest, who had a good idea where this might be heading and was reluctant to go there, Pitt added, 'His Majesty would not recall your name fondly.'

'Prince William was in the wrong. Honesty, as well as a Bible oath, obliged me to say so.'

'It is odd, is it not, that our sovereign sees little good in his male brood, but will not have anyone else question their behaviour? How bad was it?'

'I should suspect you had any number of people to inform you of that. If I did not read the numerous furious letters sent home, I was appraised of their contents.'

The eyebrows were raised, the look of enquiry insistent. 'Still.'

'The horse's mouth?'

'Precisely.'

To be utterly frank or fillet the tale? Where did Pitt stand on the matter: with his King and the Prince, or on the side of what was accountable behaviour, even for a royal? It was Pitt draining his glass that gave him an opening.

'The effect of drink on Prince William is not good. He becomes free of restraint and loses the ability to appreciate how his behaviour is perceived.'

The eyes narrowed as did the cheeks. 'I see you're no stranger to diplomatic obfuscation, sir.'

Brazier refused to be cowed. 'Do I sense irritation?'

'You sense I asked a question, to which I would like a plain answer.'

'I reckon myself to be in the steep tub on the matter as it is. Why would I venture into an area that might well make matters worse?'

'And if I said I have no opinion on the subject?'

'Then I would be bound to ask why it has been raised.'

'Would it surprise you to know that His Majesty takes a keen interest as to whom is appointed to command his ships of war?'

Time to equivocate. 'He sees them as personal possessions, then?'

'It is a fault in monarchs to believe so, Captain Brazier. What do you think he would say if he saw your name put forward for a line-of-battle ship, a seventy-four?'

'Given your previous remarks, I cannot believe it would pass without comment.'

Pitt threw his head back and laughed. 'Comment would not be the half of it. More like a display of outraged spleen and some ripe blasphemy.'

'I believe you're telling me I can wish for the moon in the article of a command.'

'Even King George is not immune to the taking of advice from his ministers. He has many people who wish to whisper in his ear, but it is true to say that he generally listens with care to what I say.'

Brazier sat back, toying with his glass, as the two men engaged in a mutual stare, which had within it curiosity but no aggression. 'I cannot help but believe that countering the King's prejudice would not come without a price.'

'I daresay you have been in Deal long enough to measure how my name is taken?'

That switch did not make sense, but had to be responded to, which he tried to do with a pun. 'Forgive me if I'm too forthright, but cess tends to combine too readily with pit.'

The response came from a fellow very far from amused, even if he tried to cover it.

'Which I take as a compliment. I have tried to curtail smuggling over several years, with little success. As you will no doubt have heard, I had the boats of the villains torched out of sheer frustration, not that it was easy. The navy would not assist, while I had to press very hard indeed to get the soldiers I required to carry out the task.'

The tone became seriously bitter. 'Everyone sees romance where there is nothing but foul delinquency, even as it has become more organised. It's no longer just single luggers risking a small cargo, though that is still prevalent. But I sense an ordered enterprise in excess of that, depriving us of unimaginable sums of money, and such are the vested interests both here and in Whitehall that I struggle to gather the means to curtail it.'

Pitt wandered off into the constraints that applied even to a King's First Minister, working with a slender parliamentary majority held together by the constant trading of advantage. There were many things that he wished to do to improve the nation's finances but could not, for they too often touched on the incomes or interests of the members, both peers and commoners, the latter ever careful of the views and needs of those who elected them.

'They will not see such things effected and, I am sorry to add, too many are themselves the consumers of untaxed goods.'

'There are many who see a bargain, not a problem.'

'Creatures of no integrity, who would sit idly by to see the nation bankrupt. As for the application of law here, it is near blind to contraband. The magistrates and justices, when I charge them with negligence, behave as though it is some kind of innocent lark.'

'I'm wondering where this is leading?'

'The only way to end it is by the gathering of incriminating evidence, so strong it cannot be brushed aside. That, given my reputation, I cannot even begin to gather. If I can show how extensive it really is and the true and staggering amount of the losses, I may be able to get the support in Parliament I need to put a stopper on it. For that I require help.'

The direct look aided enlightenment. 'You're not asking I enquire on your behalf?'

'You are without employment and unlikely to receive any without my help. You thus have time and know the value of what we speak when we talk of intelligence. That which I cannot gather could much more easily be sought by someone with an unsullied local reputation.'

'I'm afraid I must decline.'

Pitt sat back in contemplation for a few seconds before speaking again, and his tone matched the primary sentiment. 'It gives me little pleasure to say this, but I wonder if you would welcome an enquiry into the sudden and peculiar death of Admiral Hassel.'

CHAPTER EIGHTEEN

'Why would that have any bearing? Admiral Hassall died in bizarre circumstances, I acknowledge, but—?'

Pitt was looking at him in a way not inclined to induce a feeling of ease, while Brazier sought to create an expression that showed, he hoped, a combination of query and mystification. There was a case to answer and he knew he was dealing with a sharp brain – few more so – which presaged this conversation going in a difficult direction, one he would struggle to deflect.

It was another of those occasions when silence served better than words and, as with Flaherty, he was dealing with a fellow who knew the game, willing to play it with a cold and steady stare. The length of time that lasted indicated, perhaps, that Pitt was hoping for some kind of explanation, but he was not going to get one and nor was he going to hear anything that had not been included in that despatch.

'Bizarre?' Pitt said finally, picking up his wine glass and draining it. 'A curious word, is it not?'

'Fits the bill, I would say.'

A twitch of the lips, but far from a smile. 'You were at sea when it happened, I believe.'

'I was hove to off Kingston harbour the very night he died, waiting

219

for the tide to make possible an entry into what is a difficult port, given the direction of the prevailing wind.'

'Yet you were told it had occurred.'

'I was, come morning.'

'Yet still you waited until you had dropped anchor to act. Faced with news, you chose not to boat in and investigate the circumstances? I find that strange.'

'It seemed unnecessary given he was already dead. I was told he had been laid out and the doctors were examining the body.'

How in the name of the devil did Pitt know all this, and why was he probing? If Brazier had failed to go ashore in his barge, did he know the reverse had occurred? That he had been visited by his fellow captains aboard *Diomede*, five in number if you included a pair of masters and commanders, and that did not include Hassall's flag captain, who had stayed aboard his own vessel? If Pitt was querying the nature of the admiral's death, so had he and to little effect.

He could recall the wary responses his questions produced, just as vivid the memory of the way those present had assumed him complicit in what had happened, this because the villainy of Hassall had been the subject of prior discussions. Had he not said before weighing, something would have to be done to curtail his superior's greed, while writing to the Admiralty, which had been posited, would not serve without irrefutable proof?'

Pitt had been right about intelligence: it was the lifeblood of any attempt to enforce the Navigation Acts and Admiral Sir Lowell Hassall had been in receipt of a great deal. The Royal Navy had spies in every port from Charleston to Caracas, so the various Caribbean commands were well furnished with information. Just as vital was the local ear to the ground, picking up unguarded gossip from subjects of the Crown only too willing to aid others in transgressing the law.

All of this information came to Hassall, ostensibly to be disbursed to his cruising captains, thus ensuring all shared in prosperity. The devious old sod had aimed for the precise opposite, setting up an arrangement with a one-time French privateer, to whom he gifted what information was gleaned, which allowed the rogue to intercept a goodly number of the blockade runners before the navy.

Under normal circumstances, when his inferiors captured a vessel a commanding admiral under whose flag they sailed would get an eighth of the value on what was a very well-remunerated station. By this arrangement he was thought to be garnering half of the value – worse, he was depriving his own officers of any share at all.

'Your despatch stated his wish to be buried at sea, which was carried out with some alacrity?'

'Yes.'

'Arrived at how?'

'I daresay he mentioned it in passing, but I can't quite recall.'

'Lady Hassall was adamant in his wish to be buried in the graveyard at Church Stretton, where the rest of his family are interred in a family vault. Indeed, he is reputed to have asked that, in the event of him expiring in the Caribbean, his body should be returned home, preserved in a puncheon of rum. Lord Howe was beset by her on the very matter and he could only plead climate as an excuse, supposing that to demand a swift disposal of a cadaver. Of course, with no body . . .'

It was Pitt's turn to leave a question hanging in the air, one to which his guest could only respond with raised eyebrows. The doctors had spoken of contusions on the arms and a bruise of the head, which they had accepted might have been brought in the struggle to fight off the venom killing him.

'I wrote to ask Sir Joseph Banks about snakes,' Pitt continued. 'He replied there were none venomous in Jamaica, but any number on the French and other sugar islands. It is therefore curious there was such a creature, not only in Sir Lowell's bedroom, but in a position to sink its fangs into him.'

'There are slaves on Jamaica who keep snakes. We could only suppose one had escaped.'

'To be killed itself not long after the foul deed.'

'I doubt you can call foul a snake doing that for which it was created.'

'It would apply if it had been introduced into Sir John's bedroom by human agency.'

The laugh was manufactured. 'A fanciful notion.'

'Not according to a certain correspondent, who sent an anonymous missive saying that very thing had happened.' Brazier felt a strange sensation in his stomach, though his humorous look remained fixed. 'It arrived on the same mail packet as your despatch. It was also reported that you and Sir Lowell had engaged in a very heated argument prior to your leaving on that aforementioned cruise. Is there any truth in the story?'

'The admiral could be choleric and sometimes it was necessary to question his judgement, forcibly so. As his immediate subordinate it fell to me to do so, but I was not alone in wondering at some of his dispositions. Other captains shared and voiced my concerns.'

'And the nature of the argument?'

'It was felt he was ordering us to place our vessels in locations where the chances of interdicting illegal traffic were limited.'

'And it was not just you who thought so.'

'It was all of his captains, with the exception of the fellow who commanded his flagship, but he rarely left harbour and was certainly not in the business of enforcing the Navigation Acts. That is work for frigates and sloops.'

Brazier could well recall the dispute alluded to, as well as the level of noise the pair had generated in Hassall's' private quarters; it could have been overheard, for they ended up exchanging loud insults. Brazier was called a liar and nothing but an ingrate, his commanding officer cursed as a common thief, as well as a disgrace to the service. Even faced with verbal evidence, allied to the total absence of any captures by his own officers, Hassall had forcibly denied any knowledge of the accusations.

Capturing cargoes was only one part of the criminality: they only had value when sold, something that could only take place without attracting unwelcome attention in a small number of harbours, these in French Haiti, Cuba and the Spanish coastal possessions of the Gulf of Mexico. Unknown to Hassall and without orders, Brazier had placed a watch on these, using his own crew as well as midshipmen in pinnaces and mast-rigged cutters.

They had observed obvious captures being taken into Jacmel in Southern Haiti, escorted by a sloop under a fleur-de-lys pennant, before returning to Kingston to tell their captain. Following the row and Hassall's denial – he had threatened his accuser with a court martial and dismissal from the service – Brazier weighed in HMS *Diomede*, his aim to locate the Frenchman and take his ship. He would fetch him back to Kingston if he could, which, once he confessed the connection, would result in a hanging for him and disgrace for the admiral.

In doing so he had left behind an ambiguous message about action being necessary and one someone on station had taken as a signal to act, showing great ingenuity in their method as well as an extensive knowledge of arcane local customs. Venomous snakes were brought in from Guadeloupe and Martinique to be used in wildly ecstatic religious ceremonies amongst the slave population, both heavily frowned on but impossible to stop.

Brazier had missed his quarry, which had taken him swiftly back to Kingston, to find Hassall dead. As now the senior officer on station, and suspecting a combination of his words and the actions of others had led to the man's demise, he quickly ordered that burial at sea unaware, till his valet protested, of what Hassel had desired on the matter of being sent home for interment.

That put to one side he was left free to study the latest intelligence the admiral had acquired: what he found sent him rushing back to sea again, piling on all sail to make an unexpected rendezvous off Veracruz.

'So,' Pitt said, using his fingers to sum up, 'we have a dead admiral who expired in the most strange circumstances, from a non-native species of snake, and no body, it being at the bottom of the sea? One goes from bizarre to extraordinary.'

'It is easy to make what is innocent sound suspicious.'

'True, but it's always an engaging diversion to think of how you could kill someone without any danger of being apprehended for the crime, is it not?'

'For a devious mind, possibly. I'm a simple sailor, who prefers to look into the eyes of those with whom I am quarrelling. I'm curious as to whom you would visit such a fate upon, given the chance.'

'Oh, it is mere fancy,' Pitt shrugged. 'But I suspect a mind that will contemplate such an act may also be one capable of the act and, if the agency of the deed falls to another, so much the better?'

It was time to fight back. 'All this speculation is based on an anonymous letter, you say?'

'It is.'

'You seem to be convinced of the veracity of this missive.'

'Not convinced. Made curious, enough so to wonder at what further enquires might produce.'

There was a simple way out of this, but it was also impossible. He could name the fellow captains he had left behind and, if no one had admitted to the exploit when they told him of it, at least one had to have either put it in train or even helped to carry it out. Another memory was their refusal to do anything other than display collective responsibility, in which they were keen to include their new commanding officer.

Ditching them did not enter his thinking; they were his

contemporaries, his fellow officers, and he would not shame himself by trying to preserve his own skin through sacrificing theirs. His only option was to challenge Pitt, which he proceeded to do.

'The only way to answer the problem you set is to institute those enquiries. But first you must find the person who composed the accusation, which I posit would be far from easy, given they clearly have no wish to be identified.'

'As yet I am undecided. But I could ask the Lord Chancellor to act on the letter and clap anyone considered to be complicit in gaol, pending the result.' The look became crafty. 'Six weeks to the Caribbean at least, six back and Lord only knows how many to seek the truth. Then, of course, weather might extend the time. Hardly a comfortable situation to be in, I would say.'

'That sounds like blackmail.'

'Then for once in my life, I have struck the perfect note.'

How many witnesses had there been to his row with Hassall? It could run into dozens given the location, his accommodation also housing the Naval Headquarters. Then there was the lack of discretion shown by both parties, not only in the volume, but the subject. Had he threatened the man with the fate he eventually suffered? He could not clearly recollect doing so, but he had been in a high enough passion at the time and he had come close to doing so subsequently to others.

He took out his watch and flipped it open. 'I fear I have occupied too much of your time.'

'Your answer, sir?'

'What answer?'

'To the notion posed earlier.'

'That I, a stranger in these parts, should seek to expose activity which, by its very nature, is clandestine? I dislike the notion of incarceration, sir, but that is preferable to a knife in the ribs or a marlin spike on the crown. I know no one and, if I do not have knowledge of

Deal, I can be sure they will barely trust each other on such a matter, let alone an outsider.'

'Of which I am doubly cursed.'

'I can appreciate your desperation, but I must say to you, find someone else.'

'Not even for a ship of the line?'

Brazier stood. 'I thank you for the dinner, Mr Pitt, as well as the tale someone has invented to amuse idle minds. I will see it as an obligation to return the compliment of the table, if nothing else. Now I bid you good day.'

If he had expected disappointment, it was not granted; Pitt looked positively smug. He too stood, to execute a minimal bow and call for a servant to fetch Brazier's hat.

'There is one more thing. Mr Garlick tells me you have a connection to the Tulkingtons of Cottington Court?' It was pointless to say the sod talked too much: both men knew it already. 'Is that true?'

'I cannot see that I am required to give an answer to something that is not of your concern.'

'The family are very prominent locally, though really that applies to Henry Tulkington, who is the local Collector of Taxes and, I must say, assiduous in the pursuit of the duty. There's never any question as to the accuracy of his accounts. If all those holding such offices were to apply themselves as he does, the Exchequer would be in very much better shape.'

'So?'

'It is often speculated that smuggling is opportunistic, Captain Brazier: a case of small luggers or fishing smacks making dashes across the water when circumstances permit. There is that, of course, but given the amount of goods I suspect are being landed and sold, I posit, as I said earlier, there is something of greater substance afoot.'

'The proof being?'

'If you were to put the assumed consumption of tea alone against the revenues collected, as I have done, you would have no doubts. It has become a national disgrace. I've been told some traders even coach down to Kent from London to collect what is landed, which hardly fits with speculation.'

Pitt paused to see if that brought on a reaction, only to be faced with none. His guest was not going to be drawn.

'What it indicates, Captain Brazier, is an industry and to create and maintain such a trade requires resources, while nothing I see on Deal Beach leads me to suspect it is organised from there. No, what is taking place requires a high degree of application and no small sums of money with which to invest. Are there people locally who could run such an enterprise, yet still remain in the shadows?'

'Perhaps?' was the guarded response.

'No, the wit to contrive such an extensive trade is not within the capacity of country farmers or Deal boatmen to manage. I suspect it to be organised from London, but that does not debar any tendril of the process being local. Indeed, it would have to be, and I suspect, if there's a weak link with which to break the whole thing apart, it is to be found around this coast.'

'I am still at a loss to know what you're driving at.'

'With a connection to Tulkington, you would be bound to mingle with the most prosperous people in this part of the county, perhaps the very folk who could form an association to facilitate this nefarious trade.'

'You mean I should become your spy, using as an entrée a family of which I wish to be a part?'

'An unguarded word at some social gathering might produce untold results.'

'How different is the dignity that a King's officer holds dear, as compared to that of a politician.'

The smile was thin. 'Pragmatism overrides dignity when the nation is in need.'

* * *

227

It was a pensive naval officer who walked Bonnie back to find the note and sketch from Betsey. Joe Lascelles had got to work and cleaned Quebec House to his own standard, using vinegar. He was also quick to bring him coffee, the odours of both bringing back the familiar smell of life at sea. The coffee was sipped as he read Betsey's note, which had him laying plans.

Tempted to try that gate now, he had to acknowledge it was too late in the day – and besides, he could not get his conversation with Pitt out of his mind, not least that in asking him, the fellow must truly be desperate. How odd that a man who should be able to marshal all the power of the state seemed so hamstrung.

'John?' he called, the white smiling teeth coming quick. 'Do you recall the loss of Admiral Hassall?'

'From what I heard, it weren't no loss.'

'Heard?'

The smile evaporated. 'You sure you wish an answer to that, Capt'n?'

'Why not?'

A reply was not swift in coming; it took a direct look from Brazier before he spoke. 'Word was you threatened to skewer the old sod. An' you used high words, did you not?'

'Common knowledge?'

'Ship was full of it.'

'Anything else talked of?'

'If I were to say that the crew reckoned we would never have taken *Santa Clara* with the admiral alive, does that add up to an answer?'

In his naval career Edward Brazier had experienced thieving, first as a midshipman, then as a divisional lieutenant and a captain, even if it was far from endemic in warships. Mostly the crew dealt with matters without recourse to a blue coat, but sometimes it got so out of hand as to require action. Rare on a frigate, even manned with three hundred souls at full complement, it was many times more likely to arise on the largest line-of-battle ships, carrying over eight hundred men, especially in wartime when many were pressed landsmen.

One of the things revealed was the way culprits went from first stealing trifles to seeking more and more valuable booty, until things that were barely missed morphed into serious thievery. Sir Lowell Hassall had been no different to the meanest common seaman in that regard. Having lined his pockets on the backs of his officers, and due to be replaced, he had alerted his Frenchman to a Spanish ship carrying silver, leaving Veracruz for Cádiz, and sent him after it – perhaps as a final act of treachery, which would net him the great fortune he so obviously craved.

With solid information and in a fast sailing frigate, as well as a crack and fully trained crew, Brazier had intercepted the privateer as well as his recent capture. The fight had been brief and bloody, the French barquentine standing no chance against a Royal Navy frigate boasting thirty-two well-worked cannon, each firing of a ball every two minutes. Brazier had shown no mercy in reducing the enemy vessel to matchwood till she began to sink, which sent a message to those crewing the Spanish capture: surrender or die.

He arrived back in Kingston with his lower deck full of prisoners, many with wounds, and the *Santa Clara* crewed by his own men. He then sent his fellow commanders to sea to intercept other ships Hassel would have kept hidden so their crews would have their rewards, staying in port himself until his new C-in-C arrived in a replacement frigate, at which point Brazier could return home. HMS *Diomede*, after three years in the Caribbean, was in much need of a proper dockyard.

Sitting here now and thinking on what Joe had said, or more vitally what he had not said, was a cause for some concern. If it was always true the lower deck knew much more than they should about what was going on, the notion they might have an inkling of what had really happened to Hassall was worrying.

He could ask his servant for a straight answer, but did he really want one? More to the point, there were still men out there who had been serving at the time, while the notion of anything being kept to one ship was nonsense. If William Pitt did seek out the truth, how many members of those ships' crews would be only too willing to talk?

Even if they were not believed or could provide no proof, enough might be uncovered to expose the identity of the person who wrote that anonymous letter. He could speculate till the cows came home, but the possibilities were endless. There were clerks in Hassall's HQ who could have overheard the argument: masters and pursers aboard the ships, all of whom had the ability to write and, more importantly, to get the letter onto the packet returning to England, without questions being asked.

The other point Pitt had made, regarding the Tulkingtons – really Henry – he had dismissed before he got out of the keep. He had no interest in smuggling whosoever was engaged in it, and he was certainly not going to use Betsey's family to expose anyone they knew.

Harry Spafford was already drunk and it was before midday, but that was nothing unusual. His father found him in an upstairs room in the Hope and Anchor, the two whores with whom he had spent the night still slumbering in the bed, added to a bill downstairs which his father had to settle. Once in the room and facing his son, Daniel Spafford sought to chastise him but, as ever, it was water off a duck's back.

'If you have your purse, Pa, I need your kindness, for mine is empty and I owe these two charming ladies their fee.'

For a man who lived by a rough trade, he could not apply to his lad the beating he would have readily handed out to another who angered him. There was not much Spafford senior had affection for in this world, but before him now, even in his unkempt state, was the one chink in a very hard and determined exterior.

'This has to end, Harry,' he said, waving a weary arm to take in the room; no description was necessary.

'It will, Pa, I promise.' The eyes wetted in a way the youngster had perfected through long practice. 'But just this once—'

'You might be needed this night, or one close to come, and you have to be sober. There's work to be done an' it won't be gentle.'

Harry pulled himself to what he thought was upright, which was close if you took out the swaying and the inability to keep straight his head. A fist was made and lifted, while he tried in a slurring voice to sound bellicose.

'Ever ready, is Harry Spafford, and God help the cove who dares to cross him cause . . .'

The fist made useless circles while an attempted punch unbalanced him so he staggered into his father's arms.

'Get your coat, you're going home.'

'It would serve to take a bottle or two along, would it not, to ease getting through the day?'

For once the temper went. Harry was grabbed by his shirt collar and shaken violently, an act that brought forth weak pleading and genuine tears. It was telling that the son was almost immediately joined in these by his parent, who could not abide to see all his hopes for a future dashed, yet could find no way to alter that with which he was landed.

'Come on,' was the gruff response.

He produced a couple of shillings to throw on the bed, picked up Harry's coat off the floor, put his arm round his son and directed him towards the door.

CHAPTER NINETEEN

Waiting for a bloody response from Tulkington, Spafford had been mightily reassured, as well as pleased with himself, when none came. He had decided, prior to his thieving, to try and keep secret it was he who had robbed him, not that he doubted he would be suspected. So his instructions had been to steal, if possible, barrels of brandy and bales of tobacco, goods easy to shift, there being many outlets. Every tavern owner was a willing customer, but he was not foolish enough to tempt anyone in Deal.

Instead he sold everything on as bulk to a fellow smuggler in Faversham, with the excuse he was being hounded by the Revenue and he needed to shift it quick. Such a bonus was gratefully received from a contact who had more trouble than his coastal contemporaries. Faversham lay at the end of a long tidal creek which led to the Thames Estuary, one which a couple of local Revenue men could keep watch on with much more ease than eight miles of open beach, so any running of cargo was ten times more perilous.

The price received went to his men, on the very good grounds that they would not be shy when he suggested what was to come next: another scheme he wished to execute. Any minor concern that his identity, or that of the men he led, had been rumbled was laid to rest when he heard John Hawker was out and about seeking information in the taverns of Deal.

It tickled him to hear how careful he was being in his enquiries, which confirmed not only that Tulkington was in the dark, but he did not want the fact of his losses, as well as how they had been purloined, to get out. To do so might encourage others to have a try.

Not being hounded allowed him the time to rein in his errant son. Harry had been brought home to Worth and right now he was locked in a room, pleading for drink which was not forthcoming. No one was allowed in except his father who, perhaps for the first time in his life, had decided to harden his too-soft heart.

There was another reason to lock him up at home; with what he was engaged in, he could not have his son as a loose cannon running around and vulnerable. Spafford was not fool enough to think Tulkington would never make the connection between him and depredations on his goods. What better way to take revenge than a drunk easy to lay hands on?

'It's for your own good, Harry. Now eat these vittles I've brought you and reckon your torments be over in a few weeks. Think on it, boy, to be able to look on the world with a clear eye.'

This was responded to with a stream of spittle-filled blasphemy, which Spafford *père* took in an outwardly stoic fashion. It was only outside the relocked door he allowed himself any expression of how wounding it was to hear. Even then, that required to be tempered, in case he was under observation; the leader of a band of hard bargains could not be seen to be weak.

Behind his back there were those who would have cheerfully seen to Harry Spafford permanently, sober or drunk, given he was inclined to treat them as of no account. Not even his father talked to them as the brat did, as useless ignorant sods, knowing he could do so only because his blood provided protection. Then there was Daisy Trotter, who had been like an uncle to Harry since birth; what he thought was never clear and none were prepared to risk a word misplaced when he was around.

Not openly discussed was that Daisy had his own problem, one he shared only with Spafford.

'Why would a body be asking about you?'

'Is it me, Dan, or some wench called Daisy being sought?'

Spafford was tempted to make a joke about there being little difference since they were both likely to be whores, but held back; there were things not even he could say to Trotter in safety.

'Has to be a wench, or whoever it is would be a calling in at Basil the Bulgar's house. Not like to find much anywhere else.'

'An' not much there, if he's not of the brotherhood.'

Daisy was not one to frequent taverns, indeed he drank little and visited Deal rarely, so Dan Spafford was curious as to how this worry had come about. His honest ear, if he was not by his side, was to be found in the Molly-house just along from Portobello Court in Middle Street. There, if what Spafford had been told was true – he had never crossed the threshold of the place himself – ships coming into the Downs to anchor brought with them a steady supply of comely lads, some of the right persuasion, others seeking a way to fund their drinking by selling their bodies.

It had to be supposed that Daisy consorted with the latter type, for he was no portrait with his wheezy, skinny frame and cheerless manner, and nor was he humorous company. If his money was not spent on drink, there was only one place it could be going, but that too was not a question to be asked. Let him go his own way and no harm done, as long as he was there when needed, which he ever was.

'Happen we could put a couple of feelers out there to find out, just in case.'

'If you like,' Spafford responded, thinking it daft. His mind was more on the questions John Hawker was asking. 'But not for long: we've another tickle to carry out.'

'We'll have to mask up this time, lads, like proper highwaymen, for we will be out in the light of day.'

The jovial mood in which this was imparted would, Spafford hoped, calm any nerves. They knew as well as he did that John Hawker was asking about and one or two had been eyeballed by him, making no secret of how uncomfortable they had found it. He had been out in the cutter, with four men to row, the previous night, to sit silently off Leathercote Point and observe another Tulkington cargo come in, this time without interference.

He intended to sting and it would again be where his rival least expected it, but there was no boat to transport them this time. To get to where they needed to be, they must go on foot and in pairs and by different routes, so as not to attract attention. The notion he might take Harry along died in the reluctance of the object and, in truth, he was far from ready for action, if he could ever have been said to be so. His father thought he looked like death warmed up.

Harry was weak, and not just in the article of drink. He had grown up with his mother's bonny looks, for Welsh Mary had the same corn-coloured hair and sapphire-blue eyes. But she had been a fiery creature, something her bairn had failed to inherit. He could not say that now about the likeness; dissipation had made the cheeks puffy and left bags under those blue eyes, and the lower lip – too often in a pout – seemed slack.

Mary had gone before her son was truly weaned; to where, both father and son had no idea, the former being left to raise him. He was sure he had done his best, though in the early years he had been on the Baltic run and away for long stretches, which left the boy in any hands that could be found.

Once he took up smuggling there was money, and so attempts were made to school the lad, the aim for him a less felonious future. It had failed, as had everything else tried. Harry had so exhausted the patience of the Canterbury schoolmaster he had been sent home, accused of laziness, whoring and drunkenness, that before he had even reached full maturity.

'If he's not to come, I need you to stay and look after him, Daisy. I don't trust another and what I have in mind would scarce suit you anyway.'

That got a gap-toothed grin. 'Happy to oblige, Dan: my back is still achy from hauling those casks in St Margaret's Bay. You get along and leave Harry to me, an' I'll have a stew on the grate hook for when you return.'

Which Dan Spafford did, as well as the men he led, walking the roads around the villages with the same destination in mind: a wood on the edge of a wide track which ran from St Margaret's village, across the road to Dover and on to Martin, up and past a mill at the top of the hill, where it split to run to various points on the map. The part of the track where they had gathered was not visible from the high ground on either side, the route dipping into a deep dell.

Dolphin, who had set out at first light, was where he should be, the cart in which he had travelled now up a track to a fallow field and backed into a small copse. The horses had been unhitched but were still in harness, taken further on to graze on long halters which would prevent them wandering. The rest of the band came in, Spafford included, to partake of the bread and cheese provided till one, who went by the name of Barky for his loud voice, was sent off up the lane to act as a lookout.

'Are you so sure it'll come, Dan?' asked a weary-looking Dolphin.

'The man we're pricking is a creature of habit – has become so through too long being unchallenged.'

Barky was only to shout if he sensed danger, so his running figure was enough to alert them it was clear. Masks were pulled up, hats pulled down as two pistols, preloaded and primed, were taken out from under canvas. The rumble of the cartwheels on the dry rutted road soon became audible, as well as the squeal of a lever brake applied to stop it running away on the steep downhill slope, which would pressure the backs of the horses.

As it came close to the bottom the carter cracked his traces to get up a bit of a pace, this to take the first part of the up slope, not that it lasted for long. The cart soon slowed to barely a walk, at which point Spafford, his face well hidden, stepped out to block the route.

'Stand, fellow,' he called, waving his pistol, 'and haul on that there brake.'

There was a pause until he complied, to then sneer, 'Someone's had you for a dupe, mate. You won't get much for a load of chalk.'

The rest of his men came out from the trees to surround their quarry, which had the carter demand who the hell they were.

'Best get down, friend. For we knows what's hidden under that chalk, and it ain't somethin' to sow on the fields.'

'An' if I say no to that?'

Dan Spafford smiled, seeking to convey the notion was foolish, until he realised it would not be seen. 'Then I has to ask myself if I can give you time to say your prayers, afore I put a ball in your heart.'

Compliance was slow, but eventually the carter climbed down to be replaced by Dolphin who, with help from his mates on the horse bridles, backed the cart up so it could turn into the field. Tulkington's man was dragged along behind until, out of sight of the road, he was lashed to a tree, a blindfold put on as a precaution. The canvas covering the contraband was lifted carefully for, if it had been used to hide the load on Tulkington's cart, it would serve the same purpose on Spafford's, though it was enquired about as to why the load needed to be shifted at all. Why not steal the cart and the horses hauling it as well?

Daniel Spafford showed a patience to which his crew were unaccustomed as he explained. What was stolen would have to be disposed of and, while shifting illegal goods would be easy, a horse and cart could cause problems, for that would involve dealing with people not in the trade: folk who might blether.

'No; we leave it here and the carter with it, to be found whenever. But a cart will be seen going through Martin as it should, and be remarked upon.' He chuckled as he added, 'Where it goes after that will be the mystery.'

* * *

Harry Spafford, sat back to the wall on his bed, showed little interest when the door to his locked room was opened to reveal Daisy Trotter, he carrying a tray on which sat a bowl of soup, with wedges of bread and cheese, as well as a pitcher of pressed apple. His interest perked up when he noticed that, unlike his father, Daisy had shut the door but failed to lock it and the key was still outside. This had the younger man lift his head and smile – one which, with his looks, even a bit ravaged as they were, had always been winsome.

'So Pa's off on his thieving?'

'He told you?'

'Asked if I wanted along, hoped I did.' The plate and pitcher were placed on a table and Harry stood. 'Never said where, though, or what he was after.'

'As like as not you don't care.'

Harry had come close to the table to hold out a hand. 'Look at that, Daisy. Bet yours ain't as steady.'

'An' the better you look for it, Harry, too. More akin to your old self.'

Daisy slightly recoiled as Harry's hand gently stretched out to stroke his cheek. Renewed eye contact showed the blue eyes to be soft and with a hunger in them, which persisted as the gap between them closed, until the older man could feel the heat of his breath.

'Gets lonely in here, Daisy; a body wants a bit of warmth.' A hand was placed on Harry's chest but there was little pressure in the push. 'Don't tell me you ain't dreamt on it, Daisy, cause I've seen it in your look more'n once.'

'Don't mean owt. You're Dan's boy.'

There was a slightly desperate quality to the protest, one of a man caught in a white lie. He had known this lad from a bairn, watched him grow and felt longings he convinced himself were, if anything, maternal. If there had been temptations, they were ones to which he had never succumbed. Yet how many times, in the Molly-house, when a ship came in and a crew with it, had he sought out youths who looked like and had the colouring of Harry Spafford?

'I could be your boy, Daisy, if you so desire.' Daisy shook his head furiously, to see Harry smile and slowly wet his lips. 'I was not shy of it when I was at school; candles snuffed and in a dark dormitory, there was pleasure a' plenty.'

'I'm not a schoolboy.'

'Neither was the master,' came the husky-voiced reply, 'an' I was one of his special boys.'

Daisy broke eye contact by dropping his gaze slightly, so the headbutt was a shock which did what Harry Spafford desired: it stunned Daisy Trotter enough to let him skip by and out the door, which was quickly slammed and locked. Inside, Trotter was hauling on the latch with one hand while trying to stop the flow from his nose with the other, his shouts of fury muffled by both blood and wood.

Not that they would have been heard; Harry Spafford had grabbed his coat and was heading out into the open, on his way to Deal at a rush, given he had no idea when his pa would return. He needed to be somewhere he could not be found well before that, and it would have to be a place where he could get the drink he so craved. Money he never thought of, for his credit was good. Everyone knew his sire, just as they knew Daniel Spafford would always meet his son's bills.

It was dark by the time the cart got back to Worth, to be taken into a barn where it could be hidden from sight, the men who had come with it drifting into the house, their leader the last.

'Where's Daisy?'

That got negative mumbles, shakes of the head, some shrugs and a couple of moans about there being nothing to eat. Dan Spafford went looking and that took him to Harry's room, where he found his oldest friend with a bloodstained shirt, a broken nose, the makings of two black eyes and an unconvincing explanation.

239

CHAPTER TWENTY

Henry Tulkington, being utterly unaware of the latest ravages on his enterprise, was sat in the Lincoln's Inn chambers of his half-uncle. To an outside observer it would have been remarked there was nothing of a similarity between the pair. Dirley Tulkington was twenty-five years Henry's senior and of an age to have a full head of flowing silver hair and, given he wore a wig for his legal duties, glad to go without it when not in court. His fleshy jowls showed the need to be regularly shaved: not stubble on a man too fastidious to allow such a thing, but a discernible late-day shadow which continued on and down to the double folds of loose skin under his chin.

In discussing their trade, Dirley was ever alert to what was in the wind in Whitehall especially William Pitt's efforts at reform, which took in not just that of the nation's finances but his attempts to make more efficient the whole business of government. A weather eye had to be kept on how it would impact on their business. At this very moment Pitt was pressing the fellow who held the office of Master of Posts to sell his position to the government, using the threat of legislation to force him to accept the price of eighty thousand pounds.

'Insult, of course,' Dirley intoned. 'It's worth twice that in profit. But it will have to be accepted. Even the Whigs support the Tories on that particular matter.'

'Are they then willing to have their private correspondence read by Pitt's spies?'

'He's promised measures against intrusion.' This was said in such a way as to indicate it was not a thing to be relied upon. 'But we will be required to act, for a time, as if there are none.'

Henry nodded slowly, aware of what the older man was implying. Until they knew the post was sound in government hands, all their communications would have to be by private messenger. The other matter on which Pitt was pressing rated as more important. He desperately wanted to reform the Revenue Service, which was scoffed at by the older Tulkington.

'He'll whistle to get any changes to the Revenue sinecures. Damn silly thing to fiddle with in the first place, given it can only be bought out at an enormous price. He can scarce afford it and bring down the public debt at the same time.'

'He is passionate about it, Uncle,' Henry said, with grim sincerity, 'and judging by the way he has behaved in Deal, one cannot doubt it. It would serve if Lord North tossed him out of Walmer Castle.'

'Put your mind at rest, Henry. If he gets too high-handed on that front it will bring down his administration. He might be able to browbeat the Master of Posts, who has little political support, but here he will be dealing with parliamentarians who draw valuable remunerations and they will not stand still to have their purses washed out.'

It was one of the great advantages to the smuggling fraternity that the person given the office and perquisites of the Revenue, by custom a method of securing political allegiance, was never the one to carry out the duties. Such gifts of income without exertion were the mainstay of all governments, Pitt's included, even if he was known to deplore the practice. It was also the kind of gift that the sovereign valued highly, a way to ensure that which King George wanted to get through parliament was supported.

The lucky placeman, in the case of the Revenue, would then

241

employ at a much lower cost the actual bodies to carry out the work. Of course, there was a great difference between the stipend that such sinecures brought in and that which was expended on those carrying out the duties, which did nothing for application and in many cases caused it to be seriously hampered.

The man who held the office for Kent, called the Riding Officer of Customs, had been in possession of the position since before the present George ascended the throne. Elderly now, he was not a fellow to ever mount a horse – indeed he had to be aided into his carriage. He was also a person well known to Dirley Tulkington, they dining and gambling at the same St James's clubs. Henry's uncle had always been able to assure himself and his nephew of two things about the Riding Officer: his inability to win at cards and, as a consequence, the man's parsimony in the matter of both wages and allowances for his people.

'But,' Henry said, with a worried expression, 'he will not live forever.'

'Fear not, Henry: there's a queue for the position when he expires and why would there not be, when the recipient will draw a good income for very little effort?'

'Could you not acquire it?'

'Wouldn't serve, Henry: one remove is best. Besides, I have my chambers to consider.' Seeing a degree of supplication, Dirley added, 'But I do have some influence and it will be bent to ensuring we do not get anyone zealous as a replacement.'

'I fear I must alert you to some losses, Uncle.'

That did not occasion any surprise; losses were a part of the business, usually from the misfortune of a rare misreading of the weather. The Revenue men might be underpaid and generally lazy, but they could not draw a wage if they never caught anyone and, it had to be said, there was the odd occasion when someone employed was too keen for the good of the trade.

One such fellow had caused so much grief to the occasionally enterprising Deal boatmen that they had sought help from John

Hawker, known to be a person who could be relied on to provide a solution. He in turn, unknown to the supplicants, was required to ask of Henry Tulkington what he should do and, as usual, the request produced a typically clever solution.

It was the habit of the Revenue, when they discovered contraband hidden in a cellar – the most obvious place to store heavy objects like kegs of brandy – to not only arrest the owners of the property and confiscate the goods, but to fill in said cellar with beach shingle so it could not be used again. Henry Tulkington, having thought on the matter, suggested to Hawker that burial in such a setting would be a fitting fate for this overeager Preventative, and it should be in one he had seen filled by his own activities.

Carried out as suggested, it could not be done without involving others, which ensured the rumour of a live burial leaked out: little stayed secret in Deal amongst the long-resident inhabitants; it was outsiders who were kept in ignorance. It would have horrified the upright citizens of Upper Deal, but there were not many of those in the Lower Town. The effect on the other Revenue officers was profound and they got the clear message: do not be too active or you might share such a hideous fate.

'These losses did not come about in a way to which we are accustomed. It was, in fact, stolen from under our noses when being landed.'

There was a degree of nervousness in the way that was imparted. Even if Henry controlled the enterprise, he had learnt as much from his Uncle Dirley as he had from his father, so there was a residue of the novice he had once been in the relationship. His explanation was heard in silence, to have those fleshy jowls hit the substantial chest.

'Betrayal? A dissatisfied person you have engaged, perhaps?'

'Remind yourself, Uncle Dirley: I don't engage anyone.'

'Your man Hawker, then?'

Until proved otherwise there was only one possible response. 'I have him as loyal and I'm sure he is careful in his choosing of those beneath him.'

A Dirley finger and thumb were rubbed together in the universal sign for money.

'Greed can make traitors of us all, something I see daily in the Law Courts. If not Hawker, who? That is what you must ask yourself, Henry. But what was filched, as you have listed, does not amount to a great deal and it may just be opportunity was the cause. You have studied the accounts?'

Henry Tulkington rubbed eyes, which had spent until well past midnight over columns of figures. Prior to that he had availed himself of the services of a particular bagnio he visited when in London, one which specialised in providing in multiples that which he craved individually nearer to home. Served and punished by a quartet of beauties, well versed in the giving of both pain and pleasure, he had been near to exhausted even before he began to study the ledgers. Not that he had failed in his diligence; the income was close to his life blood.

'I hope you agree, Uncle, that with Calais paid for the cargo being landed, such a healthy positive balance requires a home?'

'Of course. There's some speculative building being proposed on the Oxford Road in the parish of St Mary-le-Bone. I would suggest we meet with the projectors and offer them assistance since they are having trouble getting funds.'

'On the usual terms?'

Dirley nodded. To an already large portfolio of rented properties would be added several more, secured as repayment for loans on generous terms. Money would make money.

When it came to inviting Edward Brazier to Cottington Court, Betsey Langridge exhibited a degree of cunning. Discussing the matter with her aunt, she suggested it would not look proper for him to call on more than two occasions while Henry was absent. Even that was a number frowned upon; Sarah Lovell thought one visit quite sufficient, but bowed to her niece's persistence.

On the first visit, heavy and persistent rain constrained the notion of walking in the grounds; the suggestion from Brazier that the ladies could, like him on arrival, don oilskins was looked upon askance by the person who must act as chaperone. Thus, confined indoors, conversation was only marginally better than the parlour at Quebec House; if the drawing room was larger, Aunt Sarah was no further off.

Subterfuge was required and Betsey manufactured it by complaining, with a pointed look at her aunt, that the hot water ordered for the making of tea was taking an interminable time to arrive, the obvious hint being that she who ran the household should go and find out why. Sarah Lovell was not going to fall for that and it required no more than a crabbed look to establish the fact, which had Betsey, in a fine display of pique, declaring huffily she would undertake the task.

'I fear the weather is not about to change, Captain Brazier,' Sarah Lovell opined, with, once Betsey was gone, a pointed look out of the window. 'Indeed, if my impression of the swaying treetops is anything to go by it is set to worsen severely, which may make the return to Deal hazardous.'

Brazier knew what was coming and spoke to cut off the suggestion he expected would follow, that of an early departure. 'You must recall my profession, Mrs Lovell. At sea we would call what you see no more than a shower.'

'Then I pity you when you have what we ashore see as a downpour.'

This, delivered with pursed lips, was soon followed by a reference to what would be the muddy and possibly unsafe state of the roads, that countered too with the assurance of the surefootedness of Bonnie. Sat then in mutual silence, Brazier was relieved when Betsey returned, the gloomy black-coated servant at her back, who took a

245

reprimand from the aunt for his tardiness with a blank expression.

The tea, once made, flowed more freely than any subsequent conversation, which led Betsey to make the same observation about the inclement weather, as well as the fact it was not likely to moderate – quite the reverse – which somewhat threw Brazier. The manner in which this was put forward implied that she too would not be unhappy to see him gone and, much as he tried to ignore it, the truth soon became too obvious to ignore.

'Your aunt has already alluded to the possible state of the roads, Mrs Langridge,' was imparted with a stiff countenance. 'And I daresay she cares I should not risk another fall.'

'With which I can only concur, Captain.'

'Then I thank you for the tea and ask that my horse be fetched from the stables.' The speed with which both women stood confused their visitor and he failed to hide it, even more upset that Betsey made a point of looking away and ignoring his distress, to then add insult to injury by proceeding to swiftly leave the room, her parting shot providing the final insult:

'I will have Grady fetch your outdoor garments.'

These had to be put on in the presence of two apparently impatient women. It was in a long oilskin coat and wearing a foul-weather hat of the same material that Brazier nodded farewell to the aunt and took the proffered hand of Betsey, to bestow the ritual kiss. Head bowed, his hat served to hide his anger, which was abated as he felt in her hand a folded piece of paper, this surreptitiously taken.

The hallway was no place to read it and neither could he do so on the way back to Quebec House, it precluded by the teeming rain and his being on horseback. Thus the note stayed inside his riding glove until he made his own hall, to be eagerly studied, not that such required long. Weather permitting, Betsey Langridge would be walking in the woods the next morning on a route that would take her past the broken postern gate around eleven.

'Where are your shipmates, Joe?' he enquired after he had been helped to disrobe, the act leaving a puddle at his feet. Two of his old barge crew had arrived.

'They have gone to the Ship Inn, Capt'n, to take ale and talk nonsense, as ever they do.'

'Then give me back my coat and fetch your own, Joe, for we shall go to join them.'

'And here's me thinkin' you was mad at something, the face you had on as you came through the door.'

'Let us just say I am cheered now, Joe, for I have found the woman I am in pursuit of to have sharp wits.'

It bothered Edward Brazier not one bit that the field he must cross was being ploughed, the fellow egging on the heavy shire horses well able to see him as he rode along by the outer wall of Cottington Court, Bonnie's hooves sinking into the soft ground. If it was necessary to hide the coming assignation from Sarah Lovell – he could think of it in no other terms – he saw no need to do so from anyone else.

South-facing, whatever paint had once coloured the door had long since peeled away, to reveal grey and dried-out oak. Reins in one hand, he pushed with the other at a surface initially quick to yield – that was, until it got stuck. To move it enough for him to squeeze through required a swift boot, which revealed the closest bush, to which he could attach Bonnie's reins: he could not leave her free with the ploughing horses nearby.

Equines by nature were curious creatures who sought company and were competitive as well. She would be bound to go to them, quite possibly with head thrown back and high-stepping hooves, added to a stiff, flaring tail, this to show her sex and superiority. A carrot was produced to mollify her and make up for the lack of grass.

Once through the gap Brazier then had to push his way through the bushes until, clear of them, he could look at his watch, to realise he was a mite early. About to step back into semi-concealment he heard the sound of a bark and, seconds later, the tail-wagging spaniels were racing towards him, Betsey some way behind.

Oddly he felt awkward and wondered if she did too, for this would mark the first occasion in which they would be alone and not under scrutiny. Even if he thought the notion ridiculous he could not shake it, which had him stand still to let her approach, producing a rather fixed smile as he lifted his hat. Betsey stopped several feet away and looked at him in an odd fashion, as if he was a stranger, until she showed her feelings of apprehension by biting her lower lip.

'Can I console you by saying I too am at a loss as to how to proceed?'

'I have no preparation for such an association. I assume you to be less a stranger to it than I.'

Edward Brazier was not one to blush, and anyway, his complexion would not have let it show. But he did feel acute discomfort, for Betsey Langridge would not be the first woman in his life. With his looks, manner and being young, eager and navy, he had been an object of attraction to others, like an occasional married woman seeking pleasure without commitment. He had also frequently dallied with the native women, especially in the possessions of the East India Company.

He had, too, in the past and ashore in England, been a visitor to the better class of bagnio, where the females present went beyond merely singing, dancing and the kind of flattery designed to loosen a customer's purse. He well knew that, in terms of experience, Betsey had only her late husband. Her kind of upbringing, quite apart from her sweet nature, forbade anything else.

'Can I take that as an invitation to advance matters?'

'I came out for a walk, Captain Brazier. Would it not be best I continue?'

'In my company?'

Betsey nodded and he went to join her, she turning away but then making no effort to create a distance between them of the kind that had been a feature of their previous stroll. He was acutely aware of their near-touching elbows and assumed Betsey was too, while proximity allowed the odour of her perfume to fill his nostrils. He realised it also carried the smell of her person, which he found exhilarating.

'I take it we are free from observation?' he murmured.

'But not constraint,' was the slightly nervous response.

Brazier threw back his head and laughed, she stopping and appearing perplexed, the look on her face then turning to enquiry. 'I have not felt like this since I was sporting spots and lost in the reverie of first love, which of course was foolish and came to nothing.'

'It is awkward.'

'Only if we choose to make it so.'

'I am at a loss to know how to make it otherwise.'

'Take my hand, Betsey.'

His he held out, but it was a seeming age before hers left her side and the tremble was obvious, matched by the look of unease on her face. Taking it, he bent to bestow a kiss, no polite peck this time, but one where his lips remained on her yielding flesh for several seconds.

'Do you feel anything?' he asked as he looked up, to see a deeper blush than ever he had witnessed before. Still holding the hand, he raised it to his lips and kissed it again, this time on the fingertips, his eyes steady and holding hers.

'Let us walk, hold hands, talk – and it matters not what of.'

Which they did, even reprising conversations and memories from Jamaica: the people they had met, their qualities or lack of same, the latter deplored in the case of Prince William as well as certain other folk who had demonstrated a lack of discretion or proper manners. This was not confined to Brazier's sex, for the West Indies had as many a female battleaxe as any colonial station.

It was cheering to feel Betsey relax, not least in the stiffness of her arm, which told him she was becoming accustomed to and comfortable with the physical contact. His own stiffened when she mentioned her brother, only to ease again as she reprised the conversation they had engaged in before he went away, the details of which surprised him and which he struggled to fully believe.

'He will come round in time. I fear he is a creature who abhors change.'

'Would it hurt you if it transpired we could not ever be friends?'

'Yes it would.'

'Enough to . . . ?'

It was unnecessary to complete that, important as it was: called upon to choose, Brazier needed to know how she would react.

'I cannot bring myself to think so.'

It took little effort to tug on her hand and halt their progress, which left them staring into each other's eyes, he towering over her and so close. They had come full circle and the gate was just beyond the bushes, while it was obvious this meeting could not last forever. She needed to go back to the house and he must depart.

'When I was in pain you were kind enough to bestow on me a kiss.'

Another blush. 'I recall with my fingers.'

'I would ask for that at least now, but would hope for more.' His head moved forward a fraction, only to wait for a response. It was time for him to be as bold as he could be at sea. 'Betsey Langridge, I think I love you and, if you are unsure, I can understand why.'

It was no more than a swift bestowal, but her lips brushed his before she turned away as if ashamed.

'I will come tomorrow.'

Facing him again, a hand was lifted to brush his cheek. 'I pray for it.'

'Edward?'

'Edward.'

CHAPTER TWENTY-ONE

Dutchy Holland came into Upper Deal on the back of a chalk cart, these being frequent in the east of the county, the product dug out of the ground to be spread over fields requiring their year of lying fallow. The man on the reins was a talkative soul, so Dutchy knew quite bit regarding his destination before he alighted to walk the last part of his journey on foot.

As ever, Deal was named as the most villainous and dangerous place in the land, a story he had heard in every habitation through which he had passed, never once being drawn into saying the speaker did not know Falmouth around the harbour. It was common of folk to be sure they were exposed to more crime and wickedness in their own backyard than any other.

Nothing he saw when he came into the Lower Town was enough to excite excessive curiosity, and he had no trouble when asking a crossing sweeper in the busy main road by the large church for Quebec House. They, who cleared up the equine ordure so folks could keep their boots and dress hems clean, were a fount of local knowledge, brought on by their engagement with all and sundry, high and low, who had to stop and wait till a gap appeared in the number of produce-carrying conveyances, which Dutchy was doing now.

A snivelling nose was rubbed with an already crusted sleeve. 'You'll be a looking for Captain Brazier, then?'

'I am.'

'A kindly gent, all say.'

Dutchy grinned and agreed, for he knew what the sweeper was hinting. His old captain never crossed without he tipped a bit of copper to what he reckoned an unfortunate; he had to be that or he would not be doing the job.

'Don't get across his hawse, mate,' Dutchy replied with a smile, his slow West Country drawl taking any rebuke out of the remark. 'He's tartar when his bloods all a' boil.'

The commotion distracted them both as a big fellow came out of a doorway right behind Dutchy, hauling by the collar a young fellow with tousled blonde hair who was pleading to be let go and, by the sound of his slurring speech, somewhat the worse for drink.

'Shut up, weasel, or you'll feel my fist.'

Partly because of the struggling youth the brute holding his coat collar was put slightly off balance, which caused him to barge into Dutchy, who put out a hand to push back, the reaction a demand to get out of the way.

'Don't take kindly to that, friend – a "pardon my manner, mate", would serve better.'

In the instant of this taking place, several things registered: the crossing sweeper's near-skeletal frame was nowhere to be seen, so he had made himself scarce. The fellow holding the collar was broad of shoulder and tall and his look was a black and threatening one, while to his rear, a pair of tough-looking coves had come to the doorway he had just exited and were eyeing Dutchy dangerously.

'Help me, mister,' was the near-tearful plea from the youth, now so close Dutchy could smell the drink on his breath. 'He ain't got no right to be laying a hand on me.'

'Then it might be fittin' for him to be let go,' was Holland's quiet response.

Dutchy had let his ditty bag slip off his shoulder, but it was still in his hand and he felt it being tugged, which obliged him to look at who was doing the pulling. The stick of a crossing sweeper was behind him now, exerting a lot of pressure for one of his build, while his eyes had a look in them that was a warning to be cautious.

'Happen I'll take you to where you seek to go, matey,' he said softly. 'Best come away.'

By the time Dutchy looked back, the assailant's face was close to his and it was clear he had heard. 'Best advice you'll get, stranger, so heed it.'

Holland was a scrapper of repute, but he was no fool; one-on-one he would have taken the challenge and backed himself. But with two others to take on as well, and no support, it would be a certain thrashing. He was, however, too proud to just back down without saying something.

'Might be you should let the lad free. Don't look right, does it, a fellow your size manhandling a slip like him, which you will see is common opinion if you care to look round about you.'

The collar holder could not resist the sideways glances which told him a crowd had gathered, and by the looks on their faces disapproval was widespread. That changed swiftly as he glared; quite a few folk suddenly seemed to recall the errand they were on when the bargy erupted and slipped away. Others dropped their eyes, while Dutchy himself was being dragged clear by the hissing crossing sweeper.

'Best out of it, best out of it.'

The gap this opened up allowed John Hawker to drag his still pleading victim off; unbeknown to Dutchy, he was heading for the slaughterhouse, his two fellow toughs hard on his heels.

'Who was that?'

253

'Name's John Hawker and there ain't a worse bastard in Deal, mark my word.'

'And who's he collared?' Dutchy asked, as the sweeper took up his station at the crossing again, broom at the ready.

'Harry Spafford is the lad's name, an' he's a wrong 'un too but for a different purpose, him never bein' sober and a disgrace to his name. What he's doin' being hauled along by Hawker God only knows, but there'll be hell to pay when his pa and Daisy Trotter get to hear about it, for they're blood foes.'

'Well I thank you, my old dear, for your concern and your aid. Quebec House?'

'Up the alley, t'other side, friend, once I see you across. Follow your right hand and look to your left. Name's on the house lintel, folk say.'

'I need more'n that since I ain't got letters.'

'Door's painted blue, same as the captain's coat. Can't miss it.'

Dutchy slung his ditty bag back onto his shoulder, quick to pick up a sense of disappointment, there being no copper forthcoming. 'My poke is full of nothing but air as of now, friend, but I'll seek you out for the price of wet when I see my captain.'

It not being far, Dutchy was rapping on the dark-blue door to find a welcome behind it and not just from Joe Lascelles. Cocky Logan was there, as usual his thick Scottish tones hard to understand, especially after a bit of a gap, not moderated by years spent in England or at sea. So was Peddler Palmer, both of whom had plied oars under his direction. The warmest welcome came from Brazier himself, though it was not long before Dutchy asked him the reason for the gathering of old hands, with no ship in the offing.

'You'd know if you'd seen me a few weeks past.'

The explanation got narrowed eyes. 'Happen what I was told about this place was true. There was violence on the street afore I got here.'

'You can tell me of that later. There are rooms in the attic; get yourself berthed and then Joe can knock up a feed.'

'Saving your presence, I have a debt to pay to a crossing sweeper.'
Now it was Dutchy's turn to explain. 'Might not've got clear with
him hauling me back. Said the fellow I was eyeing was a real bad sod.
Happen I might look out for him and catch him on his own.'

'How will you find him?'

'Folk know where the bully types hang out, an' besides, all I has to
do is ask for him. Sweeper named him as a John Hawker.'

'Christ in heaven, I came across the bugger on my way here too
and that near came to blows.'

'A name to mark, then.'

The look in Dutchy's eye left Brazier in no doubt about what
Hawker might be marked for.

The man they were discussing had not been out looking for Harry
Spafford: he had been on the hunt for a clue as to who had stolen
seventy pounds of tobacco near the village of Martin, due to be
delivered to a long-time buyer from Maidstone, who would not be
happy for a wasted journey to East Kent. This time there was scant
discretion; he had lost his rag and was intent on letting it be known he
was mad enough to do murder, even if he would not say why.

His search had taken him to an upstairs room of a near-derelict
house where the man who owned the building had a drinking den,
which sold only smuggled brandy and locally distilled gin of ferocious
strength. It was thus the haunt of the dregs of Deal, addicted urchins
included, and perhaps someone with a clue to impart and so fuddled
as to let slip a clue Hawker could use, for the villainy had to be local.

The notion of a gang coming from far off to steal the loaded cart
made no sense, and Hawker did not need Henry Tulkington to tell
him that; the horses and cart, which had taken the goods away, could
only travel so far before fresh beasts were needed and he had searched.
His ride round the locality had taken in several coaching inns and
paddocks like that of Vincent Flaherty, all to no avail.

While he was hauling a protesting but unsteady Harry Spafford past St George's Church, the boy's father was ducking in and out of the taverns in Middle Street, with black-eyed and swollen-nosed Daisy in tow, looking for the same body with the intention of dragging Harry back and once more locking him up.

Having done his favourite watering and whoring hole, the Hope and Anchor, Dan Spafford had proceeded to the Ship Inn, another alehouse, only to draw another blank. They were caught when just exiting to be told that John Hawker not only had his son but had collared him with no gentility. Given his place at the slaughterhouse was no mystery and that was the direction in which they had been seen to be going, it took no genius to work out where Harry would be now.

'Why we stopped, Dan?' Daisy required, in a voice made nasal by Harry's head butt. 'We's got to get Harry back.'

'I'm thinkin', that's why. Ask yourself what Hawker would want with my boy, when he's never laid a hand on him afore an' he could've done at any time. It be because he ain't daft. He knows not to touch Harry, an' he must have been tempted, 'cause it means I'd have to sort him regardless of hazard.'

'So?'

'He must know it's us robbing Tulkington and, even if it's guessing, it won't be for long. I wanted Harry to come with us yesterday, don't you recall? Told him about what we was going to flitch and how.'

'If Hawker lays a hand on him he won't hold out without lettin' on.'

It was a gloomy Daniel Spafford who reached the obvious conclusion. 'Strikes me from what we heard, it's too late for that. Best get back to Worth and set up our defences.'

'What about a rescue?'

'To be thought on, Daisy. But first we must know what we face.'

* * *

Knowing that Spafford was the culprit, Hawker was tempted to go after him right away, yet caution told him to wait for Tulkington's return. That accepted, he could derive some pleasure from playing on the imagination of his captive. There was no better place to do that than a slaughterhouse, especially given the rumours of what the man who ran it was capable of.

A wreck anyway, Harry Spafford had little forbearance when it came to his possible fate; the sight of cattle and pigs being slaughtered, with the blood and gore spraying everywhere, plus the attendant squealing, worked wonders on his wildest nightmare. He could see parts of his being, mixed in a sealed barrel of butchered and salted pork, being served up boiled in some far-off place as food for a ship's crew.

'Mind, it's as like to be condemned,' was Hawker's gleeful opinion, when he drove home the notion. 'Not even a South Sea cannibal would let a Spafford pass his lips.'

'Happen we should ship him out whole, John,' suggested Marker, one of the gang. 'Let them roast the bugger on a spit.'

'Scoopin' out the head is said to be special for the chieftains,' was another notion, soon topped by the preference such elevated folk had for roasted prick and gonads, cut fresh and still bleeding.

Prey to such terrors, it was made very much worse by his being once more deprived of drink. So when Hawker questioned Harry Spafford, he was gifted not only with disclosure of what the father was about, but also a high degree of embellishment, which came from a devious mind able to paint a picture of a war in the making. Having been a resident at Worth since his father took to smuggling, Harry had been witness to all the frustrations and possible solutions to his inferior standing in the trade.

So, to save himself, he set out to convince Tulkington's right-hand man that no landing from now on would be safe, no round-the-county transport either. He even invented a special chest of money, which had been created over years, to fund the long-planned schemes designed to bring down Tulkington and all who worked for him.

It was really the quite innocent mention of Billy Pitt that sparked another train of thought in Hawker. With Tulkington still absent he had no one to talk with, so was left to gnaw on the possibilities of what information he had, which included the knowledge that Edward Brazier had paid a visit to Walmer Castle and had been within those walls for a long time.

To a fellow not short of an imagination it was easy to sniff a connection between the two, which placed this naval interloper suddenly come to Deal and seeking to get close to the Tulkington family in a very different light. What if the pursuit of the sister was just a ploy?

In amongst the precautions he took, Hawker ensured the slaughterhouse was well guarded by armed gang members, all denied their normal pursuits till matters became clearer. He already knew Brazier was no longer alone, while the description of those who had joined him and were now resident at Quebec House did nothing to ease his worries.

Even a gin-addicted child, scraping an existence in a seaport with no shortage of the type, could observe and describe the type who could not only fight, but had the air of those who would take pleasure in it. Brazier had also been observed visiting an armourer, who was open to an enquiring Hawker about what had been purchased – four brace of pistols and a set of naval hangers – while his spies reported the navy man, who had, since his beating, openly carried his sword, now never went anywhere without he had two of his people with him.

There was one thing Hawker could do, without the need to clear it with Henry Tulkington. Not much happened in Deal about which he did not know and that applied to the question being posed around the taverns by Vincent Flaherty. The idea of letting slip to some nosy Irishman keen to buy drinks, through another body, the identity of Daisy Trotter and where he could be found counted as a good idea.

If he knew it to be more of a wild hope than a real possibility, the notion on which he drew comfort was appealing. What if the two, Spafford and Brazier, could be put to a bout in which they would cancel each other out? But again, that would have to wait on Tulkington.

Anticipating the need to go to Cottington Court often, sometimes as a proper visitor, at others, he hoped, for more clandestine meetings with Betsey, Brazier reckoned it necessary to get his trio of tars mounted so they could accompany him. Till they arrived he had been very cautious when out and about, avoiding situations in which he could once more be attacked, sometimes feeling foolish for the precaution, to then wonder once more at the name Daisy and what the enmity could portend, for Flaherty had finally come through with some information on the name.

One stark fact was obvious: if there was a threat and he was constantly taking the same road, it could be remarked upon, while there were parts of the route where being isolated was easy; if he needed his men at his back in Deal, he could also require them out in the county.

Riding a horse was not a notion that was taken to with unbridled glee by all. Dutchy Holland was fine, though happier on a donkey than a pony. Cocky Logan took to a passive mare eventually, but despite the teaching of Vincent Flaherty it seemed impossible to keep Peddler Palmer in a saddle for any length of time.

'Happy on a yard, your honour, to reef and pound canvas, even in a gale of wind,' Peddler insisted. 'But I ain't made for horseflesh.'

'Best leave him to guard your house, Edward,' was the Irishman's opinion. 'If you're in any danger and need to go beyond a walk, your Peddler will be grounded in a trice.'

Brazier was obliged to ask a question of Flaherty that troubled him once the lessons were complete. 'Why have folk who refused to talk to you of this Daisy become so keen to let on now?'

'You'll need a saint's intercession for that, for it was not brought on by my buying of ale. Nor was it more than a name and a place: a man for all love who resides in the village of Worth, which is not much more than a couple of miles beyond Cottington Court.'

'D'ye still reckon Saoirse knows more than she's been prepared to say?'

'It would stand as no more than a guess, but yes.'

'Happen I should talk to my landlord,' Brazier said, after a meaningful pause, which got a knowing look from a man now well aware of the reasons that going to the Playhouse was a risk. 'Never fear, Vincent, I will write and ask her to visit me with the excuse of a need for repairs.'

The lone shaver slumped against the wall of the Naval Yard was too much of a fixture, in terms of type, to excite much in the way of curiosity, except perhaps to wonder if he was older than he looked, for he gave the impression of being stunted when seen to rise and walk off, as he did having seen Saoirse Riorden call at Quebec House.

'First I must introduce you to the members of my old crew.'

'Is this to be a social call, as well as business, then?'

'I admit to a false proposition in my note, Saoirse.' The statement, even if the response was silent, was not well received. 'I need to ask you about a certain party whose name and whereabouts are now known to me, the person – a man indeed – who goes by the tag of Daisy.'

A short pause in the face of a female scowl was followed by an attempt at a witticism. 'I assume it's not his given name, which would be too cruel.' No reaction and certainly not a joyful one. 'But I have ordered tea to be prepared and hope you will consent to join me.'

'I'm minded to pass up on the tea.'

'You know it was the name mentioned by those who beat me?'

'I recall.'

'While our good friend Vincent assures me not much happens in the town of which you're not aware. Indeed, I am tempted to ask how my suit at Cottington is faring, given you may know more than me.'

'You never enquired before, you left that to Vincent, so why now?'

'Because the identity is no longer a secret.'

Joe Lascelles entered with a tray bearing a pot and china crockery for two, as usual with a wide grin on his face, one Edward Brazier reckoned to be able to melt all hearts. Even Joe had to moderate his look in the face of the lady now sat in the parlour; stony was an understatement. Afraid she would up and depart, Brazier sought to keep her pinned by social obligation.

'Joe, ask our good fellows to come and be introduced.'

'With a brace of pistols apiece, no doubt,' was the acerbic comment, as Joe left the room.

'There are as many mills for rumours in this place as flour,' was the slightly terse response. 'And what you have said tells me Vincent is correct. Not much happens in Deal about which you do not know, so I'm wondering what you can tell me about this fellow.'

'You're sure I would want to tell you anything?'

'Tea,' seemed a feeble response, and it was replicated in a cup that showed the leaves had yet to fully infuse. 'Or should I say coloured hot water.'

That she laughed cheered him and, not having heard it before, he was taken with the level of her pealing musicality. The effect on what had been till now a stern countenance was equally remarkable.

'Pour it back in the pot, Edward, and let it sit a while.'

The door opened again to admit three very obvious Jack tars, unmistakeably so in the manner of their dress and pigtails; Dutchy's curly-haired head was closer to the low ceiling than the others, dwarfing the Jock, Cocky Logan. Mid-size Peddler showed a dropped jaw in the face of an evident beauty and could not avoid the habit of scratching his crown. It was amusing to see them – all hard as nails and afraid of no man – adopt a posture more common to a shy schoolboy, which could only be put down to the setting. Had they not been bareheaded, he was sure they would have doffed the different articles they wore on their heads.

'And they are going to help you see to Daisy?' Saoirse enquired, introductions made and acknowledged, prior to their trooping out. The look Brazier gave her indicated it was so. 'Then I should find yourself some more bodies if you want to get anywhere near Jaleel Trotter.'

'That being his proper name.' A slow nod. 'You rate him dangerous?'

'I rate him as a man not afraid to do murder, and by repute has done so, which makes it odd he sought to have you beaten.'

'You make it sound as if I should be grateful to still be alive.'

'Pour the tea, it will be right by now.'

Eyes on the cups and determined to leave the saucers dry, he did not see her bite her lower lip, or discern here was a woman who was wondering how much to impart. The fact that John Hawker had collared and was keeping Harry Spafford was no mystery: how could it be when it had been carried out in broad daylight and with an excess of squealing from the victim?

Everyone in Deal knew what had happened, possibly except the likes of the man before her, a stranger to the place and not included in the general tavern and coffee shop gossip, not least because he rarely visited them. She could not think of a good time to seek retribution on Daisy Trotter, but right now was the worst of all.

It was obvious after the grabbing of Harry there was a clash coming between Spafford and Hawker, which would involve the men they led, and it took no great wit to discern the reason was over rumoured losses of contraband. If the latter could stride through the town with impunity, the others could not. Hawker owned the streets; Spafford was rumoured to be holed up in Worth and waiting.

'If I was to advise that it might be best to put aside any notion of vengeance on Daisy Trotter, would you heed me?'

'I might,' Brazier replied unconvincingly, as he handed her a cup of tea. 'But I would need to know why.'

'The time is not right.' A quizzical look. 'As of this moment, it would be hard to get to him – not that it was ever easy, given he's known for his skill with the blade.'

'Sword or knife?'

'It would scarce make a difference on a marble slab.'

'I have faced both before, Saoirse, and much worse besides. Cannonballs, muskets, axes, boathooks, marlin spikes – and come away with little to complain about, bar the odd scratch and bruise. Take it as true, I can handle a fellow with a knife.'

'Not if he got close to you afore it showed. You'd scarce rate a skin-and-bone creature like Jaleel Trotter as a threat, doubly so when he wheezes to breathe—'

She stopped, taken with the look on his face, which had suddenly become enquiring. 'Describe him to me?'

As she complied, and her portrayal was full of detail, Edward Brazier was back in that crowded inn on the way to Deal, looking past the sod he knew to be John Hawker at the man who had been named as Jaleel, not a common name, even if it was biblical.

'You say this Daisy is not a man for beatings but the knife.'

'I did.'

'What about John Hawker, whom Vincent assures me is a creature best avoided?'

'It would fit his ways more.'

'And what would you say if I was to suggest they were both involved, that they combined to chastise me for a trifling squabble?'

Saoirse laughed again, and full-blooded it was, but there was ridicule in it more than mirth, which went on for some time before she could speak. 'You don't know the pair, that's for certain. They are sworn enemies.'

'If I have the right of it, and by the name and your description

I think it so, why would two sworn enemies be hugger-mugger in a tavern and determined what they said to each other was not to be overheard?'

Now she looked confused and stayed that for some time as Brazier explained what had happened. His senses acute, he was slightly puzzled by her expression, which was not one of disbelief but one of suddenly being guarded.

'I have an impression there are things you're not telling me.'

The reply was sharp, the expression an indication of a complete mood shift, with the crockery in her hand rattling slightly. 'I did not come here to suffer examination.'

'Forgive me if it appears I am engaged in doing that, but I would remind you I was subjected to a severe drubbing, you witnessing the results. It is not something I'm minded to let pass without I retaliate, not least because I got not only the name Daisy, but a warning to depart Deal. Given I have no intention of complying, I have to guard against a repeat. I am hoping that is not a thing you would be happy to see.'

Saoirse put the cup and saucer down and sat for a long moment in contemplation, to then look him right in the eye with a determined expression on her face. 'With what I am going to tell you, I suggest something stronger than tea might be required.'

'Wine?' Brazier asked, intrigued.

'Brandy, Edward, and I think you will sink it in quantity when I tell you from where it comes and how. But I do so on one condition and that is you never tell anyone it was me who passed this to you.'

Henry Tulkington came back to Cottington, his Berlin having met him off the Sandwich coach, still with no knowledge of recent events. He was welcomed by both his sister and his aunt, who posed the obligatory question over a pot of tea as to the success of his trip. And how was Uncle Dirley?

Sarah Lovell was quizzed, once Betsey was not present, about how many visits she had made to the Brazier house and queries as to behaviour, these being responded to positively for nothing untoward had been permitted to take place. No question then arose afterwards from his stated intention to visit the stables and talk to the head groom. What he heard there rendered him a lot less sanguine.

'There has to be a gate of which we know little, set in the southern wall, for that is where she went on her walks regular.'

'And she went there how many times?'

'Three while you was absent. I trailed her each day, as you asked.'

'To meet with the man I told you of?' A nod. 'I am bound to ask if there was a degree of intimacy.'

'Hand holding and an exchange of kisses, your honour, but . . .' Embarrassment precluded him from naming what else could have occurred and he had no need to. That imparted was enough. 'It looked chaste enough, if I may make so bold.'

'You may not! Have you told anyone of this?'

'That, sir, would be against your express desire.'

It was uncomfortable to be under the suspicious gaze of Henry Tulkington. Lasting for near a half a minute, it felt like an hour. 'Make sure it stays that way.'

A touched forelock was the only response to his employer as he departed the stables. He had not asked about the notes, which had been sent by his sister at least once a day and twice on one occasion, using the youngest stable boy and, if he did not know of them, he could stay in ignorance. A long-time servant, his head groom had a nose for trouble when brewing which had been discussed with the cook and the head footman, it being essential they ensure no trouble came their way in the backwash.

As he walked back to the front entrance, Henry Tulkington was considering what needed to be done, given it was now obvious time would likely not temper Elisabeth's infatuation. If she would go to the trouble of arranging clandestine meetings, it could only mean it had probably moved on to become a passion. Had the moment arrived to contemplate the complete removal of Edward Brazier? If it was undertaken, could it be so covered up so as to ensure no blame attached to him?

These were deep waters indeed and required that he discuss them with John Hawker, for he had the notion a disappearance would serve better than a body to be mourned and that meant the use of the slaughterhouse.

'Henry,' Betsey called, 'dinner is ready to be put on the table.'

It was rare for him to gift anyone a full smile but he did so now. 'My apologies, dear sister. And as we dine you must tell me how you are faring with your Captain Brazier.'

CHAPTER TWENTY-TWO

Edward Brazier, as they drank wine instead of brandy, realised much of what Saoirse was telling him was supposition, the things people say quietly to each other on the grounds that it is gossip, not established truth. Asked, he would have admitted it was rife as well as a bane in the King's Navy, generally employed to undermine rivals. The owner of Cottington Court was seen as the guiding hand behind what had become a major enterprise, but pressed to give credence to her story by stating actual offences that could be set against the name she was left exasperated, for there were none.

Without question she could say John Hawker was employed by Tulkington at the slaughterhouse, but also as an auxiliary Collector of Taxes for the municipality of Deal. There Saoirse could speak with total confidence about his dual functions, one legal and official, the other quite the reverse.

'I pay him the tax due on what I sell and, to satisfy, I have to show my accounts for the quarter. Fewer have a sharper eye for inaccuracies than Hawker. Some say it's how he got his name.'

'No wonder he was not welcome.' Brazier reprised his first night in the Playhouse and the stiffness of the interchange he observed. 'But you must own it is an odd combination: an outright bully by repute, but with a counting house brain.'

'At the same time of calling, he will advise what is in the offing in contraband and invite me to bid for what I would like to buy.'

'Like wine casks of superior quality?'

'That and brandy, which he also sells to the alehouse.' Not supposed to sell spirits, it was commonplace that tavern owners did so; like the servants listed on a ship's muster while still ashore, it was too common a minor peculation to raise comment. 'They will also purchase tobacco.'

'Garlick?'

Saoirse nodded, her next comment being delivered with an arch look.

'I take it you bought this wine we're drinking from Mr Parkin?' Brazier did not need to acknowledge the truth of the proposition, so she added, 'Well he bottles it from the source, so there's none without guilt, if avoiding harsh duties could be termed that. Is the buyer any more free of sin than the seller?'

'Would it surprise you to say I have no interest in avoidance, in any other respect than the way it impacts on my future plans?'

'I cannot see having Henry Tulkington for a brother-in-law, if half of what is hinted about him is true, as a way to bring much comfort.'

There was a significant pause before Brazier responded. 'Does having him as a brother look any different?'

'If you have not already asked yourself that question, it's about time you did so.'

'I cannot believe Betsey Langridge has any knowledge of what you have suggested.'

'Would it alter your thinking,' she asked, 'if that turned out not to be the case?'

It was not a question he could readily answer. If Betsey knew, or even suspected her brother was the man to control a major part of smuggling in East Kent, did it necessarily alter his view of her? The scale of what Saoirse put forward, regarding an organised and extensive enterprise, was telling, nothing less than the same point made to him by William Pitt. Could she share the same house and be in ignorance? He then had to remind himself she was not long back from the West Indies and had been young prior to departure.

He reprised every word they had exchanged, from the first meeting in Jamaica to the last walk in the woods, seeking clues, to come to no conclusion, but knew the mere thought Betsey could keep such knowledge from him must impact on their relationship. It was to get away from such troubling speculations he changed the course of the conversation.

'You said people who have fallen out with Henry Tulkington pay a price?'

'I say the rumour is that those in dispute with him suffer for it, yes, though at one remove.'

'Hawker?'

'Him or those he employs, I would guess.'

'Could I fall into such a category?'

'You would know the truth of it better than I.'

Brazier was back in that too-hot study, reprising his fractious meeting with Tulkington, resisting the notion the exchange could have led to what happened. He decided to relate the memory to Saoirse, impressed by the way she listened without comment until he finished. It was a time before she responded.

'I think I have to say to you this. Jaleel Trotter, your Daisy, is not a well-known face in Deal and neither is he of the tough sort. You should ask yourself why he carries the name.'

'I have experienced the same name-calling in the service. I assume for a similar vice.'

'He visits the town from time to time – but rarely, and keeps to certain places.'

'I recall passing an alleyway towards the North End of Middle Street – would he be found there?'

269

'More likely than elsewhere,' Saoirse acknowledged, 'but that too is gossip. It's not a place I frequent.'

'Say I did upset Tulkington enough to warrant a beating in his eyes; it would then follow he set Hawker to do the deed. And, since he is dead set on my not marrying his sister, the proscription to depart Deal would fit the purpose. But that still does not explain the use of Daisy's name.'

It was impossible to miss the worried frown that produced, immediately followed by her standing, which brought Brazier to his feet as well. 'There are questions to which I don't have an answer, any more than you. I must also own to have gone further than intended in possible enlightenment. I must put my affairs and livelihood before your need to know things, and if it was known I talked—'

'Fear not, Saoirse. If I choose to act on what you have given me, it will be done in my own name.'

Having seen her out the door, Brazier was left to contemplate the exchange as well as how to proceed, which was not easy given his thinking kept being dragged back to the past. One thought did surface: Betsey had told him her brother would come round to blessing their union in time, as he had with Stephen Langridge, which begged the question as to why he had objected to that union in the first place. There was only one place to find more information and that would have to wait until morning.

Henry Tulkington listened to John Hawker as he outlined how he had collared Harry Spafford and, since there was no effusive approval, he was obliged to explain it had been a sudden thing, taken on the wing, rather than considered. That he had blabbed the truth of his father's thieving was entered as justification.

'Where is he?'

'Stowed with the barrels he feels sure he will end up in.'

Tulkington could not say, even if he would like to, that the action had been unwise and, in such a public manner, doubly so. Had it been done in secret, Harry would have been a solid chip with which to bargain. The way he had been lifted and his pleas for mercy would be the talk of Deal, which meant any concession made from Worth would look like weakness. So his pa would stand as firm as he could to save face, and he could, knowing that to harm or dispose of Harry, when the whole town knew of his whereabouts and who had him, was impossible.

To just hand the youngster back would send the opposite message, neither course bringing the result Tulkington reckoned he needed, which was that his operations should go on without trouble from any quarter. The people he traded with did so in the full expectation of their requirements being met.

At their meeting Spafford had given out no sign of being ill, which might give the lie to his claim of approaching death. Yet if true, the offer he had made stood to remove for good what was an irritation and one threatening to become a problem. It hinged on the depth of that which Spafford sought for his wastrel son – a sum of money, but one never arrived at. Much as he hated to bend, sense and the needs of his business meant it should be established.

'I do not expect you to like this John, but I require you to make contact with Jaleel Trotter again. Spafford and I need to talk and soon.'

The supposition such an errand might be unwelcome was obvious; Hawker looked as though he had swallowed a wasp, an indication of the depth of his objection given he took great care to hide any emotion at all from his employer; businesslike was best.

'Would I be permitted to say that there's another way open?'

Tulkington was angered by the suggestion, which implied he had not thought matters through, but it was he who now needed to hide his feelings. 'Threaten harm to Harry?'

'For a return of that stolen, added to a payment for the affront.'

Hawker had something of a mind, but did it extend beyond the learning of letters and the ability to read accounts? What was required now would not be served by a bloody reaction and again, the whole of Deal knew where Harry Spafford was being held. The angry look at the suggestion of talking to Trotter had disappeared, but Hawker's look was flinty, while the stiff posture and bunched fists at his side indicated the depth of his frustration.

'Best, then, I tell you what was imparted to me on the last occasion Spafford and I talked.'

Tulkington kept a sharp eye on his man as he related the nature of the exchange in the coach, and only in the odd twitch of skin on the cheeks could he discern how upset Hawker was. It required to be dealt with.

'You are wondering at not being told before?'

'Had I been, I would not have wasted breath charging round the town askin' daft questions, Mr Tulkington. If it gets out, I will look a fool, which I say will serve neither you nor I.'

'Even knowing what I have just told you, John, I was no more certain of the culprit than you.' The cheeks hollowed as Hawker's jaw tightened; he might as well have called him a liar which, if it annoyed his employer, nevertheless made it necessary to placate a man he needed. 'I regret it now, but I thought it wise at the time. And I had given Spafford my word not to divulge what he told me, even to you.'

'Your word is your bond, I reckon, right enough.'

The way that was said belied the words. The tone of Tulkington's response had to be very measured; it also had to be accompanied with a regretful smile. The end was more important right now than Hawker's wounded feelings; those he could deal with afterwards.

'I require you to do as I ask. You will come to see it is for the best.'

They were walking along Middle Street as twilight fell, passing several taverns, which was not to be remarked upon even if Brazier had hinted to his crewmen his intention to down some ale. Pushing through the bustle of Portobello Court, Brazier stopped before an alleyway, around which stood several obvious Mollies in gaudy attire, eyeing the quartet with a mixture of suspicion and, in one or two cases, interest; it was not always youth and beauty that engendered attraction.

'I am minded to have a look,' Brazier said, turning to his trio with an amused expression.

As ever it was Peddler who had the wit to respond in the appropriate manner. 'Well I'll be buggered, Capt'n!'

'Ye will if ye gan in there,' was Cocky Logan's chirpy opinion.

'I sense a purpose, your honour.'

'Sharp of you, Dutchy. There's a certain cove who frequents this place I'm told, and he's one I would welcome a word with.'

'You've now't to worry about, Dutchy,' Peddler hooted. 'None of these nancies will lay a hand on an ugly sod like you.'

The response came with no rancour, hard anyway with Dutchy's accent, but it did with a casually raised fist. 'Happen I might turn you a bit less becoming than you be now, mate.'

'Work cut oot there, Dutchy.'

Looking along the street, Brazier picked up, in the dim light, the head of John Hawker, making his way through the crowds, acknowledging, by the way he was nodding, those who knew him. But he had not spotted Brazier, who had whipped off his distinctive naval headgear to keep it so. Given the possibility Hawker might be responsible for his beating, while he was with some of his old barge crew this presented a chance to exact retribution on the spot. Tempted, he knew he had to be certain of his guilt: he could not act on mere suspicion, and besides, who was to say in this street, where he was on home turf, how many folk might come to his aid?

'Step back and make yourselves small.'

It was a reflection of time served together and dangers faced that all three obeyed without question. Indeed, they followed their captain's lead in engaging with various folk using Middle Street as a place to trade, in Peddler's case a whore of neither beauty nor youth, who carried in her hand a long whip, while on her head sat a pair of Viking horns, leaving no doubt of the kind of service she was offering.

'I'd stick to the Mollies, Peddler,' crowed Dutchy, 'all you'll get there, my old dear, is a sore arse.'

It was not fear that had Brazier avoid a confrontation, but curiosity, thinking he might tail the sod, for it was just possible by doing so he would find out something of interest. He could not avoid noting there was a confident bustle about Hawker, while his physical presence had folk move out of his way, at least those who knew him. That did not apply to tars come for a run ashore and, once or twice, he could be seen to give a push to clear a path, ignoring any protests that ensued.

Hawker got in amongst the Mollies, before pushing his way down the alley. Brazier's surprise did not last long: he had called on Saoirse to collect taxes due and the activities of a place selling drink would not exempt them from the need to likewise cough up to the government. But it did put paid to any idea he had of going in there himself to seek out Daisy Trotter.

'Best get Peddler away, Capt'n, afore he strikes a bargain with the lash lady.'

Dutchy's plea made Brazier look, to see the whore laughing, her shoulders and, even more, her massive bosom shaking with mirth.

'There he goes, ay?' Logan responded, shaking his head. 'He'll be getting wan frae that whip fer not a penny spent, you watch, ah tell ye.'

'Navy will do that for him, Cocky,' Dutchy opined, 'any time he chooses, an' I'll put my sweet self forward to swing the cat.'

'Time to move on,' Brazier called, thinking it a bad idea to just stand in the street with Hawker bound to exit in short order. This took them to the Hope and Anchor, a tavern occupying the corner of a sizeable square, in the middle of which sat a cock-fighting pit surrounded by an eager and noisy audience, with wagers being placed and accepted. As Brazier pushed his way into the tavern, Cocky and Peddler peeled off to join the crowd, leaving Brazier to buy tankards of porter before he and Dutchy sought a place to sit.

'What were all that about, Capt'n?'

'You know, Dutchy, with your height I reckoned you would have spotted him too.'

'Can't gainsay that, your honour, but I can enquire as to us havin' done so, what happened to the notion of clouting the bugger round the ear?'

'In time, maybe.'

Hawker was inside what Basil the Bulgar liked to call his palace of entertainment, which others referred to as the Flea Pit. The basement was a packed and noisy brick-lined room, in which perspiration ran down the walls. He had some trouble in getting to talk to the owner, whom he found on a settle with his arm round a young and pretty glassy-eyed lad, naked to the waist. That arm was soon detached: Basil could see Hawker wanted to talk and that was not to be done in public, or where they could be overheard.

Following Basil up a set of stairs, they were so steep they needed a rope on which hands could haul so before Hawker's eyes was a fat and waddling posterior belonging to a sad old man, an impression not improved face to face in the extravagant bedroom. Basil was bald and remarkably ugly, with jowls no longer firm enough to hold to his bones, added to brownish once-freckled skin which was now so pitted it looked as though it had been a target for the pellets from a fowling piece.

Slack, rouged lips and yellowed teeth were added to a high-pitched, effete voice, the eyes not helped by the kohl with which he sought to highlight and render them striking, for the effect was the opposite. Before John Hawker was a man who pretended to be joyous and outrageous in public, which acted to mask the misery of a life in which he endlessly sought affection, only to reject it when forthcoming. He was also, quite palpably, in some fear of his visitor, evident in the vocal tremor as, sure it was not time to pay his taxes, he asked the purpose.

'I need words with Daisy.'

'Haven't seen him,' was the piped, nervy response. 'Days past since he called in; a week even.'

Hawker thought it unlikely that would alter. After what had happened, Deal would be reckoned too dangerous to casually enter, but he was damned – Tulkington or no Tulkington – if he was going to go grubbing to Worth to get the message over himself.

'You must have ways to get to him.'

'Never even tried, dearie,' was waved away with a limp hand gesture.

'Then it's time you did. Not asking you to go personal, but send someone to him. Say I want to talk and do it as soon as sun-up tomorrow.'

'But—'

'You don't "but" me, Basil, for you will know where it leads. Find a body to take the message that I will be in the Griffin's Head at noontime. Also, that he has my word for his safety.'

'You're going to talk about Harry?'

'None of you concern, but there's a law that has words on what you get up to here, an' you won't want to hear 'em from the dock. Mind, life of a prison hulk might suit folk of your stamp.'

A fearful Basil the Bulgar, who in truth hailed from Dover, was left shaking as he heard Hawker's boots pounding down the bare wooden stairs.

CHAPTER TWENTY-THREE

Edward Brazier awoke at his usual time, soon fully aware he was in for a demanding day. He was determined to go to Cottington Court, despite the fact Betsey and he were due to meet at Quebec House that very afternoon. These visits took place regularly now, to maintain the fiction that his abode was one of their two main places of contact. It was not just a question of an inability to wait: what he wanted to talk about had to be done in private.

Joe Lascelles brought him a morning coffee, along with his grin, to be asked about the weather.

'Wind west sou' west and the sky fair. Looks to be a good day in the offing, but cloudy.'

That had been a worry; he had sensed no coming rain on the way home the previous night, but you could never be sure on the coast, the conditions being so rapidly changeable.

'Towels are laid out, your honour.'

Routine had been quickly established with Joe about, almost to the level it was at sea, where the naval day could be unchanging if nothing untoward appeared to disrupt it. He would don a gown and his old ducks and head for the beach to swim, returning to a bathtub laid out and water warmed, with which to wash the salt from his body and hair. He would then shave, by which time Joe would have cooked and laid out his breakfast, the others taking theirs in the rear parlour.

The ability to entertain had been tested and passed, so he could claim to occupy a fully functioning house. Joe Lascelles provided excellent food, though nothing fancy – not necessary anyway – with no shortage of game or meats. He had also educated his shipmates, with varying success, in the art of serving dinner and pouring the fine wines he had purchased in the Lower Valley Road.

Braddock had been with his wife, with Vincent Flaherty present and able to keep the conversation off purely service matters. On a separate occasion he had entertained the officers commanding the ships of the Downs Squadron, drink flowing as he recounted his exploits, in turn required to listen to those of his guests. The only person yet to dine, one whom he wished most to entertain, was Betsey. Yet the thought of her Aunt Sarah being present for the time a decent proper meal would take to consume was not something he could face.

Breakfast consumed, he was ready to depart for the Naval Yard stables, all four mounts now kept there at his expense. So were his bargemen, with only Peddler reluctant to mount a pony and unhappy the whole way. Thus the road was taken at a walk, lest he fall off, his captain spending the entire time in imagined discussions-cum-arguments with Betsey. These ranged over any number of possibilities, did little good and were in fact possibly futile: with no prior arrangement, she might not be where he hoped to find her.

Leaving the others outside the broken gate, Brazier squeezed through to take up station within the bushes, given the slight possibility Betsey might not be alone, in which case he would have to retreat. The dogs would be the first sign and there was another worry, for they had become familiar and, if they picked up his scent, they would surely flush him out.

He had to pull back when he saw the Reverend Moyle heading in the direction of the main house, his deliberate way progressing, each leading foot carefully planted, an indication that he had perhaps already been at the bottle or was possibly still recovering from the excesses of the previous day

A look at his watch, once Moyle had disappeared, told him the time was approaching when Betsey should pass this way, he once more engaged in mock arguments or imagined comforting in the face of distress. This ceased when he heard a bout of barking and a minute later Betsey appeared. For a moment, Brazier's courage deserted him, yet he knew he must steel himself. He had an hour, at most, before they would have to part so she could return to the house, and he could not go the whole day in speculation. Assured she was alone, he stepped out to greet her.

Jolted in alarm, she put a hand to her throat. 'Edward!'

'Forgive me, but I wanted to see you alone.'

'I am happy that you do so, but curious as to why you carry such a look of concern.'

He damned himself and quickly altered his features. It was not his intention to immediately raise the reason for calling, that being a subject that would have to be broached with subtlety.

'Fear of discovery, shall we say. I saw your divine passing a few moments ago.'

'We have a meeting already arranged for today. Should I be pleased or angry at your impatience?'

It was gentle mockery, not true complaint: an indication of how they had moved on since that first stilted walk. The joshing he would normally have taken as encouraging, but not now. For all his jumbled thoughts on the way, he was at a loss to know how to start the necessary conversation and, to his ear, the words he chose sounded very feeble.

'Do you think of Jamaica on a cloudy day such as this?'

'I do so even in bright sunshine.'

He let her lead the conversation, in which she recalled the Caribbean climate and how she had easily taken to it, for abundance made life easy, if somewhat soporific. The tenor of her daily life was reprised and compared to her present circumstances, until he felt his impatience mounting, this to the point where his interruption came out as brusque.

'And how fares Henry?'

Asking about her brother changed her expression from smiling ease to one of confusion; he was commonly the last subject either of them wished to raise.

'If you're asking has he altered in his opposition, the answer must be, not as far as I can see. That said, our connection and hopes are not mentioned so I have reason to believe the mere passage of time is our ally. He will come round to acceptance eventually, I'm sure.'

'As he did with your late husband?'

Betsey stopped, obliging him to do likewise, to look up at him. 'You are in a strange mood this morning.'

'Am I?' It was a weak response, which would do nothing to get him to where he wanted and needed to go. 'I'm curious, that's all, as to how long it took your brother to put aside his objections in that case? I assume you wore him down.'

Betsey emitted a soft chuckle and moved on again. 'There was nothing gradual about it. I won't say he affected a complete volte-face from one day to the next, but it was not far off the case. I suspect it followed on from the discovery of what Stephen had inherited. Henry ever has an eye for profit so perhaps he came to see advantage in the union, where he had seen nothing of that sort before.'

Seeking to lighten his own mood, Brazier joked, 'Then happen I should acquire some plantations myself.'

Her response was pithy. 'Were I not set on selling, you might have had mine on marriage.'

'That's the first time you have spoken so positively in that regard.'

Brazier knew he had got the tone badly wrong.

'Do I sense reservation on your part that I should?'

280

'Nothing could be further from my mind.'

'Something is on your mind, and I sense troubling you.'

'Have you come to know me so well?'

That was equivocation, which made him reflect on his lack of pluck. He had attacked and boarded an armed enemy ship with less reserve and more brio than he was displaying now.

'If you have become prone to reservations, I would be obliged if you would say so.'

That being accompanied by a direct look, he decided he could no longer avoid raising the vital question and he did so with no preamble. 'What do you know of your brother's business affairs?'

'Why do you ask?'

'He's obviously successful and one wonders how that is managed.'

'I try to know as little as possible, Edward, and always have, given the gloomy effect it has on Henry. I am aware, though only vaguely, that he is involved in many spheres of activity, but I don't enquire as to what they are. Anyway, I have been absent for several years, have I not?'

'And you never have taken an interest, for instance, before any talk of your marriage?'

'Where is this leading, Edward?'

'You must have wondered, as I have, at the vehemence with which Henry objected to my arrival, which mirrored his original attitude to your late husband.'

'It took him by surprise, Edward. If he has not yet come round, I think I can say he has mellowed somewhat.'

'In Stephen's case, if I may call him that, Henry manifested similar objections. That could hardly be said to have come as a surprise to him, given you were sweet on each other from childhood and he had known the man you wished to marry for years.'

'He can be cantankerous.'

'There I cannot dispute with you.'

'Is that the reason for your surprise visit, to dispute with me?'

'No. I seek some explanation for his behaviour.'

'As I have said, I believe he will soon be reconciled.'

'Fully so, to the point of being present and welcoming me openly to his house?'

A slow head shake was her response, adding, 'Given your contrasting natures, I do not see you as ever being friends.'

'Which prompts me to look for a reason, given I cannot accept either jealousy or what you choose to call his controlling nature. Let me say, if you don't already know, it troubles me greatly.'

'Tell me I am wrong, if I say it seems you're looking for an excuse to—?'

She failed to finish, could not bring herself to say 'break off'. Brazier, who was horrified at the train of thought he had set in motion, looked at her lovely face, now carrying an expression he had not witnessed before. Betsey was hurt and in no mood to disguise it, which had him reach out and gently take her hand.

'Don't assume anything of that nature. If I ask questions, it's out of concern and affection.' A deep breath was required before he could continue. 'Information has come my way that your brother may not be as upright as he appears.'

Hurt turned to confusion. 'It has been intimated to me, by what I reckon to be a reliable source, he has control of much of the smuggling on this coast.'

'Edward,' she said, with a touch of condescension, 'no one controls smuggling on this coast; it is the occasional occupation of everyone who can sail a boat.'

'The rumours regarding Henry do not fit with your contention. I have to also say, he is rumoured to have inherited his prominence in the trade, which means some of the same allegations can be laid at the door of your father.' He jerked her hand to stop her responding, desperate to get out what he wanted to say. 'And it is also said, your brother is no stranger to the use of violence.'

'Someone has been having a laugh at your expense, Edward. My brother, outside a glare, would struggle to harm a flea. He abhors violence.'

'He may have visited that very thing on me. I told you I fell off my horse trying for a fence. I have to say now, I lied about that.' Her even more confused expression demanded explanation. 'Call it my pride. I did not want to admit I'd been the victim of a serious assault by a pair of toughs.'

'I am at a loss to see the connection.'

'I have a suspicion it may have been carried out on the orders of Henry.'

'What?'

'I am informed he has the ability to direct such things and I've apparently not been the only victim. There are others who have physically felt his displeasure; indeed it falls on anyone who disputes with him, as I did on my first visit. Is it not a coincidence, at the very least, that the event referred to followed on from my warning he should be careful in his language?'

'This, Edward, is surely nonsense.'

'We have little time, Betsey, and I have a tale to tell, so I require you to listen. Please tell me you will do so.'

There was a lengthy pause before she nodded, which had Brazier speaking quickly. He reprised on everything Saoirse had said, caveats included, though he was not fool enough to even hint at the gender of the source. Betsey listened without interruption, though there was no eye contact now. Her head had dropped, leaving him unsure as to how it was being taken. That lasted until she looked up and fixed him with a firm stare.

'You have no proof of this?'

'I have not. From what I'm told, Henry is too wily to allow any. Everything he commands is carried out by others.'

'And how does all this rumour affect your opinion of me?'

'Not at all,' was said with as much conviction as he could muster. 'But I fear this is not a repeat of his behaviour with your late husband.'

'You seem very sure.'

'Your brother will seek to put insurmountable barriers in our way, rather than have me as a family relative. I am a serving naval officer, one who carried out the duties of interdiction of smuggling in the Caribbean; that alone would not endear me to him if what I have been told is true. I would find it impossible to stand by and witness the running of contraband here at home and that applies even more to condoning the kind violence to which I suspect I have been exposed. I need to know if what I have been told is true.'

'But you must know the solution is simple, Edward.'

There was weariness in his response. 'Please don't suggest I challenge him.'

'No, but I shall.'

That he had not anticipated. 'Would you take my word that such a thing could be unwise?'

'So I'm to be left with what you impute and to merely accept as fact that what you have been told – by a person who I notice you do not name – and which is supposition based on rumour, should be treated as fact?'

'I know I ask a great deal.'

'You do, but when you heard all this did you think I might be aware?' The tone changed from query to bitter. 'Or even perhaps complicit?'

He was faced with the one question he had no desire to answer, yet no great imagination would be required to see it as a possibility he would have been forced to consider. Given there was no way of avoidance he could only reply, 'I doubted it, but I also needed to know.'

'Why not ask outright?'

'Perhaps for fear of the answer.'

'I'm not sure I should oblige such a lack of faith.'

'If you accept what I have said to you as conceivably true, positions reversed, what would you have done?'

'I can scare credit what you say about Henry, but to impute the same behaviour to my dear father—'

'I didn't set out to offend you, Betsey. I care only for our future.'

'You say you were in receipt of a beating. I am abound to ask where this took place.'

'Does it matter?'

'It would if it was in or hard by the Old Playhouse.'

That was a consequence of being truthful on which he had not reckoned and it required deflection. 'Hardly the point.'

Seeing her swell up, he knew a rebuke was coming, for he had more or less confirmed her suspicions. 'While I, Captain Brazier, in the presence of someone who finds it comforting to lie to someone for whom he claims to have feelings, am left to wonder if there is one.'

'Betsey?'

'No!' That came with a hand to push him away, while it was clear she was on the verge of tears. 'How could you countenance even the notion I would know of what you claim and be part of it?'

'No one can control their thoughts.'

'You know your way to the gate; please oblige me by making your way there without me. And, just so you are not inconvenienced by the freedom of your thoughts, I shall not be calling at Quebec House this afternoon.'

Men who had served with Edward Brazier for years knew his moods. The black expression when he rejoined them precluded any jolly enquires as to how he had fared. He mounted Bonnie in silence and kicked her into a trot without a word said, leaving the others to catch up, Peddler never quite managing to do so.

Brazier knew he had made a complete hash of things, so very far from what he had hoped and imagined would be the outcome, to the point where he reckoned his hopes were sunk. He would write, that was all he could do, in the hope that a penned explanation would check the urges that came from a verbal exchange requiring an immediate response.

'Here I am,' he said out loud in a cry to the heavens, 'without a prospect of happiness, without a ship and, very likely, without a career.'

'What's that, Capt'n?' Dutchy Holland called, he being just close enough to hear the voice if not the words.

'None of your damn business,' would have carried to the mainmast cap.

'Hud yer wheest, Dutchy,' was Cocky Logan's advice, which might have been taken as good advice, if the man so addressed had understood it.

The Griffin's Head was not as crowded as it had been the day Edward Brazier first came through Chillenden, but it was busy, it being one of the places Tulkington's customers came to transact for their smuggled goods, most of it ordered and paid for in advance. These people would fan out all over Kent selling what they acquired at a profit, so high were the taxes being evaded. All operated outside the law, but with little fear: the agency of enforcement was too weak to cover the coast, let alone inland roads, in a society that would not even begin to cooperate, seeing such duties as an evil government imposition.

John Hawker was still in a black mood and, for the first time, the object was his employer. The brains to master things he would grant Henry Tulkington, not even his father had raised the game to such heights, but the man should have trusted him on Spafford. Such reflections brought on the possibility of it extending to other matters, which was enough to have him reprising every recent conversation.

286

His mind was on such matters when he espied Jaleel Trotter in the doorway, his watery eyes ranging round the room, the suspicion on his thin face obvious. What had taken a long time to arrange previously was being demanded in haste. But with Harry in Tulkington's hands there was no choice. Spying Hawker in a booth – he was hard to miss – Daisy made his way through the crowded tables to face a held-up hand.

'Your knife, Daisy. I know you ever has it on you, so afore you get close, take it out for putting on the table.'

'You won't be defenceless.'

That was not denied. Another knife and a short billy club were produced and laid out. Seeing those, Daisy Trotter obliged, to have Hawker push everything right to the middle of the table.

'Other side,' was demanded with a hand to indicate where Trotter should sit, far enough away from the weapons to render them equally useless. As Daisy slid into the bench seat, Hawker enquired, 'What's happened to your nose, mate – been sticking it up somebody's arse?'

'What have you done to Harry?'

Hawker chortled. 'Nothin', more's the pity.'

'I ain't come to bargain for him, Hawker. It would have to be Dan for that.'

'Is the useless bugger worth the effort?'

Trotter was not going to acknowledge that as true. He had never seen Harry as worth much effort, but he had cared for him for Dan's sake. He was less enamoured of him now, after the headbutt and the subsequent embarrassment.

'Tulkington wants to meet with Spafford; same place, same rules.'

Daisy was sharp enough to pick up the lack of a mister. Hawker had ever been respectful when using his employer's name. Why not now? Did it hint at a rift, and could he push?

'Reckon he'd agree if you let Harry go.'

'Thought you said you was not here to bargain.'

'Don't stop me venturing an idea, do it? Happen Dan won't agree with that not being a condition.'

Hawker leant forward, his expression angry. 'What makes him think he's in a position to bargain? Happen I might just chop Harry up then descend on Worth and string the lot of you up from the rafters.'

'Happy for you to try, John. There's a couple just a'waiting to put a ball in your head as it comes round the door.'

'Tulkington wants to talk, an' don't go enquiring what about, 'cause I don't know.'

'I have to ask Dan.'

'Tell him, for there's no askin'. Top of the mill hill at noon tomorrow, with us providing the coach to meet. You'll be safe on Tulkington's word, which I wouldn't gift you if it were me.'

'Will you bring Harry?'

'We might.'

CHAPTER TWENTY-FOUR

The talk with his sister had been difficult for Henry Tulkington, it being of a kind he had not been obliged to endure for many a year, certainly not since the loss of his father who had ever been an uncomfortable presence in his life as he grew to manhood, given whatever his legitimate son did never seemed good enough.

If he reckoned himself strong as a negotiator, he was less gifted at dissimulation with a person as close to him as Elisabeth. Where other men might have laughed off what she was enquiring about, he lacked the skill for manufactured amusement and pretend ridicule, making his denials too assertive. He could not be sure, by the time she left, they had been taken as truth, but it took no time at all to identify who must be the source of her information.

It could only have come from Brazier: Elisabeth had contact with other people, but certainly none who would even have alluded to his more clandestine business affairs even if they knew of them, and very few did with certainty. His Aunt Sarah would not be the culprit. Quite apart from his near certainty of her being equally ignorant, she would never dare challenge him when, for her, a place in the workhouse would be the best she could hope for.

Should he have challenged Elisabeth regarding her damned nuisance of a naval captain? On reflection he was glad he had not, for to do so – the mere mention of his name – might have given credence to the suggestion he had been responsible for arranging his beating. At least he was no longer claiming a riding accident, but that did leave the conundrum of what to do about the sod, given the options once floated with John Hawker had evaporated. If anything happened to Brazier now, Elisabeth would immediately lay it at his door.

Troubled merely by the fact of Brazier's arrival and purpose, he was possibly a greater cause for concern than originally envisaged. He had visited Walmer Castle, while Henry Tulkington could only speculate on what he and William Pitt might have discussed. A letter had arrived from his Uncle Dirley this very morning, which shed a more worrying light on that meeting. It informed him Brazier was under a cloud of royal disfavour, one which more or less debarred him from future employment, this for a man who did not come across as the type to welcome inactivity.

Was he conniving with Pitt for a new role, akin to the duty he had carried out in the Caribbean against the colonials? What did William Pitt know or suspect? Was Elisabeth just a ploy? For a fellow given to worry, these were deep concerns.

According to Dirley, and in the same missive, Elisabeth had written to ask him to find out, on the possibility of forthcoming nuptials, about selling her plantations, enquiring as to what price they might fetch and how long would it take for them to be disposed of, so she was clearly planning to remain in England, no doubt wedded to Brazier.

It would have troubled Henry more if he had known to where Elisabeth had gone immediately afterwards, riding out on Canasta and leading another pony with the excuse of returning her rental to Mr Flaherty. She was determined to call upon Annabel Colpoys. Since getting the cold shoulder from such an old friend, Betsey had searched her mind for a reason, something to explain the alteration in reception from one day to the next, never mind the subsequent rebuffs.

How could it be? Surely Annabel would not take Henry's part

against her, when they used to guy him as young girls and with not too much subtlety. It was one of the few advantages gifted to her sex, who were seen as frivolous and silly by men and boys, creatures who were unaware of how the platitudes drawn from the men, as well as those gaucheries extracted from the boys, brought on later giggles.

The Colpoys' gate was opened without comment, which was a plus; at least there were no instructions to deny her entry should she call. Likewise both mounts were taken without even a nervous glance, so the rap on the brass knocker of Long Farm House was loud and confident, the door soon opened by the head servant, the fellow who had been witness to her previous embarrassing departure. Suspecting a request to see Annabel might be refused, Betsey pushed past him in a way that left him no time to react, to then burst in on her friend, finding Annabel at her embroidery, quick to shut the door to cut off prying eyes.

'Annabel, I cannot abide that you will not speak to me, especially when I'm at loss to know why.'

'It's not fitting that you should just barge in here.'

'It's not only fitting, Annabel, it is required, for if I cannot ask you in public, I must do so in private. What have I done to turn you against me?'

'I have not turned against you, Betsey.'

'The evidence of the last weeks does not support such an assertion. You ignore me and so does Roger: Lord above, not even your children are allowed to speak to me.'

'I fear I'm unable to explain.'

'You must, Annabel, for I will not depart this room until you do. I suspect that will not be welcomed if Roger returns from his fields.'

That Annabel blushed deeply and began to fiddle with her needle, while avoiding her eye, gave Betsey the clue she sought. 'Is he at the seat of this?'

'He is my husband,' was the whispered response.

291

'You are – were – my friend.'

Annabel roused herself to fight back. 'Perhaps if you had married a stronger man, you would know what it is to obey a spouse. But no, you could twist sweet Stephen around your little finger, which is no doubt why you wanted him as a husband.'

'You have been unkind to me, but that is worse by far: wounding from a woman who helped as a maid of honour to give me away. I grant you Stephen was not like Roger, but he was man enough. If Roger is at the seat of this, I require you tell what his cause is.'

'Your damned brother, that's what it is,' Annabel spat.

Blurted out it was, very obviously, immediately regretted. Annabel put her hands to her mouth, while the look of shock on her face, as well as eyes filling with fear, stood as testimony to the realisation of what she had done. Betsey moved to take one of those hands off her mouth and hold it tight, lowering herself onto the settle beside her.

'Tell me.'

'I can't.'

'You must.'

'Roger forbade me to receive you, Betsey. Please accept I hated myself for acceding to it.'

'What was his reason? You blame my brother. Why?'

The tears began to flow as Annabel's resolve weakened, so what followed was much interrupted by the need to both clear them and for her to blow her nose. Much was said about male pride, about a good man laid low and unable to admit the cause even to his wife, but it could not be a coincidence that Roger was in a legal dispute with Henry at the time. High words had been exchanged, with Roger Colpoys swearing he would see Henry damned and horsewhip him if required. That was until he came home, covered in blood. The suit was never mentioned again and nor was the Tulkington name derided.

'Yet you both attended my fete.'

'Roger did not want to go but feared it would smack of a rebuke if he declined.'

'So Henry, you suspect, was responsible for what happened to Roger?'

'I cannot say with certainty your brother was the cause, Betsey. Any attempt to force the truth from Roger is unwelcome and I'm not sure he knows, for he had been drinking on that night. For me, I can only guess.'

It was a sad friend of many years' standing who replied, as well as one who had so recently talked to Edward Brazier on the same subject. 'You may have no need to do more.'

'You must go, Betsey, if Roger—' Another sniffle. 'I fear he will chastise me harshly. The servants are bound to say you called.'

'Then we must give him no cause to be angry.'

Any observer would have said both women played their parts to perfection, for now it was Betsey who appeared to be sobbing as Annabel came close to physically throwing her out of her house, with the necessary imprecations to go with it. This was followed with an instruction to the servant who had opened the door never to let her across the threshold again.

They had, of course, arranged a place to meet away from prying eyes and nosy servants. Annabel was quick to hide in her sewing box the little sketch showing the location of the broken gate. Roger would never find it, for it was in a place he would not deign to look.

Betsey had met Vincent Flaherty at Quebec House on one occasion, he dragged in when she visited, in an attempt to lighten, with his Irish banter, an atmosphere ever made heavy by Sarah Lovell. She could, through him, get a message to Edward, one in which she would not confirm his suspicions regarding her brother but neither would she deny they might be true. He was asked to use the gate the next morning, with a gnomic message that she had something of great import to say.

'And Mr Flaherty, I am minded to buy Canasta from you, so please take good care of him, and do not even think of giving him to anyone else.'

'You should never tell a horse dealer you're fond of an animal, Mrs Langridge.'

'Even one as sweet as you?' Betsey asked, as she mounted the other horse.

'And here's me thinking it was I who had the silver tongue.'

Subterfuge was required when Betsey returned home; she had to behave as though she had been satisfied with Henry's denials, with no mention of Roger Colpoys or her visit to Annabel either, only to find him absent but expected back for dinner. She was determined to get to the bottom of things, though for the life of her Betsey could not begin to see anything untoward that might have been missed.

Cottington Court ran smoothly: visitors came, most of them on business it was true, but no hint of their being under threat had ever been shown. Even an acute eye revealed nothing; Aunt Sarah went about her domestic duties, Henry was on his business affairs, much of which took place out of the house, making it easy to manufacture lurid imaginings of what he might be up to.

The decision to look through his papers was a spontaneous one; she found herself close to his study door when no one was within sight of it to bar her entry. She went swiftly through almost without thinking, closing it behind her. There had been a fire in the grate but it was now more ash than logs, yet the residue in a room with the door and windows closed rendered it still warm.

Going to the desk she saw it was neat, which was Henry's way – indeed, she could never recall it as untidy. There was a half-burnt candle in a holder, an inkstand with an upright quill, more of those in a narrow tray, as well as a pot of fine sand, but the paper laying on the surface was blank. One top drawer held the detritus of the things Henry required:

a bottle of ink, red ribbon to tie documents, wax as well as the seal in a box, both engraved with the initials HT. The opposite drawer held a pile of linen handkerchiefs, beside them a series of bottles, no doubt containing the questionable potions with which Henry unnecessarily dosed himself.

The central drawer was locked, and that applied to the other four, which had her looking about the room and the numerous ledgers that lined the shelves of a large glass-fronted cabinet. Taking one out, she opened it to examine a list of figures, soon realising they related to the domestic expenditure of the house, so it was quickly returned. Given the quantity of the whole – there were dozens of ledgers – Betsey knew she would require a great deal of luck to find anything that hinted at information Henry would not wish to share.

The door to a corner cupboard she knew to be permanently locked, for that had been home to a safe since her father occupied this room, so she did not even try a pull at the handle. The thought that she was being foolish surfaced; it would take days to go through everything she could open and that did not include the desk or the safe, even if she could open the locked door. It was also obvious that if Henry had anything to hide, he would not leave around paperwork that anyone could see, so she made for the door to exit, closing it with care behind her.

'Elisabeth?'

'Henry, I was just looking for you.' Startled for the second time that day, it was her propensity to blush that made her exclamation, to her brother, somewhat unconvincing. That said, outside those slightly reddened cheeks he had to admire her quickly restored composure. 'I wanted to apologise to you.'

'For what?'

'I fear I was foolish to query you on matters that, on reflection, no one with sense would attribute to you.'

'I must own I am curious as to where such fantasies came from.'

'While I would be too embarrassed to say. It would please me if you did not enquire.'

Henry Tulkington was thinking that for all the bravura he did not believe a word of it and, if that was the case, she had certainly not been in his study looking for him. Even the silent way she had shut the door gave the lie to that. So what was it she was looking for – not that anything could be found without she had a crow bar to break open the desk drawers? At that thought, a hand went in an automatic gesture to his waistcoat pocket, to check he had the desk keys.

'Well, you have found me now, sister, and please do not trouble yourself for anything you said earlier. Given I knew it to be nonsense, my only concern was that you were being misled. Were you, like me, engaged in several businesses and prospering, you would know that idle and jealous minds seek ways to denigrate and diminish success.'

The smile on Betsey's face felt like a grimace, so fixed was it, and she wondered if Henry had noticed, as his hand went to his waistcoat, that her eye had, for a fraction of a second, followed it, for it was a movement that sent to her a message. He did not believe her, which could include her apologies for being in his study uninvited. Asked to explain, it would have been hard; it was a gut feeling, not a certainty. Nor was she fooled by the benevolent expression on Henry's face.

'Then all is as it should be,' she exclaimed.

'I had a letter from Uncle Dirley this morning.'

'Did you?' came with another slight blush.

'You have definitely decided to sell up in the West Indies?'

'It is far from decided, Henry,' was delivered with something of a manufactured laugh. What was Dirley doing telling him something that was none of his business? 'I merely want to get some idea of what they would fetch.'

His hands, palms open, came away from his side in a gesture of enquiry. 'What are we doing standing here in the hallway, Elisabeth, talking of sugar plantations like a pair of strangers? Do you wish to come into my study and discuss the matter there?'

'Not at this moment, Henry. I have things to attend to and, I suspect, you do too.'

'Then I will see you at dinner.'

As she nodded and passed him, Betsey felt it necessary to brush his arm with her hand, which she hoped would be taken as a gesture of affection: it was anything but and, by the time she had got to her suite of rooms, her feelings had turned to concern. If Annabel was right, and Edward too, and mischief was in the air, there was no telling what Henry would do.

He was sat in his study thinking that matters were coming to a head in both the problems he faced, and as of now Spafford seemed the one more likely to be resolved. Elisabeth could only have been seeking something incriminating in his study, as if he would leave anything to be found. She must think him a fool. Such thoughts played on his mind and, once more, he imagined himself the dispenser of justice, not just for his sister but Brazier too.

A whipping seemed not to be enough and the thought occurred he might have to dispose of them both. He could recall the way Elisabeth, as a young girl, had teased him, which he had hated but could do nothing about. She was the parental favourite, always indulged when he was often chastised for seeming trifles. It would go too far to say he hated her, but there was an absence of familial love. At this moment she presented a threat and one it would be wise to deal with.

It was a pleasant diversion to speculate on a solution that would have to be impossible to prove, and on how it could be achieved, this interrupted by a servant bringing him a note just delivered at the main gate. The superscription read JH, which showed Hawker to be sound in the matter of discretion, while the contents told him the meeting with Spafford was arranged for noon the next day. There was a question too, politely posed, asking what was planned if he did not show?'

'We have his boy, John, his Achilles heel,' Henry said out loud, before going to the fireplace to find the last bit of glaring red in the ash, the edge of Hawker's note set to it until the paper began to burn. That was held until the flame had consumed most of it, the residue then dropped into the grate.

Given what he had been cogitating on prior to its arrival, there occurred another thought that tickled his fancy. What if Spafford could be persuaded to take care of both Brazier and his sister? It was a bit of make-believe, disturbed by the gong sounding to say dinner was ready. This rendered it necessary for Henry Tulkington to compose himself, so nothing of his imaginings should be apparent. He looked forward to being very nice to Elisabeth.

Daniel Spafford knew he had no choice but to comply, and nor could he contemplate what had been his first thought: that he should take along a knife and threaten to cut Tulkington's gizzard unless Harry was returned safe and sound. It would not wash: Hawker had checked he was unarmed before and he would do so again.

Those who would escort him were within the farmhouse, but creeping around whispering to each other. Even Daisy was keeping a distance and it took no great wit to surmise what they were all thinking on. Would the man who led them sell all down the river for that useless turd of a son?

CHAPTER TWENTY-FIVE

The message from Betsey was a request to meet her tomorrow, just as he had done previously, nothing more. Did that imply forgiveness or the very opposite? There was no way to tell, so it was a morose Edward Brazier who spent the rest of the day back in the state of flux in which he had arrived in Deal. He occupied himself by writing to his prize agent, instructing him to set up a regular payment to Dutchy's dependants via the Quay Inn. Logan and Palmer had claimed to have no one who needed support and were happy to take his money and spend it in the nearest taverns.

After a restless night, Brazier set off alone for Cottington, requiring his boat cloak for, if it was not raining with the lowering skies, it threatened to do so. A gale of wind was blowing in from the north-east to whip up the sea, and the garment kept out the worst of the chill. He risked solitude in case the result was bad; he had no desire, in the face of his barge crewmen, to suffer a repeat of the day before.

At the house Betsey was suffering from impatience. She had taken breakfast in her room to avoid Henry. Now she could not go out as his carriage was in the drive, horses hitched and only waiting for the passenger, who was taking his own sweet time to emerge. There was a rear entrance leading to a lawn, but to reach it required she transverse the hall and that too might cause her to bump into her brother.

Finally Henry emerged, with Betsey stepping backwards in case he looked up to her window. She listened for the sound of the wheels on the gravel, which signified departure. Only when she could see he was halfway down the drive did she don a thick-hooded cloak and make her way downstairs.

'You're recovered?' asked her Aunt Sarah, as she appeared on the half-landing.

'A mild upset, Aunt, which I think will benefit from some air.'

'Which I reckon foolish. You should remain indoors, especially with this wind. I hope you do not contemplate the woods, for it's strong enough to fetch down a tree.'

'It would be a devilish lack of fortune that I should be there when that happened,' Betsey snapped, glancing at the hall clock to note she was constrained for time; she wanted to be in place when Edward arrived, if indeed he did so, for there was always a risk that her behaviour yesterday had given him grounds to decline.

'If God wills it so, it will be so,' was Sarah Lovell's mordant opinion.

Outside, she had to give some credence to the possibility; the treetops were now in leaf, if not fully so, and thus the wind was bending the branches, while even the trunks were swaying to nature's power. The dogs, unconcerned, raced to the side door to get ahead of her, one ear blown over their heads and their coats flattened.

Betsey chose to remind herself that the woods were well managed, with an annual pollarding of branches as well as the cutting down of any tree that looked to be failing, the results burnt in the grates of the house. It was a worrying walk to get to where she needed to be, with the possibility of him not being present, this put to rest as the bushes parted and there he stood; he had come early.

'I have to ask that you forgive me, Edward.'

'You spoke with Henry?'

'To not much purpose, but there was another way and that

vouchsafed to me was enough to bring on disquiet, which is why I asked you to come.'

'I had hoped it was more than that.'

'Be assured it will be. But I want you to find me accommodation in Deal this very day: either a set of rooms or, if it can be arranged, a house. I cannot say for certain what you implied yesterday is true in all respects, but I can say I will not stay in this house an hour longer than I have to.'

Brazier lifted off his hat. 'A kiss and I'll find you a palace. At a pinch, I will move out of Quebec House and gift it to you.'

'Quebec House I will leave to you but the kiss, Edward, I will willingly grant you.'

It was a proper one: a passionate and lingering meeting of lips and tongues of the kind Betsey had not experienced since Stephen Langridge fell ill. Then, arm in arm, they walked under the swaying branches and hissing trees, laying plans as to how he would get her away from Cottington Court without the knowledge of her brother. He would be bound to try to dissuade her and might even attempt to prevent it.

'I will come tonight before dusk, with my men. It will have to be a horse, which means you can carry very little.'

'Fetch the pony I had from Flaherty.' She clutched his arm tight. 'And I shall not concern myself for possessions, for I look forward to possessing all that I need for happiness.'

It seemed an inauspicious day to meet at the chosen location, which was treeless and thus provided no shelter at all from the gale of wind. The seascape, easily visible from this elevation, was a dark grey mixed with a mass of white crests, as the North Sea drove into the anchorage to batter and reshape the shingle.

This was weather the kind of which could have the merchant ships in the roadstead dragging their anchors, so the boatmen of Deal would be wondering if that other source of income was about to be gifted to them: the cargoes of vessels driven ashore or out onto the Goodwin Sands, on which they would be stuck fast and begin to break up, this before being sucked down into perdition.

Henry Tulkington could see the meeting coach swaying to and fro, beside it – and using what little lee it provided – John Hawker and Jaleel Potter, hanging onto their hats and communing over the final arrangements. At a wave Tulkington stepped out of his coach, to be immediately buffeted so hard he staggered. He was thus in a far-from-benign mood by the time he made his destination.

Spafford was already seated and waiting, his face set in a look he probably hoped would convince Tulkington of his intention to drive a hard bargain. If he had not been so discomfited by the weather, his opponent would have been amused; the man had no cards to play.

'Have you fetched along my boy?'

'I reckon him safer where he is, but I'm curious, Spafford. What will you pay to get him back?'

'There's no need for me to pay. Not even you are crazy enough to let him be harmed. Where he is and what might happen to him is the talk of the town and if'n you think to get Hawker doin' the dirty, ask yourself this: will he swing for you. 'Cause that'll be the price.'

'You were a fool to rob me, Spafford.'

'It was a joy, you not knowin' it were me.'

Tulkington produced a thin and humourless smile. 'I knew all along. It was John Hawker who was left to wonder.'

It was with narrowed eyes that Spafford responded. 'You didn't tell him what passed a' tween us?'

'Recall you asked me not to.'

'While never having any belief you'd abide by your word.'

Now Tulkington was amused. 'You must cease to judge everyone by your own low standards. Now, about your Harry. What you filched was never going to get you to a sum of a size to maintain him.'

'It were designed to bring you to this.'

'It strikes me Harry would require a small fortune given his propensity to spend.' Spafford sat stony-faced. 'You do not acknowledge what is plainly true.'

'I'm wondering where this is leading.'

'Does your offer of an alliance still hold?'

'It might.'

'Well, let me tell you it will never happen. What you represent to me, Spafford, is irritation, not the rivalry you imagine. You are allowed to trade for the simple reason that ridding myself of you is a game not worth the indulgence.'

'You make it sound easy, but—'

A peremptory held-up hand added to a fierce look stopped Spafford. 'You made one correct guess. That I would go out of my way not to enter into a conflict in order to rid myself of you. So I am going to make you an offer, or should I say, accept your previous offer. If I cannot get rid of you, I must seek to control you.'

'You ain't enquired about the state of my well-being?'

'Only because it's a matter of utter indifference to me. If you die, you die. You will from now on work to my instructions and they may well be imparted to you by John Hawker. What I can guarantee, and you must pass this on to your men, is that all will prosper.'

'My boy?'

'What an unfortunate ball and chain he is to you. In order that I know you have accepted my terms, come to Cottington Court by six of the clock and come alone. Harry will be there. If you do not come, I will take it as a refusal and so will not swear to his having a future.'

'Take orders from John Hawker?'

'From what you tell me about the Grim Reaper, it will not be for long.'

Making to leave, Tulkington was stopped by Spafford's voice. 'You seem damn sure of yourself.'

'The benefit of being in a strong position, while dealing with one who is so weak he has nothing with which to trade.'

The coach had been swaying throughout; as the door was opened the wind gusted in, tipping it so much there was a moment when it might tip over, which visibly alarmed Henry Tulkington and caused Dan Spafford to laugh. Once more buffeted on his way to his own coach, he indicated to Hawker to join him within, and there instructions were issued that surprised his man. He and his gang were required to be at Cottington, by late afternoon, breaking the stricture of never going near the place. He was told to fetch along Harry Spafford, as well as the reason why. Alliance, or as his employer termed it, absorption, did not sit well.

'Everyone I command is chosen by me, Mr Tulkington. I don't fancy Spafford's lads to be a match.'

'I shouldn't worry, John. Some will not come near you, which is to your credit. If there are good people it will soon be obvious.'

'And those who're not?'

'I doubt such people are the type to be missed and I always work on the assumption that time is on my side. I recommend you adopt the same approach. Oh, and spruce young Spafford up, fit to be a Cottington guest.'

'I ain't goin' alone Daisy, I don't trust that sod not to slice my gizzard.'

'You don't reckon his offer real, then?' Spafford shrugged. 'Then why go at all?'

'The offer's to be found out, but I must get my Harry free. If Tulkington means ill, happen we'll both perish, but I can't not try.'

'So what do you want me to do?'

'Keep hush about what I told you. The way Tulkington's talking I can go through the front door, but you need to get a couple of lads to hoick someone over the wall so they can unbar a gate. This time of year, you will see through a winder what's happenin' and if it looks bad, then you do what you can to get me and Harry free.'

Daisy Trotter wanted to say what was proposed looked like a good chance to meet his maker. 'Course, Dan; whatever you want.'

The invitation from Henry to join him in his study was unwelcome, yet Betsey reckoned not to comply would only raise more suspicion, while she had to admit she might be seeing threats where none existed. Was he about to quiz her, and if so, how to react? She decided it had to be faced as well as dealt with and, given the hall clock said it was past five, to get away she would use as an excuse the need to get changed for dinner, which would curtail her presence to not much more than an hour. After that, she would find a way to slip out the house to go and meet Edward.

He had already set out, not wishing to be late for such an important rendezvous and, given the nature of what he might face, this time it included Joe Lascelles, previously left behind, but now, with the whole party having made their way to Vincent Flaherty's paddock, mounted on a small pony and leading a saddled Canasta.

Brazier had bespoken the same rooms at the Three Kings as he had occupied previously, which he would either use himself or offer to Betsey if she declined Quebec House. This he hoped she would accept, for the notion of her staying anywhere else raised the difficulty of ensuring she remained safe. If Garlick was delighted, he was also curious enough to render his client brusque, only mollified when it was made plain Brazier would be dining with a guest and that he wanted to rent for the purpose the private room in which he had met William Pitt.

Unbeknown to his party they were half a mile behind John Hawker, who had loaded his men into two covered vans, along with a terrified Harry Spafford, he sure he was in for a terminal ducking in the briny, a notion which no one seemed inclined to disabuse him of. From the other side of Cottington his father was leading his men towards the walls of the Tulkington estate, before separating to obey Tulkington's instruction to come to the house on his own.

'Elisabeth, do come and join us.'

Henry was, as usual, sat close to the fire and that occasioned no surprise. What was unusual was the presence of the Reverend Joshua Moyle sat opposite him, a large bowl-like glass in his hand, his rubicund countenance made more so by the heat. If Moyle was no stranger to the house – he was invited occasionally to dine, with, it had to be said, the customary drunken consequences – this was not a room into which any guest would normally be invited. And it had to be remarked that Henry too was drinking out of a tall narrow crystal glass, seemingly from the bottle of champagne in the bucket on his desk.

'I have just been regaling our personal priest on the things you questioned me on yesterday.'

'And far-fetched I found them, my dear Elisabeth,' was the response.

Betsey felt the need to smile, even if she was not happy to be anything dear to this man. 'A conclusion I have arrived at on my own, and one for which I am sure my brother has told you I have already apologised.'

'You most certainly have. Will you join me in a glass of champagne?'

'Perhaps just before dinner, Henry.'

'Oh come along, Elisabeth, otherwise I might think you still harbour doubts. I know as a tipple you are fond of it.'

'One glass, then.'

'Splendid.' He rose and produced a second glass from behind the bucket, to carefully tip it sideways and slowly pour, from where she was standing the light from the fire illuminating the rising bubbles. 'Do sit down.'

'Are you drinking champagne, Dr Moyle?'

'Not my preference, Elisabeth,' he replied, holding up his glass, as

306

Betsey lowered herself into a wing chair. 'Henry was good enough to have a glass of brandy fetched in. More my thing, brandy, and this is a very fine example indeed.'

He wasn't quite drunk but neither was he completely sober, if such a condition ever existed in his life. Yet she welcomed his presence, for it would be unlikely the subject of her queries, with him present, would be gone into in any depth. Taking the glass from Henry, she was obliged to raise it as he did, in a toast.

'To honest endeavour.'

Moyle cried, 'Hear him,' while Betsey just smiled, prior to taking a sip.

The servant Grady knocked, to enter and inform Henry that the visitor he was expecting had arrived, which had him rise, apologise and slip out, leaving Betsey with Moyle, who smiled at her with slack, wet lips.

'Your brother tells me you are contemplating another marriage.'

She was surprised, and to cover it a second sip from the glass was taken.

'Did he grant you an opinion on the notion?'

'He did. Thinks it a good idea, which I had to point out might also apply to himself.'

'A good idea?'

'You seem surprised, Elisabeth.'

'I cannot lie—'

'Which my calling must caution you against,' Moyle interrupted, his eyes cast skywards as though he was checking with the Almighty.

'—if I were not to say that hitherto, he has had reservations.'

'A noble thing to do, show brotherly concern.'

To cover the fact that it was the opposite of the truth, Betsey drained her glass.

'I'm sure Henry would want you to have a refill.'

'No, one glass is enough for now.'

Moyle waved his bowl. 'Then I hope you will oblige me by calling for more brandy.'

She would love to have refused, for if good manners demanded she comply, this cleric before her was not one to deserve such consideration. That said, she rose and went to the side of the fireplace to ring for a servant.

'Very kind,' Moyle acknowledged.

Having called for someone to attend, Betsey was obliged to await the arrival and to ask that Moyle be given that which he no doubt sought: a full bottle. It also required her to be there when it arrived.

'I wonder how long Henry will be.'

Grey, thick eyebrows rose in a gesture of ignorance, but the Reverend Doctor was smiling at her in a way that, had his wife been present, would probably have earned him a reprimand, it being openly salacious. His words would certainly have done so.

'Such a pretty flower you are, Elisabeth, I envy the fellow you have chosen to favour with your affections. Would that I was the one to pluck your petals.'

CHAPTER TWENTY-SIX

Had a human been afforded a bird's eye view of Cottington Court, they would have observed several groups of men, the first and largest within the grounds and fanning out to surround the house. A second was approaching the northern wall, aiming to be close to one of the barred gates that led to the ploughed estate fields. The third, the smallest in number, though mounted instead of on foot, was making its way along the southern wall, heading for that broken old postern door.

Inside the house Henry Tulkington was welcoming Daniel Spafford, if such a word applied, for there was nothing other than condescension in the owner's manner.

'Take a good look, if it interests you; I reckon it to be your first and last visit.'

'Do I get what I've come for, Tulkington?'

'I think from now on, I have to insist on "Mr Tulkington", or perhaps "sir", if you prefer.'

'You can wish for it, but you'll never hear me say it.'

'Even if I had a noose round Harry's neck and the rope thrown over a beam? I think you might oblige me then.' Tulkington looked over Spafford's shoulder, which caused his visitor to turn. There was John Hawker with a weapon in his hand, too long for a knife, too short for a sword, but it would be sharp whatever it was. He also had a couple of his men with him.

'The cellar, John, which you will reach by the door under the stairs. Tie him up, for there's quality wines down there and if he is going to meet Satan, it would not serve that he should do so drunk.'

Spafford did not protest as he was forced towards the door; there was no point and he half-suspected he would find his son in the same place. Once Hawker returned, he was sent to the stables to fetch Harry, who was brought in, clean in both dress and body, as well as stone-cold sober and very frightened.

Hawker was taken aside for a quiet word. 'I think I can handle him from now on, John; I would suggest you see what trick his father reckons he can spring on us.'

'Bound to be one.'

Brazier had reached the gate and all had dismounted, the reins looped together so that one man could hold all the mounts until the joint reins could be tied off. Getting Dutchy into the bushes required an extra shove to shift the jammed wood, but once he was through the others found it easy. The wind had dropped to a gentle breeze while, on a cloudy night, there was not much daylight and that, in any case, was fading. There was just enough left for their leader to see by his watch that the time was not far off when he could expect Betsey to appear.

The best defence Hawker had was noise; the Spafford gang might be smugglers and used to moving quietly, but this was not their customary activity. He had a ladder against the wall enclosing the formal gardens, which, when climbed, allowed him to see, albeit very dimly, a lot of the surroundings. Out in the grounds his men had shaded lanterns and, if they were uncovered, their open faces were to be pointed to where he stood.

'North gates I reckon,' he called down softly to Marker. 'But not till the light's gone.'

'Well, Harry, we meet at last, though your character, or lack of it, does precede you.'

'I've told your man Hawker everything I know, sir.'

The voice was weedy and needy, while the weak blue eyes seemed made for pleading. Henry Tulkington chuckled. 'And made up a good deal more, I shouldn't wonder.'

'I'm willing to help bring my pa down if it's needed.'

'Anything to save your own skin. What a poor specimen you are. Still, that's what I need for my purposes. Come with me.'

The light was fading fast, which had Brazier wondering if it would be safe to strike a flint outside the walls and fire the tallow wads in his lanterns. He had hoped they would not be required until the journey back to Deal but, with the sky blanketed, the light, at this time of year, was less than he had hoped for.

'How we sitting, Capt'n?'

'If all is well, Dutchy, we are minutes away from making contact.'

'Can seem an age, a minute,' hissed Peddler.

'Quiet, lads. I think I hear footsteps.'

At the very front of the hedge, Brazier was in a position, by the careful moving of a branch, to get a sight of the approach and his heart lifted to see a ghostly moving figure. Betsey would be in a cloak and hard to see, but anticipation died when there seemed to be no attempt to move closer. The temptation, to step out and seek to identify, had to be suppressed. He heard the sound of disturbed leaves and twigs as the figure moved, yet soon it was not increasing in level, but decreasing.

'Cocky: outside and get the lanterns lit, but make sure no light spills into the grounds.'

'Aye, aye, Capt'n.'

Nerves on edge, Brazier knew Betsey was soon going to be overdue and he could easily imagine several causes, a confrontation with her brother the most concerning. He had no choice but to wait; he could not affect whatever was delaying her and he had to trust Betsey to use her own wits to contrive her escape.

Sarah Lovell had been summoned from her room to Henry's study and on entry she found Moyle there, well on the way to being inebriated. There was a young man she did not know, a close-to-handsome youth, with corn-coloured hair and very blue eyes. Stood by the doorway she could not see her niece, who was sat in a wing chair facing the window. Yet she did wonder at the expression on Henry's face, which could only be described as smug.

'Harry, I think it's time you had a brandy.'

'What's going on, nephew?'

'I have to see what's happening,' Brazier hissed. 'I can't stand the waiting. Fetch me one of the lanterns, shaded.'

'Capt'n,' whispered Dutchy, who was close to his ear. 'You ain't told us if there's risk out there.'

It was quickly responded to and with words that caused immediate regret. 'Do you fear for it?'

'You know I don't from past service,' was the response, the bitterness not moderated by the low tone of voice. His coxswain had the right to check him, having stood by his shoulder in more than one sea fight.

'Forgive me, Dutchy, I am very much on edge.'

'What I'm sayin' is this: if you're going to look for your lady, it would not be a good idea to do it alone. The light's nearly gone now, so take two and leave two, Joe being one to go along, 'cause if he don't smile, no bugger will see him.'

The jest, even true, was welcome. 'Which doesn't apply to you.'

'With respect, your honour—'

'I know, me neither.'

John Hawker saw the flash of light from the northern wall, quickly replied to, which allowed him deep satisfaction. There was not too much brains, he reckoned, in the Spafford mob, to come from there. A brighter spark would have chosen a less obvious direction or none at all. It was not Daisy who had clambered over the wall; that had been the task of a younger, fitter man, who had the wit to stand on Dolphin's shoulders. But in getting across he had let his boots scrape the brickwork and there was a Hawker man close enough to pick up on the sound.

'Got to keep 'em away from the house, Marker, so gather up the lads to head for the kitchen garden.' Hawker chortled. 'If we get them trapped in there we can make soup of the sods.'

Brazier was just about to emerge from the bushes when he heard a muffled call, followed by the sound of running feet and, if his ears were not deceiving him, more than one pair. But that noise was fading too so, emboldened, he moved onto open ground, followed by Joe and Dutchy, every step carefully taken. If there had been practically no light before, once he came under the tree canopy there was none at all, which made moving impossible unless he opened his lantern, but only for a second at a time.

'Damnation!'

This was the cry of John Hawker, still atop his ladder, who saw the southern flashes and now assumed the Spafford gang had split up, this when he had sent his men in the direction of the north wall. A sudden cry, followed by loud sounds of fighting, told him part of them had been confronted and were being dealt with. But his lads were engaged so, if there was another threat coming, he had to deal with it himself.

Being no coward he was soon moving towards the south wall, his weapon in one hand and his lantern in the other. Having covered half of what he reckoned the necessary distance, he shouted out at full power, hoping some of his gang would have the wit to respond, while also thinking it might get whoever was holding that flashing lantern to back away.

Coming at a rush it could not be done in silence, which alerted Brazier and his two companions. Another flash of light showed they were still surrounded by trees, indeed they had been feeling their way for a while. But the illumination allowed him to get behind a trunk and hide, an order going out all should do the same. Dutchy obeyed; Joe Lascelles did not. He just stood still and listened at the approaching thuds of heavy boots. The lantern Hawker was using came waving towards him and Joe lifted the club he was carrying in readiness.

The shock as his face and body appeared in Hawker's pool of cast candlelight had even such a hard bargain scream, so telling was the shock, made worse when Joe smiled, for his teeth gleamed. Just about to clout his man, Dutchy stepped out from behind a tree and did it for him, with a punch that would have felled an ox, the lantern dropped. Dutchy picked it up to examine the face.

'If it ain't John Hawker. Now that was a very satisfying blow.'

'Reckon he thought you were a chimera, Joe,' said Brazier, coming to look. 'Frightened him half to death with that beam of yours.'

Hawker was not completely out: he was groaning and making feeble efforts to move. Dutchy grabbed him by his coat collar and dragged him to his feet. 'Reckon we can walk forward with now't to fear.'

Daisy Trotter had dodged round the kitchen garden and it was only by a fluke of luck he was not collared. He tripped and fell over a tree root, just as Hawker's men closed in. Flat on the ground and clad in dark clothing, he stayed where he was until they were past. Yet he knew whatever else was going to happen, they had been rumbled and it was likely he was on his own, soon confirmed by the sounds of fighting to his rear.

Gingerly he raised himself up and moved on: there was no point in his trying to join in a fight unless he was set to kill, and that was not yet called for. He could see the lights of the house now, which acted as a beacon. Daniel Spafford was in there and probably Harry too, but that did not solve a problem. What was he going to do on his own, when it was clear Hawker's men were here in strength?

Noises to his left made him stop dead and crouch, to pick out a party of four souls moving forward, one seeming to stagger, while being held up by another, this to the sound of garbled moaning. They too were heading for the house and the well-illuminated windows through one of which Daisy could now see figures. Those he had avoided seemed bent on making for the same destination, so as quietly as he could, he came on in their wake. There was a significant pool of light close to the window and into that the quartet moved.

Peering through the mullioned glass, Edward Brazier saw the back of a pair of broad shoulders in a black coat. It was the pepper-and-salt hair, the whiskers showing on both sides, plus the way the body was swaying which had him guess it was the Reverend Moyle. Henry Tulkington was standing over Moyle shaking his head, while sat beside him his Aunt Sarah appeared seriously distressed, with tears glistening on her cheeks.

The movement of the shoulders showed half the outline of a young man with corn-coloured hair, quite well dressed, an impression of something close to respectability which was immediately spoilt as he lifted a bottle to his lips and drank deeply from the neck.

One thing only was on Brazier's mind: the route they had taken had to be very close to that which Betsey would have used had she got away. They had not encountered her, which meant she was still within the house and, if he was going to rescue her, which now

315

seemed to be necessary, he would have to get inside as well.

'I have to doubt ringin' the bell is a sound notion, your honour,' Joe stated when his captain shared the point.

The noise from behind, faint at first, but growing and carrying the sound of numerous voices, had them looking back over Daisy Potter's recumbent and invisible body. He, with three of the faces in profile, was trying to identify them and at a loss to do so, one obviously a blackamoor and the other two big men, one holding upright the fourth. The shorter of the two moved sideways out of the arc of window light, to hold up his lantern and peer into the gloom. What that did was illuminate his face, as well as his distinctive naval hat.

The 'Christ' from Daisy was inadvertent, for he recognised the face, but he too had heard the approaching noise, which told him he was best out of it, for if they were heading this way and not fussed about the din it could only mean Dan's gang and his mates had come off worse.

Brazier was at a bit of a loss as to what to do. Whoever was coming towards the house was not likely to be friendly, but he needed to find Betsey. Against that he had his bargemen with him and just as much, his duty was to keep them safe.

'Capt'n, happen you best look through this here window.'

Joe's tone was not happy and the man he served soon realised why when he did as advised. The black coat and shoulders had moved to reveal, sat in a wing chair, though looking unlike herself, Betsey. Her aunt was now sat with her head in her hands, plainly still in distress.

'Not good at our backs,' said Dutchy.

Brazier swung round to be presented with a line of men with lanterns, none of them of the soft type. Still holding Hawker, Dutchy swung him to face them and hauled out his pistol, to cock it awkwardly, prior to pressing the point of the barrel against Hawker's head, but not before a crescendo of shouts had come from recognition. These were

316

loud enough to penetrate the glass, which brought the face of Henry Tulkington to press against it, but not for long. A casement, it was flung open and his head poked out.

'I have come to take away your sister, Tulkington.'

The statement, which should have alarmed him, was taken with disturbing equanimity.

'Really Brazier?'

'It is her express wish to live elsewhere.'

'I imagine the West Indies might suit.'

Annoyed by what was clearly a joke, Brazier pulled out his pistol which, cocked and pointed, had Tulkington retreat. This showed the Reverend Moyle now slumped over the desk and the corn-haired youth, staggering about, bottle in hand, plainly sloshed. The threat of the pistol as a gesture was likely to prove futile. He might have a groggy John Hawker in his charge, but to his rear were two dozen of the men he led and he had no idea what weapons they carried. Even if it did not run to firearms, he, Dutchy and Joe could only account for three with pistol shot; after that it would be fists and clubs, with the odds terrible.

Tulkington too could see what was behind him and he could calculate the probabilities. A voice cried out from one of Hawker's men, asking if it was time to take them; unwise, given it could cost both Hawker and Tulkington, at point-blank range in one case, their lives. The request was denied.

'An impasse, Captain Brazier.'

'I have told you why I have come.'

'You have. But there's someone I need to introduce to you. Harry, come forward and meet a naval hero, who would serve for you as an example.' It took time for the named person to obey; it turned out to be the youth, who stumbled forward. 'Captain Brazier, meet Harry Spafford.'

'Cease playing games, Tulkington.'

'But I can play games, since you have to contrive a way to get out of Cottington Court in one piece.'

'I could use you as a hostage.'

'You could, but it would be the Tyburn tree and I daresay not just for you, but also your companions. I suggest you depart as best you can; Hawker will serve to get you out without becoming endangered, but I would ask that he comes to no more harm. You can call by tomorrow, perhaps, and ask for my sister. Or perhaps send her a note.'

'I will not be put off.'

'I never doubted it, Brazier, but there is one thing you need to know. When you call, or if you write, you must address my sister not as Mrs Langridge.'

'What?'

'You missed an occasion, Captain.'

Tulkington turned to wave an arm, which encompassed the room: the comatose divine, the drunken youth, Sarah Lovell looking at him in clear anguish, her cheeks wet and what looked like a soaked handkerchief clutched in her hand. But most of all there was Betsey, still sat in the chair, who seemed, even if she was looking right at the window in which he stood, not to recognise him.

'A pity, as you can see, Captain; a wedding is such a happy affair.' He gestured towards Betsey. 'Were she not in the shock of such good fortune, I might introduce you to Mrs Harry Spafford.'

DAVID DONACHIE was born in Edinburgh in 1944. He has always had an abiding interest in the naval history of the eighteenth and nineteenth centuries as well as the Roman Republic, and under the pen-name Jack Ludlow has published a number of historical adventure novels. David lives in Deal with his partner, the novelist Sarah Grazebrook.